Wheelboys

Wheelboys

by
Dd Jaseron

Jaseron Publishing
6105 N. Wickham Rd, #410566
Melbourne, FL 32940
888-619-5619
https://jaseron.com
info@jaseron.com

Hardcover ISBN 978-1-7372679-0-4
Paperback ISBN 978-1-64254-643-9
eBook ISBN 978-1-64550-646-1

First Edition: February 2019
P-26-03-06
Printed in the United States of America

ACKNOWLEDGMENTS

I want to thank my teacher and classmates from the writing class "A Hero's Journey." Wendy gave me the tools to tell this story and the guidance to find my voice. My classmates, Pnina from South Africa and Pauline from Ireland, also gave me the courage and borrowed faith to develop this fictional work. This journey took many sessions and many rewrites to transform a simple stream of thought into a multilayered, extended story. I enjoyed sharing the art of novel writing with the most wonderful women who had their own amazing stories to tell.

I also have to acknowledge my wonderful husband and son, who have shown amazing patience from beginning to end. My husband's cover design gave me inspiration, and his editing support was essential. I also relied on his knowledge of mechanics and vehicle dynamics; he is an engineering graduate from MIT.

This is a work of fiction. All of the characters, names, incidents, organizations, and dialogue in this novel are either the products of my imagination or are used fictitiously.

CHAPTER 1

It was a rainy April afternoon in Auburn, Alabama, when Elle Dillanger rushed through the emergency room doors at the Methodist Hospital. Her husband had called her while she was in the middle of a session with a client, and her mind had been racing for the whole hour's drive to Auburn. Now she was in a panic. Where was their son?

"Is this emergency intensive care? Is Gary Lee Dillanger here?" she asked at the receptionist desk.

"Are you immediate family?" asked the attendant.

"Yes, I'm Elle Dillanger, his mother," she said, catching her breath.

"Sign in here on the keyboard." The woman pointed to a screen right next to her.

Elle could barely think, let alone type. Her hands were shaking. After entering her information, the woman handed her a name tag to wear.

"Room 121, Mrs. Dillanger." She directed Elle down the corridor.

As she approached room 121, she saw glass walls enclosing a flurry of activity. Several doctors and nurses hurried to manipulate tubes and wires connected to various machines. Elle tried desperately to see the patient in the bed.

"Elle." Her husband was suddenly beside her and touched her on the shoulder.

"What…what happened?" she asked.

"His car went off the road and crashed. I didn't want to tell you on the phone because I knew you had a long drive over here," he replied. "Gillian is dead. They airlifted Gary Lee here, and they are trying to stabilize him."

Gillian dead? She couldn't absorb any of it. Gillian Mason was Gary Lee's high school girlfriend, and they had been on what seemed to be a harmless precollege visit to Auburn University. It was just an hour from their home in Blue Springs. Stunned and confused, Elle couldn't remember any of the details of Gary Lee's plans for the weekend.

Elle leaned against the glass wall to balance herself and tried to focus on what was happening inside. She could see the doctor looking into her son's eyes with a small flashlight. The doctor turned to an attendant and then looked back at Elle and Drew through the glass. He walked toward them and opened the door.

"I'm Dr. Anderson," he said, holding out his hand. "Gary Lee's parents, I assume?" The doctor wore a white coat over dark blue scrubs with instruments in his pockets. He seemed very experienced, and his expression was serious.

"Elle and Drew Dillanger," Drew replied.

"I'm sorry to tell you that your son has suffered severe head trauma, and we've induced a coma to reduce the possibility of brain damage," Dr. Anderson said. "The pressure and swelling of the brain were causing seizures. He also has internal injuries, some bleeding, and several bone fractures. We're going to take him over to get scans now. My current concern is compression fractures in his neck and back, and we want to get him into surgery as soon as we have the x-rays. We'll have a better idea of his prognosis after surgery."

Elle was in shock and could not speak. It was like a nightmare, and the hallway seemed to spin about her. Drew thanked the doctor, and he walked Elle a few steps over to some chairs so she could sit down. They sat and watched silently as the attendants wheeled Gary Lee on the bed out of the ICU room and down the hall toward Radiology.

Elle stood up to try and catch a glimpse of her son's face. "Oh, Gary Lee…," she said softly as if not wanting to wake him up.

She turned again to Drew and asked, "How did this happen? Gary Lee is a good driver. What could have gone wrong?"

Elle was thinking how her son had been driving motor vehicles since he was a little kid. As long as he wasn't racing on the street, she thought, he could handle a car without any problems.

"I don't know. The police were here. They had some sketchy information about Gary Lee losing control on the highway. They said they had more information coming in from witnesses, and they were hoping to come back and speak to him."

"Speak to Gary Lee?" Elle asked. "He's in a coma!"

"It didn't make sense. I don't know how they work. I've never been in a situation like this before. The officer said he wouldn't have all the details for us until they finish their police report."

Elle had to pull herself together. There were problems to solve. She needed to reach out to friends and family to let them know what was happening before they heard it all on the news. She started making phone calls and texting. She was able to reach several of Gary Lee's friends, including his best friend, Chad Gibbons, who told her they would be coming over to the hospital, even if they could just sit in the waiting room and pray. She called her office and canceled her schedule for the next week.

Elle expected to see Gary Lee come back to the ICU room from Radiology, but only Dr. Anderson returned.

"Gary Lee is being prepared for surgery," the doctor explained. "I suggest that you go down the hall to the waiting room since it will probably be several hours before we have any additional news for you."

The two of them walked down the hall silently. Drew and Elle were separated, and their marriage was dissolving; he had moved out nine months earlier. There had been much tension between them, but that seemed insignificant at this moment.

Elle could feel her anger rising in her stomach as she thought about how much Drew loved racing and racing history and how much it had influenced Gary Lee. The thought suddenly tore at her again that Gary Lee had been street racing. If that were true, there would be no coming back for Drew; no reconciliation between them. Her intuition had already kicked into full throttle, and she would not be putting it away in a little box on the shelf now.

They entered the empty ICU waiting room. There were various arrangements of dreary couches and armchairs with some vending machines in the corner. Elle thought this room needed a facelift; it reflected the somber dread of so many of its visitors. As an interior designer, she had worked on many office and medical design projects like this—it would have been easy.

They walked to the back of the room, and Elle threw down her purse on a couch to claim her territory. She tucked her light brown hair behind her ears and dropped onto the cushions. Drew pulled over the chair next to the couch. Elle looked at him with a sense of bewilderment and disbelief. Now in his forties, Drew had aged well; he still had his preppy look from college that she liked so much. How did this happen to them?

"Do you want some coffee, Elle?" asked Drew.

Elle ignored his question, staring into space for a moment. "Do you think he was racing?" she asked Drew point-blank. She looked at him sternly, with that same look that she had on many of their disputes over Gary Lee's go-karting endeavors.

Drew shrugged his shoulders. "I don't know. I can't imagine that Gary Lee would do such a thing." He sunk into the chair and looked down, abandoning the idea of coffee.

Elle was concerned about what would come next. Sick to her stomach and holding her heart, she said, "Gillian Mason is dead. How am I going to face that family?"

*****

A light rain was falling as Chad Gibbons was driving with his girlfriend, Annie, in his truck. They were headed back to Annie's house for dinner after a fun Saturday in Leeds, Alabama, when Chad's phone rang. Annie picked up the cell phone from the console and looked at it.

"Elle Dillanger?" she questioned.

"It's Gary Lee's mom. Go ahead and answer it," said Chad.

"Hi, Mrs. Dillanger?"

Chad could hear the sound of a woman's voice in between the swishing of the windshield wipers. He looked back at Annie, and a wave of shock washed over her face.

"Oh my God!" she blurted out. "Where are you now?" she asked into the phone. "What about Gillian?"

Chad knew something horrible had happened. Annie listened some more on the phone and then hung up. Morose anxiety hung in the air as Chad waited desperately for Annie's response.

"Gary Lee had an accident, and he's in the hospital," she said. "She couldn't tell me anything about Gillian. We have to go to the hospital in Auburn right away."

Chad felt his throat tighten up, and his mind started to conjure up imagined scenes. He shook off the haunting thoughts and tried to focus on what to do next.

"Look up how to get to Auburn the fastest," he said to Annie. She was already on it with his phone in her hand.

"Turn on 29 up ahead. I need you to stop for a moment."

Chad made the turn and pulled off to the gas station that was by the exit. They both sat in silent shock. It had become dark, and Annie's strawberry-blonde hair looked platinum in the dim light from the station. Headlights from a passing car illuminated the look of dread on her face.

"I should call Julia," she said.

Before she could make a call, her phone started to ring.

"Hello?" she answered and then listened. "Oh, no, no, no, no, no! That can't be," Annie moaned and then started to cry. "Who told you that?"

Another long pause as she listened. The sound of the wipers and the pounding rain filled the silence as Chad waited to hear what had happened. Annie put down the phone.

"Gillian's dead," she said to Chad, looking at him in horror and misery. "That was Gabrielle. She heard it from Gillian's brother."

Chad felt numb. It was surreal, like a bad movie. Annie leaned over and put her arm around his waist. She muffled her crying into his shoulder. He put his arms around her to hold her, and she sobbed. They sat there for a minute, just holding each other. Annie looked up at Chad and took a deep breath. In the pale light, he could see a tear glistening on her round, freckled cheeks.

"We have to go," she said in a determined tone. "Gary Lee needs us now."

Chad pulled out, and they continued driving toward Auburn. Annie held his hand tightly in silence. What could have happened? Gary Lee was one of the best drivers that Chad knew.

Annie picked up her phone and started calling other friends. She told them to come to the hospital in Auburn. After some more texting, Annie had organized a small vigil to arrive that evening.

Chad turned into the parking lot at the Methodist Hospital in Auburn. They headed quickly over to the entrance to register and pick up name tags, where they found their friends Brent and Gabrielle signing in. Annie ran and hugged Gabrielle, and they cried together. Chad knew Brent from school, but the usual "hey" seemed not appropriate at the moment. He gave Brent a handshake and then a strong bro-hug spontaneously.

"You won't be able to visit right now. He's in surgery," the woman at the desk said. "The waiting room is right down that hall."

Chad and his friends walked into the waiting room to find Elle Dillanger sitting on the couch. Usually, she was an energetic woman, attractive and well-dressed. Chad wasn't sure what to expect today. She looked up, and Chad could see the worry on her face. A feeling of anguish welled up inside him, and his eyes began to flood with tears. Chad lost control and began to sob when he walked over to Mrs. Dillanger. She stood up and held him as he cried, and then he regained his composure. Annie also came over to them.

"We're here for you and Gary Lee," Annie said.

"What happened?" asked Chad.

The teenagers gathered around to hear answers to all of their questions. Drew Dillanger also came and stood by Elle Dillanger; he started to tell them what had happened.

"All we know now is that Gary Lee was driving and lost control on Highway 280," Mr. Dillanger said. "He skidded off the road and hit a tree on the passenger side."

Annie gasped, and Chad put his arm around her. "And Gillian?" Annie asked.

"The highway patrol said that she was killed instantly. I'm sorry."

Gabrielle started to cry, and Annie reached out and grabbed her hand.

"What about Gary Lee now?" asked Chad.

"Well, he was not awake when we saw him, and they've taken him into surgery," said Mr. Dillanger. "That was about an hour ago. I'm sorry, but the ICU will be limiting visitors when he comes out."

"That's okay," said Chad. "We knew we couldn't see him when we checked in."

"We just want to be here for Gary Lee," explained Annie. "Some other friends are also coming, and we'll just hang out here in the waiting room."

"All right. Thank you for coming," said Mr. Dillanger. He nodded and returned to his seat in the waiting room with his wife.

Annie staked out the back section of the room for their group to sit. As they were getting settled, three more of their high school friends entered the waiting room. Annie sprang into action, waved them over, and explained the situation to them with Gabrielle's help. After that, everyone was seated, busily texting and posting online with their phones.

Chad sat on the couch, leaning forward with his face in his hands. He stared at the floor, not knowing what to think. He had such an important summer planned with Gary Lee. Chad was a contender for the All-Pro American racing scholarship, and this summer was supposed to be the launch of his racing career. Gary Lee was going to be his support team, and Chad didn't know how he could pull this off without his best friend. Since they were eight, they had been karting together, even though Gary Lee was grounded from racing that summer.

It was not the first time the demons of fate tried to steal away Chad's dreams. When he was fifteen, Chad was competing in a southern karting championship, along with Gary Lee and others. In practice before the event, Chad had a horrible karting crash, and Gary Lee stuck with him to the Emergency Room. Chad dropped out and tried to support Gary Lee in the competition, but he knew he wasn't much help with a broken leg and crutches. It was really Gary Lee who helped him over his disappointment. The memory of his accident still haunted Chad, and thinking of the crash this day, he had visions of the sudden impact, smoke, and agony. Gary Lee had won the karting championship that summer, so why did this happen to him now?

Graduation was next month, and the summer was to be a glorious flurry of new opportunities for Chad and all his friends. Everything had been going so perfectly up until this happened. Chad just couldn't get his head around it. He was with Gary Lee and Gillian earlier that day at the races in Leeds, Alabama—Annie, too. They had so much fun. It just wasn't fair; it couldn't be true; this must have been a horrible dream—please wake up!

*****

Elle couldn't stand the waiting. She rose from the couch and started to pace. Time felt like it had stopped when finally, another set of footsteps was heard coming down the hall toward the waiting room. Everyone stopped talking and looked up with expectation. Elle recognized the tap of those steps. Evan Waitts suddenly appeared in the doorway and gazed over the sullen group of high school kids. He was lean and wore his dark hair brushed back, which gave him a younger look. He had arrived sharply dressed in a navy-blue blazer—perhaps from a meeting. Elle sprang from her seat and hugged Evan.

"Elle, I'm sorry it took so long to get here," he said.

Evan was Elle's closest friend from college at the Rhode Island School of Design, and he was always present in good times and trouble. They were friends before she met Drew, and Evan claims he introduced them. He had encouraged Elle to go to mixers at Brown University since she didn't know any straight guys at Risdee. That's where she met Drew—an architecture student at Brown who wanted to become a stock car driver. He was very amusing to her, and they shared common professional interests but not stock cars. After graduating, they married and moved to Massachusetts so Drew could get his master's degree at Northeastern. Chad was born there, and it was a struggle for them in Boston. Evan had always wanted the three of them to start a business together in Blue Springs, where he had grown up. Ten years ago, he convinced Elle and Drew to make the move.

Since her separation from Drew, Elle had become isolated from many of their friends. Most of them seemed aligned with her husband rather than Elle, and she did not share that crowd's fascination with autos and fast living. Evan Waitts was the one true friend who stuck with her after the split, and Elle appreciated his loyalty. She had only left a cryptic voice message for Evan, and he showed up.

"Drew, I don't know what to say," Evan said. "How is Gary Lee doing? Tell me what happened?"

"Gary Lee is in surgery right now. It seems like forever, but we're just anxiously waiting for an update," Elle replied.

Elle rehearsed what she knew about Gary Lee's accident. As she said the words, Elle struggled to hold onto hope. She knew her son's life was in the balance.

"Gary Lee is a strong young man," said Evan. "He has a fighting spirit. You mustn't dwell on the worst case." Evan was always very positive, and Elle appreciated his encouragement.

As they talked, Dr. Anderson suddenly appeared at the waiting room door with a woman also dressed in scrubs and a white coat. Elle looked at Anderson's face for a sign, but he wore the same all-business expression he had when she first met him. He signaled Elle and Drew with a head nod, and Elle walked briskly toward him; Drew followed.

"Your son is out of surgery now, but he's still in critical condition," said Dr. Anderson. "This is Dr. Kramer. She is the orthopedic surgeon who helped in the operation. We have him in recovery, and you can come and see him now."

"Is he awake yet—what did you find in the surgery?" asked Elle. The others in the room had moved closer to Drew and Elle.

"It's not good news, other than that he's alive," replied the other doctor. "We were able to stabilize the internal bleeding and set his arm and legs. The fractures in his vertebrae have us worried."

"I've also consulted with a neurosurgeon," continued Dr. Anderson. "We'll need to keep him in an induced coma for quite some time so his brain can heal. And honestly, we won't have a prognosis of the condition of his spine until he wakes up."

"So does that mean he could be paralyzed? Isn't there a test for paralysis?" asked Elle. Another horrible thought, but it was certainly better than losing her son.

"Right now, we are looking for brain recovery," said Anderson. "We won't be able to address his spinal condition until we get through this phase of recovery. We will know more when we can wake him out of this coma." Dr. Anderson paused and looked at the anxious friends. "I'm sorry, but only two visitors are allowed right now. The others will need to wait here in the waiting room."

Elle looked back at Evan. She did not know how to feel yet.

"Go on," said Evan. "I'll watch over the crowd in the waiting room."

Elle and Drew followed the two doctors out and down the hall. Elle could see Gary Lee lying on the hospital bed with shiny metal splints on his left arm and legs as they approached the ICU room. Elle leaned up against the glass and peered in. The doctor opened the door and motioned for them to enter. As Elle entered the ICU, the sounds of the machines became more noticeable—hissing and beeping. The doctors had wires and tubes connecting her son to illuminated and chirping devices.

Elle stepped slowly over to the bed with her eyes fixed on Gary Lee. Where was the energetic boy so full of life? His eyes were closed and surrounded by dark bruising. She reached for his right arm that was not in traction and put her hand on his. She started to sob when she touched him. Drew pulled up a chair for her to sit by the bedside.

They stayed there until the morning light came through the window out in the hall. The all-important first twenty-four hours were passing, and Elle had a glimmer of hope.

Elle and Drew had dozed off but woke up when the nurse came in to check on Gary Lee. It was now the Sunday morning after the accident, and the hospital was full of activity. Elle stood up to stretch her legs, and Drew said they should go and check on the visitors in the waiting room. They sleeplessly walked back to the waiting room where a larger group of friends had gathered, along with clusters of visitors for other patients.

Elle scanned the young faces of Gary Lee's friends, all looking to her and Drew in desperation for some positive news. Her eyes stopped on Chad Gibbons and his girlfriend, Annie. Elle had known Chad since he was eight. He stood up and looked athletic and youthful, with a head of short, brown hair brushed straight. It was hard to believe he was now eighteen. The teenage couple walked over to Elle and Drew, and some other friends followed also. Elle looked at their faces, full of despair and exhaustion. She wished she had something hopeful to tell them. Annie had clearly been crying; her eyes were red and swollen.

"Mrs. Dillanger," said Chad. "Any news or improvement with Gary Lee? We're kind of going crazy here."

"Oh, Chad," said Elle, suddenly filled with emotion. She hugged him. "Gary Lee seems to be stable—no change in his condition. I'm afraid this is going to be a long recovery. You and your friends should probably go home. I appreciate the support, but I don't know when you'll be able to see him."

"If it's okay with you, Mrs. Dillanger, I'd like to stay a little longer," said Chad. "If others arrive, we'd like to be able to talk to them."

"Me too," said Annie, barely able to speak. The others with them nodded in agreement, and they all began to sit back down on the couches and chairs.

A highway patrol officer was also apparently waiting in the back of the room and approached the two parents.

"Mrs. Dillanger?" the uniformed man asked. "I'm Officer Ryan. I spoke with your husband yesterday. I wanted to see if I could also speak with you or your son."

"My son? Didn't they tell you he was in a coma? Honestly, this is not the best time," she replied.

"Ma'am, we need to compile as much information as possible in the initial accident report," explained the officer.

Elle decided to seize the moment. "What can you tell me about the accident? Did he lose control? How fast was he going?" she asked.

"Well, they were going very fast. We have one eyewitness who said they passed him at around a hundred miles per hour," said Ryan. "The car skidded off the road on a turn and slid sideways through the wet grass until the passenger side hit a tree. We're not sure why he lost control."

Elle was horrified at the images in her head; she stared out the window as if in a trance. She had always trusted Gary Lee on the road, but now she was wondering if she ever should have. Elle looked around and saw Evan and Drew talking while putting coins into the coffee vending machine.

Evan looked over at Elle. "Coffee?" he mouthed, pointing at the machine. She nodded.

"I'd like to go back to sit with my son if we're done," said Elle to the officer. She took the cup of coffee from Evan and thanked him.

"Mrs. Dillanger, I have enough for now. This case will be reassigned to a detective for the criminal investigation. I hope your son recovers," Ryan said, and he turned and left the room.

A criminal investigation? Elle could hardly stand up. Her coffee started to spill, and Evan reached over to support her.

CHAPTER 2

Elle positioned herself in the armchair by Gary Lee's bedside and remembered how he first became involved in karting. It was ten years earlier when they had first met the racing legend who lived on top of the hill in Blue Springs. Her family—Elle, Drew, and Gary Lee—had just moved to Alabama from Massachusetts, and it was quite a change in pace. Her longtime friend from college, Evan Waitts, had the inspiration to start an architecture and design firm in Blue Springs, his hometown. She and Drew had wanted to start their own business for a while, but Boston was so competitive. Evan's idea seemed perfect—a small, wealthy county that lacked design resources. They all quit their jobs, took their savings, and moved to Blue Springs.

The opening of their offices in town was a big event for Elle, Drew, and Evan. The firm's name was Dillanger, Dillanger & Waitts, and the partnership sign read "DD&W, Architecture & Design." Elle had proudly mounted it just to the side of the front door. Elle had ordered the most stylish office furniture she could find on their frugal budget. After all, a design firm needed to look the part.

The desks and chairs had arrived, and Drew and Evan had spent the weekend setting up all the furniture. Elle unpacked her desk items and arranged her work area meticulously, although she knew that perfection would not last. She admired the small scene and took some photos for future use in potential advertising. Elle took pictures of everything that inspired her aesthetic—although never of herself. She was self-conscious of her pale skin and hoped that would change, having recently escaped New England winters. Elle was about to pick up Gary Lee from school when Drew came into the office grinning.

"I just landed a new client, and you'll never guess who!" he boasted.

Elle shrugged and raised her eyebrows, waiting for his news.

"The Kilgores! They want us to redesign Monroe Kilgore's personal garage, and his wife Uma is going to have us remodel their kitchen."

"What's so huge about that?" asked Elle. "It's mostly cabinet remodeling—why are you so excited?"

"Well, he's pretty legendary, and there are not many famous people around here. It will give the partnership great publicity, and besides, I've always wanted to meet them. We're going up to their mansion tomorrow to get started."

Drew's enthusiasm was infectious, and she had wondered since moving to Blue Springs about the people who lived in the twin mansions on the top of the hill. She knew the Kilgores were auto racing celebrities, and they had a good reputation in the town. Drew had always been into racing history, and he made it seem so exciting.

The next day, Elle and Drew drove the meandering road up the hill, past the smaller estates, and through the gates of the Kilgore property. Perched on top of the pillars framing the gates were two white concrete foo lions, sitting majestically. Elle suddenly became filled with anticipation. She was struck by the many luxurious cars parked in the circular driveway in front of the house. She noticed a black Mercedes-Benz and a gold convertible Cadillac with vanity plates "WINNER" and "ZUMA." Elle made a mental note to herself to be sure to charge enough for this project—they could afford it! The house loomed above them as they pulled up, and mounted over the front door was a family crest. Drew and Elle walked up the front steps; the large door swung open, revealing Monroe Kilgore, standing as if on a podium in his personal winner's circle.

"Hello, Drew!" Monroe exclaimed with childlike excitement. "Welcome to our home. I've been waiting to get this project started for a long time. I was just waiting to find the right chap." His Scottish brogue seemed to echo out across the grounds.

"Thanks, Mr. Kilgore," said Drew. "I think you'll be quite pleased. This is my wife, Elle. She'll be working with Mrs. Kilgore on the kitchen part of the project."

"You can call me Big Mo," he replied as he reached his hand out to shake Elle's.

She shook his hand—a firm grip and pleasant smile. Monroe's stature matched his voluminous voice; his weathered face was topped with neat white hair. Monroe was charming, and the smell of his musky aftershave was enticing.

"Uma's in the kitchen. Let's go back, and we can sit down and talk," he said.

The three of them strolled through the expansive hallway that led into a living room. It was dark and gloomy. Then they walked past a dining room with an enormous table suitable for a king, a game room with a pool table, and then a library with helmets and trophies on the shelves. Elle paused at the library doorway.

"You like that?" asked Monroe. "We call it the Hall of Helmets."

Elle smiled and nodded. She wondered who had been the designer here—it was well done but not her style. Too much like a Scottish castle, she thought. They entered into another space that looked like another dining room but turned out to be part of the larger kitchen. There was a delicious smell of something cooking that Elle couldn't quite identify. A thin, older woman was standing by the island in the center of the kitchen, pouring a cup of tea.

"Drew and Elle, would you like some tea?" asked Monroe. "This is my wife, Uma."

"Nice to meet you," Uma said, and she handed Elle a cup of tea. "I hope you like Earl Grey." Uma's gray hair was pulled back in a bun, and her olive-toned face had been graced with smile lines. She spoke with a lilting European accent, and her kind, blue eyes put Elle in the mood for tea.

"Yes, thank you, Mrs. Kilgore," Elle replied, though she hadn't been given a choice. "You have such a lovely accent—possibly from Austria?"

"Very close, my dear. I am from Hungary. I met Monroe there when he was racing Formula 3 as a young man. Oh, and please call me Uma."

Elle nodded and then recognized it was the smell of paprika that filled the kitchen.

Drew also received a cup of tea, and the four of them sat down at the round kitchen table. Elle pulled a few catalogs out of her bag and set them in front of her new client. The table was made of thick dark wood, and Elle wondered if it would stay or go as part of the remodeling. It reminded her of décor for a British pub—casual and functional. The first part of any job was listening before making suggestions, Elle reminded herself.

Monroe had an air of openness and generosity. Elle thoughtfully presented some ideas for the remodeling, and Monroe Kilgore seemed to listen to her every word and appreciated all of her design ideas. She showed Monroe a midnight blue double Italian oven from a catalog that she thought would be perfect for their new cooking space. Strangely, Uma didn't have much to say about the kitchen project—not even when discussing the colors or appliances. It was all Monroe Kilgore's ideas, and his input was dominant.

After the kitchen discussions had wrapped up, Drew asked to see the garage. Monroe rose, but Uma remained seated at the table as if she knew her place. Elle wasn't sure if she should follow the men or stay in the kitchen, not wanting to be rude and leave Uma alone.

"Let me show you two a bit more of the house before we look at the garage," said Monroe, gesturing away from the kitchen space. Elle turned to Uma and excused herself as she rose from the table. The small woman just looked up at her and smiled kindly, politely granting her leave.

Monroe walked Drew and Elle back to the library that they had passed earlier. The shelves were lined with trophies and racing memorabilia that made Drew's eyes grow wide. Elle was a little embarrassed at her lack of interest, but Monroe Kilgore was very good at making emotional connections. He picked up a few trophies and explained where they came from and the stories behind them. Elle remarked at how Monroe presented himself as if the dangers of auto racing simply didn't apply to him, such an elegant gentleman. He spoke of Formula One, diesel engine production cars, open-wheel competitions in America, the 1954 24 Hours of Le Mans, and the tourist trophy in Ireland. Elle could see that Drew was mesmerized and spellbound by the auto racing legend, and their relationship would eventually lead to more than what she expected.

Finally, they moved on to the garage. It was even more expansive than the house—easily room for twenty cars, but it was almost empty. "I had our garage man move most of the cars out so you could get a better perspective on the layout," said Monroe. That explained to Elle why there were so many cars around the circle out front. She looked at a sad, old Mercedes-Benz and an old Mustang in the corner next to some piles of auto pieces.

"Those are the project cars," Monroe explained. "They don't run now, but my mechanic and I like to find old gems like those and tinker with them."

Monroe turned to Drew and started a private conversation about his ideas for the garage. Elle took the liberty to wander over to look at the dusty Mustang. She could still see the Scotsman waving his arms and pointing, talking of new cabinets, color schemes, and lighting. Excluded, she was free to explore.

Her father had a Mustang just like this, she recalled—possibly a 1967 model. This one was pale yellow with a convertible top. On the other side of the pile of auto body parts and wheels, she found an unusual four-wheeled vehicle composed of metal tubes. Across the front was the label "Tony Kart."

"That's my grandson Mackie's old go-kart," said Monroe, as he strolled back toward Elle in the corner of the garage. Drew was now interested and also approaching. "He drove that when he was around eight. It hurled him to many a victory, but I'm not sure what to do with it now. He doesn't have room for it, and I didn't want to sell it."

Elle had heard of Mackenzie Kilgore from Drew's conversations about auto racing. The go-kart seemed unassuming for a future racing celebrity; it was just a bare skeleton of a kart with a few fenders in a pile behind it.

"So your grandson started driving go-karts when he was eight?" asked Drew.

"Well, no. Are you kidding?" said Monroe. "He started when he was four years old. He was winning by the time he was eight. You know, he won a national go-karting championship when he was twelve." Monroe was full of pride.

"Seems to be a popular thing around here," said Drew. "Gary Lee, my son, is almost eight. We stopped to see a bunch of kids driving at a go-kart track the other day. He couldn't take his eyes off of them."

"Well, that settles it!" exclaimed Monroe. "This go-kart will be part of your payment!" He clapped his hands with a smile, looking at both Drew and Elle. Drew lit up, but Elle was surprised and not smiling. She was not sure this would be a preferred venture to jump into, despite Kilgore's generosity.

"You have nothing to worry about, Elle. They don't drive that fast at that age," explained Monroe. "Many kids in this county race go-karts, and it will help your son make good, wholesome friends. Karting builds character, like scouting."

Drew was beaming. "It would be perfect for his birthday! He'll flip," he said.

Elle cocked her head and smiled at Drew, giving him her tenuous approval. She didn't have much choice, being put on the spot like that in front of a client.

Drew began to plan. "I'll have to get it dressed up—do you know anyone who can help me with that? Umm…of course, you do—sorry. Do you think I can get it ready in two weeks?"

"Now, you don't worry at all about that," said Monroe. "I'll have it all prettied up for you to take home in two weeks. Not a problem."

18

Elle comforted herself, knowing that Gary Lee would be excited about the go-kart. It would help him get over being forced to leave his friends behind in Massachusetts.

As the discussions about the design projects came to an end, Elle became anxious to leave. Her mind began to wander, and she thought about Gary Lee's birthday and picking him up from school that afternoon. The three walked back into the kitchen, where Drew and Elle bid their goodbyes to Uma. Monroe walked them back through the house and out the front door, waving.

"Why did you do that?" asked Elle as soon as she shut the car door. "We should talk about these things before getting into a big commitment like go-karting."

"What did I do? It wasn't my idea. He just offered the go-kart out of the blue," Drew defended himself. "I wasn't about to say no to him—that would have been rude. I think it's a perfect gift, though."

Elle was jolted out of her memories into the present crisis by a loud noise from outside the hospital room. Someone had dropped a tray or something. The glare of the fluorescent lights was now giving her a headache, and the wait for Gary Lee's improvement seemed perpetual. Would it all have been the same if they had never met the Kilgore family?

CHAPTER 3

Chad only had a few weeks left of high school, and under the circumstances, the teachers were giving the kids a lot of leeway. The school had brought in a grief counselor, but Chad wasn't ready to talk to anyone. The road to school took him past the Babylon Karting Park in Blue Springs. As he drove by that morning, Chad looked over at the park where the large graffiti number "87" was still visible from the road. The number 87 was his and Gary Lee's number. Although faded now, it represented a dream in him that was still there. They had spray painted this treasured gem a long time ago.

He remembered a Saturday morning in August seven or eight years earlier at the karting park. Chad had arrived with his dad to race in the Cadet class for ages up to eleven. Chad's dad and Mr. Dillanger, Gary Lee's dad, set up a large awning in the paddock area to work on their karts. They unloaded the karts from their trucks and brought them under the pit awning to get ready for racing. Being in the Cadet class, Chad and Gary Lee would be on the track around 10 a.m., right after the little kids. Their fathers handed them their racing numbers: Gary Lee was number 8, and Chad was 7. The kids had to wear their numbers on both their suits and their karts in those days, so the two of them were walking around with a large "8" and "7" on their fronts. After seeing themselves together in the photos, that became Gary Lee's and Chad's number—87.

Karting was fun, and trying to pass each other was the thrill. Chad would pull up on Gary Lee and try to pass him, then on the next lap, Gary Lee would do the same to Chad. Karting in the Cadet class was a simple pleasure, and it was easy to have the excitement of success. The top ten finishing positions would get a ribbon. That day Gary Lee received a green ribbon for fifth place, and Chad received a purple one for seventh.

After racing with the Cadets, the two friends typically would sit and watch the Juniors race. The Juniors were exciting—bigger and faster karts. This was their last season racing as Cadets, and they would be moving up to Juniors the following year. Chad's father was always there to coach and make comments about the performance. Chad remembered feeling the annoyance of his father's judgments. His father loved the award ceremony, and karting seemed to mean so much to him. Chad could still hear it all in his head.

"I want you to come with me…pay attention to the presentation…," Chad's dad would say matter-of-factly. "Don't get distracted…keep your eye on the prize, and don't waste time."

He recalled again how he hated that feeling of being constantly checked by his father. His progress, his failures, his winning, his losing was always a part of the conversation.

That particular day in August was stuck in his memory, how he and Gary Lee had walked back over to the stands where the Junior class had finished their racing. Everyone had congregated in the grandstand, both karters and parents, and another group of adults was standing on the track in front. The two had climbed up into the stands and sat by Gary Lee's dad, who was waiting for them.

"Hi, kids," a man shouted in front of the crowd. "My name is Monroe Kilgore, but everyone around here calls me Big Mo." Then he introduced his family. "Sonny and Mackie Kilgore, the greatest racecar drivers in Blue Springs, Alabama."

Chad knew the Kilgore racing family in Blue Springs, and Mackie had been the local karting hero at the track ever since Chad started there.

"All right, kids and parents," said Sonny Kilgore, "Mackie just won his first professional race at age eighteen, and we are here to introduce a new karting program that we are going to start right here in Blue Springs. Kilgore Karting! We want to help you and your kids follow in Mackie's footsteps and get to be real racecar drivers."

Chad and Gary Lee were thrilled. Chad grabbed his father's arm and gave him a look.

"Can we do that, Dad?" he asked.

His father nodded. "Next year, when you start Juniors, we'll sign you up for Kilgore Karting. It's pretty expensive."

Gary Lee was tugging on his father's arm also.

"Come on, Dad," Gary Lee said. "Chad's going to sign up. Can't I do that too?"

"Maybe. We'll have to talk to your mom about that," Mr. Dillanger said.

After karting, Chad's dad took his kart back home in their truck, and Chad went home with Gary Lee and his dad to spend the night.

Chad loved Gary Lee's house; it was cool and different. They had unusual natural wood furniture and hanging paper lamps. The kitchen had a trash compactor, and they would put things in it to see them get crushed. Gary Lee's mom had made a meatloaf that night for dinner, and they all sat down.

"This is great, Mrs. Dillanger," said Chad. His mother taught him always to compliment the chef.

"Thank you, Chad," she replied. "It's always nice to have you over. How was karting today, boys?"

"I got fifth place," Gary Lee said. "I won a ribbon. They are starting a new karting program. Kilgore Karting."

Mrs. Dillanger raised her eyebrows and looked over at Gary Lee's dad.

"Mom," said Gary Lee. "Chad's going to be on the Kilgore team next year. Can I?"

"Your father and I will have to talk about it. What's wrong with the karting you're doing now?"

"Karting is fun, but this is different, Mom. It's going to help me get to be a real racecar driver."

Gary Lee's efforts seemed to have no effect on his mother's resolute attitude. She was always so engaged around the boys, except for karting. Dinner was finished up with ice cream, and then they helped clear the table. After dinner, the kids went down the back stairs into the finished basement. Gary Lee had his projects there: plastic models and radio-controlled toys. They put on the TV, but their true interest was the new karting team. That was all they could talk about that night.

After playing around with the model racecars, the kids went up to Gary Lee's room for bedtime. He had bunk beds, and Chad would always get the top bunk when staying overnight. While getting ready for bed, they could hear Gary Lee's parents in the kitchen arguing, Chad remembered.

"Drew, it's totally unnecessary," his mom could be heard. "I don't know why you think this karting thing is so important."

"Let Gary Lee grow up and have his dream, Elle," his dad replied. "What if his dream was to be an Olympic athlete? You'd support that."

"It's not the same. I think this is more your dream than his," she said.

Gary Lee pretended like he couldn't hear them. They climbed up into their bunks, but neither could sleep.

"I hope Mom lets me join the Kilgore Karting team," said Gary Lee. "I think we really could become racecar drivers like Mackie Kilgore, you know."

"When we finish high school, we could start our own racing team," said Chad. "We could do endurance GT racing. That takes at least two drivers on a team."

"We could build the coolest GT prototype," said Gary Lee.

"That would be awesome! We could call it Gibbons-Dillanger Racing."

"Or it could be Dillanger-Gibbons," offered Gary Lee.

"That sounds better," said Chad. "It has to be Dillanger-Gibbons."

"Yeah. That would be so great standing on the podium and having them call out, 'First place, from Dillanger-Gibbons Racing…,' you know."

The next morning, Gary Lee played it like a pro. Chad recalled how Gary Lee came down the front stairs leaping with enthusiasm and gave his mom a big hug.

"Mom, I really, really want to be on the Kilgores' karting team. It's what I always wanted. I'll do a year of chores without complaining."

She couldn't hold out. "Okay, okay. We can try that next year and see how it goes," she said.

Gary Lee hugged her some more. "Thanks, Mom!" He turned and ran off with Chad.

"Remember, you have to do a year of chores," she called out.

The Team 87 chronology had some more variations that summer. It later evolved the following year into drawings of the Dillanger-Gibbons team and their cars, still sporting the Number 87. One summer night after the best of friends had started Kilgore Karting, they snuck out and painted the large "87" on the back wall at the karting park. To their surprise, it was left in place. No one asked about who painted the graffiti or talked about removing it.

This day as Chad drove by the karting park, the large number 87 left a sting in his heart. Their shared dream seemed to be in a wreckage, just like Gary Lee's car on the side of the highway. Chad's future was now unclear like muddy water—how would he get through this summer?

CHAPTER 4

Elle found some small consolation when the hospital staff moved Gary Lee from the ICU to the Critical Care Unit. A sign of improvement, she thought, even though he was still in an induced coma. Elle kept watch in the chair by the side of her son's bed, anxiously spending the hours and waiting for progress. It was late afternoon, and the sun stretched long shadows across the landscaping outside the window. She kept looking at Gary Lee's face anticipating that his bluish-gray eyes would open and he would give her his boyish grin just to let her know everything would be all right. A few locks of Gary Lee's dirty-blond hair were visible out from the bandages crossing his forehead. His eye sockets were still darkened like a sore boxer, but she could see the freckles across his round cheeks. Elle leaned forward and gently kissed his forehead, hoping that he would somehow sense her presence and know that he was loved.

Drew had brought some of Gary Lee's required school reading books, and Elle thought she would try reading some of them to him. She began reading aloud from *The Book Thief*, but she quickly realized that the main narrator was the Angel of Death, explaining how he "took" people. The dark angel wasn't welcome here, she thought, and she put the book down.

Elle couldn't help thinking of the bookshelves in the Kilgore library, just walls full of racing helmets and trophies. There wasn't a single book on them. The extended mahogany shelves were lined with racing helmets of all colors and designs intermixed with metal trophy cups, filling at least three expansive walls. No books. Monroe Kilgore and his son, Sonny, had their oversized portraits filling the main wall of that room, embodying their audacious attitudes. There was no accounting for bad taste or self-aggrandizement. She scanned the other possible books to read on the table near Gary Lee's bed and sighed.

Once again, Elle observed a sheriff's officer in his beige uniform lurking around the doorway, glancing into the hospital room. He'd been doing this for the last few days since Gary Lee moved out of the ICU. She wasn't sure if the officer was hoping to interrogate Gary Lee or if he was guarding him like a suspect. The hospital aide passed by and stopped to exchange gossip with the sheriff.

"He's the one?" Elle overheard. "How fast? Really?"

There seemed to be a curiosity in the halls about Gary Lee and his accident.

"I think they took part of his brain out…," mumbled the sheriff.

Elle was getting annoyed. What were these strangers doing around her son's room? Another uniformed policeman in dark blue stopped in the doorway and started talking to the sheriff.

"He'd be in jail if he weren't in a coma," she heard the man in blue say.

Elle observed the policeman with a mustache and wondered about his visit. The golden eagle patch on his sleeve glared under the hospital lighting, and his handcuffs, baton, and holstered gun hung by his side. His two-way radio made an intolerable racket, squawking and preventing her from hearing what the sheriff was saying to the policeman.

Another man with a brown jacket and matching tie walked up to the officers and greeted them. The man in brown turned and walked into her room, approaching Elle. He was shorter than the others, with a chiseled face that looked continually displeased. He nodded his head as he looked around the room. What now? She had no idea what the suited man could want from her.

"I'm Detective Lowry, Mrs. Dillanger. I'm taking over the investigation." He turned and looked at Gary Lee. "How is your son doing?"

"Well…," she paused. "They have him sedated while his head injuries heal. The doctors said he had a chance of full recovery if we can get past the next few days." She was trying to be optimistic but still feared for Gary Lee's life.

"Okay. I'm going to need to speak with him when he wakes up," Lowry stated plainly. "I see that I can't do that now, but I also need to speak with you and your husband. Can we talk now?"

Elle was irritated by the intrusion, and she could see the policeman and the sheriff looking into the room, eager to overhear the discussion. Elle looked away for a moment at the illuminated screens of the medical monitor next to her son, hoping that these visitors would just leave. She looked back and nodded. What could the detective want to ask her? Lowry pulled out a small notepad.

"We estimate the time of the accident to be around 4 p.m. on Saturday. Do you know where your son and Gillian Mason were headed while driving on Highway 280 at the time of the accident?" he asked.

Elle remembered what led up to that day. Gary Lee and Gillian were both accepted at Auburn University and several other colleges, but they were pretty sure they wanted to go to Auburn. The admissions department was hosting an open house that weekend, and Gary Lee had signed up to attend. They would have tours, meet students and professors, and each stay in a dorm room.

"Gary Lee and Gillian were going to visit the University at Auburn," she said. "They were considering going to college there." The university was an hour's drive from their home, and Elle liked the idea of Gary Lee coming home whenever he wanted.

"Oh, a road trip." One side of Lowry's mouth pulled up in a suspicious half-smile. He continued to make notes on his pad. "Did they leave from your house, or do you recall what time he left your house?"

"It was early, right after breakfast. Gary Lee was going to pick Gillian up at her house."

"Do you know if any others were traveling with them in another car? An eyewitness said there was another car on the highway with them."

Elle looked up, concerned. This was the first she had heard about another car. Had Gary Lee's other friends been involved? "No, I don't know of anyone else. Do you know who they were?"

"I'm sorry, but we don't have any more information yet. Did your son make many trips like this? What were his driving habits?" Lowry stood next to the bed, looking down at Elle.

She paused for a moment. "Why, yes, he was always driving all over the state. He's a very experienced driver," Elle said.

"Does he tend to drive fast?" asked Lowry.

Elle knew where the detective was going with his questions, and she would not incriminate her son. "I have never seen him speeding if that's what you're asking," she said. At this point, Elle became weary of the detective's questioning.

He continued asking about Gary Lee—questions about his friends, school, Gillian, and how long he had known her. Elle answered his questions, but her mind was wandering. She began to think about the doctors and when she would talk to them next. The conversation was interrupted when Drew walked into the room, apparently surprised to see the officers and the detective speaking with Elle. She was relieved to see him.

"What's going on?" Drew asked.

"I'm Detective Lowry, assigned to this case. And you are Mr. Dillanger?" asked the detective.

Drew nodded with a dumbfounded look on his face.

"I have some questions to ask you," said Lowry.

At that point, the nurse came into the room, unhappy with all of the activity near her patient.

"A young boy is recovering here, and this is not an interrogation room," she said. She turned to the men in uniform. "Don't you all have some criminals to catch? Why are you hanging around this hospital room?"

Like chastised children, the two officers bid their hasty goodbyes to the detective and scurried off. Lowry led the two parents down the hall and into a quiet corner of the waiting room. The detective looked at Elle and Drew and motioned toward the couch, where they sat themselves down. He pulled up a sizeable upholstered armchair and sat down with his pad in hand.

"Mr. Dillanger," said Lowry, "how long has your son been racing?"

Elle could see the look of anger on Drew's face at the question—clearly suggesting guilt on the part of their child and possibly themselves.

"My son is a good driver. He's been driving vehicles of all sorts since he was eight years old. He is not a criminal," said Drew.

"Vehicular homicide is still a crime in Alabama," said Lowry in a matter-of-fact way. The detective leaned in toward Drew and said, "Don't get me wrong. I certainly hope your son has a full recovery."

Drew looked pained.

Elle leaned back on the couch next to Drew. They had argued so many times about Gary Lee's karting. Drew always insisted that their karting investment would teach core competencies like awareness on the road and how to manage speed in any situation. Elle had been worried from the moment Gary Lee received his driving permit. Would he know the difference between defensive driving and aggressive driving? Elle wanted to agree with the detective, but not at the expense of her son's innocence. She sat quietly and listened to the questions and Drew's strained responses.

A man appeared in the doorway of the waiting room, their partner and friend, Evan Waitts.

Drew looked up and said, "Oh, I almost forgot. I drove here with Evan, and he was parking the car."

Elle let out a sigh of relief. The detective's questioning had run out of steam, and he stood up.

"I'll be putting together a preliminary police report on your son's case in a few days. I still need to speak with him before I can finalize the report," he said. He handed them each a business card, said goodbye, and turned into the doorway to leave.

"And who are you?" Lowry asked Evan.

Evan looked surprised. "I'm the Dillangers' business partner, Evan Waitts."

Lowry looked at him up and down once and continued out of the room without another word. Evan turned and watched the detective leave the room and then looked back at Elle and Drew with concern.

"That's not good. Any change in Gary Lee's condition?" Evan asked.

Elle shook her head, returning to thoughts about her son. She rose and walked back to Gary Lee's room. Drew and Evan followed. Elle settled back into the chair by the bedside and turned again toward her son, hoping to notice an improvement.

"You know, you're going to need a lawyer," said Evan. "That detective is just the start of our trouble. Whether Gary Lee turns out to be innocent or not, there's still going to be a lawsuit from that girl's family. I'm not interested in seeing all of our hard work in the business go down the drain."

Evan was right. Elle's stomach wrenched into a knot. Everything in her life was being challenged. Gary Lee was still struggling for his life. Drew was already out the door. What about her reputation? Would she be able to show her face in the community? Even if they found the best lawyer in Alabama, how could anyone save them from this disgrace, and how would they pay for the legal fees? Elle felt burning anxiety inside of her with no answers. The unloving fluorescent light glared down, and the beeping machines next to the bed reminded her that she had failed to protect her only child. Gary Lee lay there on the cool linen, bruised and expressionless. His mother knew that his life would never be the same.

CHAPTER 5

Chad Gibbons came into Gary Lee's hospital room planning to spend the morning with his best buddy. There wouldn't be much conversation, but Chad wanted to be there for his Gary Lee. Mrs. Dillanger had called Chad earlier—she had appointments that morning and didn't want her son to be alone in the hospital room. "What if he wakes up?" she had said to Chad. Gary Lee was no longer in an induced coma, and everyone was hoping he would wake up soon. It was a school day, but Chad didn't mind skipping a day of school. It was the last few weeks before graduation, and he couldn't concentrate on any schoolwork.

Chad stood in front of the bed and looked down at his friend of many years lying there. Less than a month ago, Gary Lee was sitting three desks away from Chad in English class. What happened? Chad's mind started to fill with questions about their last Saturday together when Gillian, Gary Lee, Annie, and Chad had gone to the All-Pro Race in Leeds, Alabama.

Gillian had been able to get permission from her parents to go with Gary Lee for a campus tour at Auburn University and then spend the night at her grandmother's house nearby. It was the same weekend as the big race, so they had skipped the Saturday college tour to meet up with Chad and Annie at the track. Gary Lee and Gillian still planned to go to her grandmother's house that Saturday night and then visit Auburn on Sunday. Gillian said she couldn't skip the college altogether—that would mean lying to her parents. The four of them had become very close in those last days of high school. They seemed subliminally aware that they were all going in different directions very soon.

Gary Lee loved all kinds of racing, but open-wheel racing was his favorite. This would be Gillian's first time at a major auto racing event. They had planned to meet up at the main entrance at 11 a.m. The morning was crisp with cotton-like clouds in the sky. Chad and Annie drove over to the raceway full of excitement. They pulled into the back parking lot, paid the fee, and parked the car.

Next to the lot were the large trailers with racing logos and murals of racecars across their sides. This was a celebrated track, home of the All-Pro American Racing School, and Chad was full of expectations and high hopes for making connections in the professional racing world. It seemed like a carnival atmosphere on the other side of the fence. A Ferris wheel was slowly twirling over the crowd. They could hear strains of live music, and the smell of fair food filled their senses: sweet and spicy barbequed turkey legs, beer-battered onion rings, funnel cake, and deep-fried corn dogs.

"It looks like so much fun!" said Annie, squeezing Chad's arm while they walked across the parking lot.

Chad and Gary Lee didn't pay much attention anymore to those kinds of things—they were now serious about the racing business. They both were determined to somehow break into professional racing as a driver, a pit engineer, or a business manager—anything to get a start in the business.

Where r u? the text message popped onto Chad's phone as they were approaching the main entrance. He could see Gary Lee and Gillian up ahead by the ticket booths.

Gillian was unlike any of Gary Lee's other girlfriends—more intelligent, beautiful, and talented. She was taller than him and had an elegance about her; her long arms and legs moved like an athlete or a dancer. Gillian had light brown hair that flowed over her shoulders, and she spoke with a rich, silky voice. Gary Lee had only been going out with her for a few months; plenty of guys in school had been seeking her attention, but he turned out to be the lucky one.

When Gillian saw Annie and Chad approaching, she started jumping up and down and waving. Everyone was dressed in jeans and T-shirts, although the girls wore little jackets. It was chilly that morning, and rain was expected later.

"You're early, and you have no patience!" Chad said to Gary Lee, smiling when they walked up to the couple.

"We have a lot to do today, and I don't want to waste any time," he replied.

Chad paid for his and Annie's tickets, and they all headed into the park. On the main walkway were shops and all sorts of food stands.

"Are you hungry?" Chad asked Annie.

She shook her head. "Too excited—maybe later."

"Come on, guys," Gary Lee said, and he took Gillian by the hand and led her back toward the garages. "You're going to love this!"

The race wouldn't start for a while, and they scurried their way past the souvenir huts, refreshment stands, and racing fans. Chad and Gary Lee talked about points leaders, favorite drivers, championships, past winners, and sponsors. The girls talked animatedly to each other, but Chad could barely hear what they were saying because the announcements were so loud.

The atmosphere changed when they reached the track area. There were flags on tall poles flapping in the breeze along the edge of the raceway. People were starting to fill the grandstands with colorful shirts of orange and yellow and greens and blues. It was now like a Kentucky Derby with cars instead of horses.

Zooom! A racecar flew by on the track, and Gillian squealed and held her hands over her ears.

"Come on, let's see who is on the track," said Gary Lee. "Someone is warming up before the race."

"Probably working out last-minute changes," said Chad.

"I didn't know they were so loud," said Gillian. "That was kind of exciting. I have goose bumps."

"Wait until you hear twenty of them on the track all at once," said Gary Lee.

The four of them walked over to the track fence and watched a glistening green and white car zigzag around the corners on the far side of the track.

"He's on the straightaway now," said Gary Lee. The distant roar of the motor increased in pitch.

"Look at him go!" said Annie. The sound was getting louder as it came closer. Annie squeezed Chad's hand in anticipation of the car coming past them again.

Zooom! The car roared by the fence again while the kids watched intently.

"I think that's the Kilgore car," said Chad.

"Really?" asked Gillian. "That's Mackie Kilgore? He's so fast. Do you think he'll win?"

"I hope so," said Gary Lee, "but they are all very fast just like that."

They watched the car circling the far turns again, and then it pulled into the pit lane.

"He's pulled into the pits," said Chad. "Come on. Let's head over to the garages to get a closer look."

Mackenzie Kilgore was the grandson of Big Mo Kilgore, and the community of Blue Springs celebrated him as a hometown hero. He had grown up in Blue Springs, went to high school, and helped start the excitement around karting and auto racing in their county. Chad and Gary Lee continually followed Mackie's career with his family's racing business. They had only seen the boy racer a few times in person since he had moved away after high school to Miami, Florida, so this would be a special occasion.

The four of them hiked around the track until they came to the guarded gate at the garages. Chad pulled out some pit passes from his pocket.

"Here, put these on," Chad said, handing two passes with lanyards to Gary Lee and Gillian. Gary Lee held one up for Gillian and put it over her head. Chad did the same for Annie, and she smiled.

They turned and showed their passes to the security guard, who waved them through. They walked along past the open garage doors with all different colors of shiny racecar noses protruding. They could hear a constant clamor of clunks and thuds and saw people running around with wrenches and tires.

The foursome came to the garage with the large green and white Kilgore banner hanging in front, but the car was not in the garage. They stepped up to the open door and looked around.

"Are you the karting kids?" a man asked them.

"Yes," answered Chad.

"You can come in and watch. Just stand along that back wall and don't touch anything."

The four of them walked in and proceeded to the back wall, where they found a few other kids already standing. A few quick hello nods were exchanged. Everyone seemed engrossed in the activities unfolding.

"That's Big Mo and Sonny Kilgore," one of the others pointed out. "They're the team owners."

Chad already knew that; he had raced under the Kilgores for years. Sonny was stocky with an unshaven round face. He wore a sports cap with his name on it, and he anxiously paced around the garage. Big Mo was muttering something—there appeared to be a problem, and Chad listened intently.

"Tenth on the pole?" asked Big Mo to Sonny. "He's starting ten cars back. Surely Mackie could have done better than that. He's going to have to get more speed out of that car."

"Thanks for the brilliant observation, Dad," said Sonny. "That's why we are making last-minute changes."

"I didn't come here today to ride around in the pace car and then be embarrassed by your team's performance," said Big Mo. "We had better be on the podium."

"Just let me do my job," said Sonny. He walked over to the crew that was hovering over a computer screen. The crew chief pointed at the screen, and Sonny, as his habit was, began waving his hands and then stormed away.

"Well?" asked Big Mo.

"They have all the telemetry data that they need. It looks like we just need some more downward force in the rear. They can adjust the back wing, but they will also need to adjust the suspension to accommodate that."

"Ha! Telemetry, computers. We didn't have that crap in my day," said Big Mo.

"Well, you all didn't drive over two hundred miles per hour, either. This is how everybody manages their cars these days."

"When I drove a car, I could always tell what it needed. You could feel it in your ass! Your son, Mackie, can't seem to tell the engineers anything!"

"He's *your* grandson, so don't complain to me about that."

Just then, the Kilgore racecar rolled into the garage, pushed by the pit crew. The kids admired the racecar up close while the team scurried around it furiously. The car was pearl white with a double green stripe up the front. A large number 4 in a circle was centered on the front hood and the side. Other logos were embellished along the sides and across the front of the car. Their legendary hometown champion, Mackie Kilgore, climbed out of the car and took off his helmet and gear. He still looked like a teenager in his twenties, with a full head of wavy light brown hair. He stared down despondently and shook his head. The team approached him.

"I like the front wing settings," said Mackie to the crew chief. "But the back end is still very loose when accelerating out of the turns. I don't know what's wrong."

"Don't worry," said Sonny. "Gleason has this figured out. They're going to make some adjustments, and it should be fine."

Mackie walked away from the car and looked around the garage as if in a daze. Big Mo came over to him.

"I want you to stop driving like an old lady," said Big Mo.

"I didn't want to wreck the car on a practice run," said Mackie.

"Don't make silly excuses. One more thing, I gave out some garage passes to the karting team, so please try and make a good showing for your fans." He sent Mackie toward the kids along the back wall of the garage.

"Hi, you're from the karting team, right?" said Mackie, and he extended a handshake to Gary Lee. "I'm Mackie Kilgore." He turned quickly to Gillian. "And you are?" he asked, grasping her hand with a conspicuous one-eyed wink.

"I'm Gillian Mason," she replied. "This is something new for me." She was taking it all in with a mild blush. They finished their introductions. Mackie looked smart in his white and green racing suit.

"Gary Lee Dillanger—I remember you were the kid who won that karting championship in the Juniors a few years ago, right?" said Mackie.

Gary Lee nodded and then added, "Chad here is in the running for the All-Pro American Racing League Scholarship."

Mackie raised his eyebrows. "Sweet," he said, patting Chad on the shoulder. "Good luck on that."

Chad was confused by Mackie's response—by "good luck," did he mean "fat chance" or "hope you get that"?

"How is the car running?" asked Chad, wanting to engage with Mackie more professionally. "We just saw you out on the track."

"It's good, it's good," he replied. "A few adjustments still needed, but we've got a great crew taking care of things. I like the front wing settings from those last laps."

The boys asked some more questions about the track and the competition. Chad noticed how the grown-up racer lacked the enthusiasm that Chad recalled from his younger karting days. Mackie Kilgore seemed just plain old tired. His demeanor was lethargic, without a sense of anticipation or excitement. Chad wanted Annie and Gillian to see how thrilling it was to be a professional racer. Was he worn out at twenty-six years old? Chad thought at least Mackie Kilgore could fake it for the girls' sake. Chad was irritated. The racer seemed more interested in flirting with Gillian and Annie than in the race that was about to start.

Someone called over to Mackie and told him he needed to get ready. The four of them thanked him, wished him good luck, and headed out of the garage.

"Whatever happened to 'fake it 'til you make it'?" said Chad under his breath.

"So that was the great Mackie Kilgore?" asked Gillian. "You guys seemed a lot more excited about this race than he did."

"Chad, you get a lot crazier about your karting events than he does about racing," said Annie.

"He's just super cool," said Chad. "You have to be that way with racing. He's a professional." Chad offered this as an explanation, but he knew Annie was right. There was no excuse for being so chill.

"Maybe he had an adrenaline overdose," Gary Lee said, and Chad laughed.

As they walked back toward the grandstands, Chad felt overcome and anxious about his future. Mackie Kilgore seemed to have doubts about the scholarship. Trying to put his worries out of his mind, he focused on a fun afternoon with his friends.

The racing garages and pits were the places to be on race day. They were filled with the smell of racing fuel, the sound of the engines being tuned to perfection, and the synchronized movements of guys in pit suits. Chad just wanted to be on a team, if not as a driver, then as anything else that might put him there.

Walking back around the track, they came to the grandstands and climbed up the stairs. They found four good seats, and Gillian insisted she sit next to Annie.

"Okay. I'll sit on this end with you for now," said Chad to Annie, "but I'm moving over to the other end with Gary Lee after the race starts." They settled into their spots.

"What do you want for lunch?" Gary Lee asked Gillian. "You want a hot dog or burger?"

"Chicken strips, if they have them," she said. "Or a hot dog. And fries—cheese fries, if they have them."

"Oh, yeah! Chicken strips for me too," said Annie to Chad. "And a Coke."

The two boys were off in a flash. Chad had shaken off his disappointment from earlier and was now excited about the race. They came back with a couple of trays with chicken strips, burgers, fries, and drinks. Chad sat down next to Annie and thought how perfect it was, being there with her.

The crews wheeled out the gleaming racecars onto the track below. Chad could see the Number 4 car was tenth on the grid, and a total of twenty-six racers would be running on this two-and-a-half-mile road course. The racecars were beautiful, all decorated in their colors and sponsor logos; the drivers had firesuits to match. Chad pointed out different racers and teams. They were anticipating the most famous words in racing. The head of the racing school, an old, graying racecar collector, stepped up to the microphone.

"Drivers, start your engines!" he shouted.

The thunder of the motors erupted. Chad could feel the sound vibrate his chest, and his heart started pounding. The officials walked down the column of cars, passing each row and getting a thumbs-up from the drivers. Now the anticipation of the start. The few seconds felt like minutes. The green flag waved, motors roared, and tires began to spin out clouds of gray smoke. Gillian and Annie put their hands over their ears, and Gary Lee and Chad were yelling. They couldn't hear each other or the rest of the crowd screaming.

The cars were zooming around the track, and they could see the various turns from their location in the stands. The announcer was calling the action as drivers attempted to overtake each other. Gillian and Annie held their hands over their ears each time the major pack of cars came by the grandstand on the straightaway. Chad thought this was probably nothing like the sound of the school orchestra that Gillian played in, but she and Annie seemed quite thrilled by it all. Annie looked at Chad with a broad smile on her face. Her sun-kissed hair blew in the wind.

Suddenly, a cloud of dust and smoke appeared at the far end of the track. Over the loudspeaker came an announcement. "The Number 17 car of Alex Davis is out at Turn 9, and it looks like he may have taken out George Romero in the Number 33."

Annie clutched Chad's arm tightly.

The announcer continued, "What a disappointment for the rookie driver. He's out on lap twenty-four, and we have a full-course caution."

"He's probably fine. They're only going forty-five miles per hour around those corners," Gary Lee reassured the girls.

They watched the tow truck hoist up the Number 17 car and carry it back to the pits. The track crew continued picking up pieces of the vehicle from the track.

"Will he be able to race again?" asked Gillian.

"Not this race, but they will repair the racecar for the next one," replied Chad.

"It must be very disappointing when you put in all that time and money, and you don't get to finish the race," said Annie.

Gary Lee interrupted, "Look, Number 33 is back on the track again, but they have to drive behind the pace car. It's a yellow flag." Gary Lee continued to explain to the girls the strategies around the yellow caution laps.

The four high school kids watched the race to its finish. They were excited to see Mackie Kilgore come in third and stand up on the podium. They watched the finalists' interviews on the JumboTron, but Chad was disappointed with Mackie's explanation of his race and finish.

"Well," Mackie said to the reporter, "fortunately, when the car works up there on the shoulder, you can maneuver the car." He continued in a monotone, "You know, if it didn't work up there, I'm not sure if I would have been able to come from tenth. We also gained a few seconds in the pits, and some guys didn't take tires when they should have."

"You're not going to act like that when you race?" asked Annie, and she nudged Chad in the arm.

"No! I will shout, 'I dedicate my first victory to Annabelle Sims from Blue Springs, Alabama!'" replied Chad.

"So what did you think?" Gary Lee asked, turning to Gillian, who was still taking it all in.

"I loved it," she said and leaned over and gave Gary Lee a gentle kiss.

Annie turned to Chad. "Thanks so much for taking me," she said. Annie put her arms around Chad's neck and kissed him, then laughed with Gillian.

Both couples held hands while they walked back along the main walkway. Their ears were still ringing from the noise, so they talked a little louder than normal.

"I want ice cream before we go," said Gillian.

"Me too," said Annie, smiling at Chad.

They stopped at a soft-serve ice cream stand and sat down at a picnic table with their dipped cones.

"Working in racing like this—that's what I dream about," said Gary Lee. He looked at Gillian, and she only continued to listen. "We both do—Chad and me. I think Chad's getting closer to that dream. He'll probably be racing with the pros this time next year."

"Really?" asked Annie with excitement. "That's great news. Why didn't you tell me that?"

"Because it's not really news yet," explained Chad. "I'm hoping to earn the Kilgore racing scholarship, which will open the doors for me. My dad seems pretty determined to help me get started, even if I don't get the scholarship."

"The secret to getting into racing is finding a sponsor," explained Gary Lee. "Or just having a mountain of money," he added with a smile.

"Or being born into a racing family," said Chad, pointing over his shoulders toward the garages. They all laughed.

"Well, I plan to race cars someday if I can just find a wealthy sponsor," said Gary Lee. "Sure, you do have to be a good driver. I am a good driver, and I already won a championship in karting. We do know how to get it done."

"So why don't you race now?" Gillian asked. "You were just drooling over Mackie Kilgore and his racecar at the garage."

"Yeah, and he was drooling over you!" Gary Lee joked, grabbing her thigh.

"Be quiet! He was not!" She laughed back at him and took his hand from her leg.

"Well, my mom won't let me compete as long as I live at home," Gary Lee explained. "I come from a family of architects and interior designers. My mother says I need to follow my Plan B for now, her backup plan for my life in case racing doesn't work out. I should be pursuing racing right now. A lot of racers just quit high school and get their GED.”

“Then you wouldn’t have met me,” Gillian teased him.

“So you’re planning to go to Auburn in the fall, but that’s not what you want?” asked Annie.

“Like I said, that’s my Plan B,” answered Gary Lee. “As soon as I can find a sponsor, I’m going to be joining the ladder series. Big Mo Kilgore knows a lot of wealthy people, and he said he could probably get me connected.”

“I take it your mom doesn’t approve of racing,” Annie said.

“No, not at all! I think that’s why my parents are splitting up.” Gary Lee confessed. “My folks don’t even know that we went to the race today. I told them that we were going to a campus visit at Auburn University today.”

“Yeah, my mom doesn’t know either,” said Gillian.

Annie looked at Gillian with surprise. “I can’t believe that you would lie to your parents like that!” she said.

“I didn’t lie. We’re still going to Auburn tomorrow. She just doesn’t know about today,” explained Gillian.

“What, you never lie to your parents?” Gary Lee asked Annie. “Anyway, she’s now eighteen, so she can do whatever she wants.”

“I don’t tell my parents everything,” confessed Annie, “but my mom is almost my best friend. I tell her about everything exciting that happens.”

“So you told her about last Saturday night at my place?” asked Chad, smiling.

“Hush up.” Annie elbowed Chad. “That’s not what I meant. She knew I was at your house.”

“Well, I don’t like to hide anything from my parents,” said Gillian, “but I wouldn’t have been able to come to an auto race any other way.” Gillian laughed and looked straight at Gary Lee. “I think I’m going to really like living on campus at Auburn, too.”

“I thought your mom said you were going to live with your grandmother in Willow Walk,” said Gary Lee.

“That’s what she wants me to do,” said Gillian, “but I was able to get into the honors dorm. Now I have an airtight justification for

44

living there on campus. I can walk to class, and I won't miss out on anything.

"How about you, Gary Lee?" asked Annie. "Where are you going to live in Auburn?"

"My dad thinks I should join a fraternity," replied Gary Lee. "You know, for future connections."

"I thought about a sorority," said Gillian, finishing up her chocolate-dipped vanilla ice cream cone. "I'm still set on the honors dorm. My cousin's sorority seemed too catty for my routine. I don't want the girls to hate me if I decide to move out of their group."

"What time is your grandma expecting us, Gillian?" interrupted Gary Lee.

"No later than 6 p.m. for dinner," she replied.

"We're going to need to get going, then," said Gary Lee. "It's about a two-hour drive."

"Oh! You're not going to believe what we're doing tonight!" Gillian said, pausing for the suspense. "There's a drive-in movie theater near my grandmother's house!"

"Oh, that's so great!" said Annie. "What are you going to see?"

"Does it matter what movie they see?" asked Chad. "It's a drive-in theater. I think we all know what they'll be doing."

"I don't know what you're talking about, Chad," said Gary Lee with a wink. "We love the movies."

The ice cream cones were all finished off, and they left the old, gray picnic table. The two couples walked holding hands along with the flow of the crowd toward the main exit. Outside the main gate, they stopped.

"Guys, such a great time," said Chad. "We're parked back that way by the racing trailers."

"Yeah, awesome race and great times," said Gary Lee.

The two girls hugged, and then Gillian hugged Chad.

Chad gave Gary Lee the usual handshake with a one-arm hug, grunting, "Team 87!"

That was the last time he would ever see Gillian alive and the last time he saw Gary Lee awake. Chad's eyes filled with tears, thinking back on that Saturday. How could life turn from so joyful to so horrible? What happened on that drive to Auburn? Gary Lee was such a good driver. If he would wake up, he could explain everything.

CHAPTER 6

Chad leaned in toward the mirror and studied his face. He had finished shaving, and there was no hope in anything other than a clean-shaven look. He thought of himself as average-looking, but Annie always told him how he had the perfect nose. He remembered at age thirteen trying to make himself look older, but now at eighteen, his face seemed more aged than he wanted. He looked like a tough guy, he thought while he put on his tough-guy aftershave.

It was a misty gray afternoon in April when Chad prepared himself for the funeral service of Gillian Mason. He knew he would see many kids from school there, but this tragedy had torn loyalties and created a hostile rift between schoolmates and former friends. Gillian and Gary Lee had been inseparable, and kids in every clique at school liked them as a couple. Now the question was, whose side were you on—Gillian's or Gary Lee's? What could be more absurd? At least Annie, Chad's girlfriend for the last two years, remained loyal to both of them. She seemed more grounded than most girls her age. She was true to her friends. Annie was often at the hospital with Gary Lee, and still, Gillian's friends also embraced her. Chad hoped to follow her example, but he had been getting the cold shoulder from the kids on Gillian's side. He wondered if he would even be welcomed at the funeral, but it would be just wrong not to pay his respects.

Chad remembered how he, Annie, Gary Lee, and Gillian went out to the movies together just a month earlier. Gillian was laughing, tossing popcorn into Gary Lee's mouth. They were so carefree, talking about graduating and visiting Auburn. The four were typical high school kids who did everything together: studying, going out for pizza, swapping music, and endless messaging. They all looked forward to their last summer as kids before everyone went in different directions.

Chad thought about how Gillian spoke; she was mildly shy but handled her social interactions with brilliance—such a likable person. She had a gentle voice that put people at ease. It seemed unbelievable that she was now dead and Gary Lee was fighting for his life. How could anyone believe this was Gary Lee's fault? It was just a tragic accident.

Chad was driving himself to the service even though his parents were also going separately. "I might go out with friends," he had explained. Secretly Chad worried that he might need a fast exit if not welcome. He imagined Gillian's big cousins saying, "You're Gary Lee's friend," and showing him to the door. Chad didn't actually believe that would happen, but lately, he wasn't trusting his own instincts. He planned to sit with Annie and her family, so that thought comforted him while he drove.

The Trinity Episcopal Church was on the east side of town in an upper-middle-class neighborhood with large homes and two-acre lots. When he approached the church, the traffic became more congested as cars slowed to enter the driveway. Chad looked for a parking space on the back side of the lot. He stepped out of his truck, and a Subaru pulled up next to him. Chad recognized the man driving it from various Dillanger gatherings over the years.

"You're Gary Lee's friend, right?" asked the man.

"Yes, Chad Gibbons."

"I'm Evan Waitts, business partner with the Dillangers."

"Sure, Mr. Waitts. You've been at many events with the Dillangers."

"Please, call me Evan. I'm not good with such formalities."

Evan looked over at the church. People were gradually arriving and making their way into the building. He was dressed in a sharp black suit, white shirt, and a simple burgundy tie. It seemed more appropriate than what Chad was wearing, which was the new tweed sports jacket his parents had given him for Christmas—the best he had.

"You know, I parked back here so I could leave quickly, just in case there were any problems with me being here," said Evan. "I wanted to come and offer condolences from the Dillangers and our firm, DD&W, but I'm not sure that was such a good idea."

"I know what you mean," replied Chad. "I feel a little uncomfortable myself." They both gazed up at the church with hesitation. "I'm meeting my girlfriend, Annie. You can sit with us if that would help."

"Thanks. I think I'll take you up on that," said Evan.

Chad's phone chimed. He looked down and read the message, *inside waiting for u*, from Annie.

He sent back, *coming now*.

"Okay. Let's do this," said Chad, mustering up his courage.

They both started walking toward the main entrance. There was a placard with Gillian's picture on the side of the walkway. Chad forced himself to look at her face, her broad smile and flowing hair—it truly stung. He would have to find a way to get through this.

Inside, they heard the organ playing while guests quietly filed into the sanctuary. Several people were handing out programs in the large entrance hallway. A tall young man in a dark suit smiled as he quietly handed programs to Chad and Evan. Chad could see Annie across the narthex, waiting for him. The two of them approached her, and she came forward and gave Chad a huge hug. Annie stepped back and looked up at Chad. He could see her blue eyes were red from crying. He touched her face and wiped the dampness of tears from her freckled cheek.

"This is Mr. Waitts, the Dillangers' friend," said Chad.

"Hi. I'm Annie. You were at the hospital, too," she said to Evan with a sniffle.

"Yes, I'm their business partner. And please, call me Evan. I'm so sorry to meet again under these circumstances," he said.

"I hope you don't mind—I told Evan he could sit with us," said Chad.

Annie looked up at Evan, and a smile appeared on her grieving face.

"Sure," she said.

Annie led the way for the three of them into the large hall. Chad looked up at the lofty ceiling and walls. They walked around to the right side of the pews until they came to the empty space next to Annie's parents. Annie slid into the bench, followed by Chad and Evan. Chad whispered a greeting to Annie's mom, who reached over and squeezed Chad's hand without saying a word. Annie's dad was farther down the pew and gave a nod to him.

The program in Chad's hand had Gillian's picture on the front and read, "A Celebration of Life. Gillian Anne Mason. Daughter of Colleen and Remington Mason." Chad looked toward the front of the church, trying to see Mr. and Mrs. Mason, Gillian's family, and relatives. He saw several men standing up front who seemed to be coordinating activity. The men in the Mason family all had red hair and freckled complexions.

Chad gazed at the interior architecture of the church. It was beautifully adorned with stained glass panels and all of the symbols of Christianity. He thought of his Sunday School days as a young boy, but those happy days seemed long gone.

The air was heavy. A somber silence filled the sanctuary, except for the soft organ playing, punctuated with an occasional cough, sob, or cry of an infant. The music stopped, and a young woman placed a water glass and a box of Kleenex next to the lectern. Chad hoped the service would hurry up and start. Finally, a small choir of high school students filed onto the choir platform.

The processional began from the back of the church. A white-robed man came down the aisle toward the altar bearing an ornate cross in front of him. Following him was the reverend father in a white and gold robe. He read from the scripture while they proceeded, "Though I walk through the valley of the shadow of death…"

Next came the six pallbearers with the casket, slowly moving toward the front of the sanctuary. White roses and pink and lavender hydrangeas adorned the beautifully carved oak and bronze casket.

Chad could hear Gillian's mother sobbing in the front of the church, and the moment triggered a flood of sadness that overwhelmed him. Perhaps it was the memory of his own mother's funeral five years earlier, reliving the pain and sense of confusion over the loss. How could this have happened? The casket was such a grim contrast to the bright future Gillian had. Annie reached over and squeezed Chad's hand, having sensed his emotion. Chad looked back at her and realized what a strong soul Annie was. He could see the pain in her eyes too, but he also saw her kindness and compassion.

The reverend stepped forward to the lectern to speak. "We gather on this day to celebrate the life of Gillian Anne Mason. As the family remains seated, we ask that all please stand."

The reverend motioned with his arms, and Chad and everyone around him rose to their feet. The organist began playing, and a woman on the podium waived her arms to lead the congregation and choir in songs: "How Great Thou Art" and "Amazing Grace."

The ceremony continued with a scripture reading, followed by a quartet of young musicians from the youth orchestra. Chad thought about what he would say to Gillian's parents afterward and became seized by anxiety. He felt sick to his stomach while the quartet filled the church with music. Unable to script what he would say to her parents, the idea of attending the funeral suddenly seemed foolish. Nothing could ever make reparations for their unspeakable loss, not even, God forbid, the death of Gary Lee.

A woman came up and talked about Gillian as an accomplished and gifted musician and an AP scholar. Her awards and talent reaffirmed her saintly character, and Chad wondered if she was now with the angels. Could she now help Gary Lee where she was in heaven? Would she help him? Chad bowed his head, said a quiet prayer for Gary Lee's recovery and asked Gillian to forgive him.

A man in full dress blue uniform, laden with medals, came to the lectern. Chad looked down at the memorial program and determined it was Police Commissioner John Raymond. Chad flashed back to the sheriff at the hospital and the criminal investigation of the crash. He imagined them wheeling Gary Lee into a courtroom in his hospital bed and then wheeling his bed behind bars. In his daze, Chad did not even hear what the speaker was saying.

After the commissioner, another man rose from the front pew. Chad checked the program again to find that it was Remy Mason, Gillian's father. He stood in front of the lectern for a moment and looked out at the people. His piercing blue eyes looked right at Chad, so it felt. The congregation seemed to hold its breath, waiting to hear him speak.

"Thank you for your support to our family in these difficult times," he began. "I love being Gillian's dad, and Colleen loves being her mom. I have often felt sorry for other parents when I heard of their troubles in raising their children. The delight it has been to raise Gillian is more than I could ever imagine." He continued to speak of her unfinished plans for college at Auburn University. Not a mention of Gary Lee.

Mr. Mason returned to his red-haired family of uncles, aunts, and cousins seated in the front pews. The closing prayers and recessional were a relief for Chad. He and Annie's family sat and waited for each row to file out of the sanctuary. Chad was searching the faces passing up the aisle for anyone he might recognize. He wondered if there might be someone here from the Kilgore clan, although he did not expect them to be in attendance. He did see the debutants whom he knew from high school. The county's debutant contingent always seemed to show up for photos at social gatherings and charity events. Here they were in their little black dresses and strings of white pearls. Chad wondered if they even knew Gillian.

Chad's pew finally had their turn to rise and make their way to the parish hall. Annie's parents led the way, and Evan followed behind.

Evan leaned toward Chad and said, "I'm starting to worry about being recognized. I don't think I should be an ambassador from DD&W, or least of all, bringing condolences from the Dillangers."

This comment made Chad worried about being seen with Evan Waitts. They followed the crowd out of the building and passed by men dressed in black suits, wearing purple memorial ribbons on their lapels, smoking cigarettes. Chad presumed these were Gillian's relatives, perhaps uncles—they were noticeably angry and upset. Not a word had been spoken about Gary Lee Dillanger. Chad perceived glares toward Evan as they passed by, and he wondered if these were stares of recognition and anger or if it was just his imagination.

While they waited in the line to enter the parish hall, the debutants he had seen earlier released several large clusters of balloons, repeating Gillian's name as they did so. Everyone looked up and watched the lavender and pink balloons dotting the sky.

Chad entered the parish hall and was surrounded by mourners in conversation—some were in the line to speak with the parents, others were lined up for food. Standing nearby, he overheard the commissioner talking.

"In fact, 708 teenagers have died in auto accidents in Alabama in the last four years," the commissioner said. More half-sentences drifted toward Chad. "Our kids are being slaughtered on the streets…all this young racing on our streets is a problem…entitled karting kids have permission to race with no license to drive…the fast and furious have taken over our streets."

Annie interrupted Chad's eavesdropping and handed him a cup of punch. Chad was glad to distance himself from that conversation. He didn't want anyone to bring up his karting aspirations.

Evan asked, "So you are both graduating from high school?"

"Yes. They're giving Gillian's family her diploma, even though she didn't really finish," said Annie.

"It's an awful way to end your high school years. I'm so sorry about that," said Evan.

Chad doubted that Gary Lee would be extended a diploma and wondered if he even would graduate this year. Chad heard his name called, and he turned to look. His parents were in the line to speak with Gillian's family, and they were waving him toward them.

"My mom and dad are over there. They are waiting to speak with Gillian's parents—do you want to join us?"

"Thanks, but I think I'm just going to leave in a minute. It's been a bit overwhelming, and I need to get back to the office," Evan added as an excuse. "Again, I am truly sorry about this tragedy," he said while clasping Annie's hands.

"Well, at least I'll have something to talk to Gary Lee about tomorrow," said Chad. "I know he can't talk back yet, but I think he can hear me at least in his subconscious. I try to talk and read to him when I'm visiting," explained Chad.

"So you're going to the Auburn Hospital tomorrow, and you'll see Elle Dillanger, too?" asked Evan.

"Yes, although she wanted me to stay with Gary Lee while she ran some errands. I think she's staying over with someone in Auburn."

"Would I be able to trouble you with bringing some project files to her from our office? I promised to bring them to her, but I have been swamped since the Dillangers have had to take some time off."

"Sure, I guess so. Anything to help."

"Great. Do you know where our DD&W office is? If not, you could follow me over there."

Chad did know where the Dillangers' office was in town, but this seemed like an excellent opportunity to leave the funeral and avoid any more awkward conversations.

"Annie, you don't mind if I go? I think I should try to help out," he said to his girlfriend. She looked a little surprised. "Can you tell my mom and dad that I had to go?"

"Chad?" she called his name, her voice both questioning and pleading for him to stay.

Chad gave Annie a long, reassuring hug, then turned toward Evan and nodded. The lean interior designer led the way out of the building through a side door, and they crossed over to the parking lot. Chad looked up at the church steeple towering over the building, with the silver sky behind it. The circle of a hazy sun was just starting to pierce through the gray flannel blanket of clouds.

Chad turned back toward the church as they walked away and whispered, "Goodbye, Gillian," now with a full teardrop in his eye.

CHAPTER 7

Chad was relieved to have left the funeral of Gillian Mason. He pulled out of the parking lot behind Evan Waitts' Subaru and followed him to the Dillangers' office. Chad was on a mission to help Gary Lee's parents; something important needed to be driven down to Auburn, and he offered to take it there tomorrow. It was a lame excuse to leave the funeral early, but he knew Annie would be okay with her friends there. The two vehicles drove down Main Street and turned into the office building parking lot. Chad saw two police cars in front of the Dillangers' offices when they pulled up. He parked beside Evan and watched through his open window.

Evan opened the door of his Subaru abruptly and said, "What in Sam Hill is going on here?"

He stepped out of the car and started walking toward an officer in a blue uniform talking on a radio. Chad decided to follow Evan, leaving his truck to see what was going on. Evan stopped in his tracks before reaching the officer. Chad also stood aghast, looking at the front of the building. The front door was spray-painted with giant red letters "LL" and underneath the word "Losers." Their office sign also was vandalized. The DD&W had a line sprayed on it, and underneath was painted "LL&W." Chad looked to the left and realized that the front windows were all broken.

"Are you the owner of this business?" the officer asked Evan.

"Yes, I'm Evan Waitts. I'm the 'W' in DD&W," he explained. "What happened here?"

"I'm Officer Nolan. We responded to a call from your alarm company. It looks like old-fashioned vandalism, sir. The front door is still locked. Can you open it so we can take a look inside?" asked the officer.

Evan pulled some keys out of his pocket and unlocked the front door. He stepped back and let the two officers enter first, then followed them in. Someone turned on the lights, and Chad also decided to venture in. The reception area was as he remembered it, except for a brick on the floor and shards of broken glass everywhere. He heard Evan shout out something in anger in the next room, and Chad became worried about how far this vandalism might go. Would someone also trash Gary Lee's house?

Chad walked into the next office, trying not to crunch too much of the glass under his feet. Evan was pacing back and forth, appearing to be both angry and in a panic. Another brick had knocked over a computer screen, and there were a few more bricks and papers scattered on the floor. The two police officers returned from their search of the premises.

"Do you see anything missing?" Nolan asked. "I don't think anyone came inside, but I have to ask." The officer stared at Evan, looking for answers.

Evan looked around at the desks and opened a few drawers. "No, I think you're right. This is just plain old rotten vandalism."

He walked into the back office area, and the police and Chad followed after him. The desks and worktables in the back seemed to be untouched.

"So, will you be able to find out who did this?" Evan asked with a troubled voice.

"Do you have any surveillance cameras?"

Evan shook his head no.

"I don't think we'll find any fingerprints on those bricks if that's what you're hoping," said Nolan. "Let me ask you, do you or your partners have any enemies?"

Hearing this, Chad suddenly felt a queasiness in his stomach.

"I don't, but I think my partners, the Dillangers, may have some new enemies," said Evan.

56

"Oh, the Dillangers—the parents of that kid who cracked up his car, and the Mason girl died?" The officer seemed to get the picture now. "That would probably make half the town a suspect here. So what were you all expecting, a homecoming parade?"

Chad realized that Evan and the Dillangers were not going to receive much sympathy from Nolan, or anyone else, for that matter. Chad had never experienced this level of hostility before. It seemed like something from a bad movie. The officer told Evan that he would call him when the official report was ready to be picked up. Then the police left abruptly.

Evan continued to wander around the office and finally sat down at a large desk in the backside of the building.

"You know, I was bullied as a kid in this town," he said. "I thought that was all behind me."

"You grew up here?" asked Chad.

"Oh, yes. Same high school as you kids. I even went to the 20-year reunion a few years back. I wanted them to know that people like me could be successful."

"People like you?" Chad was puzzled.

"Well," continued Evan. "As you may have figured out, I'm not a family man, like so many define as the standard of success. I'm more artistic and less conventional, but I do have deep friendships."

"Like the Dillangers."

"Yes—we go back a long way. I like to think that I brought them together, but Drew has his own version of the story. He was studying architecture and racing stock cars when he met Elle. He traded racing cars for racing sailboats to win her over. She didn't go for the stock car thing."

Evan leaned back in the chair and put his hands over his face. He seemed exhausted, and certainly, this incident didn't help. Chad wasn't sure if he should also sit down, so he stood there feeling a little awkward.

"It's really tragic what happened to them," Evan continued.

"You mean with the accident?" asked Chad.

"Well, even before that—with their break up. They were such a brilliant couple, and they did fantastic projects together. Me—I'm just happy to have been a part of it."

Chad felt like there was much more to Evan's story, but he didn't want to be rudely inquisitive.

Evan looked around and said, "I need to get on the phone and get ahead of this disaster." He picked up his phone to make a call but looked at it closely. "I have a message from Drew. He says that Gary Lee is waking up!"

Suddenly, Chad was less concerned about the trashing of the office. Evan called Mr. Dillanger and told him about the vandalism. He hung up the phone and turned to Chad.

"Drew says Gary Lee is showing some physical movement. The doctors think he may be waking up," said Evan.

Chad wanted to be more excited, but to him, waking up means opening your eyes and looking around.

"Maybe I'll have my friend back to talk to tomorrow," said Chad, trying to sound upbeat.

"Oh, yes," Evan said, suddenly remembering that he had asked Chad to come with him for a reason. "The project files for Elle."

He walked over to another desk and looked through a stack of folders. Picking up a portfolio bag, he put some specific folders into the side pocket and set it on the chair.

"Let me see what else she might need."

Evan started sorting through the unopened mail on what must have been Mrs. Dillanger's desk. He opened a few envelopes, studied their contents, and then stuffed them also into the portfolio. Then he stopped after opening what looked like an oversized invitation.

"The Kilgore's annual White Party, presented by the Luxurious Lifestyle Foundation," Evan announced out loud. "DD&W normally attends all of the Luxurious Lifestyle events, but I'm afraid the White Party isn't going to be on the company's calendar this summer."

"Why not?" asked Chad.

"Certainly, events like this are good for business. Architecture and interior design rely on word of mouth, and mingling with potential clients brings in business. However, with this kind of sentiment toward DD&W, I think we need to lay low until this ill wind blows over. Honestly, I don't know if we'll survive the year." Evan paused then handed the invitation to Chad. "Have you ever been to an LL event?"

"Well, in a sense. Mr. Kilgore has us work at the LL events."

"Oh, yes—that's right. You were at the big car show at the Hilton last year. I remember. Who can forget that event?" Evan sighed out loud and sat back in his chair.

Chad thought back to that year and did remember it well—the Luxurious Lifestyles Classic and Luxury Auto Show.

"So you'll be working the LL White Party this summer at the Kilgores'?" Evan asked, interrupting Chad's recollections.

"Yeah." Chad nodded.

"Well, have fun and good luck in your sponsorship pursuits. I'm surprised that Kilgore even sent us an invitation to this year's LL event." He sat back in the office chair and shook his head. "Do you think the LL has a charity for blunt force head trauma? The Dillangers could probably use some financial support right about now."

Chad wasn't sure if Evan was serious or just being sarcastic.

"Okay, here you go," said Evan, as he stood up and handed Chad the portfolio. Evan picked up a nicely framed picture from Mrs. Dillanger's desk. "Oh, wait," he added. Evan gazed at it for a minute and then handed it to Chad. It was a picture of Gary Lee and his mom at the beach. They looked so happy and full of life in that moment. "I hope I will see her gorgeous smile again. Maybe this picture will bring a little joy to Elle during her unwanted hospital vigil over in Auburn."

Chad began to understand that Evan's emotional connection to Elle was something other than a romance. Last year, people had gossiped about the three DD&W partners when Mr. Dillanger moved out, but Gary Lee had assured Chad that nothing was going on.

Chad tucked the picture into the portfolio and then turned to leave. Evan thanked him for his help as a courier and told him sternly to drive safely. Chad walked through the wreckage of the front office. It seemed like a challenging task, cleaning it all up. At least the news from the hospital gave Chad some hope for Gary Lee's recovery.

CHAPTER 8

The Luxurious Lifestyle Classic and Luxury Auto Show—Chad did remember it well. The show was held at the Hilton convention center over a weekend in April last year. The opening Friday evening was the charity event, and Chad, Gary Lee, and the rest of the Kilgore karting team were working to help raise contributions for the LL charities. Chad enjoyed these events because of the impressive cars on display. That was also the kickoff of Kilgore's new, more expensive Pro Karting team.

Late that afternoon, Big Mo and Sonny Kilgore had pulled up to the entrance of the Hilton Hotel in their two Ferraris—Big Mo with his yellow 458 Italia, which let out a loud growl, and Sonny following in his red matching Ferrari. The loud blast from the exhaust pipes made some heads turn.

During an LL event, the boys had to wear the "Kilgore uniform." That year, he wore khaki shorts and white Polos with the Kilgore crest embroidered in green. Jobs were handed out, and that evening, Chad was assigned to run errands for the event staff.

He received a message from Gary Lee: *can u meet my parents in the lobby?* Chad dutifully headed for the main hotel lobby, curious as to why Gary Lee didn't just meet them himself. He looked around for the Dillangers, but they were not there yet. He decided to step out front and catch them when they arrived.

A hunter-green Lamborghini Gallardo coupe was parked by the front entryway, and a beautiful blonde model in a black-and-white checkered miniskirt was standing next to it. The LL hired attractive girls in their twenties to work at the events, and Chad figured they were at least paid for their time, unlike the karting boys. The girls were nice, though. They seemed to think the karting boys were sweet or cute, and they didn't mind flirting with them. The girl by the Lamborghini was Kaitlyn; Chad had spoken with her earlier that afternoon when everyone was getting ready.

"Hi," said Chad as he strolled over to look at the supercar.

Kaitlyn smiled at him but then made a face. Chad could tell that she didn't want to chat now—she was working, doing her best to strike a pose. Kaitlin continued to ignore Chad when an elegant couple came over to look at the car.

She greeted them quite warmly and said, "Welcome to the Luxurious Lifestyle Classic and Luxury Auto Show." She offered them each a flute of champagne.

Chad didn't mind the brush-off—they each had their purpose at the event. He strolled around to the other side of the car. The windows were down, and Chad peered into the delicious, buttery, leather interior. He could imagine what it might feel like to hold that wheel and accelerate from zero to sixty in three seconds.

"Not just beauty and speed, it has everything you would expect—antilock braking, curtain and side airbags, traction and stability control. Plus the cool tech, like driver assist and emergency self-braking," a familiar voice surprised Chad.

He spun around and stood up straight.

"Hi, Mr. and Mrs. Dillanger," said Chad, greeting Gary Lee's parents. "Gary Lee asked me to come and meet you in the lobby."

"Hello, Chad," said Mrs. Dillanger. "We just need to wait for Evan, our business partner, before we go inside."

"Yes, wait for Waitts again," chuckled Mr. Dillanger.

Mrs. Dillanger gave him a little nudge in response to his bad humor. The couple was well-dressed, so graceful and good-looking. Mr. Dillanger was wearing a black tux, and his wife's blue sequin dress looked like she had just stepped off the red carpet in Hollywood. Another gentleman approached them from across the courtyard, also in a tux.

"Not something you would let your kid drive," said Evan with a laugh as he approached the supercar on display.

Gary Lee's dad looked pained at the comment.

"You look stunning, Elle," Evan said to Mrs. Dillanger, which she indeed did.

"Thank you," said Mrs. Dillanger. "You clean up pretty well yourself, party boy," she replied.

Evan turned and greeted Kaitlyn, the LL girl still looking perfect in her soft sweater and miniskirt standing by the supercar.

She smiled and said, "Welcome to the Luxurious Lifestyle Classic and Luxury Auto Show Gala."

As the group walked on toward the lobby, Kaitlyn smiled and gave a wink to Chad this time.

"Nice to see you," Evan said to Chad, with a pat on the shoulder.

The four of them crossed the lobby and walked down the hallway leading to the ballroom. The hall was adorned with black and white checkered flags and signs about the LL Foundation. Chad could hear a familiar booming voice from a distance when they approached the ballroom.

"It's pronounced 'Boot-kiss'!"

What would an LL event be without Mr. Butkis? He was someone who seemed even more excited about auto racing than Big Mo. Mr. Butkis was a substantial sponsor of the Kilgores' karting team, and he liked to hang out with the boys whenever possible. Chad's dad often referred to Mr. Butkis as "The Rainmaker" because his sponsorship had helped turn many kart racers into auto racers. Butkis was one of the wealthy founders of the LL, and he had significant social influence. Chad's dad had explained that Mr. Butkis' presence at these Luxurious Lifestyle events was one reason the event was so well attended. Money, wealth, and sexy models attract a large audience.

"How are you, Mr. Butkis?" said Mr. Dillanger.

"Ah, the Dillangers. Glad to see you all again," said Butkis to the three of them.

"You remember our business partner, Evan Waitts."

Chad hung back a few steps while the gala attendees greeted each other. Mr. Butkis was an aging southern gentleman, nearly bald with a touch of white hair and a round physique. His face was glistening as he spoke.

"I've seen your son somewhere in the ballroom. He's wearing the Kilgore uniform," said Butkis.

Mrs. Dillanger seemed puzzled by this statement. They continued into the ballroom, and she asked her husband, "What did he mean by the 'Kilgore uniform,' Drew?"

"I told you before, Elle. Gary Lee was invited to come here and stand up with Chad and the other boys from Kilgore's team," said Mr. Dillanger. She seemed to accept the explanation.

"Chad, can you take us to Gary Lee?" Mrs. Dillanger asked.

Chad had already texted Gary Lee, *where r u? they are here.* Just as she asked, the reply came, *stall!* Chad wondered what was up.

"Um, he's not answering my texts," said Chad. "You might need to wander around to find him."

Mrs. Dillanger excused herself from her husband and Evan to find Gary Lee in the large ballroom. She disappeared behind two superluxury cars parked in the center of the hall, a sleek two-seater convertible and an eight-passenger SUV.

"What was that about?" asked Evan.

"Well, the Kilgores invited Gary Lee to be on their Pro Karting team," said Mr. Dillanger. "I was hoping Gary Lee would get this opportunity after his karting season last year. He aged out of the Junior division, and there are only a few drivers who go on to the national level with the Pro series."

Chad was very excited to be in the Pro series with Gary Lee. It's something they had dreamed of for years. The Pro karters used shifter karts that could go well over a hundred miles per hour. These karts had a transmission with multiple gears (therefore the name "shifter"), and they were so much like driving a real racecar that even Formula One drivers trained in shifter karts.

"Oh, yeah! The Pro series is awesome!" interrupted Chad, unable to contain himself. "The shifter karts are like driving a mini Ferrari GT."

"That's right, the closest thing to a GT," came a big Scottish voice from behind them. Big Mo Kilgore stepped into the conversation. "Shifter karts might not look like much. They are lightweight, with transmissions and sophisticated brakes, and drive much faster than the Junior series karts."

Big Mo had a glass of champagne in his hand, and when he saw that the other guests did not, he waved over a young woman with a tray of bubbling flutes.

"A toast," said Big Mo, holding his glass up toward them. Mr. Dillanger and Evan picked up obligatory glasses. "To the new Pro Karting Team this year!"

Chad watched the three of them all sip their champagne, but Evan had a concerned look. Big Mo led them over to a display of a classic Le Mans racecar in the center of the hall.

"Isn't Pro Karting a bit expensive?" asked Evan while they walked over to the collector car.

"That's why we have these events," explained Kilgore. "Each team member has to come up with their half of the costs. We have many interested sponsors at the LL event willing to pick up the other half if we can pair them with the right Wheelboy."

"Wheelboy?" asked Evan.

"Yes, that's what we are calling the Pro Karting team members," said Big Mo. "Wheelboys. Chad here is one of them, and here is another." He turned toward the young man standing by the Le Mans car. Like Chad, the young man was neatly dressed in khaki shorts and a white Polo with the green Kilgore crest.

"This is Eric," said Kilgore. "Eric, explain to this gentleman how the fundraising works."

The Wheelboy answered, "Well, sir, each luxury car in the hall represents a charity. We stand by an assigned car and answer questions about the car, the charity, the team, and auto racing in general. The guests put donations in the box on the side of the car for that particular fund."

"And your sponsorship?" Big Mo prompted him.

"Each of us must find a sponsor to secure our spot on the team," said Eric. "I've just met with Mr. Butkis. His company, South East Furniture, will be sponsoring me."

"He's sponsoring me also this season," chirped in Chad, not wanting to be left out.

"Is that why they call him the rainmaker?" said Evan under his breath to Chad. "Persuading others to spend their money on his favorite hobby."

"Would you like to donate to Mr. Butkis' charity?" young Eric asked the guests. "It's called 'Racing Builds Character,' or RBC—a summer karting camp for kids who are less privileged." The box next to the Le Mans car was labeled "RBC."

"Not tonight, thank you," replied Mr. Dillanger.

"This is Mr. Dillanger, Eric," Big Mo said to the young man. "His son is Gary Lee, who is also looking for sponsorship just like you are."

"Oh, Gary Lee's dad," Eric said. The fellow Wheelboy nodded and seemed to understand the situation. "Good luck."

Chad felt a little embarrassed for Mr. Dillanger, now that he had been identified as one of the needy at the charity event. Big Mo Kilgore excused himself to continue to mingle with other guests.

Evan turned to Mr. Dillanger. "I didn't know Gary Lee was going back into karting. Didn't Elle say that she was against it?"

"She still is," answered Mr. Dillanger. "I was hoping to sway her to the idea before this event, but I ran out of time."

"How much money is this going to cost you?" asked Evan.

"Well, our half is only fifteen thousand. It does cost money to train, and it isn't a free ride. The sponsor will cover the other half. It's not a problem. I can get a home equity line of credit on the house."

"That sounds like a problem if Elle isn't in agreement."

"I know. Let's keep this quiet until I can bring her around to the idea," said Mr. Dillanger.

"You need to figure out how to close this deal. Elle had told me how relieved she was last year when Gary Lee had aged out of his karting division and would be moving on to other things in his life. She said that karting and a teenager with a learner's permit did not mix. Racing karts and being a safe driver were like oil and water to her."

Chad did not want to be part of this conversation. He had thought Gary Lee's parents were both supportive of his karting. Chad tried to act nonchalant as if he were more interested in the lacquer finish on the Le Mans racecar. Everyone was interrupted when the jolly voice of Butkis came on the scene. He had arrived at the Le Mans display to meet and greet the guests.

"Isn't this car a beauty?" Butkis came up between the two men, putting his hands on their shoulders. "I picked it up in France about twenty years ago—it was one of my first in the collection. Peugeot—this car won the race that year."

"This is your car?" asked Evan.

"Well, technically, my charity, RBC, owns it," Butkis replied. "It's a great arrangement. I buy all my cars that way. I get the tax shelter, and the charities get the cars when I die. And they also get fundraisers like this. Did the Wheelboys tell you about RBC? Racing Builds Character."

The two men nodded while Butkis illuminated his audience on the exquisite attributes of the French racecar.

"Very interesting indeed," whispered Evan to Chad. "Wish I could buy any car I wanted and just write it off my taxes like that!"

Chad wasn't quite sure what Evan was talking about.

"Mr. Butkis, you own South East Furniture, yes?" asked Evan. "And you're the sponsor for Eric and Chad, here. Am I right?"

"Why yes to both questions," said Butkis, and he put his arms around the two boys' shoulders. "This young man, Eric Daly, has real talent, and we're looking forward to seeing him on the podium many times this season. Likewise, Chad here has real potential for a future career in racing." Butkis gave them both a firm squeeze with his burly arms. With a proud look, he continued, "South East Furniture is my family's business. My grandfather started it in 1925, originally as Confederate Furniture, but we changed the name in 1975. The company has to change with the times.

"And now we are giving back to the community. Sponsorship is the key to healthy youth activities like karting." Butkis continued to extol the virtues of his RBC cause. Ultimately, he concluded, "Remember, green means go," with a wink to his Wheelboys. Butkis looked around at his audience with a wide grin, then suddenly turned, waved to another group of guests, and excused himself.

"Wow," said Evan. "How much money can furniture sales bring in? Well, what does that matter? That's how the other half lives." Evan looked around for Mr. Dillanger, but apparently, he had wandered off during Butkis' speech. Chad just shrugged, not knowing where he might have gone. "Might as well enjoy the party," said Evan, and he reached for another glass of champagne.

Suddenly, the soft murmur of the crowd was broken by a shout from across the hall. "You did what?" a woman yelled out.

The people around fell silent, and everyone turned to look. It was the Dillangers. Gary Lee and his parents were standing by a Ferrari near the side of the ballroom.

"No, I'm not going to calm down!" Mrs. Dillanger yelled again.

"Oh, this is not good," said Evan. He turned and walked quickly toward the family. Chad followed from a safe distance. Gary Lee stood sheepishly to the side of his parents. Mrs. Dillanger turned to Evan as he approached.

"Did you know about this?" she asked, pointer her finger at Evan.

"Know about what?" Evan asked.

"That this idiot was going to sign my son up for driving a hundred miles per hour when he doesn't even have his full driver's license?" she said, her voice rising.

"You know it's not like that," said Mr. Dillanger, trying to placate her.

"Oh, the hell it isn't! I've put up with this 'pay to play' karting pyramid scheme that you've been in love with for eight years, and I told you last year we were through with it! You promised it would bring 'character building,' but you never said anything about the broken bones and the late nights in the emergency room getting x-rays. I did not sign up for this, and I'm not signing a mortgage on my home to pay for it. No way!"

Chad felt horrible for Gary Lee—not only an embarrassing fight but also aired in front of the wealthy folks of Alabama. He could see Big Mo Kilgore headed their way with a stern face, too.

"Let's take this outside," Evan said to Elle Dillanger.

She grabbed Gary Lee by the sleeve and hauled him toward the hotel lobby. The other adults and Chad followed. Chad could hear Kilgore behind them announcing, "It's all right, folks! Just a little family conversation."

Mr. Dillanger caught up with his wife as she and Gary Lee were exiting the hotel's front entrance.

"Elle!" he shouted. She paused and looked at him. "I'm sorry. I wanted to discuss this with you earlier but just didn't know how to."

"That's because you already knew what I would say!" she screamed. "I'm so sick of you trying to live through our son's activities. You're like the other fathers in this group, acting like children yourselves, but it's your kids taking all the risk. Who slaps a logo on their kid and expects them to perform for the sponsors at outrageous speeds? Gary Lee is not a carnival monkey!"

"Gary Lee has a real opportunity here. I wish you could understand that," begged Mr. Dillanger.

"Drew, you have been drinking the Kool-Aid way too long. Gary Lee is going to prepare for college in his senior year, and that money you want to throw away is needed for his education. What? Did you think he's going to win tens of thousands of dollars karting, like at the Super Nats in Vegas? Is that how you're justifying this insanity?"

"I'm not going to let you ruin Gary Lee's career like you did mine, Elle," said Drew Dillanger, becoming stern and angry. Crossing his arms, he said, "It's not your decision."

Big mistake, Mr. D, Chad thought to himself. Gary Lee's mom was not a passive woman, and challenging her was really asking for it.

"Me, ruin a career? What—as a Wheelboy?" Mrs. Dillanger screamed. "That's it! I'm through putting up with you and this charade. You are no longer welcome in my house. Find another place to stay tonight. Why don't you hook up with one of those LL girls that you like so much? You can pack up your things tomorrow and move out."

Everyone was dumbfounded, and Chad could see that Gary Lee was horrified.

"I mean it!" she screeched.

Elle Dillanger had her son's arm locked in her hand. She turned and walked away with him toward the parking lot. Chad and the two men just watched them walk away in silence.

"Hey, man. I'm truly sorry," said Mr. Dillanger to Evan.

"No, I'm much sorrier for you, Drew. I didn't know things were so bad."

"She'll calm down. I'll stay over at the office again."

"Let me give you a lift. Let's get out of here," said Evan. "Good night, Chad," he turned and said while they walked off.

Chad didn't know what to think. That was the first time that he learned of Gary Lee's parents having serious problems. In the weeks following that gala, Mr. Dillanger did move out. Gary Lee didn't join the Kilgore Pro team with Chad, but he did come to many of Chad's karting events that summer. Gary Lee still loved karting and drove for fun whenever he could, but the dream of racing that they had both shared had been handed off to Chad to carry on alone.

CHAPTER 9

Uma Kilgore found herself alone in the cavernous halls of her mansion home once again. It was a Saturday morning in May, and the racing season was in full swing. Monroe was seldom around; he was off on some business activity in Florida. Their son, Sonny Kilgore, was off at his team racing events. The Kilgore clan would converge on the house tonight after their week of activities.

Uma read the morning paper and noticed that there was another article about the Mason and Dillanger tragedy. The students at the high school were holding a vigil for Gary Lee Dillanger that very night. They would be releasing sky lanterns and praying for his recovery. She wondered what the Mason family would be praying for—forgiveness or something else?

The article in the paper said that the Dillanger boy was still in a coma. It described how Gary Lee Dillanger was a popular high school kid who wanted to be on the Kilgore Racing Team, like so many local kids. She thought of the story from a few years back about how Gary Lee had won the karting championship at age fifteen. She recalled the headline: "Permission to Race Without a License to Drive." How did it become acceptable to have kids racing fast even before having a permit to drive a car?

Uma made her favorite Scottish blend tea with lemon and honey, gathered her favorite cat, and sat by the window in the formal English-style parlor. She thought about Elle Dillanger's current situation. She hoped Elle had a sister or a brother to hang on to after remembering that the Dillangers were separated. Uma decided to bake something to bring over to the hospital for her.

Uma was no stranger to tragedy, and she had paced the hospital floors many times herself. She remembered Monroe's last accident, the one that pushed him into retirement. Uma had sat in the hospital in Italy with him for weeks while he healed after rolling his rally car several times. She'd been able to persuade him to finally give it up and leave the racing to the younger drivers—after all, he was a team owner. At that time, Sonny was well into his racing career, and Monroe hoped his legacy would be passed on to his son. That seemed to be part of the racing culture. The goal of all racers: build your legacy, become a legend, and pass it on to your heirs. It certainly was in this family.

Worse than that was the Kilgore rule, the "code of silence." The men in the Kilgore family were always silent about death and disaster. It weighed heavily on Uma today. In racing culture, the drivers were celebrated like toreadors headed for the bullfight and mourned as fallen heroes when killed or injured. For the Kilgores, no complaints were allowed. No criticism or blame about an injury or the death of a driver was tolerated on Monroe Kilgore's team. If someone spoke up, they would be gone shortly. Uma just shook her head.

Thankfully, her son had survived racing. Over the years, Sonny had his share of hospital stays, as well: concussions, broken arms, broken legs, burns—too many even to remember. Monroe joked that they should always know where the nearest emergency room was. He seemed oblivious that their son was risking his life, and Uma bore all the worrying for the family.

Recently Sonny had retired from driving and was happy with just being a team owner. Now his son, Uma's grandson, Mackie, was racing for Sonny's team. A third-generation racer—what a great story. The truth is that Mackie didn't turn out to be a stellar driver and only a few times had earned a spot on the winner's podium. Uma was less worried about Mackie because he had become more cautious as he matured. Maybe he didn't have the aggression or ambition to be number one; he was a shy boy after all.

What was Monroe's secret of success and longevity? He had won his first Formula 3 race purely by the misfortune of the front-runners. In the final lap, the two lead cars bumped and spun into the wall, forcing the third-place runner off the track, leaving Monroe to cross the finish line first. He celebrated the win, and the other driver went to the hospital. Uma even wondered if Monroe's strategy had been to hold back and let the front runners take themselves out. Or maybe he was just not that fast, or he didn't take the crazy risks that the others did. At least Monroe survived and occupied his time with his business activities now. The only crazy driving he still engaged in was his annual road rally to Belle Isle.

Uma wanted to put the present tragedy out of her mind, at least for a little while. Her heart ached, and her stomach was in a knot. Uma looked out the back window at the small vegetable and herb garden in the corner of the yard. She always planted a garden each spring, and it looked like some floppy-stemmed dewberries were ready for picking. She could make a dewberry strudel for dinner, she thought. Uma was anxious to make some comfort food, and she yearned for the contentment found in cooking.

Remembering that the house would be a flurry of people again tonight, Uma returned to planning the dinner party. Monroe would likely bring home some guests, and his sister, Margaret, would also be arriving for her summer visit. Uma would need to stop by the market and pick up some fresh Hungarian paprika and honeycomb. Summer seafood gumbo and dewberry strudel were on her mind, and for a moment, she felt the comfort that Alabama spring brought her.

Uma rose and walked outside; the air was crisp and had warmed to nearly summer weather. She crossed over to the narrow footbridge and stood leaning on the railing. The stream was just a trickle from an underground spring, and this is where Uma had started her memorial stone garden in 1966. At the Sebring race in Florida that year, her two friends were killed while watching the race. A car spun off the track; Percy and Joanne were injured when the crash fence gave way, and they later died from internal injuries. It was a very personal loss for her, yet no one was permitted to speak of it in the Kilgore household. "Spectators who wish to stand on the side of the race track do so at their own risk," her husband had said in dismissal.

Uma started the stone garden to give a silent voice to her mourning. She placed the first two large stones near the stream for her two friends, giving her peace. From that day forward, Uma had placed a rock or a stone along the stream for each person in her life that she lost to racing. At first, the stones were plain without any engravings since Uma knew for whom they were placed. After a few years, she began to engrave the names on each one for everyone to see.

The large, dappled granite stone was in memory of the celebrated Formula One racer Ayrton Senna. She thought about the death of the triple world champion at the San Marino Grand Prix. Sadly, Roland Ratzenberger died at the same event the previous day, but Ayrton Senna's death was the headline. Ironically, Senna was renewing his efforts to increase attention to driver safety after Ratzenberger's death, just one day before he died himself. Auto racing was such an ironic business.

Uma gazed at each stone and whispered the name as she passed by. "Hello, Pederson," she said, stopping at a prominent pink quartz stone settled in the green clover. Their family friend Phil Pederson was such a dear friend. She thought that he was the most notable American racer ever, although he came originally from Europe. He died in a violent crash only a few years back—that was too much for her, and she had never been to a race since. Pederson was so humble; he never bragged about being a legend, and he never even had a severe injury before the crash that took his life. Uma remembered his times at their dinner table and how much he appreciated her hospitality.

Uma was drawn back to thoughts of her dinner menu for the family's return home, wondering who would be her guests that night. In Monroe's racing years, drivers and their girlfriends or wives (or escorts) would fill up the grand dining room for her cuisine, such as truffle soufflé or stuffed eggs casino. Her signature was a spice mixture of rosemary and thyme, basil, cinnamon and mace, cloves, allspice, white pepper, a dash of salt, and Hungarian paprika. Sometimes her guests applauded her like a five-star chef. Monroe's friends always wanted more of that Eastern European flavor and Turkish coffee.

Uma walked back to her house and onto her patio. Looking out across the stream, Uma gazed at the other Kilgore estate, the house that Sonny had built for himself and his family. Her son's home followed the same architectural plans as her and Monroe's home, and the houses were known in the community as the Twin Mansions. Uma remembered how much she enjoyed having her son and his family as neighbors. Her former daughter-in-law, Kylie Shay, and their grandson, Mackie Kilgore, kept her company many years ago during those long racing months. At least Kylie was still her neighbor. Even though Kylie and Sonny had divorced many years ago, Uma remained close with her—like the daughter she never had. The two of them shared a common bond as racing wives and moms. Uma recalled holding Kylie's hand while young Mackie Kilgore was having his broken bones set years ago. Kylie also understood the Kilgore code of silence.

Uma thought it sad that Sonny felt so compelled to replicate his father in everything. He seemed to make all the same foolish mistakes, too. Oh, yes—Monroe had his flaws, such as infidelity. Uma knew all about the other women in her husband's past. Being the *other woman* doesn't make you special; it makes you a runner-up, she thought to herself. About thirty years ago, when Monroe had his first affair, Uma invented her own secret retribution. Regardless, she was not worried about losing him. She knew that the high and mighty legend of auto racing loved himself the most—more than any other woman. While his escapades did stir up a lot of rumors, Uma had rules about gossip. She never talked about the controversies that seemed to follow the Kilgore men, except perhaps with her daughter-in-law. Kylie had shared stories with Uma of Sonny's liberalities with other women. Uma questioned whether she had spoiled her son too much or if he was just imitating his father.

Kylie had wanted a divorce from racing more than anything else. It wasn't just Sonny's flirtations with other women that irked

Kylie. Auto racing had consumed her family, including her son, Mackie, who was expected to follow in the Kilgore family business. Uma wondered if people even knew about all the things racers' wives had to tolerate.

It was not long into her husband's racing career for Uma when she started to develop her own coping mechanism—her secret retribution. When she had been tipped off on his cheating ways by another racer's wife, she went to his trophy case—the thing that he seemed to value the most—and picked up his winning helmet from a rally in Switzerland, which had two karats in diamonds across the front. In her anger, she pried out the precious stones using her knitting tools and replaced them with Austrian crystals from her decorative jewelry. Monroe was such a fool; he couldn't tell the genuine from the counterfeit. That first heist was so easy. Uma eventually sold the loose diamonds and learned to hide her banking activities in a private account in Credit Suisse.

Uma found she was a good little jewel thief, and it became her private thrill. Since those first gratifying experiences, Uma had found real satisfaction in replacing Monroe's coveted jeweled trophies with lesser metals and crystal glass. Her Swiss retirement account had ballooned with lucrative interest, and she had no qualms about it. Monroe had not even noticed when she replaced his very expensive Crystal Sapphire Award with inexpensive Slovakian glass. He couldn't recognize the difference between precious stones and glass, just like he couldn't discern the difference between real love and a call girl or real friends and his false admirers. Her cheating husband deserved this secret punishment, and she had no guilt and no intention of changing her plans now.

Uma stood up and returned to her kitchen. She walked into the pantry to start getting out her ingredients for the evening's fare. She had put the Dillanger tragedy out of her mind, but her son's karting endeavors still bothered her. Why was Sonny Kilgore so intent on getting kids into racing? After all, he hardly ever participated in the karting—the actual work was all handed over to his assistants. Honestly, Monroe was at the karting activities more than Sonny. Monroe certainly liked having his ego stroked by the young people;

he would tell stories and give out advice to the kids, and they would soak it up.

Uma topped up the water in the vase of fresh flowers on the kitchen counter. Flowers made her think of the recent funeral, and she imagined what a difficult time the Mason family was going through. Uma had comforted grieving racers' parents before, and she needed to do something for this family—a charitable donation in Gillian's name. She decided to indulge in her secret craft of jewel theft. The Bicentennial Irish-Scottish Road Rally trophy cup, one of Monroe's prized possessions, had emeralds around the bottom that Uma was saving for a worthy cause—like a donation to the youth orchestra in memory of the young musician. That set Uma's mind at ease. She would make the call to her private jeweler and confidant in the morning.

Feeling resolved, Uma took some mushrooms out of the refrigerator and gave them a quick rinse in a colander. She picked up her tin of Hungarian paprika and shook it with concern. It felt light, and she was hoping to get some fresh paprika for the Chicken Paprikash. Uma could pick up some more at the market that afternoon, but time was now short. She thought about dropping in on Kylie next door to see if she had any paprika but realized how pointless that would be. The tin would have to do. Kylie was a class act, but she was not a cook, for sure. She knew how to throw a great dinner party—with a caterer.

Kylie loathed Sonny Kilgore these days, now that he had a new young girlfriend. Another young bum—Uma shook her head. Whores and escorts were always hanging around the track, and now she would be forced to entertain one at the family dinner. She wasn't going to trouble Kylie with these family matters.

Uma muttered to herself as she rolled out the strudel dough. She had prepared the dewberry strudel for the oven when suddenly, there was an eerie feeling all around her. The smell of burning rubber blew into the kitchen.

For a moment, Uma thought something might be burning on the stove, but then she remembered it was not the first time she experienced that fragrance. She put the strudel into the midnight-blue oven and looked around. The late afternoon had darkened the rest of the downstairs.

Uma ventured to the hallway and peered into the shadows. Again, she felt a presence along with the pungent scent of burnt rubber. A slight draft blew by her, and there was a soft voice, a half-whisper coming from down the hall: *"Winning is everything."*

Uma walked gently along the hall toward the parlor. "Winning is everything," she echoed back, hoping for a response. That was the slogan of the Owen Racing team, where the Kilgores met Phil Pederson. For so many years, "Winning is everything," Pederson would say with a wink. Now, "Winning is everything" was haunting her home.

"Pederson, is that you?" she called out. "I remember! I remember!" she shouted out into the empty hall, hoping to appease the apparition. Why did he keep returning—is his business unfinished, or is there a debt owed? Did somehow the Kilgores cheat death?

Uma was confused by this encounter. She loved Monroe, although he was certainly an SOB much of the time. Why hadn't *he* died? How many times had she paced those hospital floors with worry and fear? How many times would she have to tolerate the masochistic determination to race and win? Too many times. And now a ghost was reminding her without apologies that winning is everything.

"What a day!" Uma said out loud.

CHAPTER 10

Uma had dinner nearly ready in the kitchen when Monroe arrived home with his friend and business colleague, Mr. Butkis. Uma came down the front hall and greeted them. They had just returned from business travel and seemed to be in a giddy mood. Monroe was wearing a sheriff's badge and a cowboy hat along with pointed-toe, snakeskin boots.

"Hello, Darling," greeted Monroe as he took off his cowboy hat in a sweeping gesture and kissed Uma. "I'm Sheriff Big Mo, and this is Marshal B.B."

"Oh, good lord. And who is this two-person posse in pursuit of?" Uma asked.

Mr. Butkis, who Monroe always called B.B., was dressed similarly in a cowboy getup and red cowboy boots. They seemed sober enough, but they had the scent of stale cigar fumes on their clothes.

"We are in pursuit of the U.S. dollar, and we're closing in on a big roundup in Florida," Monroe replied. He looked at B.B. and raised his eyebrows. They both started laughing hysterically, and then Monroe let out some yells, trying to sound like a cowboy. The two men sat down in the living room.

Uma shook her head. She knew that the tension of work followed by unwinding at home was just another part of Kilgore life. However, for Monroe, that unwinding was sometimes more like a tightly wound spring popping loose. He and his pals would become like silly schoolboys.

The dining room table had been set hours earlier, and the Kilgore home was imbued with the smell of Uma's Hungarian chicken paprikash, apple casserole, and dewberry strudel. Besides Uma's cooking, the pantry was brimming with Napoleons and other assorted cakes filled with custard and decorated with chocolate lace, thanks to Stossi, her catering friend. Sometimes it bothered Uma that Monroe was unaware of the gastronomic efforts made for him and his guests. Uma went back to the kitchen and returned to the living room with a cheese and fruit tray.

"Some appetizers?" she asked, putting the tray on the coffee table.

"Thank you," said Monroe. He was pouring a drink at the bar. "B.B., a drink? Anything for you, Uma?"

"No, thank you. I'll have some wine with dinner," she replied.

"Yes, Mo," replied Butkis. "Uma, our gourmet chef, the aroma from your kitchen is heavenly. I can't imagine what you have prepared, but I'm sure it will be sensational."

"I know you boys obviously have something to celebrate, but please remember that we've just had a tragedy in Blue Springs," said Uma. "The Dillanger boy, Gary Lee, is still in a coma, and Gillian Mason was killed in the same crash. They're still talking about it in the newspaper just today."

Monroe and Butkis stopped their chuckling.

"Yes, I heard that news, and it really is a shame," Monroe said, looking at Uma. "No one knows when his last day is going to be, right? We all have to go sometime. I don't waste time worrying about things I have no control over."

Uma left the living room seething. What a preposterous notion, "no control over." So many tragedies are avoidable, so why not just take steps to avoid them? Why bother trying to explain that to Monroe Kilgore? He had the antiquated belief that when it's your time to go, it's inevitable, or if it's not your time to go, you're safe. Those poor teenagers—was it just their time to go? How could her husband be so cold-hearted?

She returned to the kitchen, and the men continued their dialog with rolling laughter, snorting, and coughing, which bellowed through the house. They were so loud that Uma could almost hear the conversation from the kitchen. What could be so funny?

Uma walked to the doorway of the living room. They were laughing about a toilet paper commercial from one of the new sponsors for Sonny's karting team.

"You mustn't neglect your butt, Butkis," Monroe said, and Butkis roared with howling laughter that echoed through the mansion.

Uma shook her head. This was the prelude to their dinner that she would soon serve. Margaret Kilgore, Monroe's twin sister, would be arriving shortly. Uma hoped they would act like adults at dinner. Margaret was driving down from Detroit, Michigan, where she and Monroe had lived as children. Margaret would be spending the month of June at their home. She usually spent the month of August with them every summer, and now that she recently retired from Chrysler, she wanted to come down earlier this year.

Uma was about to return to the kitchen when the front door opened, and Margaret strolled in. She was tall and wispy, with thick dark and gray hair brushed back. She wore tangerine Capri pants with a multicolor flowing top; her hands were well adorned with various rings and bangles.

"Oh, Uma! I missed you!" Margaret said with open arms while Uma was making her way through the hall toward her. Margaret spoke with a sultry voice that still carried a Scottish brogue more subtle than her brother's.

Monroe and Butkis instantly stopped their carrying on, and Butkis rose from the couch. "My first and last heartthrob, Margaret. It's wonderful to see you again," said Butkis, putting on his charm.

Margaret was busy giving Uma a long hug, and then she turned toward him. "Why hello, B.B.!" she said and kissed him on the cheek. "What is with the cowboy outfit and sheriff's badge? It's not Halloween. Has Monroe been to the county jail, or are you guys just playing cowboys?" Margaret then paused and breathed in deeply with eyes closed. "Oh, Uma, I just love the smell of your cooking!"

Monroe gave his sister a quick squeeze. "It's good to see you, Sis," Monroe said. "Your bags?"

"You too, Monroe. The bags are in the car, but that can wait until later," said Margaret. "I'm famished from traveling."

Margaret waltzed into the kitchen and began poking around. Uma had already opened a bottle of red Chateau Ducru Beaucaillou Saint Julien and was letting it breathe for dinner. She went to open a simple chilled Chardonnay from Sonoma County for herself and Margaret.

"Oh sweetie, can you pour me a glass of that?" asked Margaret.

"Sure, here you are," said Uma, handing her a glass and then clinking their glasses together. "*Egészségedre!* Cheers! To your health. Were you driving all day?"

"Oh, no. I stopped and stayed with some friends in Nashville last night, so I've only been driving five or six hours. I've given up those road-rally experiences that Monroe relishes. I don't need to drive until it hurts!"

"Good for you! So you're retired now. How is that going for you?"

"Love it. You know I worked for a VP, and he was in a panic with me leaving his department. I've moved permanently up to the vacation home in Belle Isle. Are you coming up with Monroe at the end of the summer?"

"Oh, you mean the great Belle Isle Road Rally? I might drive up myself and stay with you, but as you said, I've also given up on the road rallies. You know, Monroe isn't happy unless he can show off at least one speeding ticket from that trip."

"Well, it would be great if you could come early," said Margaret, turning to the casserole dish on the kitchen island. She smiled and said, "Smells so good. I'm starved! Are we waiting for Sonny or Mackie?"

"I just heard from them. Sonny and Mackie are still in Atlanta. Mackie is racing tomorrow, so it will just be the four of us for dinner tonight," Uma replied.

Uma walked over to the entrance of the living room. "Dinner is ready," she announced. "Sorry, I don't have a dinner bell to ring for you cowboys."

Monroe rose diligently, and B.B. followed in after him. "Uma, I always look forward to the Kilgore dining experience," said B.B. as he pulled up to the dining room table. "It is just like a Viennese waltz. Thank you for having me over."

Margaret passed the casserole dish and said to Uma, "Sweetie, your chicken paprikash will always be my favorite." Turning to the gentlemen, she asked, "So what is the story with the sheriff's badges?"

"Oh, we were just playing some cards to unwind after the trip to Florida," said Monroe.

Uma was used to her husband's habit of playing Bang, the card game. Big Mo and B.B. liked to dress up for the occasion, given that there was always a sheriff, two outlaws, and a renegade.

"You know how Monroe loves to dress up," said Uma to Margaret. "Didn't your mother dress you alike when you were kids? Lately, he has been getting into my closet and wearing my old bathrobes after his shower!"

"That's nonsense," said Monroe.

"Weren't you singing "Danny Boy" late one night out by the pool?" asked Uma.

"I probably was. What does that have to do with anything?" said Monroe.

"Well, you were wearing my pink chenille robe then, and it wasn't the first time."

Monroe waved his hand and shook his head, dismissing the notion.

"I'm not surprised," said Margaret. "Mo has always been a little loony, even before his racing concussions."

B.B. started to chuckle and nod in agreement.

"You know, I was born a few minutes before Monroe and managed to get away with the beauty as well as the intelligence," Margaret said, smiling at her brother. "Or maybe Mama just dropped Mo on his head."

B.B. chuckled louder. "To the beauty and the intelligence," he said, holding up his glass toward Margaret and then toward Uma. "And hail to Uma's culinary brilliance."

Monroe raised his glass and said, "And here's to the Florida Springs Motor Resort & Country Club."

B.B. acknowledge Monroe, but Uma and Margaret were taken by surprise.

"What exactly are you toasting?" asked Uma.

"It's our new project in Florida," answered Monroe.

Uma gave Monroe a concerned look. His covert projects usually spelled trouble.

"Uma, we definitely want to have some of your signature dishes on the menu at the club," added B.B.

"Come on, boys. Spill the beans," said Margaret. "What is your latest folly?"

"Uma, didn't Monroe tell you about our new motorsport club?" asked B.B. He looked over at Monroe with a grin. "We are going to make a fortune on this new club with Sonny's racing and karting connections. I am surprised you didn't hear about the planning. Big Mo, you must have been waiting for a special occasion. Do I need a drum roll?" Butkis drummed on the table with his fingertips.

Uma was puzzled and looked over at her husband. "Can you please explain? What kind of grand plans do you have now?" she asked.

Monroe smiled. "We have about twenty investors now," he explained. "Gavin Carrington put together the LLC, and we just purchased 380 acres in the Florida Panhandle. It is right near the Air Force Base in Okaloosa County."

"Well, that sounds like quite a big project," said Uma. Gavin Carrington was the Kilgores' lawyer, and once he was involved, Uma knew everything was already in motion.

"So what's the angle, Mo?" asked Margaret.

"I think of it as a gentlemen's club for our friends and us to race our cars when we want to let them loose," said Monroe. "We will be charging $25,000 for annual dues. It will also be a five-star resort. The boys are gonna love this place, too. It will have a karting track, and we'll also be starting a superkart league with this club as the premier venue."

"A gentlemen's club? As in adult entertainment?" asked Margaret.

"No, no, that's not what he means," explained B.B. "More like a country club for people with expensive supercars. With a restaurant and day spa, as well."

"It's going to have a two-and-a-half-mile track. And I must say, the price was right. It's a win-win for everyone," said Monroe.

Uma still gave Monroe a suspicious look while she collected the dinner plates. She returned from the kitchen with Turkish coffee and strudel with raspberry sauce.

"Sonny is happy with the plan," Monroe continued, trying to make it sound appealing to Uma. "We can be a part of the winter karting tour. Uma, you'll love the weather in Florida in the winter. It will be a family affair."

"A family affair, with all the kids, too. I like the sounds of that," said B.B. as he reached for more raspberry sauce. "What exactly is in this sauce?"

Margaret stared at B.B. "Chambord Channel, French Black Raspberry Liqueur," she muttered. "Maybe you and Mo should have your heads examined. I know you boys love your Luxurious Lifestyle events and activities, but why are you mixing up families and little kids with that sort of thing?"

"This is the business we are in, Sis," said Monroe. "It's an entertainment business, and no one makes any money if there's no audience. Our goal is to build the audience and develop the market. The kids and families are a huge market."

"What about the local Wheelboys?" asked Uma. "Involving them is more than just marketing. Telling and selling should include listening and learning. We just had a neighborhood girl lose her life to speed. The driver was one of your proteges and neighbor. He is in a coma and holding on for his life."

"The legions of the miserable have arrived again," moaned Monroe. "That accident was tragic, but how can you think we had anything to do with that, Uma?"

B.B. coughed and explained, "This is all a part of how we build the business. The young racers are the key to drawing in the young market. Each kart racer brings in dozens of fans, and those who don't make it as drivers become lifelong fans themselves."

"But the real money comes from the sponsors," added Monroe. "We want to get sponsor logos on those kids and get them to turn heads. The larger the audience, the more money we can bring in from the sponsors."

"You know, Monroe, it's been my impression that most racecar drivers are under-compensated. They risk their lives and barely make a living," said Uma. "Why would you want to put that struggle on young kids?"

"Sweetheart, it's not like that at all!" answered Monroe. "These young kids aren't starving or trying to make a living. This is character building, and they love it. Their parents are willing to pay for the service. They sign the contracts and waivers and give full consent for their kids to race those karts."

"Well, Mo, you know how I've always felt about it," said Margaret. "Exploitation. You get these kids addicted to adrenaline, you don't have to pay them anything, you slap a logo on them, and you have a huge profit margin."

Monroe sipped his coffee and grinned. "What a wonderful business!" he said. "Hold on."

Monroe sprang up from the table and disappeared into the hall. He returned with a map and began to unfold it on the end of the table. "Let me show you where the club will be," Monroe said. The four of them gathered around Monroe to see where he was pointing.

"The Luxurious Lifestyle organization will hold charity events at the club," explained Monroe. "We might even get a few million dollars from the state or a local bond. The secret is convincing folks that the club brings in tax and tourist revenue. Florida is very supportive of tourism investment." Monroe showed where the entrance would be. "We are going to have one thousand palm trees planted with ten varieties and a road course to die for."

"Hmmm. Ironic choice of words," said Uma. "Someone probably will die for it."

"Must you?" Monroe complained and frowned.

Uma excused herself from the table and started to bring some dishes into the kitchen.

"Let me help you with those, Uma," said Margaret, and she picked up B.B.'s plate.

"It was such a wonderful dinner. I have an early game of golf tomorrow," B.B. said. He arose from the dining table and held his hand over his brass sheriff's badge. "It's been a great week, buddy," he said to Monroe.

Walking out to the massive entryway, Butkis hugged Uma and said, "Uma, don't forget we still have planning to do for the White Party. That Hungarian strudel and raspberry sauce need to be on the menu." He smiled at Margaret, kissed her on the cheek, and said, "Good night, lovely lady."

"Good night, cowboy. See you on the range," Margaret replied with a smile. They watched Butkis walk to his big black Audi sedan in the circular drive, and Monroe shut the front door.

"Well, you managed to alienate Sonny and his new girl out of our weekend plans," Monroe said to Uma with a sudden scowl.

Uma was surprised by his reaction. "I thought they had a race tomorrow," she said.

"Yes. When I talked to him last week, he said they were coming here for dinner and would head back out in the morning," said Monroe. "Today, he said you had changed his mind. What exactly did you say to him?"

Uma smiled sweetly and said, "I told him that there are some girls that you bring home to meet your mother and others that you don't. At his age, he should know the difference."

"Sonny is forty-five years old. I wish you would let him bring any guest that he wants to our home." Then Monroe's countenance lightened. "Thanks for the great dinner. Loved the raspberry sauce. I'm going to get Margaret settled in her room." He smiled and kissed his wife.

Margaret and Monroe went out the front door to unload her luggage from her car. He returned with her suitcases in both of his extra-large hands and headed up the stairs. Margaret followed behind him with another large overnight case. She looked frail and light compared to her twin brother, and her shadow was notably smaller. Margaret laughed some more about the "Gentlemen's Club." Uma heard something said about Sonny's new girlfriend before the upstairs door closed. It was late, and she would leave the adult twins to their chatter.

Uma brought the rest of the plates into the kitchen and left them in a pile by the sink. She was tired now and decided the dishes could all be left for the morning. Heading up the stairs, she could still hear the muffled voices and laughter from Margaret's room. No point in waiting up for Monroe.

Uma tucked herself into her side of the bed without her husband. In no time, she fell into a deep and peaceful sleep.

CHAPTER 11

Uma was in a deep sleep that early Sunday morning and was suddenly consumed by a nightmare. She was a young woman racer, a celebrated champion, driving around corners in the heat of a race. She looked at her hands on the steering wheel, adorned in pink leather gloves, which moved quickly left and right. Suddenly, her car was spinning out of control. She could see the road and other cars swirling around her. She felt like screaming as she began to tumble. Everything came to a stop, and all she could see was the blue sky above her. People came and started to pick her up and pull her out of the crash. The man was going to cut her gloves off, and she yelled, "No! No! Do you know how hard it is to find pink leather racing gloves?"

Uma woke up in a sweat. She felt paralyzed from her nightmare. Now awake, it felt like a great weight held her down and made it difficult to breathe. She remembered hearing a voice in her dream: "Winning is everything." She looked around the bedroom. It was early dawn, and Monroe was sound asleep on his side of the bed. Uma decided she wasn't going to try to go back to sleep.

She got up and put on her slippers. She walked down the front stairs and through the long hallway to the kitchen. In the dark, she stumbled on the threshold and was so glad that she didn't lose her balance and fall. She heated some water in the electric kettle and poured a cup of tea. She took a deep breath to shake off the anxiety of her dream.

Uma sat down at the kitchen table by the sliding glass door. Looking at her cobalt blue appliances and holding her warm teacup, she remembered how Elle Dillanger had worked so hard on the kitchen remodeling project. They had become close during that time. Uma appreciated how Elle cared about Uma's opinion during the project. Now their community was in mourning, and she felt anxious about Elle's son, Gary Lee, who was in the hospital, fighting for his life.

The beautiful morning light outside was rising over the willow trees by the brook. She grabbed her sweater from the kitchen counter stool and went out through the sliding glass door to the patio garden. It was early summer, and she had already planted some herbs and tomatoes.

Uma looked down and saw a white paper Chinese sky lantern on the ground by the young plants. What was this? Uma picked it up. It was pure white, and the wick of the candle was charred.

"Oh!" she gasped aloud. "They had sent up sky lanterns at Gary Lee's vigil last night at the high school. It must have fallen from the sky." She thought the vigil was a kind gesture.

Uma examined the lantern and saw that there was a yellow envelope attached inside it. She opened the envelope and read a note, *"Slow and steady wins the race. Keep moving forward, Gary Lee."* Another piece of lavender paper was folded inside that read, *"The stars will light the sky for you, Gillian."* She laid the lantern down on the stone wall and tucked the notes in her sweater's front pocket.

A morning mist was floating up from the brook, and Uma heard sobbing but could not locate where the sound was coming from. This was not the first time she had heard this sound near the brook. She walked through the fog over toward the stone garden and saw a man in a white racing suit sitting on one of the large boulders. Could it be? The sad soul had his face in his hands and was softly weeping in the early morning mist. She could hear him moan, "Winning is everything," in his lamentation.

"Pederson?" she said with her hand over her mouth. The apparition stopped and looked up at her, and she could dimly see his face—a face she recognized from years ago. "Oh, Pederson," Uma confirmed. She started to move slowly toward him as if to avoid frightening him off.

"Uma?" a voice behind her called out.

She continued forward, steadfastly looking at the man in white. He had stopped his grieving and smiled when he saw her.

"Uma, are you out here?" Margaret called again. Uma turned and could see the lights were on inside the kitchen and Margaret on the patio. A soft rush of wind blew from the brook. She looked back at Pederson, but the fog had lifted, and he was gone.

"Oh, don't go," Uma said, but it was too late. "I'll be right there," she replied to Margaret. Uma glanced around wistfully and relished her encounter. She crossed back through the yard to the patio and greeted Margaret.

"What are you doing out here at this hour?" asked Margaret. "Church doesn't start for at least a few hours. Uma, come in the house before you catch a chill."

"I'm skipping church today," she said. "You and Monroe can go. You have a lot of catching up to do."

Margaret was staring at her. "Who were you talking to out here?"

"I was talking to myself in the stone garden, of course," Uma replied with a sly smile. They went into the kitchen together. "I'll fix you breakfast. Monroe is still asleep."

She silently busied herself in the kitchen and was looking forward to being alone again. Perhaps her spirit friend would return. Uma was also not in the mood for exchanging small talk with other people. She had tragedy on her mind. She did not want to look at the smiling faces at church, which she imagined saying, "Boys will be boys," and just sweeping it under the rug.

*****

After Monroe and Margaret left for church, Uma sat alone outside on the patio for her own private reflection time. She walked to the small bridge over the stone garden, and as her ritual was, she said a short prayer for each lost soul marked by a stone set by the brook.

"Oh, Pederson, I hope you find rest soon," Uma said out loud. Why was his troubled soul still visiting her? Maybe it was her doing—was she keeping him here? No, it must be something else. Tragedy weighed heavy on her heart. Uma prayed for Gillian Mason and her family. She prayed for the Dillangers and Gary Lee's recovery. She prayed for her son and grandson—for Mackie's safety while racing today.

Uma turned her mind to the day ahead. She went inside to the kitchen and started preparations for an early Sunday supper. She opened the refrigerator and took out the vegetables and fresh roast from the butcher. Uma spun into action, and the time flew by while she immersed herself in the cooking.

Uma had just put the meal in the oven and set the timer when she heard Margaret and Monroe come through the front door. It was noon, and they were just returning from church.

"How was the service this morning, Monroe?" Uma asked when she walked to the foyer.

Monroe let out a disgruntled noise.

"I don't think Mo was feeling the love today in church," explained Margaret. "The pastor could barely say 'nice to see you' when we left after the service."

"I don't know what's wrong with people these days," said Monroe. "I'm generous with my donations. I sponsor activities. What more do they want?"

"What happened?" asked Uma.

"The teen choir sang for everyone in church today," said Margaret. "The same choir that sang at the high school vigil last night."

"I don't know why they have to go on and on about it all," said Monroe. "Sure, it's very unfortunate, and of course, I feel sorry for the families."

"That wasn't the point, Mo," said Margaret. "The students talked about the importance of safety and the dangers of speed. You felt out of place because your family name is all about speed."

Uma understood Monroe's issue, and it wasn't just his family name. It was his brand: *Kilgore*. He wanted everyone to associate *Kilgore* with fast driving, courage, and tenacity. He wanted *Kilgore* to be the standard. People should say, "That guy drives like Big Mo Kilgore!" But he had a problem when he met people who were advocates for safety or caution.

"Why did they have to do that in church?" asked Monroe. "Some people glared at me as if I was the devil. I'm a Christian man. I say my prayers. One certainly must, with the business I'm in."

"Well, did you talk to God today?" asked Uma.

Monroe glared at her and sulked toward the back of the house. Margaret took Uma's arm and walked with her down the hall behind him. Monroe settled into the family room just off the kitchen, where he sat down in his favorite chair and scowled.

"Oh, lighten up, Mo," said Margaret. "We will be watching the race in Atlanta on TV after supper. Maybe Mackie will win."

Uma retrieved cheese and crackers on a long slate board from the kitchen and served it on the coffee table in the family room. Grapes and apricots alongside Monroe's favorite cheeses might cheer him up, thought Uma. As Monroe stared out the window, the corner of his mouth started to turn upwards, and his frown soon turned into a smirk. Uma knew he was thinking about the Kilgore team on the podium.

"Oh, these apricots are delicious," Margaret said. "Are you going to see Dad when you come up for your road rally in August?" she asked Monroe. "He is not well, you know. It might be your last chance to make peace with him."

Monroe's smirk turned back into a scowl. "He isn't a part of my life because I was too much of a disappointment to be a part of his life," Monroe said sternly. "Dad never came to one race of mine. When I was inducted into the Grand Prix Hall of Fame, only Mom was there for me. He was not."

"Mo, you promised that you would help with Dad when Mom died last year."

"Who do you think is paying his bills? Isn't that enough?" asked Monroe.

"He is in the nursing home now, and I'm not sure if he will make it through the winter. At least visit him when you come up to Belle Isle in August," Margaret continued. "Just because Dad didn't agree with your business and your life choices doesn't mean you should cut him out of your life."

"Certainly, we will see your father when we are in Michigan," said Uma. "Do you two want wine with dinner?"

Monroe nodded. "Well, I won't be looking forward to it," he answered. "Disapprove. That's all he does. Dad was sour when I started Sonny racing, and I have never even discussed Mackie's career with him."

"It's not a surprise. Look what happened to our uncle's family—Dad's brother lost a son and another injured. It isn't unusual for a parent to not want their only son to race cars over 175 miles per hour, you know," said Margaret. "Who wants to see their child end up dead or handicapped for life, like our cousin Ian?"

"I feel the same way," said Uma.

"Well, you never complained about Sonny's racing," said Monroe to his wife.

"There's a lot I never complained about," Uma replied. "That's not how I was raised, you know. But that didn't change how I felt about it."

"You shouldn't say that," said Monroe, looking at her intently. "You know I always value your opinion."

"Ha!" Uma laughed. "You value my happiness, and I am thankful for that, but you don't value my opinion. Just be glad I'm not like Kylie Shay, or we would have been through years ago."

"Ugh. Now that woman is the embodiment of ungratefulness," said Monroe.

"Mo, don't say that about your neighbor," said Margaret, giving him a nudge on the knee. "She's a good mother to your grandson, and she's one of the reasons you see Mackie as much as you do."

"She has the same attitude as Dad about racing, even though it's paying her bills," said Monroe.

"Oh, I bet she'll be watching the race today," said Margaret. "Why don't we invite her over to watch with us?"

"No way!" said Monroe, thumping the coffee table with his hand. "I'm already outnumbered."

Uma liked the idea of inviting Kylie over after supper. Uma didn't particularly want to watch the race, and she would like to have someone to talk to.

The timer chimed on the oven, and Uma returned to the kitchen to serve the supper. Margaret followed behind her. "Do you want me to open the wine, sweetie?" Margaret asked, picking up the bottle.

"Sure, the opener is in the drawer below the bottle."

In no time, the veal with applesauce was on the dining room table, along with a serving bowl of roasted vegetables. The table was set with the Sunday dishes, Margaret brought in the wine, and the three sat down to the meal. Uma was pleased with how tender the veal turned out, and nodding heads from Monroe and his sister confirmed it.

"So Monroe, how are Sonny and Mackie really doing?" asked Margaret. "You know, Mackie looked a bit depressed when he was up in Michigan last summer. Is this season going any better for him?"

"Oh, I think they are doing fine. Mackie has been a bit discouraged lately, but every racer has his ups and downs," replied Monroe. "And Sonny is starting to make a name for himself as a team owner."

"Well, that's good to hear. How are you going handle this new racing country club in Florida?" asked Margaret. "It seems like Sonny and Mackie have their hands full, and the way you describe it—it's such a big project. Why don't you just enjoy your retirement like I am doing?"

"Not to worry, Sis," said Monroe. "We have many partners on this project, and many hands make light work. There is room for more investors. You could put in some of that retirement money, and you'd be set for life."

"Oh, Mo. You know that I wouldn't dream of doing that!" said Margaret. "Remember what happened with Mom's investment in that one project of yours."

"Seriously, Sis, this is different. You'll meet some of the investors at the White Party."

"Even if it was bonafide, I couldn't put my money into such a thing for two reasons. First, this Luxurious Lifestyle brand is just a cover for raunchy old men, loose women, and fast cars. Second, your version of 'family karting' is a disguise for kids' racing. I have no issue with go-kart parks, but superkarts? You're going to have teenagers driving what—130 or 140 miles per hour? How do you even get parents to consent to that? That's just crazy."

"Whoa, Sis. Calm down. Racing is not like it was when I started out. Technology has improved, and safety is paramount. Imagine how much better a racecar driver I would have been if I could have driven a superkart when I was a kid. I would not have thought twice about doing it. This is like a dream come true for these kids."

"I think you're drinking your own snake oil, Mo. Dad would have never given his consent. You must be quite a salesman if you're getting parents to agree to that."

Uma had finished her supper quietly while listening to the two of them bantering back and forth. Finally, Monroe, in desperation, turned to Uma.

"Uma, my dear, can you help me out with this debate? Remember how much Mackie loved karting and how it gave him confidence?"

Uma put down her wine glass. "You want my opinion?" she asked, almost in disbelief. Both Margaret and Monroe looked at her earnestly.

"Your father never gave you consent to race cars," Uma began. "Now you and Sonny are determined to manufacture parental consent. You want the youngest of kids to participate in the fastest of driving and for their parents to say 'isn't that great'—why? Do you have something to prove to the world?"

Monroe was a little surprised but should not have expected any support from his wife on this topic.

"Kylie Shay left Sonny because Mackie broke his legs racing a kart when he was ten years old," Uma continued. "Remember that? Sonny is probably the worst father in the world. Are you proud of that? Now we have escorts and streetwalkers in our son's life, and for all you know, he could be carrying syphilis or some other strumpet's disease. Is that something our family should build a business around?" Uma was raising her voice now.

Monroe stood up and said, "Please remember who is making money around here and how I accumulated our wealth. It is my legacy, and that is important to me. I will do whatever I please, whenever I please. If I want to run my red Ferrari down the street at 150 miles per hour in my underwear, I will do it. If the cops catch me, I will pay the fine.

"The new club in Florida is on private property, and I earned the privileges that I worked for all of my life—just like the butcher and the baker and the candlestick maker. The strong and the brave lead with their heart. Weakness doesn't live here!" Monroe strutted out of the dining room.

Margaret and Uma watched him go and heard the patio door shut behind him. They were left in silence, looking at each other. Margaret burst out laughing, and Uma couldn't help herself but laugh as well.

Together they cleared the dining room and put the food away in the kitchen. Wine bottle and glasses in hand, the two went out to the pool area to reconcile with Monroe. He was reclining in a shady corner of the pool deck with his eyes closed as if asleep.

"Would you like your glass of wine?" Uma asked.

"Yes, thank you," Monroe replied, sitting up from his feigned nap.

"Sorry if I got under your skin, Mo," said Margaret. "I was just trying to say no thank you to your investment offer."

"Well, I heard you loud and clear, Sis. So we'll be having the White Party out here," Monroe said, changing the subject. "Summer is nearly here. There is nothing like the month of May. The groves of tall trees, dogwoods, and azaleas are beautiful. Looking off in the distance, you can see the hills of Alabama."

"It certainly is a beautiful setting, Mo, but you know how I feel about Belle Isle," said Margaret. "Nothing will surpass it. Oh, it's almost race time. Are we going to watch Mackie and Sonny on TV?"

"Yes," said Monroe, standing up. "Speaking of Sonny and Mackie, they will be participating in Bump Day for the Indy 500 next Sunday. Sonny's trying to beat the unofficial lap record of 239 miles per hour. We are all going, and I can get you tickets, Sis."

"You know I won't be attending, Monroe," Uma said before Margaret could reply. "Kylie and Sonny will certainly be there to support Mackie. Maybe even some of Sonny's karting families will attend, too. You and Butkis will be there, so the Kilgores will be well represented," said Uma.

Margaret rolled her eyes and changed the subject. "How do you like my new red shoes, Monroe?" She pointed at the pair she had kicked off earlier.

Monroe laughed and picked them up by the chaise lounge. He pulled off his loafers and tried to slide his two big toes into her red shoes. Sitting on the chaise, he pretended to walk in them.

"A little tight on me, but exquisite red high heel shoes, Margaret," said Monroe. He exaggerated his imaginary walk with hand gestures, and the women laughed at his little act. "How do they look on me, girls? High heels and hot wheels are what I live for," he moaned in jest.

Monroe stood up and gave back the red shoes to his sister. "Let's go watch that race on the telly!" he said. Uma and Margaret laughed once more, and they all walked inside. Monroe was happy again with his arm around Uma.

"Twins always have their secrets," Uma said softly under her breath.

CHAPTER 12

The sun was shining through the window in Gary Lee's hospital room on a bright Wednesday morning. Elle had just settled down to go through her monthly planner after the doctors and nurses came through during rounds. Drew had gone down to the cafeteria to pick up two more cups of coffee.

So many projects in the planner, but everything would have to wait or be done by someone else. She had an appointment for window treatment installation in one of her clients' homes later that week. Typically Elle supervised, but the installer would have to handle it himself. It was such an animated home with many pets and animals. A little pot-bellied pig was best friends with the dog, and they ran around the house together. There was a mynah bird in the room where Elle measured for the curtains. The bird kept saying, "I talk to myself," in the voice of an older woman.

Gary Lee had always wanted a dog, but with their busy lifestyle, they could only accommodate caged pets, like a hamster or a parakeet. Elle remembered how Gary Lee once rescued an injured bird he had found on the way home from school. He had it wrapped in an old shirt, and they put it in a shoebox with a lid to recover. He tried to feed it, but the poor thing never ate and died the next day. Gary Lee buried it in the shoebox in their yard with tears. Elle wrote in her planner, *Get a therapy dog.*

Elle had become impervious to the steady rhythmic, monotone noises of the machines hooked up to Gary Lee. Her concentration was broken when suddenly, the rhythm of the beeping accelerated.

She turned to her son lying in the bed and saw that his fingers began to twitch, his arm was moving, and a monitor alarm began to sound.

"Nurse!" Elle yelled out. "Someone help us here!"

Elle stood up and pressed the call button. She leaned over Gary Lee to look at his face. His eyes suddenly opened, he looked directly at her, and then his eyes rolled up.

Two nurses rushed into the room. "Please step back, ma'am," one said to her, and they began checking on her son.

"Call Doctor Aimsley," the other nurse said to an attendant in the doorway.

"What is it? What's happening to him?" asked Elle.

Gary Lee was now struggling in the hospital bed, constrained by his casts and brace. His attendants were removing the tape from the tube on his mouth.

"He's waking up. It's an excellent sign," the nurse explained. "We have to get the tubes out. He is having a gag reflex."

She began pulling the ventilating tube out of his throat while the other male nurse held Gary Lee still. Elle's panic started to evaporate when her son responded to her voice. Gary Lee tried to reach for his mother, and he wanted to speak but couldn't.

A woman in a blue uniform entered the hospital room calmly as if to oversee the activity. The nurses finished removing the tubes, and Gary Lee coughed and took a deep breath. He let out a weak groan. The doctor went straight over to Gary Lee and began to examine him.

"Your throat will be sore," she said to Gary Lee loudly. "You don't have to talk. I'm Dr. Aimsley." She shined a small light into each of his eyes. "Can you follow the light?" she asked, moving it back and forth.

Elle was anxious to hear her son speak, but she didn't want to interrupt the doctor. She called Drew on his cell phone but no answer. Eventually, the doctor turned around and smiled.

"Well, that's progress," she said. "When he does start to talk, let him whisper. There may be some irritation from the tube in his throat."

"How is he, Doctor? What comes next?" asked Elle.

At that moment, Drew entered the doorway with two coffee cups in his hands. He was startled by all the commotion.

"What's going on?" he asked, looking at Elle for some answer.

"Gary Lee is awake now. They just disconnected him from the breathing machine," she explained.

"That's a good thing, right?" He was looking at the doctor for confirmation.

"Yes," Aimsley replied. "It is very good. We can now get a better understanding of the extent of your son's traumatic injuries with his help."

"What do you mean? You've already set his broken arm and leg," asked Elle.

"There is some nerve damage, as well, and there's no diagnostic machine that can measure those types of injuries. I'm not entirely sure how cognitive he will be immediately. We have to see what happens over the next few hours."

Elle looked back at Gary Lee, and she could see he was exploring the room with his eyes. The nurses reconnected him to the monitor and elevated his bed just a bit.

"You can talk to him now," one said. She beckoned Elle and Drew with a gesture. "Just try to keep him calm as he becomes cognizant."

The nurses and the doctor left the room. Elle and Drew stood by the bed, one on either side. Gary Lee was awake, and all of the tubes had been removed. He was breathing on his own, and the gentle pulse of the monitor was a reassuring sound to Elle. She looked intently at him, holding his hand. He looked up at his father and back at Elle.

"Ma," Gary Lee whispered.

Elle was overwhelmed with happiness.

"Yes, Gary Lee! I'm here. You don't have to talk, honey. Just rest. You're going to get better," she said.

"What happened?" he whispered.

"You're in the hospital, Son," said Drew. "You've had an accident," he stated in a calming tone.

Elle's joy was short-lived. It was torn from her when she realized that she and Drew would have to tell Gary Lee what had happened. How could Drew be so calm and collected about it all? She gave Drew a cross look. He flashed his wife back a puzzled glare. Gary Lee laid his head back down and closed his eyes with a sigh. Elle had a brief reprieve from the inevitable conversation that was to come.

Over the next few hours, Elle shared the good news with family and friends. It was such a relief after days of endless waiting for even the slightest sign of improvement. Elle talked on the phone while watching the nurse help her son with a sip of water through a straw. She wondered what pain he must feel with a full-length cast on his right leg and a brace to immobilize his hip. The bruises under his eyes and his lost and broken front teeth were scary to see. Elle told herself that it looked worse than it was. His bruising would subside, he would receive dental work, and he would be her beautiful shining boy again. The road to recovery would be full steam ahead.

After several hours, Gary Lee started to ask some questions in a soft, frail voice. "What day is it? Will I be able to graduate? Can I see my friends? Where is Gillian?"

Elle avoided any real answers, not wanting to stress her son out while he was healing. "Honey, don't worry about school. Your friends can come and visit tomorrow," she answered.

Drew suggested maybe a little television would take his mind off the situation. She put on the TV and flipped to an afternoon movie. This comforted her more than Gary Lee. It reminded her of the times when Gary Lee was younger. If he would catch a fever and stay home from school, Elle would bring him soup, and he would watch TV and get better.

After a short while of TV, Gary Lee fell asleep. Elle watched him for a few more minutes and decided she needed to eat something healthy. "I'm going down to the cafeteria to have a salad," she said to Drew.

"I'll come with you," Drew answered. "Gary Lee's fine. The nursing staff is here."

They walked down the hall and took the elevator to the first floor. Just as they reached the cafeteria entrance, the hospital intercom called, "*Code Blue, room 209, Code Blue, room 209.*"

Elle froze and said, "That's Gary Lee's room!"

She turned back and ran to the stairs. When Elle arrived at his room, there was a male nurse who stopped her.

"Ma'am, you can't go in right now," he said firmly.

"That's my son! What's happening to Gary Lee?" Elle was hysterical.

Drew had also arrived, and she could see the confusion and hear loud voices in Gary Lee's room. Drew and the nurse held Elle so that she couldn't go in. The commotion settled down, and the white coats started to leave Gary Lee's room. A doctor came out and approached Elle and Drew.

"Your son's going to be okay. He's fine now. It was a bit of a scare, but he's fine," said the doctor.

"What happened?" asked Elle. "Code Blue—that means his heart stopped, right? How could that happen?"

"That's correct. Your son had a cardiac arrest. The staff did their job and revived him. We don't know the cause yet, but we're going to run some tests. You can see him in a minute."

Elle leaned back against the wall in the hallway to catch her breath. "Oh my God. I don't know what I would do if I lost him," she said.

After a minute, the nurse signaled that they could go into the room. Elle ran to her son and held him.

"Oh, my Gary Lee, my Gary Lee," she said, rocking him.

"Mom, stop," said Gary Lee. "I'm okay."

"What happened, honey?"

"I don't know. I was watching TV, and Gillian came in. We were just talking, and then I felt a huge pain in my chest, and everyone was running around the room." Gary Lee looked around and at his parents. "Where's Gillian?"

"Gillian?" asked Elle, bewildered.

"Yes, Gillian Mason," said Gary Lee. "She was just telling me she wasn't going to graduate, but I didn't find out why. Then suddenly, all kinds of hell broke loose."

Elle looked at Drew, shaking her head and wondering what they should tell Gary Lee.

"Son, you were in a car crash," said Drew. "Gillian is dead."

Gary Lee stared at him in shock. "No—you're wrong!" he tried to shout. "She was just here." He slapped the bed with his one good arm.

Elle reached over and put her arm around him. "I'm so sorry, honey," she said, trying to comfort him. "It was a terrible accident."

His anger turned to sorrow, and he sobbed hard with intermittent breathing and gasping for air. "It isn't true," he kept repeating as Elle rocked him. Drew came around the other side of the bed and put his hand on Gary Lee's shoulder.

CHAPTER 13

Gary Lee was now awake and had been moved to a general hospital room to continue recovering. Fragrant magnolia, beautiful white lilies, and budding violet orchids had started to fill the room. Colorful cards, navy blue and white balloons with checkered flags, and well wishes for Gary Lee began to overflow the windowsill and table. Even with his progress, the days seemed to drag along slowly for Elle. Family and friends came by to see Gary Lee, but the nursing staff only allowed three visitors at a time. Elle had no intention of leaving the room, so only two of his friends could come in at a time. The others waited their turn in the waiting room.

One late morning while Elle continued her vigil by the bedside, Gary Lee started making guttural sounds. She leaned over to him and asked, "Honey, what is it? What do you want?"

Gary Lee looked up at her and seemed to be unable to speak. "Ma, Ma," was all he was able to say finally, and a tear ran down his face.

He lost his focus, and his eyes began to wander around the hospital room. The nurse was standing at the door watching Elle trying to communicate with her son.

"Traumatic brain injury takes time to heal, Mrs. Dillanger," the nurse said. "The prison rehab isn't all that bad."

Elle got up from her chair and glared at the nurse. "What?" she said, suddenly overwhelmed with anger. "Why did you say 'prison rehab isn't all that bad'? Gary Lee isn't going to prison rehab. He is coming home with me as soon as he can get in a wheelchair."

"I'm sorry, I thought you knew," said the nurse, acting as if she let something slip out.

"Knew what?" demanded Elle.

"About the rehab discharge. Detective Lowry filed papers with the hospital to have Gary Lee released to the state prison rehab."

Elle stood up in a rage.

"Where is Lowry?" she shouted.

The nurse started to back out the door. "Detective Lowry is going through the paperwork at the nurses' station," she said.

Elle stormed out of Gary Lee's hospital room and walked quickly down to the nurses' station. Detective Lowry was drinking coffee and chatting with a man.

"Excuse me, please!" Elle nearly shouted. She glared at the detective. "Could you explain this nonsense that the nurse just told me? There's no way Gary Lee is going to prison rehab!"

Detective Lowry calmly cleared his throat and said, "The Lee County Sheriff is responsible for anyone in custody and held for trial. The county must keep two rotating guards with your son while he is in the hospital for one day or one hundred days. It cost taxpayers $10,000 to guard an accused criminal in the hospital for a month.

"It is standard procedure to transport persons awaiting trial to the state correctional medical center if they have medical needs. Your son is out of the Critical Care Unit, and the correctional medical center is much more economical."

Elle was almost speechless at the talk of custody or trial. "He's barely awake, and you haven't even charged him with anything!" she said in disbelief.

"Well, Mrs. Dillanger, that's what I came here to do," said Lowry.

"Oh no," she said, pointing her finger at the detective. "You're not doing anything until we have a lawyer here."

"Out of courtesy, ma'am, I will give you an hour or two to bring your attorney," Lowry said. "When I come back after lunch, I can assure you that I will Mirandize your son and arrest him."

Elle marched back to the hospital room, pulled out her phone, and dialed Drew. She looked at her son lying helplessly in his bed while she waited. His eyes were wide open, and he was looking back at her intently. Elle walked down the hall so Gary Lee wouldn't hear the conversation.

"Did you know they were going to charge Gary Lee?" she asked Drew on the phone. "We need a lawyer right away. The detective is here at the hospital now!"

"Yes," Drew answered. "I knew this would be coming, and I've already hired a lawyer, John Bernstein. Our business lawyer recommended him. He's an excellent defense attorney, and he has an office in Auburn."

Elle was surprised but glad that Drew was on top of this crazy and out-of-control situation.

"Can you have the attorney come to the hospital now?" she asked. "The detective is coming back in an hour, and I don't want him talking to Gary Lee without a lawyer present. They want to put our son in the state prison rehab!"

"What? I'll call Bernstein's office right now. I'm sure his firm can have someone over to the hospital right away."

Elle returned to her son's room and put her cell phone on the table. She looked around anxiously and sat down in the chair next to Gary Lee's bed. The floodgates of her soul burst open, and she began to cry uncontrollably. Gary Lee looked over at her. She wiped the tears from her face, then reached out and held his hand, trying to smile reassuringly.

"What's the matter, Mom?" he asked. He looked at her with concern and compassion in his eyes. At that moment, she knew that she had her kind-hearted boy back.

"Your father and I love you, Gary Lee, and we'll always be here for you," she said. The answer seemed to convince him not to worry, but Elle was determined to fight for her son.

Elle settled back in the chair and watched the clock in suspense. She felt like an entrenched soldier waiting for the troop reinforcements to arrive before the enemy's attack. It had been nearly an hour since she spoke with Drew, and the detective might return at any moment. Elle was desperately hoping Drew and the lawyer would arrive first.

There was some noise in the hallway and the sound of footsteps walking. Elle focused on the doorway and could hear muffled voices and the sound of keys jangling. Would the sheriff handcuff Gary Lee? Then two figures appeared in the hospital room doorway: Drew and a gray-haired man in a suit. Elle's anxiety was relieved, and she was ecstatic to see Drew, despite all the troubles they had gone through so far. She sprang from the oversized hospital chair and hugged him.

"Elle, this is John Bernstein, the attorney I told you about," Drew said.

"Thank you for coming, Mr. Bernstein," she said and shook his hand vigorously. "I can't believe this is happening! The detective said he was going to arrest Gary Lee and charge him with a crime. They want to put him in the prison rehab!"

Elle looked back at Gary Lee in the hospital bed, suddenly realizing that he was listening. Gary Lee's eyes were open, and he seemed to be taking in everything. She knew that she could no longer shelter him from the situation.

"Well, I'm not surprised," said Bernstein. "They move quickly on these things, but it's more of a formality than anything else," he said with a reassuring voice. "The discharge to the correctional medical facility is standard practice for infirm defendants who can't make bail. We'll supply the bail bond, and that will eliminate any worries about prison rehab."

Elle felt an immense relief from hearing his reassuring explanation. She looked over at Drew.

"Bail bond?" she whispered.

Drew leaned over to Elle and quietly explained, "I took out a $25,000 loan against the business to cover the attorney and bond expenses. The attorney's retainer is $15,000, and he thinks the bond will be around $10,000."

Elle was dizzy with how fast things were moving. She wondered if Evan, their business partner, knew about the loan against their business. It was only a modest architectural design firm. What would Evan say? Elle looked back at Drew in confusion. She felt relieved that Drew was taking care of things and worried that he might not be making the best choices. This was a familiar dichotomy in their marriage. Drew's actions had often forced her to second-guess her maternal judgment. Isn't that what led them to this hospital room? Now she was feeling angry and detached. Elle's head was spinning with unhealthy thoughts, and she knew she had to stay focused for her son's sake.

Before Elle could ponder the situation any further, Detective Lowry appeared in the doorway of the hospital room. Behind him were two sheriff's deputies in uniform. Lowry stepped forward into the room, looking only at Gary Lee. Gary Lee wriggled to lift himself up in his bed, and he looked straight back at the detective.

Elle moved to the side of the bed and held her son's hand. She was frantic. If she could only stop time for another day or a week— just to let her son smile again. How could she stop what was coming? She didn't want Gary Lee to take this awful accusation into his consciousness.

Lowry paused for a moment and then said plainly, "Gary Lee Dillanger, you are charged with Homicide by Vehicle under Alabama Code section 32-5A-192 for the death of Gillian Anne Mason."

Gary Lee closed his eyes in anguish; he groaned and turned his head to the side. Elle didn't want him to go through this, and it burned inside her that the police would have the audacity to accuse her son of a crime.

"You have the right to remain silent," Lowry began again. "Anything you say can and will be used against you in a court of law. You have the right to an attorney. If you cannot afford an attorney, one will be provided for you. Do you understand the rights I have just read to you?"

By the time Lowry finished, tears were rolling down Gary Lee's face. He made guttural noises and gasped for air between sobs.

Elle turned her full attention back to Gary Lee. She took his hand again to comfort him. "I love you, Gary Lee, no matter what happens," she said gently.

"Is it true, Ma?" Gary Lee asked his mother in a choked-up voice. "Did I kill Gillian?"

At first, Elle couldn't speak; she just shook her head. "It wasn't your fault," she said. "It's not your fault," she repeated, hoping her words would make it so.

"It's going to be all right, Son. We are here," he said.

Gary Lee took a breath and looked up at his mother. "How did it happen? I don't remember anything." Gary Lee turned toward his father.

"Gillian died in the accident, but it's a miracle that we still have you," Drew explained. "We don't know what happened either, but we have the best lawyer to get you out of these outrageous charges."

Drew lightly squeezed Gary Lee's shoulder to reassure him. Gary Lee closed his eyes and rested.

CHAPTER 14

Elle sat herself down in the chair in Gary Lee's hospital room once again, as she had been doing for each day that week. She felt exhausted from the long days there at the hospital in Auburn. Elle kept trying to put together in her mind what had happened. She rehearsed in her mind the different statements from the detective, the attorney, and Gary Lee, but it didn't make sense yet. She needed more information—she needed the police report.

What would the future hold for her son? The stress was taking its toll on her. Elle was glad not to be alone in her situation, with her soon-to-be-ex-husband, Drew, also visiting during the week. However, she was becoming resentful and angry at him. Yesterday, she snapped at Drew in front of Gary Lee and was worried that her son would see through their veil of civility. Why did Drew have to make her so angry all the time? At least he had the sense to get a decent defense attorney for Gary Lee, and she intended to thank him for that when she wasn't so out of sorts.

Elle's briefcase sat on the floor next to the table. She looked at it and thought about taking out her notebook computer to do some work, but the motivation was not with her today. Even when she had opened it up and read email or looked at new design catalogs online, it simply didn't hold her attention. Work just seemed insignificant right now.

Gary Lee was asleep beside her. He still spent much of the time sleeping, and the doctor said that was normal for this kind of recovery. When awake, he amused himself with games on his tablet or catching up with his friends online. Elle wished he would talk to her more, but even before the accident, she and her son never really had many conversations unless she was trying to tell him something or pry information out of him. If she had asked him, "How was school?" his response would have been "Fine."

One time at home Elle had asked him how his friend Tom was doing, and Gary Lee had responded, "Mom, Tom's an ass."

"But I thought you two were such good friends."

"That was fifth grade, Mom."

Elle was embarrassed that she knew so little about her son's life. She rose from her chair and picked up her phone off the table, impatient with the lack of news from their attorney. She looked at her phone for any new messages but nothing. It had been a week since their initial meeting, and surely he would have an update by now. She had asked for a copy of the police report that Attorney Bernstein had taken with him, and she didn't like being kept in the dark. He had teased her last week with some information, but she needed to know what really happened that day of the crash. Elle had called Bernstein's office yesterday and left a message. Perhaps Drew had heard something.

Elle had been fiddling with her cell phone for the past five minutes, and she finally decided to call Drew.

"Hello, Elle," he answered. He sounded businesslike.

"Have you heard anything from Bernstein?" she asked.

"Yes, they had the arraignment hearing two days ago. Bail was set at one hundred thousand, and I posted a bond. They should have removed the deputy sheriff who's been guarding Gary Lee's room by now."

Elle looked up at the doorway. She didn't recall seeing the man in uniform outside the room this morning when she came in.

"Why didn't you tell me yesterday?" she asked.

"I was out posting the bond yesterday. I was going to tell you when I came to the hospital today."

Elle was annoyed at Drew's typical lack of communication. "So where did you get the money for the bond?"

"I told you last week. I took out a loan against the business for the lawyer and the bail bond."

"Don't be annoyed at me. I'm here every day watching over Gary Lee. I expect to be included in what's going on. How about the police report?"

"Yes, I have a copy of it. I'll bring that with me when I come tonight."

"Tonight? I thought you were coming this afternoon," she said.

"Elle. We still have a business to run and bills to pay."

"Well, try not to be too late. I'll see you then."

Elle hung up the phone. She wondered how much information Drew kept from her—was there more? Everything felt upside down. What used to be black seemed white, and what was once white seemed black. Just like the checkered flags on the raceway, she thought, putting her cell phone back on the table.

The hospital routine was pretty uneventful that morning and through the early afternoon. By 4 p.m., a group of Gary Lee's high school friends showed up. They waited in the waiting room while they came in two at a time because of the three-visitor rule.

"Hi, Mrs. Dillanger," said Chad Gibbons when he and his girlfriend came in for their turn. "How are you holding up?" he asked.

At least one of Gary Lee's friends was polite. "I would just like for us to get out of this hospital soon," she replied.

Chad turned to Gary Lee, and they began conversing in almost a whisper.

Elle could never understand what any of the kids were talking about with Gary Lee during these visits. All she could hear were snippets of juvenile banter. "Kisha's breaking up with him," or "Kyle went to the prom with Ashley," or "that movie was so sick." Sometimes they seemed to be in denial of the reality of Gary Lee's tragedy. Maybe that was good.

As Chad continued his whispering to Gary Lee, Elle looked up at the clock. It was seven o'clock, and Drew had still not yet arrived. Elle lost her patience. She collected her purse and marched down the hall into the waiting room. At least six or more teenagers were chattering there, playing with their phones, and talking. They all stopped and looked up at her, startled.

She cleared her throat. "Thank you all for coming and for your concern for Gary Lee," Elle announced to the room of high school students. "He's feeling better, but he needs his rest. He's not going to have any more visitors tonight."

A collective moan echoed from the teenagers. Some had not yet had a chance to talk to Gary Lee. At that moment, Drew came in. Following her lead, he turned to the group and told them it was time to leave.

"Please don't linger around the hospital. It is getting late," said Drew. "It is over an hour's drive back to Blue Springs. Thank you for your concern for Gary Lee."

Drew walked around clearing up the food containers and the fast-food trash from the waiting room as the kids packed up their things.

"Please don't just leave your trash behind," he said. "We are sharing this space with other visitors and the hospital staff."

No one seemed to listen to him. Finally, Chad Gibbons and his girlfriend had returned from the hospital room, and he approached Elle.

"Gary Lee said that the police were talking to him," said Chad. "What was that all about? The police aren't cool, you know. They are always looking for a reason to arrest anyone who is going past the speed limit."

"Don't worry, Chad. Gary Lee always follows the rules," said a girl behind Chad, teasing him sarcastically. Chad glared back at the girl. She tossed her ponytail and picked up her backpack.

Elle suddenly realized she knew nothing about what happened that day or who was with Gary Lee on his trip to Auburn.

"Chad, were you with Gary Lee on his Auburn college trip when he crashed?" Elle sternly asked him. "I need to know!"

"No, Mrs. Dillanger—not when he crashed. Of course not!" he replied.

She turned to the teenagers in the waiting room. "Do any of you know anyone else who went to visit Auburn University with Gary

Lee when he had the accident?" she demanded. They just looked at each other and shrugged, shaking their heads.

At that moment, Evan Waitts and Kylie Shay walked into the waiting room.

"Look who I found wandering the hospital hall," said Evan.

Kylie threw her arms up in the air. "Come here, sweetie."

Kylie Shay was the ex-wife of Sonny Kilgore and lived in the twin mansion next door to her former father-in-law, Monroe Kilgore. Elle and Kylie had become good friends during the renovation project Elle had worked on for Kylie at her home. They both seemed to share a dislike for the racing business, although Kylie would never publicly admit it. Probably because it remained her primary source of income, via alimony and whatever other means she had.

Kylie always looked great, like someone out of a reality TV show. She had on a shimmering blue top with white jeans, and her makeup was perfect. Kylie walked with her back straight, a dazzling smile on her face, and confidence in her movement. Elle hugged her and then noticed the commotion within the room that Kylie's entrance had made. Some of the teenage racing fans recognized Kylie right away, and they approached her.

"Mrs. Kilgore, how is Mackie doing in the racing championship?" one boy asked.

"It's Ms. Shay, now. I'm no longer Mrs. Kilgore," Kylie explained with a smile. "Mackie's doing fine. I'll tell him you were asking next time he visits. He's always glad to hear from his fans."

Another blatant lie, Elle told herself. Elle remembered Kylie complaining about how disconnected Mackie was from the people who were cheering for him. It was remarkable that the Kilgore family had such an impact on the boys in Blue Springs. Elle watched with amazement how her friend took command of the starstruck kids. Elle was glad to have Kylie visiting, but Elle had now lost control over the room.

"Hello, Ms. Shay," said Chad Gibbons confidently. "It was great to see Mackie at the race in Leeds. Do you know if he'll compete in the annual Rodeo-Kart in Texas in July?"

"Why, Chad Gibbons! It's so nice to see you again," Kylie said in her supersweet southern style.

"Kylie," Elle interrupted. "I had just persuaded these kids to head back home. It's getting late for them."

Kylie nodded. "Okay. I've got this," she said to Elle. She linked Chad's arm with hers and started leading him toward the door. "So Chad, would you like to drive in the Rodeo-Kart?" she asked him. "I don't know if Mackie will be there. He and his father scheme those karting events and things."

Elle was now glad to have Kylie helping. Drew was useless again. He was back to talking business with Evan, their partner.

"It is a long ride home to Blue Springs," Elle reminded the teenagers. "Drive carefully, and thank you again for coming to see Gary Lee."

"Let's walk out to the parking lot, and I'll tell you more about Kilgore Racing," said Kylie to the teenage fans. They gathered around her eagerly. "Elle, I'll meet up with y'all in the cafeteria."

Kylie glided out of the waiting room escorted by Chad and the rest of the high school kids, following like children behind the pied piper. Elle could hear Chad still talking about how Sonny Kilgore was the best racecar driver in Alabama. Blah, blah… Elle was glad to see them go.

Elle glared at her husband and said, "These kids make a mess here almost every day. Apparently, they don't care, or they think they are entitled." Elle shook her head. She came over and gave Evan a quick hug. "You've been such a great friend through all of this, Evan."

Elle glanced over at Drew, wondering if Evan knew about the business loan for Gary Lee's bond. She resisted the temptation to confess but said, "I know the business was doing well up until now. I'm sorry that this is also impacting you. Certainly, you don't deserve to be dragged through this Alabama swamp."

"It is what it is," said Evan. "We'll get through it. Did you see my email about the new interior design project?"

"Sorry, I've not been online much today," said Elle.

"Why don't we all go down to the cafeteria and see if you can get something to eat, Elle," Drew said with an exhausted voice. "Elle just doesn't eat during stress," said Drew to Evan.

"I've known that since Risdee," said Evan. "Maybe they are serving dirty martinis. It's after five o'clock," said Evan. He grabbed Elle's hand and said to her, "Don't worry. Gary Lee is going to make it through this."

Elle and her two architect partners headed toward the cafeteria. Elle's high heels were skipping a beat, and her shoes were worn down to the nail. They echoed through the hospital hall as they walked all the way to the elevator.

The hospital cafeteria was surprisingly crowded when the three entered. The white overhead lights seemed dreary now, and it smelled like old cabbage and carrot raisin salad. Still, this was the hot dinner spot for nurses and hospital aides taking a break and getting ready for their night shift. Visitors were at the tables, too, but the lines for the prepared food were not that long.

"I have not been impressed by the food here," said Evan.

Elle smirked and said, "Everyone knows that hospitals need to keep people sick to stay in business."

"Your humor returns!" remarked Evan.

"I think I'll have an Italian ice from the vending machine," she said with a bit of a smile.

"Elle," said Drew. "Let's sit down and look at that police report you wanted." Drew led Elle over to a quiet, empty table and pulled out a large envelope. "I'll get you your Italian ice—what flavor did you want?"

Elle sat down and stared at the envelope on the table in front of her, now very serious.

"Oh, um, lemon or whatever they have," she replied.

Evan also sat down and held her hand. She knew that she wasn't going to like what was in that envelope, but she opened it, pulled out the stapled papers, and started reading. Drew came over with the ice, but Elle was no longer interested in eating anything. She read diligently, turning the pages and folding them under as she went.

Suddenly Elle yelled out, "Reckless? My son is not reckless! Whoever wrote this is an idiot. They obviously know nothing about investigating. There's nothing in here except ridiculous, unfounded conclusions."

Elle ignored Evan and Drew. She could see that they were surprised by her anger. Elle continued to berate the investigation as she flipped through the pages.

"People said he was driving around ninety-five miles per hour! I can't believe that Gary Lee would do that. What about these other cars that were also driving fast? One person saw a white Lexus going the same speed. Another said the cars had a black and white checkered sticker on the back—Gary Lee didn't have any such sticker!"

"That's why we have the lawyer, honey," said Drew, trying to calm Elle down. "He can dispute anything in the report with what his investigators find out."

"Yes, at least Bernstein had the sense to ask for the kids' cell phones," she said.

Elle read more and gasped. The gruesome description of the accident was more than she could bear. Maybe the lawyer could dispute the facts, but no one could deny the horrific loss and tragedy detailed in that report.

Elle looked up and noticed Chad Gibbons and his girlfriend sitting with Kylie Shay at a corner table in the cafeteria. Elle stood up and put the report down.

"It's about time I asked a few questions," said Elle, staring over at Chad. She walked across the cafeteria to the table where the three were sitting.

"Chad," Elle interrupted them, "you had said that you saw Mackie at the race at Leeds. Gary Lee mentioned the race at Leeds, also. Were you both there together, and when was that?"

Chad was surprised, and he looked over at his girlfriend. "Mrs. Dillanger," said Chad, "yes, we were all there. That was the day Gary Lee had the accident."

"He never did go to visit Auburn University, did he? That was just his cover story!"

"No. They were going to visit Auburn on Sunday," Chad's girlfriend said. "Gillian had never seen a race before."

Elle started to nod and was fuming. Drew and Evan had just arrived at Chad's table. She turned and looked crossly at Drew.

"This was your doing!" she said, raising her voice and pointing her finger at him. "You put all this love of racing into Gary Lee's head. That's why he lied to us about Auburn. I bet you were in on this Leeds secret."

"I didn't know," said Drew, shaking his head, "but what's the big deal with him going to a race?"

"Oh, you are so ignorant! Boys like to impress their girlfriends, and what do you think happens after the races? They zoom down the highway trying to prove that they are just as badass as the pros!"

Elle was shouting, and everyone in the cafeteria was looking at them. She grabbed the report out of Drew's hand and held it up.

"Two cars driving at ninety-five miles per hour! What do you think they were doing? It's called *racing*—that's what you've always been pushing him toward. If you had not tried to live out your speed fantasy through Gary Lee, this never would have happened!" She picked up her Italian ice, threw it in the wastebasket, and then stormed out of the cafeteria.

"Thanks for nothing, Drew," she shouted back. "I will never forgive you!"

CHAPTER 15

Chad Gibbons was driving to the county car show on a sunny Saturday morning, the first weekend of June. He was obligated by his karting contract to appear at the car show, but he didn't mind. May had been a hard month for Chad and his friends. They graduated from high school at the end of May, which should have been a celebration, but with Gary Lee absent and Gillian gone, it was only bittersweet. Both Chad and his girlfriend Annie had agreed not to go to the Senior Prom, another occasion too depressing without their friends. All that was now behind him, and his future was ahead. The plans that he and his father had made to start his racing career loomed in his mind. Now it was summer, and it was karting season!

"Summertime in Blue Springs, Alabama is nothing less than spectacular," said Chad to the rearview mirror in his Chevy truck while he rolled down the winding country highway.

He was dreaming of lazy summer days filled with scorching summer heat, boating on the lake, and hanging out with friends. No more worries about homework or school. He had graduated, and that was over now. He did have to worry about karting, though. How he performed on the track this summer would determine his chances of earning the racing scholarship he had coveted for the past three years. It seemed that Gary Lee had always been at Chad's karting events, and he felt the pain of not having his best friend with him now. The car show was the kickoff event of the summer, and Gary Lee would have been there. Chad pulled off the highway exit and stopped on the side of the road. He had given his smartphone to Gary Lee's lawyer, and he was now using an old flip phone. Chad sent a text to Gary Lee, who also had a new mobile number.

Hey, this is Chad. I'm headed to the county car show.

He wasn't sure if or when Gary Lee would get the message, but a response came a minute later. *Awesome! Dent one for me.*

This was a private joke between the two from a few years ago when Gary Lee had dented the trunk of a classic car by accident. The two of them had been fooling around, and Chad had been chasing Gary Lee for throwing a hot dog at him. Gary Lee tripped on a tent stake and lunged into the side of a '50s Chevy Bel Air, denting the fender with his head.

I'll try, but my head isn't as hard as yours, Chad replied back.

Chad sat there for a moment on the side of the county fair road exit. He could hear the cicadas singing in unison out of his window while waiting for a car to pass. Driving on, he crossed over a creek and saw a couple of boys cooling their feet in the water. He recalled doing the same with Gary Lee when they were much younger, chasing crawdads for fishing bait without a care in their minds.

Chad had grown up in Blue Springs, a small, well-to-do town in southern Alabama where the ice cream truck never missed his stop in the summer. He remembered how the line for sweet, cool treats was as long as the summer's day. He and his friends would spray the garden hose on each other in the front yard, or someone would have set up a slip-and-slide to beat the heat. He would be eating watermelon under the old tree at his grandpa's house in July like he did year after year. There would be afternoons of lying on the grass and looking up at the clouds and evenings chasing lightning bugs. Kart racing on the weekends would be the only real work this summer, come rain or shine. Life was good in Blue Springs in the summertime.

The classic car show in Barbour County was a favorite for families after school was out. It was sponsored by Mr. Butkis and his Luxurious Lifestyle Foundation, but it was very different from his Auto Show Gala held in the spring. This was like a mini-fair with amusement rides and fair food stands. The rides stayed on for two weekends, and it was great fun before the hot, sultry, long dog days of the Alabama summer kicked in. The Kilgore Karting Team hosted a small karting track for younger kids, and the team members were required to work the track for the weekend. Chad recalled when Gary Lee was still on the karting team and had won the Junior championship three years ago. That year, all they had to do was show up at the car show in their racing suits and pose for pics—they were heroes!

Chad missed his friend and hoped that they would be able to experience another racing event together soon. But it wasn't the same since the accident. Chad thought of Gillian Mason for a moment, how Gary Lee could never stop talking about her. A wave of worry suddenly hit him—would he run into any of her family members at the car show? He heard that Mrs. Mason was recently hospitalized for anxiety. He doubted that the Mason family would be going to the car show this year. At least he hoped not.

Chad shook his head. Life was just so unfair. He turned off the country radio station and continued driving into the fairgrounds to find a parking spot. Chad paid his five-dollar entry fee and got his hand stamped with the date. He was good for the day. The smell of peach pies, cotton candy, and corn dogs, along with the giant Ferris wheel, welcomed him while he walked toward the car displays.

Chad strolled through the lines of classic autos, each one with a sign in front naming the car and the owner. Chad loved the brilliant chrome, the rich, glossy lacquer colors, the sexy, curved fenders, and the cushy interiors. He took pics with his phone of the ones he liked. Some cars had the hood open, showing off a pristine engine or pictures of their restoration project on a plaque. Some proud owners sat beside the cars in lawn chairs under small tent awnings or umbrellas. Chad waved to a few and made some friendly comments as he paused to look at each one.

One Plymouth Barracuda had such a sweet cherry-red lacquer that Chad had to take a selfie and would post it on his newsfeed. The hood was open to reveal an impressive supercharger and valve covers painted to match the body.

Chad laughed to himself when he remembered how he and Gary Lee would spend hours studying American and European classic cars online, memorizing the names, and trying to pronounce the foreign classics. One time, they even made flash cards with complete information on the year, make, and models of the cars.

After the car display, Chad wandered through the amusement ride area, heading for the Kilgores' racing exhibit. He stopped for a corn dog and some cheese fries at one of the food booths to satisfy his lunchtime hunger. Fair food! After his first bite, any anxiety about the scholarship melted away, and he was back to the happy days of summer.

The Kilgore exhibit had a large awning stretched out with a black and white checkered trim. A small crowd was escaping the sun under the shade, and behind the booth, Chad could see the small go-karts running on the track. He walked up to find Tom Grasiano standing there in his karting race suit; he had just finished snapping selfies with some kids. The karters had given him the nickname "Kruz" because he looked like a young Tom Cruise. Chad didn't particularly like Tom, but he was determined to be professional and a solid karting team member.

"Hey, Chad. How y'all doing?" said Tom. "Casual today?" Chad was dressed in jeans since he had to work the karting track.

"I'm good," he replied politely. "Glad to be done with school. And you?"

Tom seemed unusually proud of himself in his race suit. "Well..." He paused and pulled a folded letter out of his pocket. "I've been given a scholarship from the All-Pro American Racing League!" He grinned widely and showed the letter to Chad.

"Wow! Congrats!" replied Chad, trying to sound excited.

This was the scholarship that Chad had been working for, and all the karting boys were chasing after it. They gave out several of these scholarships each year. It was a ticket for a kart racer to move to the next level—to become an auto racer. Chad's heart sank when he looked at the letter that Tom showed him. It was dated last week, and Chad had not received one. He now realized that his hopes for the racing scholarship were not happening.

124

Chad remembered how Gary Lee always said Tom was an ass, but Chad presumed Gary Lee was just jealous of Tom's success. Maybe Gary Lee was right. Regardless, Tom Grasiano was on his way to becoming a genuine, professional racer. He had received a coveted racing team scholarship. Many of the great racers started with an opportunity like this. Tom would soon be living the life that all the other karting kids dreamed about: training in real racecars, running on actual auto racing tracks, and being on TV. Chad handed the official letter back to Tom and tried not to show his disappointment.

"You know what they say," said Tom with a pat on Chad's shoulder. "If you want the job, you've got to dress for the job." Now Tom was just being obnoxious.

Chad stepped under the exhibit awning and was surprised to see Big Mo and Sonny Kilgore both actually there. The racing celebrities were standing next to a display case with a jewel-studded helmet and trophies. Some of the parents were listening to their stories and asking questions. One of the karting boys was also standing with them, trying to look his best, listening and nodding. Behind them, one of Big Mo's famous racing firesuits was hanging on display. Chad moved closer and waited for a lull in the conversation.

"Hi, Mr. Kilgore," said Chad to Sonny after two parents walked away and two more stepped up.

"Hey, Chad," said Sonny Kilgore. He seemed a little irritated to be interrupted.

"I'm here to work the track booth," explained Chad.

"Okay, good," said Sonny. "Are you going to be ready for the race next weekend? You still need to get at least two more practices in before then." Sonny was clearly showing off his coaching in front of the parents waiting to talk to him.

"Yes, sir. I'll be there tomorrow and Tuesday," Chad replied.

Sonny quickly lost interest in Chad and returned to the questions from the parents. Chad noticed how people were browsing around all the Kilgore racing and karting merchandise for sale on the shelf. Hunter, another younger karting team kid, was sitting at a table processing credit card purchases and bagging up their goods. Brilliant business, Chad thought.

Chad turned and looked toward the dirt track behind the racing exhibit. There was a long line of the kids waiting for a ride on the go-karts. Fifteen or more young boys and girls with their parents were willing to stand in the heat for a five-lap run on the Kilgores' dirt go-kart track.

Working the go-kart booth wasn't an exciting job, but Chad did this faithfully every year. When he first started helping with the go-kart track, it was kind of exciting. The go-karts were really for grade school kids. They didn't go very fast—maybe twelve miles per hour, and there was a forty-eight-inch height requirement. There was nothing to the job. You put the kids in the karts, tell them the rules, wave the green flag, and then take them out of the carts after five laps. Chad remembered the first time he was invited to work the track at the fair; he felt like a racing official. His favorite part was waving the flags—the green flag to start, the white flag on the last lap, and the checkered flag when finished.

Chad saw Matt, another karting team kid, sitting in a lawn chair under an umbrella by the side of the track while the little karts went around. Chad waved while walking toward him.

"Hey, Chad! I'm so glad to see you, man," said Matt getting up. "I'm dying out here. I've been doing this since nine this morning."

"No problem. I've got the afternoon shift. What lap are they on?" asked Chad, referring to the go-karters.

"Lap two." He took the whistle off his neck and handed it and his counting clicker to Chad. "You know what to do, right?"

Chad nodded. "After six years of doing this, I should open my own kart track!"

"That would be sweet. See you at practice." Matt took off.

Of course, Chad didn't want to open a kids' go-kart track; that would be some form of hell for him. He wanted to make sure Matt and everyone else knew that Chad could always be counted on to take one for the team. He spent the afternoon putting the kids in the go-karts, taking them out, and waiving the different flags. It was boring, really, but Chad smiled and laughed with the kids who were having their summer fun.

After a couple of hours, Hunter came over to Chad.

"Big Mo says you need a break," he told Chad and handed him a bottle of water.

Boy, was that for sure! Chad was glad for the relief. Hunter was in the Junior karting class and had only been on the team for a year. Chad had to explain to Hunter what he needed to do. What could go wrong during a fifteen-minute break? Chad walked back under the Kilgore black and white checkered awning, chugging his bottle of water. He listened to Sonny and Big Mo explain their shifter karts to a group of parents and kids.

"You see, we guarantee the engine for a whole season," explained Sonny. "You'll never get stuck at the back of the pack because of a blown-out engine with our karts."

Brilliant, thought Chad to himself, but who could afford it? They sold their engine for twice the price of a regular one. But that was a familiar problem kids had on the track—replacing the engine and getting sent to last place by the race officials. Everyone was listening intently when Tom walked up beside Chad.

"I bet you wish you had one of those Kilgore engines when we were at Ashville a couple of years back," said Tom, reminding Chad of how he blew out his engine one race. "So what are your plans after high school?"

Tom knew that Chad was one of the Wheelboys who was vying for that scholarship. Was he just rubbing it in? Chad had not formulated a good Plan B.

"Well, I don't need my parents' signature anymore to race karts," Chad replied. "I can now race in any karting event I want."

"Yeah, you can race in the Senior class as long as you want," said Tom. "Heck, my old man still races in the Masters class."

Chad started to feel anxious again, thinking about their fathers. Chad didn't want karting to be just a hobby. He wanted to be an auto racer and to win big cash prizes. He wanted to make it big, like Mackie Kilgore.

"I'm going to race in Rodeo-Kart," Chad blurted out. It was the only comeback Chad could think up. Rodeo-Kart was a major national karting competition open to all ages. Karters from the Cadets all the way up to pro racers competed in Rodeo-Kart. This year it was in Texas.

"Sweet! I'll be there, too. So what's up for you next year? Didn't you say you might join the army?"

Chad was grasping for ideas. He needed to formulate a backup plan to break into auto racing if he didn't get the scholarship. Sonny Kilgore told him it was a sure thing—what happened with that? He could probably work in his father's garage while trying to get a pit job.

"There's an opening on the Kilgore pit crew for next year. I'll probably do that until I can get a ride." Chad was now lying outright and hated doing that. Was he lying to himself, too? Tom was now looking away, and he saw his other Wheelboy friends.

"Hey, I gotta run," he said, and he slapped Chad's shoulder. Tom took off in a jog, and Chad went back to the track to finish his shift.

Another hour or two passed while working the kids' go-kart track, and Chad couldn't wait for it to be over. He heard the bellowing voice of Mr. Butkis under the Kilgore awning and knew that it would be quitting time soon. An announcement echoed over the speakers across the fairgrounds. *"Ladies and gentlemen, boys and girls, please join us in the main tent for the classic car award ceremony!"*

"That's it. The go-karts are now closed," Chad told the last few kids on the line. "You can come back tomorrow."

Chad finished the laps of the current kids driving around and then closed down the ride. He returned to the Kilgore Racing exhibit to find that the Kilgores had already left, and Mr. Butkis was the new center of attention. Chad approached the jolly event sponsor and held out his hand.

"Hi, Mr. Butkis. Great show this year," said Chad.

"Yes!" said Butkis. He put his arm around Chad and squeezed him. "Come on, Chad. We're headed over to the award ceremony. You're going to love my latest cars there!"

Two attractive women glided up to the small group under the awning and linked their arms with Butkis, one on either side.

"Folks, these fine young ladies are here to escort us over to the main tent to award the car show prizes," announced Butkis. "Anyone interested can come along."

The announcement repeated over the fairgrounds loudspeakers, and the whole entourage from the Kilgore exhibit followed Mr. Butkis walking toward the main tent. It was almost like a small parade, led by the mayor of "car town" himself. People from all over the fairgrounds were streaming into the main tent. Chad watched Mr. Butkis stride in with a flair of showmanship and the two pretty blonde girls on either side. Tom Grasiano was walking with them. Butkis always soaked up his "fat cat" status, greeting people and shaking hands. Of course, Tom had to join in; he smiled and ogled all the girls who followed them into the tent.

Sonny and Mo Kilgore were already sitting up front, and they stood up to greet Butkis and his company of friends. The master of ceremonies was standing on a podium, speaking into a microphone.

"Have you been enjoying these fabulous vehicles of yesteryear?" the MC prompted the cheering crowd. "Did you see that blue and white Studebaker? Just beautiful!"

When the MC saw Butkis, he stopped and said, "So without further delay, ladies and gentlemen, let me introduce you to the founder and president of the Luxurious Lifestyle, Mr. George Butkis!"

A round of applause came from the audience. Chad watched Butkis step up onto the podium and bathe in the applause with his usual wide grin.

"I want to thank all of our show participants for bringing their beautiful new and classic motorcars to the Luxurious Lifestyle Classic Car Jubilee," said Butkis. "I want to thank all of our sponsors and the Wheelboys who are joining us from Sonny Kilgore's karting team. I now want to bring up some of our rising racing stars from beautiful Alabama."

He pointed at Tom and two other boys in their racing suits sitting in the front row with the Kilgores. Tom Grasiano stepped up to be recognized. The two other boys joined them on the side of the podium, and Butkis shook hands with the young men in their race suits.

"Here are the stars of the future," Butkis continued. "Tom Grasiano, Jeffrey Sears, and Tristan Baker. All winners of this year's scholarship program for the All-Pro American Racing League. Our very own Wheelboys—racing stars of the future from Blue Springs, Talladega, and Leeds, Alabama."

Another slow round of applause echoed, and the boys on the podium waved to the crowd.

Butkis continued, "Tom Grasiano is a young man who exemplifies courage, talent, and tenacity. A word from you, Tom?" He signaled to Tom to join him at the microphone.

"Thanks, Mr. Butkis. It's a dream come true," Tom spoke into the microphone, trying to sound humble. "I'd also like to thank the Kilgore Karting program for teaching me the skills to become a winner. I could not have made it here without them!" He gestured toward Sonny and Big Mo Kilgore.

Sonny Kilgore stood up and turned around, waving at the audience. He never missed an opportunity to get some publicity for himself or his racing program.

Chad watched it all with disappointment. He felt out of place watching from the audience, after so often standing on the podium. So this is how it feels on the other side. He remembered his karting training: "When you lose, just look forward to the next win." What had gone wrong? Perhaps he hadn't won enough karting events to qualify for the scholarship? He remembered his father telling him that he could someday be an auto racer, and he would help him realize that dream. Chad just looked down at the ground and listened while Mr. Butkis continued his speech.

"This year's Luxurious Lifestyle Classic Car Jubilee is proud to donate portions of the proceeds to the Children's Wing and the Burn

Unit of the County Hospital," Mr. Butkis announced. He wrapped up his introduction and concluded with, "Thank you to our volunteers for bringing the LL cars to the show. Thank you to all of the contestants who brought their pet projects, their prized possessions to the fairgrounds for us to enjoy this weekend. The cars are fabulous.

"Before we announce the winners, let me first introduce to you the Luxurious Lifestyle cars we have here in the tent." He stretched out his hand to the right. "First, we have this custom Jaguar hybrid, one of only 250 made this year." The crowd clapped, and he continued, "Next, we have a 1994 McLaren F1, one of the finest driving machines ever built for public roads." Heads turned, and the mild applause subsided with some murmuring from the crowd. "Over on this side is an example of the classic chauffeur designs. The Maybach Landaulet, valued at over $1 million."

A few moans rose from the audience, and Chad was amazed at how people never grew tired of the display of wealth.

Butkis continued, "Finally, here is the beautiful white and silver Pagani Zonda Roadster, one of the most exclusive supercars ever built. It bears a price tag of $1.4 million."

His speech culminated with more applause from the audience. Even Chad was impressed with the roadster, and he stretched his neck to get a better view.

"Back to you, John," Butkis said to the MC. He and the karting boys stepped off the podium.

"Thank you, Mr. Butkis and our racing scholarship recipients," said the MC into the microphone.

The car show was a great place for showcasing George Butkis' charities and his Luxurious Lifestyle brand. Chad was always impressed with Mr. Butkis' and the Kilgores' business style. Money seemed to flow from Butkis, and people wanted to be around him, hoping that some wealth could splash onto them. As for the Kilgores, Big Mo's charisma and graciousness would draw people in, and Sonny Kilgore was as tough as nails in closing deals. Their whole family seemed to roll in racing success, and all of the would-be racers would do anything to roll with them.

"Now, let's talk about those beautiful automobiles that are contending in our show today," said the MC. "We have three honorable mentions and then the prize winners of this year's show."

The award ceremony continued with various people coming up to receive their awards hailed by mild applause. Chad wondered if the auto owners were ever disappointed in receiving an honorable mention. It was not really winning—it wasn't even third place. That's how he was feeling now—just an honorable mention for Chad Gibbons, followed by a golf clap.

Being part of the Kilgore Karting program and with help from his father, Chad always thought he would move up into auto racing after karting. Now nothing was certain. He was just standing there, not in his racing suit but his jeans—ordinary.

Chad recalled how angry his father would become when he didn't do well in a karting event. Driving home together, Chad's father would berate him the whole way. Chad would never say a word. He could not speak, and his voice would freeze up. His father would repeat all of his mistakes of the races over and over again.

"What a loser," Chad said of himself under his breath.

He felt detached and dizzy, imagining how his father would call him a loser when he got home and found out that Chad didn't get the scholarship. Chad continued to beat himself up, and he looked again at Tom Grasiano, so elated. Chad would never measure up to his father's expectations, and he wondered if he should even talk about a future in racing.

Chad didn't stay for the end of the awards to see who won first prize. He was tired and somewhat fed up with thinking about karting and racing. Having stewed in his thoughts all afternoon, he just wanted to blast out of the place. At the parking lot, he texted his girlfriend, Annie, to see where she was. He wanted to meet up with her before going home, but there was no answer. He jumped in his truck and sped off down the road with the windows down.

Driving down the road, he came to a straightaway. Chad put his foot to the floor to feel the rush of speed. The motor roared, and he was pinned to the back of his seat. It felt great. Suddenly, blue lights appeared in his rearview mirror, and the sound of a siren caught up to him. Chad pulled over and silently accepted the ticket from the state trooper. Chad looked at the ticket—ninety-eight miles per hour, $250. He threw the ticket in his glove compartment. It was worth it. He turned up the radio to full blast and headed down the road at a legal speed. He loved the adrenaline rush and would not apologize for loving speed. After all, speed was now a part of his DNA. A classic country song was on the radio, and Chad sang along as loud as he could to forget this bitter moment of low self-esteem.

CHAPTER 16

It was dinnertime when Chad arrived home from the county car show. He could smell the barbecued brisket, baked beans, steamed sweet corn, and buttermilk biscuits from the front porch. He was so glad to be home, and he took a deep breath before he walked into the door of the Southern Colonial two-story home where he'd lived since childhood.

"Hello, Shug," his stepmother, Carole Gibbons, greeted when he came in.

Chad nodded his head at her beautiful wide smile. Carole was captivating and sweet, and she tried so hard to please her new family. She'd just married his father about a year earlier. His mother had died of cancer a few years back, and Chad truly appreciated all of Carole's efforts.

"That barbecue smells so good. I could smell all the way from Second Street," said Chad. He went to the refrigerator to get a Dr Pepper. His dog, Indy, greeted him with a wagging tail, and his younger brother, Grant, ran into the kitchen.

"The cops were here today," Grant blurted out. "They were asking a lot of questions about you and Gary Lee."

Chad looked over at his stepmom. She nodded.

"You should go talk to your dad about that," she said and then turned to Grant. "Swanee, go wash your hands for dinner and stop gossiping about things you know nothing about." Turning back to Chad, "Shug, it wasn't the cops. He was a detective, and he was just asking questions about Gary Lee. That is all. Nothing to fret about."

Chad put his hands in his jeans and suddenly felt a sense of relief. For a moment, he worried that the cops might have told his dad about his speeding ticket today. News traveled fast around here, and Chad wanted to forget about the speeding ticket for the moment. He hadn't thought of a good excuse yet. How would he explain that ticket for ninety-eight miles per hour? Chad could offer to go to driving school after paying the citation. Surely his dad would understand if his stepmother supported him. A little bit of "Shug" just might help, relying on Carole's presence. Buttermilk biscuits with barbecue brisket were the perfect dining atmosphere for the speeding confessional. Chad smiled. He decided he would tell everyone at dinner.

"Where's Dad?" Chad asked.

"Rusty is in the garage working on the karts," Carole said.

"Well, it's about time you're back," said Chad's dad when he walked through the back door into the kitchen. "We were about ready to start dinner without you. How was that car show?"

Chad's father was a native Alabamian and the owner of Rusty's Wrench and Tires, a local automotive repair shop where all his friends and family went for car repairs and new tires. He wasn't a very tall man; he had wispy reddish hair and blue-gray eyes, with a stern look as one who had seen the long, hard road of life. Chad's dad was undoubtedly one of the hardest working men Chad knew, and he respected his father. In fact, his father was the hero in his life.

"Pretty good. I think it was bigger this year," answered Chad about the car show.

"Did ol' Butkis have his million-dollar cars there?"

"Yeah. I took some pics," said Chad.

Carole Gibbons called everyone to the dinner table, and they all rushed in and took their places. The meal began with their father saying grace.

"Bless us, O Lord, for these gifts, which we are about to receive. Help us to be ever mindful of all our blessings and the needs of others. Amen."

Chad's father served himself some brisket and passed the platter to Grant. After a flurry of plates and bowls passing, the food was served, and everyone waited for Carole to begin.

Grant groaned when he first tasted his southern feast. Chad smirked and nodded in agreement. The boys knew how good they had it with Carole's home cooking and always made sure to let her know that they appreciated her hard work.

"Carole, your barbecue is best in town," said Chad, and he served himself seconds. "If we put up a sign on the street, there would be a line a mile long to get some." Chad was a little too sweet now, and he knew it.

The brisket disappeared in no time. After his dad's last bite, Chad figured this would be as good a time as any.

"Well, the darndest thing happened to me today after working at the car show," Chad began. "A trooper pulled me over by the churchyard and pulled out his citation pad. He wrote me up for going ninety-eight miles per hour in a forty-five zone," Chad said with a quick grin.

"Holy crap!" exclaimed Grant.

Chad's father looked over at his wife and then said, "Well, Son, you are eighteen years old now, and you can face the consequences of your actions. If you keep that up, you'll lose your license. Pay the fine and learn from your mistakes in life." His father stood up. "Grant, help Carole with the dishes. Now on to more pressing business. Chad, let's talk out in the garage. Okay, Son?"

"Sure, Dad," said Chad. "I'll be there shortly."

That was a surprise. Chad thought for sure he would have some form of punishment levied on him. He walked his plates over to the kitchen sink, and Grant started clearing the table. Chad went upstairs to his room. His old and faithful golden retriever, Indy, followed him, wagging his tail. Chad was tired from the day, but he wanted to check his newsfeed on his computer. Chad had given his smartphone to Gary Lee's lawyer, so he needed a computer to get online now. Chad lived off his phone, so letting it go was a huge inconvenience. His stepmom had given him her old flip phone for calling and texting, and he was glad it had a decent camera, too.

Chad also wanted to call his girlfriend before he talked to his dad. He knew that those talks could take some time. Annie didn't pick up when he called, and so he sent her a text. Chad had fallen hard for Annie, and he wanted to see her before she left on her family vacation for several weeks. Life was changing fast since high school graduation, and he felt like he couldn't hold on to time. Why wasn't she answering? Annie had many friends, and Chad usually knew what was going on in her life because he was connected to their friends online. He was in the A-crowd, and being popular was a necessity to Chad. He checked his newsfeed and found out that his friends and Annie were at the Pearson Mall nearby. The kids liked the mall in the summertime. It was air-conditioned, and they usually caught a movie on the weekend. Chad was missing his girl. He posted a photo of himself at the fair with the Barracuda—*Best 'Cuda ever*—and he updated his status: *Great Day for Cruising*.

"Chad," his father called him from downstairs. "Meet me in the garage, Son."

Chad lumbered down the stairs and went out the back door to the detached garage, where his father could be found on many weeknights working on their karts. His dad was putting a plastic body part back on the front of the kart.

"How did it go at the karting booth today? The Kilgores were there, right?" his father asked.

"It went okay. It's just kids in go-karts, Dad. Yeah, the Kilgores were there, too."

"Why didn't you wear your karting suit? It's important to make a good impression. Did you hear anything about when they would announce the scholarships?"

"I was just working the go-kart track today, Dad. It gets sweltering in the karting suit. Anyhow, they announced the scholarships today. Tommy Grasiano and some other guys were picked." Chad hung his head.

"Damn it!" His dad turned away and tossed his wrench onto the workbench. "It's not your fault, I know," he said. "I was hoping we could do a lot with that scholarship. No matter, we'll figure out how to get you into racing one way or another."

"I'm sorry, Dad," said Chad. "I don't know why they didn't include me. I've been as good as Tom all season. Sometimes it just doesn't seem fair."

His dad held his hand up. "Stop. I've told you before these things aren't based on how well you drive or how often you win. At this level, you're starting to get into the racing business. Other factors become important. The Kilgores' White Party is coming up, and I want you to look your best. You need to think about getting a white linen suit and maybe a date this year."

"Okay, Dad. I was going to ask Annie, but she'll be away on her family vacation. Also, the Kilgores are going to have me working, and I'll have to wear a uniform with khaki shorts."

"Fine, fine. Practice is tomorrow, and I wanted you to help me bleed the brakes. You said they were feeling loose. Bring me that jar from the bottom cabinet."

Chad came over to his father with the jar, which had a plastic tube tucked inside. He set it under the kart, which was sitting on top of the waist-high dolly.

"Carole said that a detective came by today, but she said I should talk to you about it," said Chad.

"Yes, a Detective Lowry was over at the house today, and he wanted to talk to you. He also wanted your cell phone records. In fact, he wanted your cell phone. I gave him the phone bill and said you would provide your cell phone, of course."

"I gave my phone already to Gary Lee's lawyer. That's why I'm using Carole's old one."

"Okay, when he talks to you, let him know that. He left his card, so call him and arrange a time. The detective is investigating the day that you and your friends were all at the races in Leeds. Is there anything that you should be telling me about that day, Son?"

"No, it was just a fun day." Chad handed his father a wrench from the workbench. "We were all there to see Mackie Kilgore race in an open-wheel road course. He was awesome. Why does the detective need my phone? Isn't there a right to privacy in Alabama, or can the cops just take your phone when they want it?"

"They are charging Gary Lee with vehicular homicide for the death of Gillian Mason. You know that already, right, Son?"

"Dad, it's awful, but accidents happen. It was an accident. Gary Lee would never kill Gillian with his car. Everyone knows that he loved her."

"Vehicular homicide, also called vehicular manslaughter, doesn't mean he intended to kill her, Chad. It simply means it was a crime."

"That doesn't make sense. People have accidents all the time, and they don't go to jail. I got a speeding ticket, and I have to pay a fine." Chad struggled with the logic.

"Son, if you were to have damaged any property while you were going ninety-eight miles per hour or hurt or even killed someone, you would have committed a crime. If your illegal action contributes to loss of life, they call that manslaughter. Get it?"

It still didn't seem fair. Chad picked up a sprocket gear on an axle and started spinning it in the air.

"Help me with these brakes," his dad said.

"Dad, I'm sorry, but I really can't work on this right now. I need to get over to the mall for the movie with my friends. It starts in half an hour."

"Okay, fine. I don't mind doing it myself," said Chad's father. "Do you have enough money?"

Chad nodded.

"You are going to have to start working since the racing scholarship fell through. You're not a school kid anymore. We can talk about that more tomorrow, after karting practice." He gave his son a reassuring smile and patted him on the back. They left the garage and walked back to the front porch. "It's all going to work out." His dad offered him a twenty-dollar bill. "You might need this for the movies."

Chad smiled. "Thanks, Dad. You know you're the best."

Chad got into his truck and turned on the radio. His favorite country singer started crooning, and Chad turned up the radio loud when he got to the stop sign at the end of the street. He didn't want to think about the events of the day.

CHAPTER 17

The Babylon Karting Track in Blue Springs was an old facility just west of town. Originally built in the '70s, the track had fallen idle until about fifteen years ago when the Kilgores adopted it and began to develop their kart racing program. Some of the great American racecar drivers had practiced on this turf, and Chad Gibbons and his best friend Gary Lee Dillanger were proud to call it their home track. Maybe it wasn't large enough to hold a national competition, but Babylon had a decent-sized paddock for the kart work, an ample clubhouse, and plenty of seating in the stands for local events.

Chad and his dad pulled into the parking lot with the kart and dolly in the back of the truck. They could hear the buzzing sound of a kart running the course, and other kids and their parents were also arriving. Chad suddenly felt the absence of his friend. Gary Lee had not been on the Kilgores' team since he aged out of the Junior division two years ago, but he always would come to practice and karting events with Chad.

Practice on a Sunday began with a meeting in the clubhouse, and today it was at 1:00 p.m. Chad and his dad walked in, and he noticed two boys laughing. He missed his conversations and the belly laughing he used to have with Gary Lee.

The clubhouse had rows of chairs set up, and its walls were adorned with colored ribbons and framed photos of various victories. Tom Grasiano and the other guys who received the All-Pro racing scholarship were sitting in the back of the room talking. The younger kids were sitting together in their usual spots, and Chad and his dad sat a few rows from the whiteboard near the front. Some of the parents stood along the side wall. The little side office had a massive sign on the door that read *Monroe Kilgore, Champion of Speed* in bold, gold letters.

Just then, Chad saw Sonny Kilgore walk out of the side office and gaze around the room. Sonny was a stalky, sturdy man in his late forties. He was a demanding coach and always seemed bothered by something. Chad never wanted to be on his wrong side.

"Where's Thompson and Baker?" Sonny asked everyone in the room. He looked around, hoping someone would have an answer. "Being on time is what winners do."

A couple of the boys in front of Chad just shrugged.

"Well, let's get started," Sonny said. He then ceremoniously wailed, "Good afternoon!" Chad knew he was about to launch into one of his rituals. "What do we like to do?" he wailed to the group.

In unison, all the kids yelled back at him, "Win!"

"How do we do it?"

"Go fast!" they all replied.

"It's a great afternoon for karting practice, but before we get into that, we are going to talk about next year's season."

Big Mo Kilgore walked out of the office and stood next to Sonny. Chad wondered what was up.

"Great things are on the horizon," Big Mo announced. "Some of you may already know about the racing club that we're building down in the Florida Panhandle. It's called the Florida Springs Motor Resort & Country Club, and it's only about two hours away from here. We'll have the grand opening next year, and it's going to be incredible! The facility will be large enough to handle real racing road cars, like the Mazdas, and the Jaguars, and so much more. Perfect for karting and real racecar training! The club is going to be our focus for next year."

Chad leaned forward in his chair and listened intently. Maybe this was the opportunity he had been looking for—to move from training karts to real racecars. He couldn't wait to tell Gary Lee.

"This is going to be a very exclusive motorsport club," continued Big Mo. "Racing on this track will be only available to members, but you will get exclusive access through the Kilgore Karting team. Sonny will give you more details."

Sonny Kilgore walked over to the whiteboard and picked up an erasable marker. In his raspy voice, he narrated while he drew a trapezoid. "The new racing facility is a total of 380 acres. There's a full-size road track here." Sonny drew the snaky lines of a track inside the trapezoid. "Over by the entrance, we have the main clubhouse for catering and social events, the gymnasium, and the Olympic-size pool. Over on the back will be the guest villas. And finally, on this side of the park will be the superkart track." Sonny drew another snaky set of lines. "Yes, I said superkart!" he repeated, looking for a response from his audience.

There was a muffled gasp of excitement from the racers, and they looked at each other and their parents. The superkart was a concept that Chad had only read about. It doubled the size of the engine used in regular shifter karts and nearly doubled the top speed and the thrill. It would be almost like driving a real racecar. Chad looked at his dad to share the excitement of this announcement. Unfortunately, his father was not smiling; he just looked back and raised his eyebrows.

Sonny Kilgore continued, "Starting next year, our Florida club will be part of the new Southern Superkart League with competitions held at various tracks across the south. Kilgore Karting is going to offer very elite spots in our superkart team, which will compete at the Cadet, Junior, and Senior levels."

"And you'll have a chance to drive our own brand of superkart, the Kilgore Special," added Big Mo. "To talk about these, I'd like to introduce Bruce Larsen and his daughter Jessica."

Chad sat upright in his chair, intrigued. A man and a girl about Chad's age emerged from the side office and took their place beside the Kilgores. Various noises echoed from the boys in the audience at the sight of her. Someone in the back yelled out, "Yeah!"

The man appeared to be Asian American with jet-black hair; he was about the same age and height as Sonny, although thinner.

"Hi. I'm Bruce Larsen, the owner of the Cottonwood Karting Park in Longview, Texas, and this is my daughter Jessica. We're also going to be hosting events in this superkart series at our karting track. Jessica normally drives in the Senior class, but today she will be demonstrating for you a prototype of the Junior class superkart."

Jessica gave a modest wave to the assembly in the room. She was uniquely attractive with medium-length dark hair that was blonde at the tips.

"Keep your karting suits on, boys," said Sonny. "You're going to see more girls in karting, so get used to it."

Chad had already seen plenty of news about girls involved in karting, but strangely, very few had participated in Blue Springs karting. There were only three girls on the Kilgore team, and they were all little kids in the Cadet class.

"The superkarts come in three sizes for the three classes in the series," explained Mr. Larsen. "In the Junior and Cadet class, we will still use a 125 cc engine, similar to what you Juniors and Seniors are running today. The Cadets have speed limiters. You can get a closer look at the Junior prototype when Jessica drives with you in practice today. However, the real excitement is in the Senior superkart, which will have a 250 cc engine like the Formula Es. Those will be able to get up to speeds of 140 miles per hour on the straightaway."

Chad's father whispered loudly, "Geez. That is twice as powerful as you are driving now!"

Sonny Kilgore then posted on the board a large photograph of a little girl dressed in a pink racing suit. "Have any of you heard of Speedy Sue from Santa Rosa, California?" he asked. "She and her competitors are driving at highway speeds in the Western Superkart series, and she is only eight years old! She came in ninth place at the last proKart event in Santa Rosa, and she was driving at sixty-five miles per hour."

The young racers looked at each other in wide-eyed amazement.

"Kids, we are behind the eightball here, and this is our competition," said Sonny, pointing at the photo. "Speedy Sue will be driving up to ninety miles per hour by the time she is twelve years old and joins the Junior class. I know you don't want to be left behind in the dust."

A young boy in the front raised his hand, and Sonny pointed at him.

"I'm eleven," said the boy. "Does that mean I'm going to be able to drive ninety miles per hour next year?"

A chuckle echoed through the room. The boy turned and looked at his father standing by the side wall, who was shaking his head.

"You'll have to work up to that just like everyone else, but you can when you're ready," said Sonny.

Sonny handed a stack of brochures to the two boys in the first row to pass out to the room. Chad looked at the glossy booklet with an artist rendering of the new club on the front. It reminded him of the Blue Springs Country Club. Inside were pictures of the Kilgore Special with a detailed description of the karts. It all seemed too good to be true, and Chad took it all in with a big smile on his face. Maybe he could make a name for himself in the superkart league.

"These karts are going to bring our program up to the next level," Big Mo said proudly.

Chad's father raised his hand to speak. "How much are these new Kilgore superkarts going to cost us?" he asked.

Chad stared at his father, intently listening.

"Don't worry, Rusty. We have a plan for every budget," said Sonny Kilgore. Then, pointing to the back of the clubhouse, he continued, "I'd like to recognize Tom Grasiano, who received one of the scholarships for the All-Pro American team. Let's give him a round of applause, everyone." The room filled with applause, and Tom stood up in the back. "Tom has some packets with our financing plans. Would you bring me one, please? Hand them out to the parents, and we can all go over them together.

"The price for membership at the new Florida Springs Motor Club will be $25,000. The Kilgore Karting Team participants will be allowed to race there as an exclusive privilege—no membership required."

Chad was relieved to hear that, and now he considered staying in Kilgore Karting as part of his "Plan B" to get into racing.

"More good news," continued Sonny. "You can pay for your karting team dues by bringing in new members to the club or the karting team. For everyone that you refer and who buys a Florida club membership, you get ten thousand kartcoin. For each racer that joins the Kilgore Karting Team, you get five thousand kartcoin." Sonny showed his rare smile.

Kartcoin was another business innovation by the Kilgores. It was like Monopoly money that could only be used in their game. Various volunteer jobs or other promotional work would earn kartcoin for team members, which they could use to pay for things from the Kilgore racing business. They must be upping their game since the team referral bonus used to be only two thousand kartcoin.

"We are going to have a top-notch facility. It's going to make your families proud for you to race there," said Big Mo. "Our karts can be driven the way they were meant to be driven—fast!"

Sonny led the audience in more applause. "And thanks to our guests, the Larsens," he added.

Chad looked over at his dad, who was still standing, and he pulled his father's arm to sit down. His dad looked surprised and unsure. Chad never saw him with such a lost expression.

"Dad, we can make this work," he whispered. "I can sell this plan to some friends, and you know plenty of people through the garage who have expensive sports cars." Chad was hopeful.

Sonny Kilgore ended his pep rally for their new racing club by again drawing attention to the poster of Speedy Sue. "Just remember that Speedy Sue in California will be your competition someday soon."

Sonny then pointed to a yellow paper on the bulletin board. "This yellow sheet shows this afternoon's practice schedule. Junior class is up first. Write your names on the whiteboard outside," Sonny said.

Everyone jumped up, and the room buzzed with chatter. The Junior class headed out to get their karts ready. Chad was in the Senior class, so he had some time before taking to the track.

"This is so cool," he said, turning to his dad. "I think I'm finally going to get to drive a real racecar."

CHAPTER 18

Chad went out to his Chevy truck in the Babylon Karting Track parking lot to unload his kart for practice. Other kids just coming out from the clubhouse meeting were doing the same. The Alabama mud was still all around the parking lot from the recent rain.

"Chad, can you give me a hand here?" asked Artie, another Senior driver.

They each took a side of the kart in Artie's truck, lifted it out, and set it on the dolly. Artie's kart was in worse shape than Chad's. Some of the tubing looked like it had been bent and then straightened, and the plastic covering was torn and taped in one spot.

"Wow! 250 ccs," said a grinning Artie. "I can't wait to trade in this hunk of junk for one of those superkarts."

"I know," said Chad.

The two boys walked over to Chad's truck and lifted his kart out, as well. Chad looked at his kart. It was well used but still a good-looking machine.

"I'll miss Dude," he said.

"Dude?" Artie laughed. "Is that your kart's name?"

"Sure. What's wrong with that? Didn't you name your kart?"

"No. But I guess if I had to, I'd call it Turbo Turd." Artie laughed again. "It's amazing what you can do with duct tape."

"Buying one of those Kilgore superkarts is probably going to cost twenty grand," said Chad. "I'm definitely going to have to sell some of those club memberships or something."

"Hey, it's perfect timing for me," said Artie. "I had already convinced Craig Willis to join the Kilgore Karting team, so that's five thousand kartcoin right there!"

Chad's heart suddenly sunk. Craig was at the top of his list for selling a spot on the karting team. Maybe this was going to be more challenging than he thought.

"Nice," said Chad. "Hey, I have to get my duffel bag. See you over there."

Chad walked back to his truck, and Artie pushed his kart and dolly toward the pit area. Chad knew Gary Lee would be super optimistic about helping Chad get his referrals. Mrs. Dillanger wouldn't have to know about it.

Chad and his dad checked all the cotter pins and fasteners on the kart while the other kids were zooming around the track. The kart dolly was thirty inches high, making it easy to work on the kart. It was certainly much easier than the brake job Chad had to do on his truck over at his dad's garage two months ago.

Chad walked over to the track to watch the little kids run laps; they were up right before his practice time. He watched the little karts whiz by with their little motors sounding like tiny dirt bikes— a much higher-pitched sound than his kart. Chad vaguely remembered his days in the Kid class.

"Look at them go—they are so cute!" said a voice next to him.

He turned and saw Jessica Larsen. She had changed into a pink and white karting suit. He was so startled; he didn't say anything.

"Hi, I'm Jessica," she said.

"I know. I'm Chad Gibbons."

Jessica had engaging green eyes and a warmly tanned face with slight freckles across her cheeks. Her Asian heritage gave her a subtle beauty. Brunette hair flowed gracefully down over her shoulders, ending with golden-blonde tips. Chad wasn't usually shy, but standing up close in front of Jessica unexpectedly launched a swarm of butterflies in his stomach.

"Are you racing now?" he asked.

"Yes, I'll be doing laps with you guys in the Senior class. The Junior superkart is too fast for the regular Junior class."

They watched some more of the little karts whiz past. The sound calmed his mind while Chad desperately tried to think of something interesting to say.

"When did you start karting?" Jessica asked.

"That age," Chad said, pointing to another kart zooming by. "I was seven."

"Cool. Me too."

"Where in Texas are you all from?" asked Chad.

"Longview. It's just between Shreveport and Dallas. I'm not originally from there. We moved from Los Angeles a couple of years ago when my dad started the track."

"Oh, so how do you like Texas?"

"It's okay, but I'd probably go crazy there if I didn't have karting. Hey—we're up next! Come on. I want to show you the kart!"

Jessica grabbed Chad by the arm and pulled him over toward her pit area. Chad could see one of the parents was out on the track waving a finish flag, and the little kids were already stopping.

Chad and Jessica walked up to the pit area to find the Junior superkart off its dolly in the track entrance, ready to drive out. Mr. Larsen was explaining something to a group of parents and kids who were gawking at it.

The kart was a real jaw-dropper. First of all, it did not look like an assembly of tubing. It had a full plastic body, a spoiler airfoil in the back, and awesome red decal designs. It had the same wheelbase as a regular Senior kart, but it just looked bigger.

Jessica handed Chad her helmet. "Here, hold this."

She whipped her beautiful, shimmery brown hair back, twisted it up, and put some small clips in to hold it in place. Jessica put on her white balaclava hood and took back her pink and white helmet from Chad. She put it on and climbed into the kart. Jessica looked back at Chad, and all he could see were her piercing green eyes. He was smiling and still just standing there.

"Well, get going!" she shouted, and she put on her racing neck brace. A couple of kids laughed at Chad. He turned and headed back to his pit area. Chad didn't know what to think. Suddenly, everything felt different.

As he walked to his pit spot, Chad's dad was waving at him. The kart and dolly were in the lane, ready to wheel out.

"Come on," his dad called out. "You're going to be last in the pack if you don't hurry up. What were you doing?" Chad's dad handed him his duffle bag.

"I was looking at the superkart," said Chad.

"Yeah. I don't think that's all you were looking at, Son. Now pay attention here."

Chad pulled his karting suit out of his bag and put it on over his shorts and T-shirt. They wheeled the dolly over to the track entrance, set the kart down, and started the engine.

Chad put on his radio earpiece. The Kilgores insisted that their karters use radio systems for karting practice, even though radios were not allowed in actual karting events. All the kids liked it. It made them feel like real racers talking to their pit teams.

Chad finished donning his helmet and neck brace and then climbed into the kart. He revved the engine a few times, and his dad put on his own radio headset.

"Can you hear me?" came through the earpiece in the helmet.

"Yes. How am I?" Chad responded.

"Good. Now remember what we talked about when you're drafting behind someone and getting ready to pass," his dad said in the static of a radio voice. He gave the kart a push, and Chad rolled out onto the track to start his warm-up laps. "I talked to Artie's dad. You and Artie are going to be taking turns passing each other."

Chad hit the gas pedal and felt the acceleration pushing on his back. The familiar rush of adrenaline made his worries melt away behind him, and he accelerated up to track speed. His speedometer read forty-five. Warm-up laps were not only for the kart but also for the driver. It put Chad in a peaceful zone as he slung the kart in and out of the turns. He felt the kart rocking him back and forth, and it felt great. The anxiety of the outer world faded away.

"Look for Artie," his dad squawked over the radio, interrupting Chad's zen moment. "What are you doing out there?"

Gary Lee used to be on the other end of Chad's radio. He missed the way they worked together, with his friend's voice inside his head, warning him about who's coming up behind him.

Chad imagined Gary Lee commenting about the kart in front of him: "He's driving like a loser. Pass him on the next turn!" Chad drafted up close to the kart and then moved inside for the pass.

"Now that's what I was talking about. Nicely done," said his dad on the radio. "Artie's coming up behind you, and he's going to attempt to pass you. So just keep your normal line. You know there's no blocking allowed."

They were coming up on the last turn before the straightaway. It was a sharp right turn, and Chad's regular line would start the turn wide from the left side of the track and then cut tight into the turn. Chad could see Artie drafting up close for the pass. Artie would try to pass Chad on the right. He squeezed up next to Chad while they were braking for the turn. Once Artie was inside, Chad had to take the slower, outer path. They both came out onto the straightaway with Artie in the lead. Chad punched it—pinned back by the acceleration, the motor pitch going high and low as he shifted through the gears. Artie was doing the same. They flew past the bleachers. Chad looked at his speedometer. It said 103—sweet!

Chad was next. He would do essentially the same maneuver and pass Artie on the right when they came into the next turn. Chad was drafting close behind Artie on the straightaway. Suddenly, there was a loud engine noise and a flash of red in the corner of Chad's eye. The superkart flew by Chad on the right and then past Artie. She must have been going 110 miles per hour!

"I'm going where you're going!" Chad muttered to himself.

He took the opportunity and darted out from behind Artie to follow Jessica in the superkart. She was already starting to brake for the turn, so Chad was able to catch up. Artie had been forced to the outside by Jessica, so it was an easy pass for Chad. He just followed her around the inside of the turn.

"Whoa! Watch out, big boys—the girls are coming through," Chad's dad announced over the radio and laughed.

Chad didn't care anymore about his dad's training exercises; karting practice had become much more fun. Following Jessica, he passed three more karts. He knew Artie was falling back behind him. Now, if he could just pass Jessica—he was determined.

"What are you doing?" Chad's father squawked on the radio. "Artie's way behind you. Let him catch up."

Chad wasn't interested in letting anyone catch up or pass him. He was desperately trying to keep up with Jessica. Suddenly, he felt the back of his kart moving the wrong way. Driving through a turn, he could not compensate for the skid. He continued to spin out of the turn and onto the grass. His vision blurred while the world revolved around him. He could hear the roar of karts continuing past. He came to rest with a thud on the wall of tires. His chest hurt from the steering wheel.

"What the hell were you doing out there?!" yelled his father over the radio. "You're an idiot trying to keep up with a superkart! There better not be anything broken on that kart!"

Chad knew there was going to be hell to pay for his fun, but it was worth it. He couldn't wait to tell Gary Lee.

CHAPTER 19

Uma Kilgore and Stossi, her friend and caterer, had been working on the White Party preparations for weeks, and the day had finally arrived. Everyone in Blue Springs knew about the Kilgores' summer charity party, and Uma wanted the experience to be up to their guests' high expectations. They had worked on the menu and plans for months, but the last two weeks had been a frenzy of activity.

Stossi's real name was Inga Stoss, but everyone knew her as Stossi. She started her continental restaurant, Stossi's Steakhouse, many years back when she first came to Blue Springs. Uma was ecstatic to have found someone with the same love of European cooking, and they had been close friends ever since.

Uma insisted that the White Party be more casual this year. In previous years, black tie and formal white attire had been the rave—Monroe liked to go all out, but Uma thought a change would do everyone some good. She put it in large print on the invitations: *Casual dress in all white.* After all, it was hot in Blue Springs in July, and casual white was easy.

Uma had her outfit and Monroe's laid out on their oversized king-size bed. Monroe had a white linen suit with a simple white shirt. Uma had told him to wear it open neck, no dark ties, and no fancy footwear. Uma had a beautiful, white lace, mid-length skirt with a white silk shell. Haute strappy white sandals and graduated strands of white freshwater pearls completed her ensemble.

Uma was starting to feel excited when she came down the stairs to answer the very loud doorbell. When she opened the massive front door, there was Stossi with a young man carrying a tray full of appetizers wrapped in plastic. Stossi had always been a little on the plump side, as many good chefs are. She was ready for business in her white cooking jacket, and her hair pulled back in a bun.

"You're right on time!" said Uma.

Stossi smiled and hugged her.

"Yes, yes. Can you show Alex to the kitchen?" Stossi said. "He's new in our restaurant this year, and this is his first time catering an event."

Stossi turned and headed back to her catering truck parked in the driveway and left Alex to learn his job.

"Come this way, young man," said Uma, leading him into the heart of her home.

The tall and lanky Alex was dressed in jeans and a T-shirt. He followed Uma through the expansive front foyer carrying the first stacks of many trays of delicacies down the hall. Alex gaped wide-eyed when they passed the trophy room and went into the kitchen.

"Wow, Mrs. Kilgore, this is an incredible home you have," said Alex. He placed the trays on the counter. Stossi followed behind them with another stack of trays.

"Alex, can you bring the rest of the appetizer trays in and then park the truck over by the garage? We'll leave the desserts in the truck and bring them in later through the garage side door," said Stossi.

When Alex trotted off, she turned to Uma. "I have the Hungarian pastries in a new cooler in the truck, so they'll stay nice and fresh this year."

"Let me show you what we've done for the event," said Uma, excited to show off her preparations.

Stossi took Uma's arm, and they started toward the back patio.

"Well, I already noticed that the Imperial foo lions guarding your gates looked stunning."

"Oh yes, we had those power cleaned."

The two large cement lions in front of the Kilgores' gate were a signature landmark in Blue Springs.

"How many strands of white lights do you suppose are hung along the driveway, Uma?" Stossi asked with a laugh.

"Well, you just can't have too many white lights for our summer celebration."

They walked out onto the patio, and Stossi gasped.

It was almost dusk, and the clouds above were turning pink and orange. Lines of small globe lights crisscrossed over the pool and twinkled like stars. The pool itself was magnificent. It had a hydrotherapy spa at one end and a waterfall that cascaded into the pool with changing colored lights behind it. White wicker furniture was arranged in cozy groups around the deck. Little amber lights lined the white rose bushes surrounding the pool patio, and white orchids and pillar candles were placed on all the tables. White umbrellas with white lights twinkled, and behind the pool area stood a large white tent, warm light glowing within and without. The gardener was just finishing setting potted white rose bushes along the tent entrance.

"It just takes my breath away. It's your very own *Nuit Blanche*," said Stossi.

"We just need some Parisian artists." Uma laughed. "Come out here to the tent. This is for the swing dancing."

As they entered the tent, a man was setting up sound equipment in the back. A small dance floor was laid out in the center of the white canvas tent. Uma loved to dance.

"We have a new jazz combo tonight, the Sam James Band. They play swing and jazz—Sam is a saxophone player. Look, we also have an old jukebox for when the band is on break."

Stossi looked at her watch. "Let's get this party started, Uma. There is much to do. Matt will set up the bar here on this side of the pool area. We'll bring the trays in and out of the kitchen by coming around the side of the house from the kitchen patio."

Stossi walked with Uma along the brick path around the corner of the house to the garden patio just outside the kitchen. This was Uma's favorite place. She had also decorated it with twinkling lights just for herself and hoped Kylie Shay would see the lights from her twin mansion across the creek and come over to the party.

Stossi opened the doors into the kitchen, and they went in. The two other servers had arrived and joined Alex. They were dressed in white tuxedos with black and white checkered cummerbunds.

"Something had to be checkered," said Uma. "That was Monroe's contribution."

"Jeff, at seven o'clock, I want you to take this tray with champagne flutes out to the foyer," Stossi said to one of the servers. "Alex, if you're done here, change into your tux, please."

Uma loved Stossi's energetic style—so prompt and crisp.

One of the servers had brought a large ice chest into the kitchen. Stossi turned toward Uma with a twinkle in her eye.

"Here's a surprise for you! Alex, help me with this."

They opened the chest, and a frosty cloud swirled out. The two of them lifted out a shimmering ice angel.

"Oh!" Uma clapped her hands. "It's fantastic!"

"We'll set that up right when the party starts. It will stand up on the ice with the champagne bottles. I'm keeping it on dry ice until then." They lowered the sculpture back into the ice chest and shut the lid. "Now, don't you need to get ready? Your guests will be here soon."

"Yes, thank you so much, sweet girl," Uma said, and she gave Stossi a big hug.

Uma glided along the hall and started to think about all the different people that were coming. Monroe had invited his investors and his potential investors, of course. Friendship and business were always interwoven for him. Uma invited everyone that she wanted to see. Kylie Shay, her neighbor and the mother of her grandson, Mackie Kilgore. Jonathan Saras, her favorite dancing partner and Monroe's Formula One rival from thirty years ago. Elle Dillanger, her friend and interior designer, was also on her list, but she had declined.

Monroe was coming down the stairs when Uma turned to go up. He was wearing his white linen suit that fit him perfectly. She stopped for a moment to admire how handsome he looked.

Monroe paused and admired his wife Uma standing at the bottom of the stairs.

"There you are," Monroe said. "Have the Wheelboys arrived yet? They are doing the parking tonight."

"No. I haven't seen them. Stossi and the servers are here. They're setting up now," she said.

"Excellent. You'd better get ready yourself, darlin'." He kissed her on the cheek, and she continued up the stairs.

*****

Monroe surveyed the extravagant decorations of twinkling lights and the manicured presentation of his estate from the front steps of his family mansion. A small Chevy truck came down the driveway and parked in front of the entrance. Chad Gibbons emerged, and he walked briskly up to Monroe. Chad was dressed in a clean, white polo shirt with the Kilgore crest and khaki shorts.

"You're the first Wheelboy here, Chad, so you can be Head Valet," Monroe said. "I want you to park all the guests' cars over there on that grassy area. Stack those cars three deep—that should give you enough room." Monroe pointed at the large yard to the right of the long driveway.

"Yes, Mr. Kilgore."

"Don't let the limos park over here. They have to wait out on the street after dropping their guests off—the drivers should know that. Remember your manners. If the ladies flirt with you, flirt back. Now you can start by parking your truck over there in the corner. And don't forget to keep the keys in order, son."

Chad nodded and hurried back into his truck to move it out of the circular driveway.

Monroe was about to go back inside when two more Wheelboy trucks pulled up.

"Park over there by Chad's truck," he commanded through the open truck windows. "He's in charge. You can get your instructions from him. Hurry up. It's almost 7 p.m."

The two trucks zipped over toward where Chad had parked, and Monroe headed in through the front door. A server was just entering the foyer with a tray full of champagne flutes when Monroe came in. The young man looked elegant in his white tux with a black and white checkered cummerbund.

"Marvelous!" exclaimed Monroe.

"Champagne, sir?" asked the young man.

"Not yet—save them for the guests. Thank you."

Monroe passed on through the house to finish supervising. He walked out to the patio where an ice sculpture had just been set up. To the right was the gazebo where the barman was placing sample beer and wine bottles on his serving station. At the rear of the pool patio was the charity table with a donation box decorated like a treasure chest. The sign on the front of it read *Blue Springs Hospital Charity*. Monroe smiled proudly. The Kilgore Children's Wing was named after him.

Guests would start arriving now, so it was time to begin. Monroe walked through the hallway of his home and out to the front entrance. He enjoyed watching the Wheelboys in action—opening the doors for the guests, getting in the front seats, and parking the cars.

Monroe offered them all greetings: "Wonderful to see you... Glad you could come... Charles, I hope you are wearing your dancing shoes!"

He welcomed as many as he could, and when the foyer became crowded, Monroe escorted an entourage back toward the patio. He then returned to the front steps to greet some more enthusiastic party arrivals. Everyone was all dressed in white, with some silver and gold, of course.

*****

It only took Uma thirty minutes to transform herself into the hostess of the evening. Uma practiced her greetings in the mirror while she put on her jewelry. She looked at her watch: 7:05—just a few more minutes. After hearing the sound of voices downstairs for another ten minutes or so, she knew it was time to make her entrance.

Uma gently descended the stairs into the foyer. Several guests were picking up champagne flutes from the server by the front door, and all eyes turned to look up at her. She thought of her younger self once descending stairs at the grand ballroom in Budapest. Uma glowed, and her more modest setting here in Blue Springs suited her just fine, now.

"How are you?" she clasped her guests' hands and leaned forward as she had rehearsed upstairs. She could see Monroe outside the front door, greeting some more arrivals. They gave their car keys to one of Sonny's karting boys serving as a valet.

"Have some champagne and come to the patio with me," Uma said to the guests. They each took a glass.

There was casual banter about how beautiful the front of the house looked all lit up. Some of the guests meandered to the family room and others down the long hall and out to the poolside. They all gasped in amazement. Uma enjoyed watching people's reactions when they walked out onto the patio. The ice angel was now adorning a table in front of the pool with several bottles of champagne seemingly embedded in the base of the sculpture. Other guests had previously entered the pool area and were already deep in conversation. Music drifted from the white tent beyond the pool.

Uma turned and saw her daughter-in-law, Kylie Shay, walking toward her.

"There she is! Did you see the lights on my patio?" Uma asked. "Where's my grandson Mackie? Do you know when he's coming?"

"Hi, Uma." Kylie hugged her. "Oh, this patio is even more beautiful than last year. Can I move in with you? I think my house is haunted!" she said.

"I think you need to have some fun. Try a little dancing. Here, have some champagne."

"Seriously, Uma, I hear strange noises at night and find things moved around in the kitchen in the morning."

"Maybe it's just your ex-husband looking for a midnight snack," Uma teased her. "Do you know if Mackie is coming?"

"You'll have to ask your son—the boys are together this weekend."

Uma and Kylie entered the tent. People were enjoying the music, but no one was dancing yet. Clearly, they just needed a nudge. Uma waved at the band—this prearranged signal meant to start the swing music. The band paused and shifted gears—the bass player started a quick beat, and the snare drum joined in. Sam launched into a syncopated melody on the saxophone. No one could resist tapping their feet, and in a few seconds, couples started twirling around on the dance floor.

Uma looked at Kylie, and she was now smiling. Uma continued to glance around at the faces and nodding heads, but her vision stopped on a tall, handsome man with dark hair, slightly graying on the sides. Jonathan Saras. Uma's gaze silently caught his attention, and he looked up. He broke off his conversation and walked over to her.

"Hello, Jonathan." Uma kissed him three times on his cheeks. He looked into her eyes.

"This is why I come to your parties each year," said Jonathan. "To see your face and refresh my memory." Jonathan spoke softly and gracefully with a touch of old-world royalty.

Uma turned toward Kylie Shay. "Kylie, you remember my dear friend, Jonathan Saras. He was Monroe's archrival in Formula One when we first met. Now he's a polo champion."

Jonathan laughed. "Hardly a champion, but I do love to play polo. Yes, of course, we've met before. It is a pleasure to see you again, Kylie." Jonathan took her hand and kissed it in a classic European style.

"Actually, Jonathan owns a polo club in Vero Beach, Florida," explained Uma.

"Oh, it's a family business," Jonathan said. "This music is irresistible! You must dance with me," he said to Kylie.

"Thank you, but I'm just not 'In the Mood' yet," said Kylie.

"Well then, Zooma, would it be too much for you to dance with me?" asked Jonathan with a smile.

"Zooma?" questioned Kylie.

"That's always been her nickname. It's on her license plate, you know," explained Jonathan.

160

"Ah, yes. I do recall seeing that."

"Excuse us," said Jonathan, and he took Uma by the hand. They started to twirl and sway on the dance floor. Once Uma started, even more people joined in the swing. Suddenly, the floor was crowded. Uma remembered how she and Monroe one time danced in London to a live big band—there was nothing like it. She loved the swing classics, and Sam's band could deliver.

The song came to an end, and everyone on the floor broke into applause.

"I shouldn't steal you away from your guests," he conceded.

Jonathan walked with Uma back over to where Kylie was speaking with a young man.

"This is Tom Grasiano, one of Sonny's karting racers," said Kylie. "He was just telling me about the racing scholarship that he received."

"Nice to meet you. I am Jonathan Saras," he said, and he reached out and shook Tom's hand. "I have known the Kilgores since Sonny was just a little boy. Congratulations on your scholarship. Those scholarships can be very helpful if you are pursuing a racing career."

"Wow! Are you the same Saras that beat Big Mo out of the Formula One championship? And now you raise polo ponies, right?" asked Tom.

"Yes, that is all true. I see I already have a reputation here."

"Do you have any advice for someone like me, a rookie to racing?"

"I'm sure you get plenty of good coaching from Sonny. Tell me, why are you pursuing a professional racing career?"

"Have you seen this mansion and the cars in the garage? They are awesome! From the moment I saw his racing success, I knew that's what I wanted too."

Jonathan laughed. "I'm sorry, but that is amusing to me."

Tom looked puzzled. Even Uma chuckled.

"I did not get rich by being a racecar driver. Neither did Monroe," said Jonathan. "Sure, there's some money to be made in racing, but not much for the drivers, as you probably are finding out.

I invested my few winnings in polo—it was my family's business, so it was easy to become successful. Polo is where I made my wealth. I raced for the love of the sport but not for the money. That is why I asked you why you want to be a racer."

"Sure, I really like racing. I like beating the guy behind me." Tom looked a bit embarrassed by his own honesty.

"Don't be in a rush for success," said Jonathan, "but there are much safer ways to make money if that's your goal. When Monroe and I were racing, half of our friends died violently—some on the track, some off. With racing, you are risking your life, so it had better be worth it. After my championship, I had enough money to get out and start a real business."

Uma gave Jonathan a nudge. "Why are you talking about these awful things here at my party? Kylie's son races nearly every weekend," Uma said, looking at Kylie.

"I am so sorry," said Jonathan. "I get worked up when young people talk about racing. They romanticize it and have dreams of glory. How many times did Monroe and I say to each other about a friend that he died doing what he loved?"

"I'm going to send you over to bother the men now," said Uma. "You can swap war stories with them. Look, there's Monroe. Maybe you can convince him to find a new career for Mackie."

Uma crossed her arms as Jonathan walked away. Why couldn't Sonny and Mackie take some of that advice?

CHAPTER 20

Monroe gazed across the pool area that was stirring with conversation. It was time for his speech. He had a microphone and speaker set up beside the charity table, and he used it to get the party's attention.

"Friends, thank you for coming and enjoying yourselves. The swing tent is where all the fun is happening." Monroe pointed behind the patio, and he could see Uma standing by the opening of the tent. "The famous Samuel James jazz band is just getting started. My beautiful wife is probably already dancing. The Blue Springs Hospital benefits from all the gracious donations that you put into this treasure chest. The sick children afflicted with cancer and childhood leukemia will appreciate your kind and generous donations. As tough as it is for a child to have cancer, it's good to know that most children and teens with childhood leukemia can be successfully treated."

Monroe peeked into the box on the table and could see that checks were already accumulating. Two guests approached Monroe, and he reached out to shake their hands.

"Rusty and Carole, yes? You are Chad's parents," he said.

"Yes, thank you so much for inviting us," said Rusty Gibbons, dropping a check through the slot in the donation box.

"Your home looks so beautiful, all lit up," said Carole.

"Thank you for your contribution," said Monroe, and he patted Rusty on the shoulder. "Carole, you look gorgeous tonight. Chad is doing an excellent job as valet this evening. These boys are growing up so fast. It was just yesterday they started in trainer karts."

"And now they are driving at highway speeds," added Carole. "It seems a little scary to me."

"Well, you have much to be proud about," Monroe continued. "He and the others are experiencing personal victories, growth, and overcoming challenges." Monroe liked to emphasize the character building that karting offered. "And they are also learning about business."

"Oh, yes. They certainly had to learn how to raise quite a bit of money," replied Carole.

Monroe smiled. He was glad to be interrupted by Butkis and Monroe's sister, Margaret, who had walked up to them arm in arm.

"Great party, as always, Big Mo," Butkis said, and he shook hands with Monroe. "Doesn't Margaret look enchanting tonight? No one would ever guess you two were twins." Butkis laughed. "You look dashing in your white suit Mo, but Margaret's shoes are the talk of the town."

They all laughed, but Monroe knew that joke was aimed at him. He looked down at his shoes and said, "I love my white Prada sneakers. Uma even likes them." Monroe turned to Chad's parents. "Rusty and Carole Gibbons, this is my sister Margaret and her date this evening, B.B. Butkis."

The couples exchanged pleasantries.

"I also wanted to thank you, Mr. Butkis, for all of the karting sponsorship over the years," said Rusty.

"It is always my pleasure to be part of the Wheelboys adventure," said Butkis.

"You know, B.B. has traditionally been one the biggest benefactors of this event," Monroe said to the Gibbons.

Monroe was waiting for Butkis to pull out his contribution check. Butkis excused himself and made his way over to the contribution box. He pulled a check out of his suit pocket, but Monroe interrupted him.

"May I announce your contribution?" he asked Butkis.

"Gladly." He handed Monroe the check.

"Excuse me, ladies and gentlemen," Monroe said into the microphone. "We have a generous donation from B.B. Butkis of South East Furniture…$50,000!"

The crowd let out a moan with applause while Monroe slid it into the treasure chest.

"For the Kilgore Children's Cancer Wing," Butkis replied in a loud voice, smiling. The patio offered some more applause, and Butkis waved it off.

"Very kind. Thank you, B.B.," Monroe said with his hand on Butkis' shoulder. "Keep my sister close in your sight tonight; you don't want her stolen away by any of the eligible bachelors in our midst."

Suddenly, there was a boisterous shout from across the patio, and the company turned to see.

"Why, it's Sonny Kilgore!" said Butkis. He nudged Monroe. "How did you get your son to come to a charity event? I thought he was racing at Talladega this weekend?"

Monroe was equally surprised. Butkis nudged Monroe again. "Get a look at the beautiful blonde with him!"

A woman in her thirties was gripping Sonny's arm while wearing a white translucent top, a visible red bra, and a shimmering short white skirt. Sonny Kilgore and his date came over to his father's gathering of friends.

"Hi, Mo, B.B., Aunt Margaret," said Sonny. He was apparently not in a good mood, as shown by his general scowl.

"Well, a nice surprise to see you," said Monroe. "What happened with Talladega?"

"Don't ask," said Sonny. "Does it matter? We're here. How is everyone? This stunning woman is Ruby Mae, my girlfriend."

"Nice to finally meet you," said Monroe, winking and taking Ruby's hand.

Monroe actually did know Ruby from prior LL events, but he wasn't going to bring that up now. She smiled, and Sonny made further introductions. He then waved a server with a tray of champagne over to them.

"Everyone should have a glass," said Sonny.

They all picked up shimmering flutes.

"Here's to family and friends," said Monroe with his glass raised.

Sonny noisily sipped his glass of champagne, then turned to his father and said, "Ruby is a sports massage therapist, and we met at a race in Leeds. She has a heart of gold, and good god, she has a sweet booty."

Sonny patted Ruby Mae on the back of her behind, and like an adult cat, she instinctively lifted her rear end in response. Sonny's face lightened up, and he flashed a rare smile.

Monroe was glad to see his son with a nice-looking woman by his side, but he wondered how these two came together. He looked over at Butkis, who winked back.

"Did you set this up?" he whispered to Butkis, who just smiled and nodded. Monroe then remembered that Ruby Mae had worked for Butkis at the LL events as a masseuse.

"Oh, I have to tell you, she has been teaching me amazing things about the 'Law of Attraction,'" said Sonny.

Monroe raised his eyebrows in curiosity. Butkis leaned over and whispered to Monroe, "I know exactly what he means!" with a snicker.

"Let me explain," Sonny continued. "Every positive or negative thing that happens to you was attracted by you," said Sonny. "Ruby, you can explain it better."

"Okay," said Ruby. "Let's say, for example, a friend loaned you some money when you didn't have any. You attracted that, even if you didn't realize you were using the Law of Attraction. Similarly, if a friend does you wrong, you also attracted that."

"Fascinating," said Margaret, nodding. "I think, B.B., you must be using this law of attraction on a daily basis."

"Well, that's the point exactly," explained Ruby. "Everyone is using the Law of Attraction all day long—for good and for not so good. So it's important that you learn how to use it. People in this world need to learn how to communicate with the Universe. You need to formulate your requests precisely and send them to the Universe."

Sonny looked eagerly at everyone to see if they understood.

"Is that what happened in Talladega?" asked Monroe, smiling.

"I'm not going to talk about that, Mo," said Sonny. "I'm just learning about these Laws of Attraction, and I have a long way to go." Sonny turned and walked over to the donation box, flipped open the latch, and lifted the lid. "Nice haul for the hospital, Mo!"

"Leave that alone, Sonny, unless you're putting something in," said Monroe. "Why don't you take your Ruby dancing? I bet she'll love that saxophone swing band."

"Sure, but first, I need a real drink. Come on, Ruby, let's get something from the bar."

"Nice meeting you all," Ruby said.

As the couple walked away, Ruby's outfit shimmered under the globe lights. Very photogenic, Monroe thought. She'll look good next to Sonny for the team photo shoot, even if he's not winning. A pleasant change from Sonny's last scandal in the news!

"Definitely some law of attraction going on there," chuckled Butkis as he watched them walk away.

"Eyes over here, B.B.," said Margaret. She took Butkis' arm. "Let's check out the dance floor."

Two of the Wheelboys were passing by toward the dancing tent, Tom Grasiano and another young man. Monroe grabbed one by the sleeve. "What's your name, again, son?" he asked him.

"Brad, sir."

"Here, Brad—take this stack of thank you notes and hand them out to the guests when they put their checks in the donation box," instructed Monroe. "And just keep an eye on the box. I don't want anyone using the 'Laws of Attraction' on any of those checks."

"Yes, sir." Brad took the stack of cards from the table and went to work.

Monroe grinned at Margaret and Butkis and motioned toward the swing tent. Now the music was picking up with that big band sound. Margaret couldn't resist. She took Butkis by the hand and led him onto the dance floor.

Monroe stood by the door of the tent and sipped his champagne, happily watching the guests twirling and twisting. Uma caught his eye, and he could see her dancing with Johnathan Saras, his old racing buddy. Monroe was about to cut in for the next tune, but when he saw Uma having fun and entertaining their guests, he decided just to wait and save the last dance for her. The summer they first met in Budapest, Monroe and Uma would dance late into the morning hours. His favorite memories filled his mind.

Monroe strolled back across the pool patio and came across his associate, Bruce Larsen, talking to some guests.

"Bruce. There you are," said Monroe. He turned to the couple standing with them. "Nice to see you. Did Bruce tell you that he is a karting track owner in Texas?"

"Why, yes. We were just talking about your project in the Panhandle in Florida," said the gray-haired gentleman in white. "Definitely something I'm interested in."

"Marvelous. Bruce, where is your lovely daughter? You all should see her—a very talented kart racer indeed! It's kids like Jessica who are going to make this racing club a great investment. Superkart events, rallies, private sports car owners—there's an enormous demand." Monroe gave his quick pitch.

Monroe was now enjoying himself even more. He had signed up five investors this week and would close the deal with two more moneybags tonight. The privileged few in Alabama loved charity events, and Monroe Kilgore loved his circle of friends. A charity event is such a fantastic opportunity to rub elbows with people of abundant financial means, and they are always looking for new ways to put their money to work. Maybe Sonny was right—the Law of Attraction was working.

"Make sure y'all get some dancing in with the Sam James band," Monroe reminded them. "Have fun this evening—life is short. Bruce, we will get together and chat about the new club before this evening is over."

Monroe suddenly was in the mood for dancing himself, but he needed to check on the boys' valet service first. Monroe walked through the house and out the front door. No one was there. The front of the mansion was quiet and peaceful; only the distant noise of the party could be heard. The air was a little cooler now, and the stars were out. The light of the front entrance lanterns fought off the darkness, and the long driveway, lit on either side, looked like a runway at night. The white lights sparkled on the trees. Monroe stood on his front steps, pulled out a cigar, clipped the end, and lit it up. There was the sound of muffled laughter coming from under the trees to the left of the driveway.

"Boys, it's time to get to work," said Monroe.

Chad Gibbons and Jessica Larsen stepped out from the shadows and walked toward Monroe.

"Hi, Mr. Kilgore," she said.

Monroe started to grin. He took a deep puff on his cigar and savored it, looking at the kids in front of him. "Jessica, your father is by the poolside, and he would like to show off his racing champion daughter. We are trying to close some sales deals. You look lovely tonight, and it isn't every day that we get to show off a superkart champion driver in Blue Springs."

"Chad," continued Monroe, "could you find your way into the kitchen and bring a platter of sandwiches and desserts down to the limo drivers at the end of the driveway? Stossi, the nice lady in the white chef's jacket, can help you with anything you need. I'll come around to check on you in a while."

The kids snickered and immediately skirted off together into the house as requested. Monroe watched them and chuckled to himself, "Oh, to be eighteen again and in love with life."

He continued to smoke his cigar and walked around the circle of the driveway, checking on his young valets' parking skills. Having finished his cigar, Monroe returned to his party guests in the pool area.

He saw Sonny and his ex-wife, Kylie Shay, talking by the gazebo. Nearby, Ruby was sitting on a barstool. Kylie was agitated, and her voice carried across the gazebo deck. Monroe walked over to intervene. He didn't want family nonsense on display at the party. When he approached, he could hear his ex-daughter-in-law, Kylie.

"Mackie doesn't need your negative energy. He is more than a racecar driver. He is your son, for heaven sakes," she said.

"It's his chosen career. He understands—he's a professional," replied Sonny.

"Chosen by whom? You treat your employees better. You're always chiding him. He at least deserves a paycheck, not peanuts. This racing gig is not a circus. Or maybe it is."

Kylie knew how to press Sonny's buttons. Sonny turned away in anger. He snatched Ruby's hand and started walking past the pool toward the swing tent. Kylie followed.

"Hey, Kilgore! Why don't you cool off!" she shouted and pushed him into the pool. Everyone turned at the sound of a large *ker-splash*. Ruby managed to escape falling in herself. Monroe watched in surprise his son flailing around in the pool. Kylie smiled, turned, and walked past Monroe.

"Hi, neighbor. Thanks for the party. I think I'll call it a night." She headed out the side of the patio toward her house.

Monroe laughed and called to his son, "Sonny, get out of that pool. Swimming is not allowed in the deep end without a lifeguard on duty."

Sonny climbed out of the pool, dripping all over the patio. Everyone was watching. He turned to Ruby with his hands up. "Don't say it! I already know. The Law of Attraction!"

Monroe tossed Sonny a towel.

"Son, why don't you go upstairs and put on some dry clothes," Monroe said. "We have an important meeting with the club investors in a half-hour."

CHAPTER 21

Monroe Kilgore had told Chad to take a tray of sandwiches down to the limo drivers waiting at the end of the Kilgores' driveway. Chad had been parking cars for the guests at the Kilgores' White Party all evening. He didn't mind that he was not paid; it was volunteer work for a good cause—the White Party was a fundraiser for the Blue Springs Hospital.

Chad entered the kitchen and almost collided with a server coming out with a tray full of appetizers. Chad was looking for Stossi, a woman in a white chef's jacket. The oversized kitchen in the mansion had a large island in the center. The counters were covered with various platters of food, some still wrapped in plastic. Chad overheard the woman in the white jacket talking about Gillian Mason. They stopped talking when they realized Chad was there.

"Stossi?" Chad asked the woman with the chef's jacket. Chad recognized her from the well-known steakhouse in town, Stossi's Steakhouse. She was known as the best caterer in this part of Alabama.

"Yes. Is there something you need?" Stossi asked.

"Mr. Kilgore asked me to take some food down to the limo drivers. He said to speak to you."

"Here's a disposable tray. Take what you need from those platters." She pointed to full trays of appetizers and desserts.

Chad set the tray down and started choosing various kinds of appetizers—crab puffs, bacon-wrapped dates, crostini, finger sandwiches, baklava, Bavarian chocolate cupcakes, and mini crème brûlée. He was astounded with the food choices while he listened to the women resume their conversation about Gillian.

"I think it was a very kind gesture," said Stossi to the other woman, "but don't you think it a bit unusual for someone to donate $20,000 anonymously to the Blue Springs Youth Orchestra in Gillian Mason's memory?"

Chad smiled at them, took the tray, and left the kitchen. The mention of Gillian caught him off guard, and he suddenly felt like breaking down and crying. He thought about how Gary Lee and Gillian used to do so many things with him and Annie. They were an inseparable foursome—chilling out after school, playing around at the karting track, going out to the movies at the mall, and just hanging out. He realized those days were over, and they were never coming back.

Chad walked down the long driveway lined with twinkling lights, looking up at the dark and star-filled night sky. The summer cicadas played a familiar sound around him. Since the graduation, which he hardly remembered, the emptiness seemed more and more overwhelming as the days went on. Annie was away for a vacation with her parents, and his heart ached when he thought of her. They had been so close all senior year, but now every thought about her only reminded him of Gillian and Gary Lee and their shared tragedy. He wasn't sure what to do, but he had been avoiding calling or texting her lately. Now he met someone new. Jessica Larsen is here, and she was so different, like a fresh start. Chad felt guilty. He remembered the counselors at school were talking about survivor's guilt, and maybe he was experiencing that dreaded thing.

There were three limos parked on the street outside of the Kilgores' gates. The drivers had congregated in front of one of the stretched cars; he could hear their muted conversations. Chad recognized one of the drivers as "Big Walt," the older brother of a classmate in school. He left the tray with the drivers, who greedily attacked the generous spread and thanked him. Chad wondered what kind of career it would be as a limo driver. They probably all liked auto racing just as he did. Chad laughed to himself and thought limo drivers must probably meet some very fascinating people. Chad's sadness had left him for the moment, and he admired some of the exotic parked cars—he loved the V-12 Jaguar E-type—as he walked back up the driveway to the house.

"Hey, there you are!" Jessica was standing in front of the open front door. "Take a walk?" she invited.

The two of them walked along a pathway around the side of the house facing the other twin mansion. The other large estate on the same hillside looked desolate. The gentle sounds of swing saxophone jazz lightly echoed through the yards. Jessica took Chad by the arm.

"You know, you look very dashing in your valet uniform," she said coyly.

"What did your dad want?" asked Chad.

"I think he just wanted to show me off. He was trying to convince someone to invest in superkart racing. Somehow the Kilgores think seeing me, a smart and beautiful racer, will sway an investor's decision in their favor." She laughed.

"I can see how that could work. I'm ready to invest right now." He smiled at her.

"Oh, you and your whole five dollars? Or how about all the money you earned tonight?"

Chad fell silent. He already knew that he needed to get a real job if he wanted to move up into racing. His dad reminded him often enough that he failed the All-Pro racing school scholarship opportunity.

The two came upon the softly lighted side patio next to the garden. There was a small bench, and they sat down.

"Hey, don't feel bad—I was just teasing you," Jessica said.

"It's just that karting is expensive," he explained. "You can use karting to break into racing, but that's even more expensive. I was hoping to get that All-Pro scholarship for racing school in the fall, but now I'll have to come up with another plan."

"Oh, you mean the scholarship that Tommy kid got? He's a jerk, you know. He was at the Rodeo-Kart last year trying to get the attention of sponsors—I guess it paid off. He has all the signs of adrenaline addiction, too. I see those types of jerks at our kart park in Longview all the time."

"So you think I'm an adrenaline junkie?" asked Chad.

"Maybe. Adrenaline junkies pay good money and even work for free to get their drug of choice. The karting business thrives on people like that. It's going to put me through college."

"Hmmm. I seem to be fitting that description. What about you?"

"For me, it's all about being first. I can't stand being beaten out by someone else. It's not just in karting—it's with everything."

"I wish I were more like that. I might have won that scholarship," said Chad.

"You shouldn't think that way. Be who you are. I wouldn't want you to be like anyone else. Anyway, that guy, Tom Grasiano, drives like the person he is—freakin' obnoxious. He doesn't know how to use his brakes. He's going to kill someone someday."

"I don't get it. I worked like a cotton picker for the last two years in karting. I won a few races and placed in a lot more. Sonny Kilgore said I have real talent, but I guess not enough."

"Talent? Forget about that crap they're feeding you," Jessica said, taking his hand. "If you like karting and have goals, great— pursue them, but don't let anyone put you on a hamster wheel. If they can ring a bell and you salivate, that is not a good sign."

"What are you talking about?"

"Pavlov! I'm just saying follow *your* dreams—not anyone else's. And especially don't follow anyone's cattle path."

Chad looked at her and paused. "So you were at Rodeo-Kart last year?" he asked. "Did you race?"

"What? Did you think I was selling cotton candy?" she said and gave him a shove. "Of course I raced. I made it to the finals."

"Geez. I always wanted to do that."

Jessica laughed. "So, are you going to sign up? It's at my dad's karting park in Longview, Texas, this year."

"I don't think so," Chad said disappointedly. "My dad and I talked about it, and we agreed it was too much money, too long a drive, and I wasn't likely to do well up against the pro racers."

It suddenly dawned on Chad that maybe his dad didn't believe in him. Instead, he was all about scholarships and who you know.

"Oh, come on. That is so lame!" she said. "Just because the karters and the pro racers race together, that shouldn't scare you off." She was right. All of those reasons were lame excuses. "Most of the karters competing in Rodeo-Kart are showing off to the media, promoters, and the sponsors. They want to be scouted. They are also trying to get their SCCA full competition license so they can race autos—you know, like sports cars or F2000s."

Chad nodded and anxiously rose from the bench. Jessica followed and put her hand on his shoulder.

"You have a decent kart, and I've seen you drive," she said. "It's the perfect opportunity if you want to get your name out there and advance your career if that's your intent. Hey, aren't you an Alabama Wheelboy?"

"You make it sound so easy," Chad replied, starting to smile. "But my kart is not that great—not compared to the high-end karts that show up at those big competitions. It won't look very good to any sponsor."

"Well, I could lend you the extra kart that my dad has for me. Don't worry—pink isn't my signature color. It's painted neon-purple." Jessica laughed.

"I guess I could talk to my dad again."

"Aren't you eighteen now?" Jessica squeezed his arm muscle. "Why are you even asking your dad—unless you need his cash?"

"No, I think I have enough money, but you know how karting dads can be. They want to experience the thrill through their kids."

"So just tell your dad you're going to Rodeo-Kart. You can stay at the park. We have a guest trailer in the back. Don't you want to come and see where I race?"

Jessica's enthusiasm was contagious. Chad nodded. Suddenly, he felt the tingle of excitement at the idea of going to Texas. It might even be easier to go to Texas without telling his dad at all.

"It's a pretty long drive, isn't it?" he asked.

"Not too bad—about nine hours. Come on! Racecar drivers like to drive."

Jessica smiled with her beautiful teeth glistening. She took Chad's arm, and they started to walk some more.

"You should come if you want a future in racing," Jessica said. "I'm serious. Sprint cars, sports cars, Formula BMW, Star Mazda, Formula Renault, Ford, Dodge, and A1GP—Rodeo-Kart is the road to racecar driving. At least that's the advertising if you buy it."

"Okay, I'll do it. Why not?"

"See, I knew you had it in you," Jessica said with a little jump.

She pulled him close and kissed him on the cheek. Chad was a little surprised, but she was genuinely excited.

"Wow. You really must be into it," said Chad.

"Listen, the only reason I'm in karting is because I'm like 'legacy.' You know, my dad owns the freakin' karting park in Texas. It doesn't cost me anything to be karting."

"What do you mean by legacy?"

"Legacy. You know, like racing legacy or heritage. That's what they call you when your parent was a racer, and you become a racer. Like the Kilgores. Legacy racers get a free ride, a spot on the track; they don't have to beg for it like you do."

"I'd like to think that I could earn a place in the auto racing world. You make it sound like everyone else is groveling."

"Maybe more like kissing up," said Jessica, puckering up and making a kissing noise. Chad could not believe how beautiful she looked under the glowing lights, even when making a full face of lips and dimples like a kissing fish. She was gorgeous. Right there, he wanted a real kiss.

"So your dad was a racer?" asked Chad.

"Yeah. Before I was born, he raced in Le Mans. That's where he met my mom."

"Sounds pretty romantic."

"*Oui, mon beau garçon, je suis français,*" Jessica said gleefully. "They're not together now, but I go to Paris to visit her at least twice a year."

"Wow. I did not see that coming. Did you grow up in France? You don't have an accent."

"No, I grew up in California. My dad had businesses there. We didn't move to Texas until he decided to buy and renovate the Cottonwood track five years ago."

"But you were karting before that, right?"

"Sure, but it was no big deal. That's why this 'legacy' thing is a joke."

"Well, you certainly won't have any problem making it into racing, Jess. I could not even keep up with you at karting practice."

"I was just driving a faster kart. Anyway, who says I want to go into racing?"

"I just thought—you know, with your father doing all this." Chad was confused. "So then, what are you going to do now that you have finished high school?"

"I'm starting at Texas A&M in the fall. I'm thinking of either engineering or business. My dad wants me to help him manage the kart park, but I'm not sure what I want to do yet."

Chad was impressed. Beautiful, fast, well-traveled, smart—he had never met a girl like this before. In their slow stroll, they had come up onto the bridge over the stream between the mansions.

"My friend Gary Lee, he was going to go to Auburn University in the fall," Chad said.

"He *was*? What happened—did he change his mind?"

"He cracked up his car during spring break. He's still in rehab, and it's not clear how well he will be in the fall. They say he's going to be in rehab for a pretty long time."

"Oh, I heard about that. I'm so sorry. His girlfriend was killed, right?"

Chad just nodded. He suddenly felt all choked up, but he didn't want to show it. Jessica put her hand on his arm gently.

"Hey, I'm sure he'll get better. Auburn will still be there for him when he's ready."

"Yeah, but it will never be the same." Chad looked away when he felt his eyes tearing up.

He turned back and looked into Jessica's warm green eyes that seemed iridescent in the glow of the twinkling lights. He was fascinated with all of her unique beauty. Before he knew what happened, Jessica kissed him softly on the lips. Her lips tasted so deliciously sweet, and her scent filled his breath. He felt as though he would lose control. Jessica kissed him again and then pulled away gently. She held his hands and turned to look out over the stream.

"It's so peaceful here," Jessica said.

The jasmine was open, and the lilacs filled the night air with their rich fragrance. Jessica leaned on the stone bridge railing and looked down at the stone garden.

"Look, you can see something written on the stones," Jessica said. She pointed to a big rose-colored stone shimmering in the light from the patio. "P-E-D—Pederson. I wonder who they are for."

"Winning is everything," softly whispered the night.

"What did you say?" asked Jessica.

"I didn't say anything," replied Chad. "I thought you just read 'winning is everything' on a stone."

"That wasn't me," she said, looking around for the source.

A faint, smokey odor floated on the breeze, and Chad recognized it immediately.

"Ugh, I can smell someone smoking a cigar at the party," she complained.

"That's not cigars. That's burning rubber."

A moment of stillness passed. Jessica turned toward Chad and took both of his hands. He leaned in and kissed her again. Suddenly someone passed behind them. Startled, they both turned around and could see a faint silhouette dressed in a white suit. A peculiar man had just crossed the little bridge, walking through the darkness toward the other mansion.

"Winning is everything," they heard him say.

"Oh, that was a fright," Jessica said, putting her hand on her chest. "I thought we were alone out here."

"Me too. I thought you weren't afraid of anything," Chad said.

He pulled her close again to feel the softness of her lips on his. She kissed him back. Everything suddenly felt new and wonderful. Chad breathed in deep the fragrance of jasmine and Jessica. He now knew his future would be brilliant even if all of his plans in karting failed.

CHAPTER 22

The evening was getting on at the White Party, and Monroe Kilgore needed to get his potential investors together. He walked among the guests on the patio and tapped several men on the shoulder.

"We're going to have a short meeting for the racing club investors. Would you join us in the Library of Helmets?" he said to each of them.

Monroe waved at Bruce Larsen, who excused himself from his conversation. B.B. Butkis also was lumbering toward the house.

The Library of Helmets was precisely that—a rich wood-paneled room with bookshelves on three sides filled with over forty years of different helmets and trophies. The room had a comfortable musky smell that Monroe always enjoyed when he walked in. Several other gentlemen followed in behind him, looking at the shelves that brought pride to Monroe. There was a mahogany desk at the end of the room and comfortable chairs all around. It was an unusual contrast to see all the men in their white apparel compared to the dark wood and furniture behind them.

Monroe sat down at the desk and opened a box of cigars, gesturing to the others. He pulled out his half-finished stogie from his pocket and lit it up. Butkis took up the offer of a cigar, but the others seemed entirely unappreciative.

"Please sit, please sit," Monroe started the discussion. "Gentlemen, for those of you who have already joined us financially in the Florida racing club, I want to thank you for embarking with Sonny and me on this adventure of a lifetime. At this point, we are now more than half subscribed with investors, and the site preparation has started. We are on schedule for opening next year!"

Sonny, who had changed into dry clothes, stepped into the room and interrupted Monroe.

"Well, thanks for joining us, Sonny," said Monroe. He opened his desk drawer, pulled out some glossy folders, and handed them to Sonny. "For those of you still considering this investment, here is our latest prospectus," said Monroe.

He motioned to Sonny, who appeared confused about who should receive the folders. Finally, after those who wanted one had received one, they opened the folders and began studying the material. Some people pulled out reading glasses, and everyone became quiet for a moment.

"I know most of you are captains of industry or finance and also are lovers of exotic, fast automobiles," continued Monroe. "This is not only an opportunity to be an investor in the hottest racing industry growth area, but your investment gives you five years of club membership."

"I have some questions about the tax implications," said a younger man sitting on the couch.

"Gavin Carrington is providing the legal services for the project," said Monroe, motioning toward a tall man standing in the corner.

"My office number is at the bottom of the prospectus," said Gavin. "Call me if you have any questions or want to set up an appointment."

A gray-haired man seated in the corner raised his hand. "Big Mo, you had said we were going to have a board of directors and executive management. Now we find out that Sonny is the president and CEO of the club."

"Yes," said the man sitting next to him. "No offense to Sonny, but this is a multimillion-dollar project and should be led by someone with business experience."

"Especially after what we saw tonight," chuckled another. "Sonny can't even manage his relationships! How is he going to handle this project?"

"Look!" shouted Sonny. "I'm forty-five, a team owner, and I've been in the racing business since I was a kid, so don't think I don't know what I'm doing!" Sonny turned away and hit his forehead with his palm. "Oh, no way."

Monroe pulled Sonny by his sleeve and said privately, "What's the matter, Son?"

Sonny explained to Monroe, "I used a double negative. With the Law of Attraction, you're not supposed to use a double negative. It works in reverse."

"Son, you've got to get a grip on yourself!" Monroe said while he squeezed Sonny's arm. "This is business, so drop the superstitious bullshit!"

"Seriously, Big Mo," said the first investor. "If you don't get someone more qualified, I'm going to pull out."

"Now calm down, everyone. Sonny has a solid reputation in the racing world," answered Monroe.

"So make him a VP or chief marketing officer. You've got a lot of talent in this room for running the business. Keith here, he's been CEO of several companies. B.B. has grown his family business to be practically a household brand."

"Thanks," said Butkis. "But I'd rather keep a low profile on this project. I just enjoy the perks of membership."

The room broke into a frenzy of discussion.

"Okay, okay," interrupted Monroe, with his hand up. "We'll find someone with experience in running an operation of this size to be the president and CEO. Sonny will still retain a VP position. Now, can we move on?"

Sonny shot a cross look at his father. Monroe continued with a few more discussion topics about the new club and then asked if any new investors were ready to sign up. Several men indicated their intention and stepped up to Monroe's desk. They each signed a few documents, and one also wrote a check.

"Thank you, gentlemen. You won't be disappointed, I assure you!" said Monroe to each of them with a handshake and a grin.

The other investors had already left the library to return to the festivities. The new sign-ups filed out of the room and left Monroe and Sonny alone. Sonny closed the door.

"What the hell, Mo?" said Sonny. "We own sixty percent of the project! Why are you caving into them on this CEO thing? Who cares if they don't like how I roll?"

"Now, keep your cool, Son. This is a big boat, and there are others in it, too. We need their investments to make it float, so don't start rocking the boat. I'm not actually going to get someone else to be CEO. We can't have anyone else snooping around the finances. That could be a real disaster, and you know what I'm talking about."

CHAPTER 23

Elle Dillanger drove down her street in Blue Springs, realizing it was the last time she would go home this way. She had rented an apartment in Auburn to be close to Gary Lee while he was in rehab. They would live there together after he was discharged. Elle and Drew had recognized that they were past the point of ever reconciling, and they had agreed it was time to sell their primary residence.

Drew had moved out last year, and Elle could no longer see any reason to stay in Blue Springs. Elle believed in her heart that regardless of how long it would take for Gary Lee to recover, this was not the place for his return.

It was a sad moment when she drove past the homes of neighbors she might not ever see again. She and Gary Lee would find another home of belonging. It felt all so bitter now without the sweet love that used to live there. Maybe she stayed in Blue Springs too long and should have moved years ago. Her ten years there would soon come to a close, but the pain and pleasure of those many years would linger on.

Elle could see their house down the street with a large moving truck parked in front of it. There was a big "For Sale" real estate sign in the yard with a "Sold" placard on the top. At least her custom real estate sign had some style, she thought when she pulled into the driveway. She was almost relieved to find Drew's car next to the moving truck.

Today, Elle's mission was to instruct the movers what to pack up for her and Gary Lee's move. Elle was hoping that her soon-to-be-ex-husband would have things started. Gary Lee's bedroom furniture was going with her without dispute. She didn't want a major conflict over the rest of the furniture going to Auburn. The Dillangers' divorce wasn't finalized, so the division of property was not yet written in stone. Elle had been preparing herself for months for some negotiating.

Elle entered through the open front door, and she could hear a lot of activity from the bedrooms upstairs. There were pieces of furniture around the living room and dining room neatly wrapped in quilted moving blankets. In the center of the dining room were her sacred Nakashima dining table and chairs. They were the big purchase that she made after completing her first major design project with their architectural firm, DD&W. Elle worshiped George Nakashima and his natural, modern design. She had already made it clear to Drew that the Japanese table and chairs would be going to Auburn with her and Gary Lee.

"Oh, I'm glad you're here," said Drew, coming out from the hall. "How is Gary Lee today?"

"He's doing better. The doctor thinks he can start more intense physical therapy soon," replied Elle. "So why is the Nakashima furniture not getting packed for my move to Auburn?"

"Elle, you're not being fair. You want to take everything. You're getting all of the living room furniture and the kitchen housewares."

"I carefully and deliberately chose that dining table and chairs with my hard-earned money! It was my first big job."

"I don't know why you say that. We purchased this set of furniture in Pennsylvania together," Drew said.

Elle was getting irritated. "You always do this—say one thing and do another. You had agreed that I would be taking my Nakashima dining table to Auburn. Gary Lee will be there. Don't you want him to sit at his family dining room table? Hasn't he suffered enough?"

"Don't make this about Gary Lee," said Drew. "I'm not going to argue with you. If you can't be reasonable about the Nakashima, then we'll have to sell it and split the proceeds. That's why we have lawyers."

"Okay, I can be reasonable. I'll take my table and the four walnut chairs, and you can hold on to the other four Nakashima chairs for now." She turned and went up the stairs into Gary Lee's bedroom.

Two hefty and unshaven men, one younger and one older, had started packing Gary Lee's things into boxes. The linens were off the bed, and they had emptied all the contents of his bureau—clothes, swimming trunks, racing magazines, and some loose coins.

"You're going to wrap the mattresses in plastic bags, right?" she asked the movers.

"Yes, ma'am," replied the older one.

"Make sure you put the dining room table on the truck. You can leave four of the eight dining chairs behind for Mr. Dillanger."

"Okay. Just the table, but not all eight of the chairs?"

"Four walnut side chairs are staying here," Elle said with angst.

Elle looked around to see what she needed to do. There were racing posters on the walls that needed to be taken down. She pulled out the thumbtacks and very carefully rolled up one poster that a racing driver had autographed. The *Schumacher* signature scribbled in blue ink was probably important. Elle didn't want to see these racing posters on the walls of his new room, but they couldn't stay here.

The doorbell rang, and Elle went down the stairs to see who it was. She and Drew arrived at the front door at the same time.

"Good morning, Mr. and Mrs. Dillanger," said the man showing a badge. "You remember me? Detective Lowry from Auburn on your son's case." He didn't pause for them to answer. "I do have some good news for you."

"Come in," said Elle.

She led them over to the dining room table to sit for a conversation. Lowry sat down, noticing the beautiful wood. He ran his hand gently over the table, smiled, and looked up at Elle.

"I see you're busy, so I won't take long," said Lowry. "We're dropping the charges against your son."

Elle felt a rush of relief. She grabbed Drew's hand.

"It turns out there was another car involved in the accident," Lowry continued. "A small trace of white paint had scraped off onto the side of the front bumper by the driver's door of your son's car. This white topcoat paint is indicative that another car cut him off and clipped the front left side of his car. That's what made him lose control."

"Oh my God, so it wasn't Gary Lee's fault? Who was in the white car?" asked Elle.

"We don't know yet. Our investigation is currently working on the unknown facts of this case. Based on eyewitness reports, we are looking for the driver of a white Lexus with a checkered flag window sticker. Have you ever seen a window sticker like this?" He pulled out a piece of paper with a sketch.

"I've seen that before around Blue Springs, but I don't know whose decal it might be," said Drew.

"I wouldn't go so far as to say your son is not at fault. We are simply no longer pursuing a criminal investigation of him because he was left at the scene of the accident. Hit-and-runs are a felony in this state," the detective explained. "You should know that most civil lawsuits wait for the outcome of criminal proceedings. The District Attorney has concluded that your son and Gillian Mason were victims of a hit-and-run. Still, you should probably be prepared for hearing from the Masons' lawyer."

"Well, I sure hope you catch the person who cut Gary Lee off," said Drew. "We want him charged to the fullest extent of the law."

"In that case, if you hear anything that might help the investigation, give me a call. Here's my card again. I'll also leave a copy of this window sticker sketch with you."

Detective Lowry left the description of the decal and his card on the table. He reached out his hand to Elle for a brief handshake and exited through the front door.

"Wow, what a relief!" said Drew.

"That's a big weight off my mind," said Elle. "I will tell Gary Lee when I get back to Auburn today." Elle wondered if Bernstein had a hand in getting the charges dropped. They may need him in dealing with the Masons' lawyer.

"That changes everything," said Drew.

As Elle studied the window sticker sketch, Drew's comment began to gnaw at the back of her mind. "You have no sense of reality," Elle finally said with irritation. "You think that just because someone else was involved in a vehicular homicide that everything has changed. Sure, it's great that they don't want to charge him with a felony, but it still seems obvious that Gary Lee and this other driver were racing on the highway. You're the one who fed him all that nonsense—the 'thrill of speed' and 'winning is everything.' Did you see the posters on the walls of his room recently?"

"It's perfectly normal for boys to like racing stars," said Drew.

"So it's just another day in Blue Springs, Alabama? Boys will be boys? Gary Lee's in the hospital, Gillian Mason is dead, and we're losing thousands. Is that your idea of normal?"

"I've had enough of this. I'm going back to work," Drew said sternly. "I let the movers in. You can take four Nakashima dining chairs and make sure they leave the other four dining chairs here with the table. The table stays put because that negotiation is *not* over. I'll call Bernstein and see where we stand legally with Gary Lee." Drew walked across the living room. "Oh, and I'm taking this floor lamp!"

He marched out the front door with a nearly perfect reproduction of the famous Tiffany lamp called Dragonfly before Elle could say anything to stop him.

CHAPTER 24

Elle stood next to the moving truck and watched Drew get in his car. He slammed the door shut and started to back out of the driveway. Just at that moment, Kylie Shay pulled into their driveway in her silver Mercedes. Drew stomped on his brakes, and his car lurched to a stop.

"Hi, Drew," said Kylie with a slight wave through her open window, but she didn't get a response from him.

Drew sped back out of the driveway around Kylie's car with his tires screeching. He took off, kicking up a massive cloud of dust from the road. Elle watched her husband of twenty years storm out of the home they once shared, and he disappeared into a veil of Alabama sand and gravel.

"Well, bless your heart, Drew Dillanger. Did a dust bowl just visit the state of Alabama?" Elle heard Kylie say as she closed the door on her Mercedes. "Hey, Elle. I heard you were here today and thought I'd stop by the old homestead. Drew seems madder than an old, wet hen. What's up with him?"

"Everything is fine," said Elle, with tears welling up in her eyes. "Come in, I'm about ready to send the movers off to Auburn, and the realtor is coming over soon. The house finally sold, and I'm moving to Auburn."

Elle didn't want to show her sadness. It was such a profound sense of loss. She suddenly felt the pain and the pleasure of everything that she had loved and labored for over the last twenty years in a moment. Elle wiped her tears and looked away for some privacy.

"Hey, honey." Kylie reached out her hand to Elle. "I'm going to miss you, girlfriend, but Auburn isn't that far." She tried to lighten the mood. "Say, do you want to hear the gossip from the White Party?"

Elle sniffled and reached for the Kleenex tissue on the sideboard. She nodded. Kylie smiled wide and said, "Life gets better, honey. It's tough in the beginning, but after a while, your heart will rise again. Gather your favorite things that are now yours and not his, and you will soon see the benefit of all of your efforts. Don't worry. It will be all right."

Elle smiled. Kylie always seemed to have perfect hair, perfect nails, and the perfect thing to say. The two women walked into the dining room, and Kylie sat down at the dining table.

"I always loved this table," Kylie said, and she glided her hand across the smooth hardwood finish. She picked up the sticker sketch that was sitting on the table. "Oh, what's this?"

"The detective on Gary Lee's case just came by and left that sketch. They are dropping the charges against Gary Lee. They said he was run off the road by someone in a white Lexus with a sticker like that on the rear window. The detective said the driver left Gary Lee and Gillian at the scene of the accident, so now they are investigating a hit-and-run homicide."

"Well, that's good news for a bad set of circumstances. How is Gary Lee doing?"

"He's improved quite a bit. They've moved him into the rehab wing of the hospital, and he's getting around in a wheelchair. But the sticker—have you ever seen this kind of decal, Kylie?"

"You know, it does look familiar. I'm sure I've seen it around. In fact, I recall seeing a sticker like this at the White Party last night. Yes, I was on the front steps talking to someone, and the boys were parking cars. I saw at least one of those stickers on a rear window. You should send your detective over to Big Mo Kilgore's. I'm sure it will give Big Mo something to sweat about."

190

"Yes, I'll give the detective a call right now. Can you excuse me a moment?" said Elle.

She picked up Lowry's business card, pulled out her cell phone, and dialed. She listened to the ringtone and walked into the living room. A man answered.

"Hello, Detective Lowry?" said Elle.

"Yes," he answered.

"This is Elle Dillanger again. I have something for you about that sticker sketch. A friend of mine said she saw one of those decals at Monroe Kilgore's home in Blue Springs at a party last night."

"Thank you. I'll check that out. Who was it that saw the sticker?"

"Kylie Shay. She lives next door to Monroe Kilgore. Kylie Shay is their ex-daughter-in-law."

Lowry thanked Elle and hung up. She hoped something might come of that lead and walked back into the dining room. Kylie was taking a picture of the sticker sketch with her phone. She looked up at Elle after putting her phone back into her vintage straw handbag.

"So?" asked Kylie.

"He said he's going to check it out. Thanks so much. I feel a little better now." Elle pulled up a chair at the table. "So what else happened at your party?"

"Well, I didn't stay that long. I went home early after I threw Sonny into the pool." Kylie laughed. "Sonny is such a moron, and his new girlfriend deserves him. He is such a raunchy old dog." Kylie smiled again.

"I'm surprised that you still live next door to your ex-in-laws," said Elle.

"It's not so bad, except for the house being haunted. I swear, strange things happen there late at night. Anyhow, there are twenty acres, a brook, and a grove of chestnut trees between my house and theirs, so I have my privacy. Even though my marriage was a complete disaster, I still love Sonny's mother, Uma Kilgore. Oh, honey, she had her mansion looking amazing last night. So many white lights and great music. The food was fabulous."

Elle smiled thinking about it. "How is Mackie doing—was he at the party last night?"

"No, he was at some race in Talladega. I'm not sure what happened, but it didn't turn out well. He just came home and went straight to bed. Mackie is now living at home most of the time, even though his father wants to get him an apartment over in Leeds for the racing season."

"I'm surprised that he didn't go to his grandparents' party."

"He's depressed. I'm not sure why, but I blame Sonny for it. That's why I pushed him in the pool. At twenty-five years old, my son can't even get himself his own girlfriend. His father has to get him one from his little black book of 'girlfriends'—the Kilgore help."

"I haven't seen Mackie in such a long time. You said he is still racing professionally?" asked Elle.

"If you can call it that. It's all a big show. Sonny would like to make a celebrity out of him, but he's not really celebrity material. How does signing autographs at the local Piggly Wiggly make somebody a celebrity?"

Kylie rose from the table and looked around. While they were talking, the movers had emptied the bedrooms upstairs and packed it all in the truck.

"I think I've taken up enough of your time. You clearly have a big task ahead of you here," said Kylie.

"Yes, I have to get the movers off to Auburn. They need to pack these four Nakashima chairs."

"You have eight chairs and a table here. Why are you only taking four chairs? Is there not enough room in the truck?"

"No, it's just that Drew wants to negotiate the furniture still. He asked me to leave the four chairs and table for him."

"Oh, that's not how to do it, honey. You put the table and *all* of those chairs on the moving truck. Drew can still negotiate, but instead, you'll have what he wants. I still have some of Sonny Kilgore's prized possessions because he forgot that there is the community property rule."

192

Elle smiled, and Kylie lingered and talked about the black and white checker patterned dinnerware that Sonny obsessed over.

"What is it with our racing friends and family and all their black and white checkered stuff?" Kylie asked.

"Oh, my god. I know! Drew insisted all the time, and I must have thought it cute. We had so many of Gary Lee's birthday parties and school events with checkered party themes." Elle laughed. "I actually have a set of plastic black and white checkered dishes packed away somewhere in one of these boxes."

Kylie laughed so loud. She snorted gently, holding up her hand. "Wait, I never told you this one," Kylie added. "I used to always make black and white checkered cupcakes for Sonny and his team just before a big race. I served them with a glass of milk for protein."

"That sounds nice," said Elle, curious of the humor.

"That's not the best part. After I found out about his first girlfriend in Indiana, I decided to change the recipe. I frosted his special cupcake with a strong chocolate laxative just before the next big race. He pooped in his racing gear, and everyone on the team thought it was from the adrenaline rush."

Elle put her hand over her mouth and started to smile.

"Even better, this routine continued for a few months," continued Kylie. "Cupcakes and crapped firesuits! Sonny would explain that his accidental pooping on the track was like an Apollo astronaut's experience in space." Kylie laughed out loud again. "It was a 'fecal matter'!"

"I can't believe that he never figured it out!" said Elle, laughing and shaking her head. The two women could barely speak, they were laughing so hard.

"Sonny believed that he had a genuine need for special racing underwear just like the NASA astronauts." She became serious for a moment. "Of course, the Kilgores developed their successful brand of racing underwear from that prank." She shook her head. "Little did he know that it was just the beginning of our very long divorce. Oh, well. It is what it is."

Elle forgot about her troubles and thought that was why she always loved Kylie—a friend who watched out for her and always made her laugh when she needed it.

"Thanks so much," said Elle. "You always seem to cheer me up."

"Of course I do. You know I am here for you, honey." Kylie kissed Elle's cheek and walked toward the front door. "Have a safe trip to Auburn. Remember, good hair is the best revenge."

"Thanks for coming over. Drive carefully," said Elle and waved a little goodbye to her friend.

CHAPTER 25

Monroe Kilgore was enjoying his second cup of morning tea at the kitchen table when he heard the doorbell ring. He tied his robe up, made sure that his slippers were firmly on his feet, and walked through the large hallway toward the front foyer. He glanced at the ticking grandfather clock when he passed by—9:30 a.m. It was a beautiful Thursday morning in the middle of the summer. The long, lazy summer weekdays were usually peaceful, and Monroe enjoyed his mornings at home without interruptions.

"Who could this be?" Monroe muttered. The doorbell rang again. Monroe was in a great mood this particular morning, so he didn't mind the interruption. Five more investors had signed up for his racing club project, the mansion had recovered nicely from the White Party, and everything seemed like it was going to be a fantastic summer. Monroe casually inspected the formal dining room and then the living room while he walked toward the foyer. The cleaning crew did an outstanding job, and even his wife Uma hadn't complained. There is no better way to host a party than to have the hired help set up, serve, and clean up when finished.

After arriving in the foyer, Monroe pulled open the front door to find a man in a suit and a sheriff's deputy on the steps. Monroe recognized the officer—Deputy Lamar Millhouse from the local sheriff's office, a longtime family friend. He stood tall in his khaki uniform with reddish hair and a little reddish mustache. The suited man was shorter with a weathered-looking face. Behind them,

Monroe could see the sheriff's cruiser and a large black sedan in the driveway.

"Why, Deputy Lamar, I haven't seen you for a while," said Monroe. He winked at the sheriff and laughed since he had just seen him at the White Party. "What can I help you all with?"

"Hi, Big Mo, this here is Detective Lowry," replied the deputy, motioning toward the shorter man. "He came to the station on an investigation from Auburn. I was asked to help him around town."

"Thank you, Deputy Millhouse," said Lowry and held up his investigator badge for Monroe to see. "Would you have a moment for some questions?"

"Sure, no problem. Come on in, boys," answered Monroe, motioning for them to come into the foyer. He looked up at the white lights that were still dangling over the front entryway.

Monroe put his hands in his robe pockets and put on a serious face.

"I won't be long," Lowry said, and he stepped into the foyer entryway. "I am investigating the vehicular homicide of Gillian Mason. A witness says he saw a decal with checkered flags and possibly a big green 'K' on the rear window of a white sedan that left the scene of the accident near Auburn." Lowry pulled out a sketch of the window sticker. "Have you ever seen a sticker or a decal like this, sir?"

"Well, yes, I have," replied Monroe. "Everyone who is anyone around here has one of those stickers on their car. It is the Kilgore Racing Team checkered flags decal, and we give those out to people who attend our racing school or racing events. I think it looks great. Beautiful black and white checkers with green lettering—the 'K' is for Kilgore. That's me."

"What's all this about?" asked Uma, coming into the foyer from the hallway. "Oh. Hi, Lamar."

"This is my wife, Uma," Monroe said to Lowry.

"Ma'am, I'm Detective Lowry investigating the vehicular homicide of Gillian Mason. We have reason to believe that a white sedan with this window decal forced the car she was in off the road. It's now considered a hit-and-run."

"Oh, my. Well, that changes everything," she replied, looking at the sketch.

"Do either of you know someone who owns a white sedan with this decal?" asked Lowry.

"We know a few people who drive a white Cadillac or a white Mercedes, but I don't recall any of them having one of our stickers," said Uma.

"There's a stack of decals right here, left over from our White Party," said Monroe. He picked up a pile of stickers on the dark walnut entryway table in the foyer, and he offered one to the detective.

"Thank you," said Lowry, and he took two of them. "White Party? What is that?"

"It's a charity fundraising party we put on for the community and our friends every year," replied Monroe. "Too bad you just missed it. There were probably some white sedans sporting our decals at the event. Lamar was there, too. He occasionally provides security services for us when he's off duty."

"Do any of you recall guests who drove white sedans? Specifically, we believe it was a Lexus," said Lowry.

"We're not really involved with the cars or parking," answered Uma. "You should ask our valet service. They might remember."

"Yes, the Wheelboys probably would remember. They are pretty keen on that sort of thing," said Monroe.

"Wheelboys?" asked Lowry.

"The Kilgore Karting Team members—we call them Wheelboys," said Monroe. "I'm surprised you haven't heard of them. They volunteered to help with the valet parking."

"Excellent. Can you give me the names of the boys who were parking that night?" Lowry sounded more satisfied.

"Why sure. Let's see… There was Chad Gibbons, Tom Grasiano, and Bradley Moore," Monroe recollected.

Lowry was busy writing down the names on a small pad. He turned to the deputy and said, "Can you look up their addresses in your cruiser? I'd like to visit these boys today while their memory is still fresh."

"I'd be glad to, but I need to speak with Mr. Kilgore first about another matter," said the deputy. He took Monroe aside and said quietly, "Big Mo, the traffic department is going to put out a warrant for Sonny's arrest because of his unpaid speeding tickets."

"What? That's ridiculous," said Monroe.

"It's true. He has tickets outstanding all over the state! He needs to pay them right away, or there will be a warrant out for him on Monday," explained the deputy.

Uma was listening in and shook her head. "I've given Sonny every one of those summons notifications when they arrived in the mail. I don't know what he's been doing with them," she said.

Lowry suddenly became interested. "Who are you talking about, and how many speeding tickets does this person have?" he asked.

"Oh, Sonny? He's our son—Monroe Kilgore Junior," explained Monroe. "But he doesn't get any more tickets than I do—maybe only one every couple of months, but he's obviously not been taking care of them."

"One ticket every few months?" asked Lowry in surprise. "And you don't think that's a lot? How do you even keep your driver's licenses?"

"Well, we don't get any tickets in Blue Springs, I can assure you of that," answered Monroe, with a wink toward the deputy. "If you're asking about the point system, there are ways to work around that. We're very generous with charities in our community."

"So is this how you teach all of your racing school students how to drive?" probed Lowry.

"Now wait a minute, young man. I don't like what you're implying," Monroe responded crossly. "I am not responsible for any foolish actions that some numbskull driver might perform just because they have one of my stickers on the back of their car."

"Why don't you all come in the kitchen for some apple strudel?" offered Uma.

Monroe glared at her and said, "No time for strudel. I have to get the checkbook and pay Sonny's speeding tickets."

"Don't you think you should let Sonny take care of his own problems?" asked Uma. "How many times are you going to let that boy escape the consequences of his own actions? He is forty-five years old, for heaven's sake, Monroe."

"Excuse me, but I have to get dressed and head out to the station. I need to be back right away for a meeting with our lawyer," said Monroe, looking at the clock. "Uma, if Gavin comes before I'm back, have him wait in the Library of Helmets." Monroe was in a rush and excused himself to get dressed.

Before Lowry could say goodbye and before Monroe could head up the front stairway, Sonny waltzed into the front entryway with his girlfriend, Ruby Mae.

"Well, if it isn't the man of the hour," said Monroe from the stairs. "Sonny, meet me in the library. We have some bones to pick."

All eyes were on Monroe and then on Sonny, who was still laughing about something.

"Mo, you should have seen it at the Babylon track this morning. One of the new kids flipped his kart over," explained Sonny. "His parents called the ambulance to take him to the emergency room."

"Was he injured?" asked Uma.

"Nah—just a little banged up. If you want to be a racecar driver, you have to go fast, and sometimes you get a ride to the ER," Sonny continued. "Right, Mo?"

"You should have stayed with the parents, and you probably will wish you had," Monroe said.

"What? We just donated thousands of dollars to the Blue Springs Hospital," said Sonny. "They will take good care of the boy."

Monroe continued looking at his son with disbelief. He wanted to say "shut up!" but instead, he simply said, "Please listen." Monroe glanced back at the officers who were taking in all of this conversation in the context of the moment. He tried to calm himself.

"Sonny, this is Detective Lowry, and you know Deputy Lamar from the local sheriff's department. Lowry came all the way from Auburn and is investigating the crash of Gillian Mason, the girl who lived in town. He was just leaving."

"Nice to meet you, Sonny," said Lowry. "I have some questions about the Wheelboys on the list your father gave me. How many boys do you employ, exactly?"

"I don't employ any of the boys. They pay me to teach them how to race. I give them opportunities, and they love it," said Sonny.

"That's an interesting arrangement. Maybe you can tell me more about this mentoring system of yours," the detective said.

"It isn't complicated, really. The parents give their kids' permission to race our karts, and we help the kids acquire the skills it takes to become racing drivers. It is character building. We build discipline, sportsmanship, and self-responsibility. We provide all the knowledge and practical experience you need to develop as a racing driver. They all sign waivers, of course, because accidents can happen." Sonny glanced over at his father, who was motioning for him to stop talking.

Sonny continued, "We are racing legends in these parts, and folks around here pay us for sharing our skills. Speed is our business. Winning is everything, and if you don't win, you lose. Who wants to be a loser? Our boys know that you need passing power."

Monroe coughed. To disrupt the conversation, he swept the racing magazines off the foyer table. The magazines dropped to the tiled floor with a thump.

"Sorry," interrupted Monroe. "We're going to have to have this meeting another time. I have a business meeting starting any minute now, so thank you for dropping by, Detective Lowry." Monroe opened the front door. Lowry and the sheriff's deputy walked out.

"See you around town, son," Monroe said to the deputy. "Get after those bad guys and say hello to your family. Sonny is going to take care of those speeding tickets, don't you worry."

Monroe quickly shut the front door, and then he pulled Sonny by the arm and marched him down the hall toward the Library of Helmets. They entered the large, wood-paneled room, which was Monroe's seat of power. He pushed Sonny down into the seat in front of his desk.

"What is the matter, old man?" asked Sonny.

"You need to learn how to keep your mouth shut, Sonny." Monroe sat down at his large mahogany desk and coughed. "Try and remember what Mark Twain said. 'It is better to keep your mouth shut and appear stupid than to open it and remove all doubt.' Now Lamar came by as a courtesy to warn you about the speeding tickets you have not paid. They will have another warrant out for you, and you remember what happened the last time."

"Is that what your knickers are in a knot about, Mo? I can pay those online in two seconds."

"I wish you would stay on top of these things and not make your mother and I worry so much. And it's not just the tickets. It's the way you speak too freely about our business in front of the detective."

Monroe heard voices and footsteps coming down the hall. Gavin Carrington's face appeared in the library doorway. Monroe was glad to see him. He always trusted Gavin as their business lawyer, although he was curious about why Gavin called this meeting.

Monroe rose and greeted Gavin with a handshake. "Nice to see you, Gavin—right on time as always. I'm still in my robe and slippers because my morning was interrupted with speeding tickets and other things."

Gavin looked over at Sonny, who showed his guilt. He laughed and said, "Well, Sonny always has his moments."

"So what did you want to meet about, Gavin?" asked Monroe.

"Yes. Let me get right to that so we can work on a solution."

He opened his briefcase and pulled out a large envelope. Extracting legal papers, he laid them out for Monroe to read.

"It seems that an environmentalist has filed an injunction to stop your building of the Florida race park," explained Gavin. "Frederick Gonzales has prepared an environmental impact study that will make your head spin. He is the single most invested man in private conservation in American history, and he claims that your racing park plans are encroaching on his private wildlife preserve. Mr. Gonzales also has an advocate from Eglin Air Force Base in Florida. General Arnold Fremont has endorsed this petition for injunction."

"He can't be serious," said Sonny.

"Oh, this is very serious," said Gavin. "In fact, it might be best to relocate your plans for the Kilgore racing resort elsewhere, Monroe. Otherwise, the legal costs could outweigh your profits."

Monroe stood up and raised his hands in outrage. "What else could possibly go wrong today?" he shouted.

CHAPTER 26

It was hot as the sulfurous blue blazes of hell when Chad packed his bag to drive from Alabama to Texas. He was heading out to Rodeo-Kart, the big, open karting event of the summer at the Larsens' Cottonwood karting park in Longview. It had been three weeks since Jessica Larsen had convinced him to enter this national competition. This karting race was something he had always dreamed of, and he couldn't wait to get on the road.

Chad thought about being up against professional racers watched by all the big sponsors and media people. Chad had kept his plans confidential to avoid any negativity or discouragement. He didn't want to tell his family, the Kilgore clan, or even Gary Lee. Today he had to tell his family something since he would be gone for several days.

"I'm going over to Longview, Texas for the weekend to watch the Rodeo-Kart," Chad announced at dinner. Chad felt confident with this statement. It was certainly true; he just omitted that he would be driving Bruce Larsen's kart as a contestant.

"Well, that's a sudden decision," said his dad. "Too bad you're not racing in the competition." This statement took Chad by surprise. He thought his father didn't believe Chad should even try to race in Rodeo-Kart.

"That sounds like fun, Shug," said Carole. "When do you leave?"

"Early tomorrow morning," said Chad. "I'm just going to drive straight through."

"Eat breakfast, pack a sack lunch, and leave the house by seven in the morning," his dad said. "You'll be there before dinner. No speeding on the highway."

Chad had helped clear the plates into the sink after dinner. His dad came up to him.

"Here's a hundred dollars for the trip," his dad said, handing him some bills. "Before you leave in the morning, please go down to the shop and put some damn new tires on your truck. Your tires are almost bald, and I have some that will fit the truck. They are waiting for you."

Chad thanked his dad. He almost caved in and told him of his true plans but decided that news would not play out well at this time. Chad could tell his family all about Rodeo-Kart when he returned.

*****

The alarm clock sounded at 6:15 a.m., and Chad jumped out of bed. Maybe it was the old-fashioned buzzer or just his anticipation of the weekend, but he was instantly wide awake like he had one too many Italian espressos. Chad wanted to take his father's advice and put the new tires on his truck, but instead, he had to stop and see Gary Lee in Auburn before heading out to Texas.

Chad was so glad to have heard that the charges had been dropped against Gary Lee. The dread of prosecution that had weighed on all of their minds was now lifted. Gary Lee had sent Chad a text message that the investigation was finished with Chad's smartphone and that he could pick it up this morning. This smartphone was a must-have for the trip. Chad had given it to Gary Lee's lawyer two months ago, and he was frustrated with the one he borrowed from his stepmom. Her simple flip phone could only call, text, and take pictures—no apps, nothing more.

An hour later, Chad pulled into the parking lot in front of the rehab facility adjacent to the Auburn hospital. He couldn't wait to tell Gary Lee about Rodeo-Kart. This secret was now burning inside of him, and it had to come out.

"Gary Lee," Chad said when he walked through the open door of his friend's room.

Chad was surprised to find that Annie, Chad's high school girlfriend, was already visiting when he arrived. Chad had not had any communication with Annie since she had left on her family vacation a month ago. He didn't know how to negotiate their breakup, and he dreaded this conversation. Annie took one look at Chad and stormed out of the room.

"What's with you two?" asked Gary Lee.

Gary Lee was sitting up in his bed and now had a nice, new power wheelchair by his bedside. He would be able to use the high-tech machine to get around soon. His speech was still slightly slurred, and he seemed to struggle a little with words and pronunciation.

"Annie says you've been ignoring her," Gary Lee said. "You won't return her calls or texts."

"Annie must be calling my other phone number, and that's the phone your fantastic attorney took for his investigation. That's one of the reasons I'm here—to get it back."

"You do know her number, right? But still no calls?" Gary Lee was on to him.

"You won't believe what's happening." Chad could no longer contain himself. "I'm going to race in Rodeo-Kart this weekend!"

"No way!" bellowed Gary Lee. "First prize is like ten grand. That is awesome!" Gary Lee was slapping his good arm on the bed. "Where is it, and how did this happen?"

"It's at the Cottonwood Karting Park in Longview, Texas. This girl I met at the Kilgores' party, her dad owns the place. She talked me into entering. I'm headed straight to Texas from here. I wanted to get my phone back for navigation. I've been using Carole's not-so-smart phone for too long."

Chad pulled out the old flip phone from his pocket, and it immediately started to chirp. Chad looked at the screen.

R u coming? I c u r on the roster. Your kart is ready, the message said.

"Seems to be working for you," said Gary Lee.

"That was Jessica Larsen. She's wondering when I am going to arrive."

"Who's that?" asked Gary Lee.

"Yeah. Who is Jessica Larsen?" a voice shouted from the doorway. Chad turned to see Annie standing there, indignant.

"I came back so you could apologize, and now I find out what you've really been up to!" she said. "Obviously, you're not man enough to tell me that you want to break up, so let me save you the trouble."

Annie went for a dramatic ending, calling him every F-word she could put together in short sentences. She ripped the gold necklace that he had given her for Christmas off her neck and threw it in his face. Chad knew that Annie would be jealous, but he did not expect an all-out F-bomb fest.

Fortunately, Gary Lee's lawyer interrupted the breakup drama when he entered the rehab room. Annie turned and left, leaving Chad standing there in complete embarrassment. He could feel that his face was flushed. Chad sat down in Gary Lee's power wheelchair and settled himself while the lawyer pulled up a seat.

"What just left? A hurricane or a tornado?" asked the lawyer, laughing. "She's too good for you, right? Glad I only caught you at the end of that storm. I'm Mr. Bernstein, if you don't recall," he said to Chad. "The Dillangers' lawyer."

He opened his briefcase and pulled out Chad's smartphone. "I think this is what you came to pick up. It's good news—all is clear. Here, Mr. Gibbons, you can have this back now." He handed the phone over to Chad.

"Thanks," said Chad. "I was having some serious FOMO."

"FOMO?" asked Bernstein.

"Fear of missing out," explained Gary Lee.

Chad tried to turn it on, but the battery was dead. He would have to charge it in the car so he could use it for navigating to Longview.

"Sorry to interrupt," said Chad. "Do you have a charger here, Gary Lee?"

"Sure. It's on that dresser behind you."

"I am also returning your phone, young man," said Bernstein to Gary Lee. He pulled another phone out of his briefcase and handed it over. "As I discussed with your parents, the detective has dropped the criminal case against you, and both your phones were helpful in that."

"I had heard that, too. Great news," said Chad.

"Well, we're not out of the woods yet. There was a payment to the Masons from the insurance company, but the Masons might still come back with a civil lawsuit. It depends on what details emerge from the case, now that they know a second car was involved. The detective says they have a couple of suspects now and are close to catching who was driving the other car."

Chad turned to Gary Lee with a questioning look. Gary Lee shrugged and said, "I barely remember watching the race at Leeds that day. I am totally blank."

"That's all for today, kids." Bernstein closed the clasps on his bag and stood up. "If I hear anything more about the case, I'll contact your parents."

Bernstein sauntered out the door, and Chad noticed that his smartphone was now powered up. He could now see there were dozens of missed messages and calls, mostly from Annie.

"Hey man, I've got to run," Chad said to Gary Lee, realizing how late it was getting.

He texted Jessica back on his flip phone. *I'm leaving now, should b there by dinner.*

*****

Chad was finally driving on highway I-20 to Texas, and tomorrow he would be on the track. Chad's guilty feelings about Annie and his dad had passed, surprisingly. The excitement and anticipation of seeing Jessica again filled his mind. He smiled.

Chad turned his concentration back to the interstate and his driving since he was coming up on some congestion behind a tractor-trailer. He started to pass the huge eighteen-wheeler when a small explosion erupted from the trailer's rear tire. Large rubber chunks came careening into the lane in front of him. Instinctively, he swerved left onto the shoulder. In the rearview mirror, he saw the other tire parts behind him. Just a typical trucking incident—a retread ripped off an old tire. The rig driver stopped to check out his tires.

Chad thought about the disaster he had just avoided—he could have ended up in the hospital like Gary Lee! Chad was able to pull ahead of the traffic, and now he wished he had taken his father's advice and put new tires on his truck. He didn't want his little, worn tires to blow out in the heat of the summer highway. He continued driving more carefully, and he frequently noticed big rig tires that had shed their skins along the interstate. These bits of retreaded rubber looked like little black alligators sunning themselves in the heat of the day.

Hours passed, and Chad had crossed Mississippi and Louisiana and into Texas. The blue skies of Alabama had followed Chad along with the blue, red, and white flashing beacon lights of the Texas State Troopers.

Chad pulled his truck over to the shoulder, and before he knew it, a Texas trooper was at his driver's window asking for his driver's license and registration.

"Son, do you know why I pulled you over?" the trooper asked.

"No, sir," said Chad. He cleared his throat and rummaged through his glove box for his registration. He thought he might pee in his pants when he handed the officer his driver's license and registration.

"You failed to slow down when you passed the emergency vehicle back there. Didn't you see the truck and the cruiser with lights on pulled over on the shoulder? Where are you going in such a hurry?" The trooper grinned and bellowed out loud.

Another trooper came out of the cruiser and walked toward Chad's truck on the passenger side. The other officer was much bigger than his partner, and he had a baton and a gun in his holster. He leaned in on the open passenger window. The large star on his badge glimmered from the lights on the cruiser flashing behind them.

"This young man has outstanding speeding tickets in Alabama," said the second trooper. "We don't stand for reckless endangerment in Texas. In this state, you are required to move over for stopped emergency vehicles and slow down twenty miles per hour below the speed limit. I don't care where you are from; that's the law whether you know if or not."

The first trooper glared at Chad and said, "I suppose the entitled kids in Blue Springs, Alabama always expect a 'get out of jail free card' when they are caught speeding down the highway. Well, this is Texas, son, and we don't play games here." He finished writing up a ticket and handed it to Chad. "You can send this in by mail or pay online. Check the appropriate plea on the reverse side of your citation and send it to the Municipal Court with payment."

"Or you can show up in court and argue your case," said the trooper in the passenger window. "You need to slow down and pay attention when we are doing our patrol business on the highway."

The trooper at the driver's side handed Chad back his license and registration. "Where do you think you are anyway?" he asked. "You were driving like a madman. Don't they have safety laws in Alabama too?" The officer had his hefty hand on the front window post and spoke directly to Chad.

Chad could feel his face getting flushed and turning red. He could smell his own sweat, and the truck suddenly reeked like an old-fashioned soup kitchen. Chad had another urge to pee, but he focused on the trooper and smiled politely. "Sorry, sir, I am not usually so preoccupied when driving on the highway," Chad replied. "It won't happen again."

The highway patrol finished admonishing Chad about reckless endangerment and drove off quickly with their lights still flashing. It seemed like this incident with the Texas troopers lasted an eternity. He looked at the ticket—two hundred dollars! Chad hoped he could pay this ticket without his father knowing. He threw it in the glove compartment along with the old ticket from earlier that summer.

Chad gathered his thoughts and pulled out a clean T-shirt from his duffel bag that sat in the passenger's seat. After a quick shirt change, he stashed his sweaty one deep behind the seat in his truck. He was so glad that he could change and put the whole incident behind him. He didn't know about the Texas law to slow down. How was he to know he had broken the law? He was also glad that Jessica would not know that the incident had made him sweat like a whore in church.

Chad pulled out back on the highway and settled back into driving. He was happy to have his phone with all the apps and his music back in his truck. It was plugged into the radio, playing his favorite playlists. Finally, after the long and distressing day of driving on the highway, his phone announced that he should exit. Chad was relieved when he saw the sign that said *Longview*. Yes!

CHAPTER 27

The nine-hour drive from Alabama had taken its toll on Chad's body. He felt stiff in his back and legs, and the Thursday afternoon had dragged on in the summer heat. Chad navigated off the highway to the Cottonwood Karting Park in Longview, Texas. When he pulled into the parking lot, he saw the motorhomes and custom trailers of the high-end karters. Chad was relieved that he hadn't brought his old kart with him. Even if the loaner kart from Bruce Larsen turned out to be no better than his, at least he wouldn't have the embarrassment of unloading it in front of the professionals and the karting elite.

Chad parked his truck, stepped out onto the blacktop, and bent over to stretch his legs. He grabbed his duffle bag and walked through the front entryway under the Rodeo-Kart banner. The familiar sights and sounds of the karting track helped him to relax. He could feel the rhythm of racing start to flow again. He had been to many karting tracks around the South, and the Cottonwood track was one of the best he had seen. To the left of the central walkway was the karting center. Through the smoked glass, he could see racks of clothing and equipment for enthusiasts and fans. On the right side was the karting paddock, where he could see some contenders getting their karts ready for practice tomorrow. The karts were always what captivated Chad's attention. His eyes were drawn to the machines, and he loved the anticipation of driving again.

Chad continued walking toward the track. Straight ahead in the distance, he could see the enormous "Stars of Karting" banner hanging next to the American flag in the outfield. He came up to the railing trackside and looked up and down the main straightaway. To the left were the stands rising up in the evening sun, dotted with a handful of people. Beyond the stands, he could see Turn 1 at the end of the straightaway. Looking back to the right was the pit entrance onto the track.

He stood there leaning on the railing when two karts came whizzing around the back corner and down the straightaway. Chad laughed and thought about how even the oldest adults looked like children when they drove the karts around the track. He knew he would have plenty of time tomorrow to practice before the racing on Saturday, but he was anxious to check out the kart he would be driving.

An uneasiness had started to grow from within him in the last few hours of the road trip, and he couldn't seem to shake it. His pace wasn't where he needed it to be for racing, but he knew that a little more chaos at the karting park would help him find his order for race day.

Chad pulled out his cell phone and sent a message to Jessica: *hey i m here. where r u?*

Waiting for a reply, Chad continued to watch the karts zipping across the straightaway in front of the stands. Suddenly, someone grabbed him from behind.

"Hey you!" shouted Jessica, and she swung around in front of him. "I'm so glad you're here." Jessica gave him a big kiss, square on the lips.

"I can't believe it. It's incredible to be here," said Chad.

Jessica looked better than Chad remembered. She was wearing cutoff jean shorts, a Cottonwood Karting T-shirt, and a red and white checkered blouse, open and tied at the bottom. Chad saw there were a couple of other guys following Jessica in her entourage.

"Oh, this is Rick and Caleb," she introduced her friends. "They're always karting at the park." Chad greeted the other guys and quickly understood that others were competing for Jessica's attention. "Are you here alone? I thought your dad was going to crew for you?"

"Yeah. It's just me. I felt like I needed to do this on my own."

"Cool. Let's go."

Jessica dismissed the two other guys, and Chad felt a little better about his prospects with her. She took him by the hand, and they headed back up the walkway. She led him inside, still holding his hand. Chad dropped his bag by the Karting Center door. A cluster of ten or more people stood in the middle of the showroom, and Jessica plowed through them with confidence until she reached a sturdy man with black hair.

"Daddy, this is Chad Gibbons. He's the one who will be driving the Cottonwood kart this weekend," she said.

"Ah, so you're the young man I've heard so much about from Jessica," said Mr. Larsen while he shook Chad's hand.

"Nice to meet you, sir. I'm not really that much of a karting star," Chad replied, trying to be modest.

"Oh, for sure! Jessica said she left you in the dust on the track." He laughed.

"Well, I hope to show some potential in the karting competition tomorrow."

Jessica gave a big hug to another man standing next to Mr. Larsen. "This is Uncle Chuck," said Jessica. "My dad's brother. He and his family always come out for the big karting events." Jessica's uncle was taller and more burley than her father, and his handshake was like a vice. Chad greeted a few more people in the group, now feeling a little more comfortable. "Come on. My cousin Jayden has been working on the Cottonwood kart. Let me show you the pit."

"Nice meeting y'all," Chad was able to say before Jessica pulled him away by the hand.

Chad grabbed his duffle bag on the way out of the building. She led him across the main walkway toward the karting paddock. The kart paddock was filled with rows and rows of work pits under an enormous tent. Half of the stalls were still empty since many of the racers would be arriving tomorrow. Chad gawked at the phenomenal, high-end karts in each occupied pit while they walked by. The karts were up on waist-high dollies, covered with vivid, colorful decals and trim. The tool chests on rollers and the bench-mounted equipment were more than he had ever seen at an event.

Everyone in each pit stopped what they were doing and turned to watch the two of them pass by. Their stares made Chad uncomfortable, and that anxious feeling had now returned to him. Chad looked at Jessica. She acknowledged everyone with a smile as they passed by. Jessica radiated a sense of happiness that Chad could only vaguely recall from before the spring tragedy. Suddenly, he missed his familiar friends in Blue Springs.

They stopped in front of a pit stall where one short man was furiously working on his karting machine. Jessica stood pointing at a beautiful machine with purple and yellow airbrushed body panels, sitting up on its dolly. Chad realized almost in disbelief that this kart was for him.

"Hey, Jayden," said Jessica. The young man in his twenties straightened up quickly and spun around toward them. He had jet-black hair and was grinning widely.

"This is Chad," she said. "He'll be driving the Cottonwood this weekend."

"Awesome," said Jayden, reaching out and shaking Chad's hand. "You're from Alabama?"

Chad nodded. "Blue Springs."

"I had this out on the track earlier today," said Jayden. "It seems to run pretty well, but I'm not much of a kart racer. There's some daylight left. Do you want to take it out now?"

Chad made a face. "I'm a little worn out from the drive here," he said. He wanted to be at his best when he took his first lap in the Larsens' kart.

"Say, Jayden. Chad doesn't have a crew for the weekend. Would you be able to crew for him?" Jessica asked.

"Sure, but I thought you needed me working on your crew," Jayden replied.

"Don't worry about me. I have never had a problem finding people to work on my crew." She smiled at Chad. "There's always three or four guys who offer, and my dad usually likes to be the crew chief."

214

"All right then. It's you and me against the pros," Jayden said to Chad and gave him a fist bump.

"Thanks. I really appreciate everything," said Chad. He immediately liked his new teammate; Jayden had sort of a California skateboarder vibe about him.

"Are you hungry?" Jessica asked.

"No, not really," replied Chad. He still had a knot in his stomach.

"Why don't I show you your luxury accommodations," said Jessica, looking at his large duffle bag.

"Oh, are you putting him up in the 'Palace'?" asked Jayden. "Don't worry, man. I've stayed there before."

Chad turned to Jessica, wondering about the arrangements she had planned for him.

"Let's go. It's not that bad. I'll show you," she said.

The two continued walking through the paddock, away from the main entrance toward the backside of the park. They walked past the parking area for trailers and motorhomes, where the early arrivals had already set up camp. Several motorhomes had their awnings extended out, and people were sitting in camp chairs, offering a polite wave as they passed by. One family had an evening barbecue grill started, which smelled very appetizing. The roasted hot dogs and burgers reminded him of good times with friends and family, and he began to relax.

They came to a small, single-wide trailer at the far end of the camping area. A set of wooden steps led up to the door, and just to the right of the door hung a sign that read *The Palace*.

"Ta-da," said Jessica with a smile when they arrived.

She pulled out a key, unlocked the door, and went inside. Chad followed her in and looked around. It was actually quite nice— roomier than a motorhome or a hotel room. He threw his duffle bag down by the couch and dropped himself into the big cushions. It felt like *his* place—at least for the weekend.

"There's beer and soda in the fridge. Do you want a beer?"

"No thanks," replied Chad. "A Coke would be great."

Jessica pulled out a cold can and walked over to the couch where Chad had sat down exhausted. She handed it to him; he popped it open and took a long sip. So refreshing.

"Turn that way," said Jessica. She sat down next to him and turned his shoulders so that his back faced her. With her hands grasping his shoulders, she pressed her thumbs into his back and pushed them in a circular motion. Chad suddenly felt both pain and ecstasy in his back muscles, and the tension of the day seemed to melt away. It was an experience he never had before. It filled him with unexpected emotion, and he felt tears welling up in his eyes.

The tragedy of the summer had left him in shock and disbelief, but now something new came over him—a wave of grief. The unmerited kindness of Jessica and her family toward him had triggered a flood of emotion for the loss of his friend Gillian Mason. Chad was fatigued, but why couldn't he stop thinking about his friend Gary Lee? He had watched his best friend suffer in the hospital, and Gillian died before he could even say a good word about her life. Jessica continued to work down the center of his back, and he couldn't hold it in any longer. He started to sob.

"Hey. What's wrong?" she said, turning him toward her.

"I'm sorry," he said between sobbing breaths. "I don't know."

Jessica put her arms around him and pulled him in close. Her firm grip gave him a sense of relief, and he breathed deeply. He felt her soft cheek against his, and he put his arms around her as well.

"Such terrible things happened this year. I guess it's all catching up to me," he said, still holding her tightly. The more he thought about his friends in Blue Springs, the more he couldn't stop the tears from flowing.

Jessica pulled back to look at him. "You probably haven't been able to mourn over all this loss until now. These things take time, you know."

"You're right. I didn't even think about that. I've been trying to be strong for Gary Lee."

Jessica got up, brought over a box of tissues for Chad, and sat back down next to him. "Here."

He took a deep breath and composed himself. "I'm sorry. I'm not usually such a crybaby."

"No, don't worry about it." She took his hands in hers. "Being a tough guy is a myth. We're all people with real feelings."

Chad took another sip of soda and started to clear his head. "I imagined life after high school would be so different than this. I was going to go into auto racing, and Gary Lee was going to be my manager or something like that. Now look at me. I'm just here trying to do this on my own—no sponsors, no family, no friends. Except for you."

Jessica leaned in and kissed him. It wasn't just a "fun" kiss like she did at the party three weeks ago. There was passion in her lips, and she put her hands on his face. He kissed her back with all his heart for all her beauty, kindness, strength, and brilliance. He held her in his arms, and it felt like energy flowing through him. He kissed her in a way he never had before.

Suddenly, there was a knock at the door of the trailer. "All right, you two lovebirds," a voice called from outside. "I know what you're doing in there!"

"Shut up, Jayden!" Jessica yelled back at him. She was now a little bit embarrassed and agitated to be interrupted.

"Your dad sent me to get you," said Jayden. "We're all going out for dinner, so let's get a move on."

CHAPTER 28

The walls of Louie's Smokehouse restaurant were wood-paneled and covered with various Texas photos, old and new. Old black-and-whites and modern colored pictures captivated the eyes. Chad stood with Jessica behind her family in the entrance and took it all in. The air was filled with the smoky, rich flavor that Chad anticipated from a barbecue place. There was quite a crowd waiting, so he knew it must be a top-notch place to eat.

"Look," said Jessica, pointing to a picture hanging in the entrance. "That's us at Cottonwood at our grand opening."

Chad smiled and looked closer at the faded photo. He could see Jessica standing next to Mr. Larsen and several others underneath the large Cottonwood sign. She looked about thirteen in the picture, and she wore her hair with bangs in front.

Mr. Larsen led their party past all the people waiting and spoke to the hostess. She immediately brought them all to a large, round table. Chad wasn't sure if Mr. Larsen had made a reservation or if he had an inside connection at the restaurant. There were six seated around the table—Mr. Larsen, Jessica, Uncle Chuck, Aunt Liddy, Jayden, and Chad.

"Sure smells good. Do y'all come here often?" Chad asked, and he picked up his menu.

Mr. Larsen just smiled a sly smile and looked at Jessica.

"I think it's really Uncle Chuck's favorite place," said Jessica. "We always come here when they come to visit."

"They're telling you a Texas tall tale, son," said Uncle Chuck. "I think Bruce is too modest to tell you that we are all part owners of Louie's."

"We're just silent partners, but it has its benefits," said Mr. Larsen.

A waitress came over to the table and introduced herself. She took everyone's drink and appetizer orders. She returned quickly with beers for the parents and Jayden. Jessica had ice water, and Chad ordered a Coke. A plate of fried veggies was served with white dipping sauce.

"Alabama white barbecue sauce and fried okra," said Chuck, "in honor of our Alabama guest."

Chad was surprised how good it was—better than he ever had in Alabama. "Wow. This is great!" said Chad.

"You should try the beef brisket," said Mr. Larsen, nodding.

The waitress returned and took everyone's order around the table. Chad felt better after having some of the appetizers and a sip of Coke.

"Uncle Chuck and Jayden are Texas wildcatters," Jessica said to Chad. "Their family has oil wells down by San Antonio."

"Really!" Chad replied.

"Jessica makes it sound so sensational," answered Chuck with a laugh. "Sure, we do some drilling, but most of my wells I've bought from wildcatters."

"Jayden's starting a new drilling project this month," added Aunt Liddy. She smiled proudly at her son and spoke with a gentle voice.

"How does that work?" asked Chad. "Do you just go out into open land and start drilling?"

"It's a little bit like that. You first start with a geologist," explained Jayden. "You're hunting for where you think untapped oil pockets might be. Then you find a place reasonably close above the pocket where you can drill."

"There's a lot of paperwork involved, too," added Uncle Chuck. "Permits, regulations, drilling rights, and such."

"It sure sounds pretty impressive," said Chad.

"You can come and check it out when we start drilling in a couple of weeks, if you want," offered Jayden. "See how it's done. We like to throw a little groundbreaking party."

"That would be awesome," said Chad.

"Can I come too?" asked Jessica.

"You know, darlin', you're always invited," answered Aunt Liddy.

As they were speaking, the waitress came over with a large tray of steaming hot plates. The conversation paused, and everyone anticipated each dish as it was served. Chad could hardly wait to dig into his beef brisket. The sauces were passed around, and a silence fell over the table while they feasted on the Texas delicacies.

"Tell me, darlin', when do you start at Texas A&M?" asked Aunt Liddy to Jessica.

"Classes start August 28, and the last day to add a course is a week later," she said.

"What are you taking?" continued Aunt Liddy.

"Oh, pretty basic courses. Humanities, sciences—I don't have a major yet. At least I passed my Algebra AP."

"So you're going to be an Aggie!" said Uncle Chuck. He turned to his brother. "Oh, the irony! Are you going to be rooting for the Aggies this year, Bruce?"

"I think I'm going to have to," answered Mr. Larsen. "But there will always be a special place in my heart for UCLA."

"His alma mater," Uncle Chuck explained to Chad. "So how about yourself, Chad? Are you for the Crimson Tide or Auburn Tigers?"

Chad realized now that they were talking about college football. Alabama versus Auburn was a perpetual rivalry back home that divided the state into two sides. Chad didn't follow much football, but his dad always made him watch that game and insisted he pull for Auburn.

"We're an Auburn house back home," Chad answered.

"Are you going to become an Aggies fan, too?" asked Mr. Larsen.

Jessica smiled toward Chad and started batting her eyes at him as if to signal what the correct answer would be.

"I can't imagine missing any of their games," said Chad.

"In person," Jessica added, grabbing his arm. "At least any games in Alabama—with me, of course."

The waitress came and cleared the plates of rib bones and unfinished sides. Chad had eaten his fill and then some. He opened the little moist towelette package and wiped off his hands.

"How about you, Chad?" asked Aunt Liddy. "Any brothers or sisters? You also just graduated like Jessica, yes?"

"I have a younger brother, Grant. He's just starting high school," said Chad. "My stepmom calls him Swannee. She's really nice."

"Oh, that sounds sweet," said Aunt Liddy.

"Carole is really great. She calls me Shug," he said with a grin.

"Can we all call you Shug, too?" Jessica teased him.

"No. Only Carole can," he said emphatically. "She's brought a lot of happiness to our family. My mom died of cancer when I was thirteen. That's when my dad and I became competitive with karting. I think he needed a distraction, or maybe he just did it for Grant and me. It all worked out, though."

Chad took a deep breath. It was always a little awkward to talk about his mom, but he knew that the next conversation was going to be worse. He might as well get it over.

"Yes, I did graduate," said Chad, "but it was not a happy graduation. My best friends were in a car crash, and one of them died. The other is in rehab, and he still can't walk."

"Oh, that's terrible," said Aunt Liddy.

"We had heard about that when we were visiting Alabama," said Mr. Larsen. "I'm sorry about your friends."

"What happened?" asked Jayden.

"Well, we're not entirely sure," answered Chad. "Gary Lee can't remember anything from that afternoon, and the cops haven't found the other driver yet."

"So there were two cars involved?" asked Mr. Larsen. "I hadn't heard that."

"Yes. At first, they were trying to prosecute Gary Lee because they thought he was the only car involved," explained Chad. "That was pretty crazy. Some witnesses said there was another white car with a checkered flag sticker on the window."

"You mean like the Kilgores' sticker?" asked Mr. Larsen.

"Exactly like the Kilgores' sticker. Then the cops figured out that there was white paint scraped off onto Gary Lee's fender. So they dropped the charges and started looking for the other car and driver."

"Quite a story," said Jessica, reaching for Chad's hand.

"You still have to meet Gary Lee," Chad said to Jessica. "We've been best friends since we were eight. Next time you're in Alabama."

The waitress came by again, and some pie was ordered for dessert. Chad was looking for a chance to change the subject.

"Mr. Larsen," said Chad. "Jessica told me you had raced in Le Mans. What was that like?"

"Well, that was amazing, but it was really both the start and end of my racing career," he answered.

"Your glorious racing career," Uncle Chuck added.

"It was a very educating experience for sure," said Mr. Larsen. "The best thing about it was meeting Jessica's mother."

"Oh, Collette!" said Uncle Chuck. "The best thing to ever happen to you. Well, maybe the second best—after this little jasmine flower came along," Chuck added, turning to Jessica.

Mr. Larsen sat there speechless for a moment, looking down at his apple pie with a blank expression. Maybe this was his difficult conversation to share.

"Tell us how you met again, Daddy," said Jessica. "I love this story."

Mr. Larsen took a deep breath and then smiled at Jessica. "I was just a college kid at the time at UCLA, thinking that I wanted to become a racecar driver. I had this old Dodge that I had been racing around at the dirt tracks in L.A. with friends. What really hooked me was the Trans Am road racing. I had met Tommy Kendall, who was hugely successful in Trans Am while he was also attending UCLA.

He gave me a chance to work on his pit crew at Laguna Seca one summer, and I was hooked. He had me test driving, too."

Chad was glued to the conversation and completely forgot about his pie.

"I think it was the road courses that I loved," continued Mr. Larsen. "A team driver had dropped out of the 24 Hours of Sebring race, and Tommy recommended me for the pinch-hit spot on that team. It was awesome. The GT cars looked like spaceships."

"Enough racing stuff. Get to the part about Mom," said Jessica.

"Well, Chad doesn't seem to mind," said Mr. Larsen. He continued, "I did so well at Sebring that they offered me a spot on the Le Mans 24-hour team. The Corvettes and other Chevy cars had started racing there in the '90s, so they wanted to get more American drivers. I had never been to Europe before, so I was very excited. We flew into Paris—just so much to take in."

"I had to go with him to keep him out of trouble," added Uncle Chuck. "I wasn't going to let him have all the fun. He even bought some cassette tapes and a book to teach himself some French."

"So we were in Le Mans—practicing, racing, working on engines and suspension. It was a dream," said Mr. Larsen. "I would go in the mornings to a little café in town, and that is where I met her. Collette Picard—the most intriguing woman ever."

"I can confirm that. He never missed a breakfast there," added Uncle Chuck. "You didn't mention that she was also a fashion model."

"She worked at the café and was a student at Le Mans University studying journalism. Yes, modeling was her side gig, too. Her English was better than my French, but I learned it fast. We talked about everything. I never met anyone who thought like her, enlightened and still traditional. She came and watched me race, and I brought her to the team dinners. I never wanted it to end."

"It didn't end for you," said Chuck. "I could not get you to come back to the States when the race was over. Our father had a fit since Bruce had only a few more classes to graduate."

"College could wait at that time," explained Mr. Larsen. "I had met the person I wanted to be with. In fact, racing didn't even matter much at that point. So I stayed and got a job in Le Mans, France."

"You left out too many things," complained Jessica. "Tell us about the picnic and the vineyard."

"Another time, Jess," he replied. "I think Chad is more interested in the racing—am I right?"

"Did you race after Le Mans?" asked Chad.

"I had an offer to come back and race in a GT endurance series that summer, but I chose to stay with Collette. She finished up her degree in the fall and told me that I had to finish mine, but I refused to leave France without her. To my surprise, she agreed. We moved back to California and UCLA. Collette was a huge hit in L.A."

"That is an understatement," Chuck added.

"She fit right in with all the beautiful people in California. She immediately found work and success. I later graduated with a business degree, and with her Los Angeles connections, she landed me a fantastic job in the entertainment finance business. The next thing we knew, she was pregnant." Mr. Larsen turned and smiled at Jessica.

"Another great day for our family," said Uncle Chuck.

"So no racing?" said Chad.

"I still liked racing for sure, but love, education, business, and then family—those all seemed so much more important," answered Mr. Larsen. "Collette and I went back to Le Mans several times to watch the race and visit her family."

"Now comes the sad part," said Uncle Chuck. "Collette just wasn't the stay-at-home mom type. Truth be told, she wasn't the stay-in-America type. She was offered an amazing job in Paris."

"You know you could have gone with her," added Aunt Liddy.

Mr. Larsen just shook his head. "It just didn't work out like that. Collette was always out of my league, and I had put down roots in California. Jessica was in school and soccer, and she had her best friends there. Collette and I had never married, so we agreed to go our own ways." He looked down and fell silent again.

"It's okay, Daddy," said Jessica. "I visit Mom every year, and I love my life. You know I'm thankful for all that you've done and provided for me. I have the best life."

"He's not sad for you, darlin'," said Liddy. "I think it's his own heart that's still broken. Some things just don't have closure."

"Well, we have a big day tomorrow," said Uncle Chuck, changing the subject. "Where's that waitress with the check?"

Chuck flagged down the waitress and took care of the bill. Chad thanked him and everyone for a great dinner and all the great stories. The group headed back to their cars and the Cottonwood park to drop Chad off. Mr. Larsen pulled up his car on the back side of the park by all the motorhomes and campers. Jessica and Chad got out of the car, and she fiddled with a small keyring.

"This one is for the back gate over there," Jessica said. "And this one is for the Palace." She handed them to him, then looked up into his eyes and put her arms around his neck.

Chad put his arms around her back and pulled her close. They stood there for a moment staring into each other's eyes in the dim light of the camping area. Chad felt Jessica's deep breathing in his arms. He put his lips on hers, and she closed her eyes. Chad felt like he was melting into her while they kissed. Eventually, they were interrupted by Mr. Larsen knocking on the glass of the car window. Jessica stopped and looked up at Chad.

"I'm so glad you're here. I would stay, but I can't right now. I really missed you since I left Alabama," she said softly.

Chad was shaken by her reveal and his own emotions. He didn't expect this at all. "Me too," was all he could say.

"I'll meet you here in the morning," she said.

She gave him one shorter kiss and then climbed into the front seat of the car. Chad waved to Mr. Larsen and said good night. He strolled toward the trailer, still savoring the taste of her kiss on his lips.

CHAPTER 29

Uma stood outside on her kitchen patio with a cup of tea in hand while the dawn broke on Friday morning. She took a sip and breathed in the hot, fragrant steam from her cup. In the distance, there was a faint murmur of water from the stream under the stone bridge. The birds had started stirring with the morning light, and the songs of mockingbirds called out from the willows on the other side of the bridge. Uma could see the other mansion, Kylie Shea's house, beyond the bridge, still asleep with darkened windows.

Uma walked over to the bridge to look at the memorial stones by the stream. Her thoughts were interrupted when she noticed a light had come on in an upstairs window of Kylie's house. Uma knew she would have to get busy in the kitchen now. People were coming over, and it would be an early breakfast.

Uma started the griddle and laid bacon strips out to sizzle. Monroe strolled into the kitchen and gave her a little kiss on the cheek.

"Good morning, sweetie," he said.

Uma smiled at him, then he turned and sat down at the large wooden table in the kitchen nook. The morning paper was lying on the table waiting for him. Uma brought over a cup of tea, and Monroe took a sip.

"Ah! Thank you," said Monroe. He picked up the newspaper and started reading the front page.

Sonny came thumping down the stairs and lumbered down the hall to the kitchen nook wearing a robe and pajamas.

"Why are we getting up so early today?" Sonny asked. "It's not even eight o'clock, and you're already dressed."

"I told you yesterday," said Monroe. "Tom Grasiano is headed off to Rodeo-Kart this morning, and I wanted him to sign the All-Pro contract before he leaves."

"Doesn't he have to be in Texas and qualify on the track today?"

"Yes. I spoke with Leo Grasiano, Tom's father, earlier this week. They are headed out to Texas this morning, and I asked him to come by here on their way out of town. They'll be here by nine o'clock, and they will get to Longview before dinner. He can qualify on the track up until late tonight."

Sonny came into the kitchen and poured himself a cup of coffee from the pot that Uma had just brewed. He was oblivious to his own interference in the cooking area. Uma had to maneuver around him.

"I would have brought that over to you," Uma said, waiting for him to step out of her way.

Sonny took a sip of the coffee. "Ma, you should make the coffee with a little more kick, like Starbucks does," said Sonny.

"If you don't like it, you should switch to tea," she said with a smile.

"You know I don't like tea, Ma."

Sonny sat down at the table next to his father. Uma sat down also. Sonny stared at his phone and started swiping it with his finger. He glanced over at his father.

"Really, Dad? A newspaper? You know you should get with the times."

"I like the newspaper," said Monroe. "It's much easier to handle than trying to twiddle a little screen like you do."

"They have big screens, too, for people like you." Sonny chuckled.

Monroe just snorted and shook his head. "I like the feel of the paper and the smell of the print." He folded the paper over and continued reading.

"Is Ruby Mae coming down for breakfast?" Uma asked Sonny. "I'm serving in a couple of minutes. Mackie is coming over, too."

"Yes, I'll tell her," said Sonny.

Sonny picked up his phone and made a call. In a minute, Ruby glided into the kitchen. She was wearing a T-shirt with no underwear, pajama bottoms, and a wispy, open jacket that didn't cover anything. Her breasts were a little too perky under that shirt, Uma thought. She was not pleased with that look for a family breakfast. Uma didn't have time to discuss it now; she had to bring the glasses of orange juice to the dining room table.

"Hi, Grandma," said Mackie when he walked past the dining room.

"Wait, young man. I need your help," said Uma. "Bring out the serving plates that are warming in the oven. You might need the mitts that are on the counter."

"Sure," said Mackie. He turned to go.

"And tell everyone to come in for breakfast," she added.

Uma had just finished setting all of the places when the other three sauntered in and found their seats around the table. Monroe always sat at the head, and Uma in the first side seat. They didn't even fill half of the king-size table with only the five at breakfast.

Mackie had brought in a couple of platters of eggs, bacon, potatoes, fruit, croissants, and pastries. Everyone started passing the platters around and serving onto their plates.

"Oh, the Hollandaise sauce," said Uma. She darted into the kitchen and picked up a small sauce boat from the counter. She returned to the dining room and paused to admire everyone enjoying themselves. Smiling, she set the sauce dish next to Monroe and sat down.

"How come Aunt Margaret isn't here to help you?" asked Mackie, sitting next to Uma.

"Oh, she went back to Michigan two weeks ago," answered Uma.

"I thought she would have stayed for the road rally back to Belle Isle," said Mackie.

"No. Margaret had enough of the road rallies. She said she wanted to take care of some things around the house in Belle Isle before we come to visit."

"I don't think she could take the heat," said Sonny, and he ate another bite.

"Mackie, she left two weeks ago. How long have you been out on the road?" asked Uma.

"We had a couple of back-to-back races, Ma. You know what it's like in the summer," said Sonny. "We were in California last week."

"Oh, that was wonderful," said Ruby. "The weather, the wine, the ocean. It was so much nicer than summer here."

"Or in Atlanta!" added Sonny. "But did you know that my condo in Atlanta would cost four times more in California?"

"Well, son, you get what you pay for," said Monroe with a wink.

Uma noticed that Mackie was sitting across from Ruby Mae and was staring at her breasts. Uma gave him a little nudge under the table, which startled him. She tried discretely to signal to him with face gestures, but it was no use.

"What?" asked Mackie, finally turning toward Uma.

Uma just shook her head. Was he clueless, or maybe just pretending like he didn't understand?

Sonny let out a huge yawn, which also triggered one from Mackie.

"Sorry, but it's only 8:30, and we were out late," said Sonny.

"What time did you all get in last night?" asked Monroe. "I didn't think there were any places open after 1 a.m. in Blue Springs."

"We were visiting friends, Dad," answered Sonny. "You know, I used to live here. Do you remember Bennie Haynes? We were over at his house."

Monroe shook his head and finished off a croissant.

"Oh, I remember Bennie," said Uma. "How are his wife and daughter?"

"He's divorced now, and he has a girlfriend, Angela. His daughter was there, too."

"They were so nice," said Ruby. "I was so glad to meet them and hear all of the stories from when Sonny was younger."

Uma had heard many of Sonny's stories. They were more like tall tales that grew taller with each retelling. In this respect, he was just like his father—always talking about himself.

"His daughter is really hot," added Sonny. "Right, Mackie?"

Mackie smiled and nodded.

"Oh, you were there too," said Monroe to Mackie.

Sonny was always trying to fix up his son with various girls, and it appears that last night was more of that. Somehow being "hot" was Sonny's number one criteria for a girlfriend. Who taught him that? It certainly wasn't Uma's doing.

"A wonderful breakfast, sweetie," said Monroe. "I think we'd better get ready for Gavin and the Grasianos coming over." Monroe stood up from the table and turned to leave the room. Sonny did the same.

"Mackie, can you help me clear the plates?" Uma asked.

"Sure," he answered, but he had already started before she asked.

"I can help, too," said Ruby. "I used to be a waitress once," she said to Mackie. She leaned over and picked up a platter, showing her cleavage to the whole room.

"I bet you made great tits—tips," said Mackie, correcting himself.

"Oh," said Ruby. She giggled. "Both." She winked at Mackie while they carried plates into the kitchen together.

Sonny watched the two walk out of the dining room, and Uma started to smile. She savored the irony of the scene. Sonny, she imagined, must have been quite irritated seeing his girlfriend flirting with his son. It only seemed natural; after all, she was closer to Mackie's age than Sonny's. Ha!

"Thank you," Uma said to Ruby after the dishes were placed in and around the sink. Uma smiled at Sonny, and she watched him waiting impatiently.

"Come on, Ruby," said Sonny. "We have to get dressed. People are coming over."

The couple headed upstairs, and Monroe disappeared into the library. Uma took a few minutes to put away the leftovers into the refrigerator. She then prepared a large serving tray with the coffee pot, teapot, cups, cream, and sugar. An elegant service, she thought, suitable for doing business.

Uma carried the tray into the library and set it down on the large desk. Monroe was admiring his Bicentennial Irish-Scottish Road Rally trophy that had been sitting on one of the shelves. Uma turned and watched him. He ran his fingers across the emeralds at the bottom of the silver cup. A twinge of anxiety struck her, and she carefully watched his face.

"I do love these beautiful trophies and helmets," Monroe said to Uma.

"They are lovely," she replied.

The cup with emeralds that he was holding was her most recent victim of jewel thievery; it now only had green cut crystal in those bezels.

"You know," Monroe continued. "It was always the accomplishment that was important to me. I wouldn't even mind if these stones were just Austrian crystal."

Uma's heart skipped a beat. Had she been found out? Did Monroe suspect something?

"I won those trophies," he continued, placing it back on the shelf. "My accomplishments. Remember what we used to say at Owen Racing?"

Oh! Don't say it, Uma thought.

"Winning is everything," said Monroe.

Uma grasped her heart. She didn't want any ethereal visitors to be summoned.

"What's the matter, dear?" asked Monroe.

"Oh, it's nothing." Uma looked around nervously.

"Now about the road rally. Won't you consider riding with me to Belle Isle? It would be like old times when we were younger."

Uma remembered how much fun they used to have on road trips.

"I will think about it. If I feel up to it, I will."

Monroe walked over to Uma and kissed the top of her head. The doorbell rang.

"I hope that's Gavin," said Monroe, and he walked out of the room.

Gavin Carrington was the Kilgores' lawyer for both family and business needs, but Uma always thought of him as Monroe's accomplice. He wielded the sword of contract and tort law to do Monroe's bidding, whatever it might be. Whether it was locking a vendor into a one-sided contract or defending a family member in a lawsuit, Gavin was their man. He gave Monroe plausible deniability—Monroe never quite knew enough of the gory details to be guilty of Gavin's legal slaughters. Today was no different. Whatever contract Gavin had prepared for this business deal today would surely maximize the Kilgores' financial benefit.

"Uma," said Gavin as he entered the room with Monroe and Mackie. "So kind of you to serve us this early in the morning. I must apologize."

"It's my pleasure," replied Uma. "You know I am a morning person. Some tea or coffee?"

"Tea, most definitely," said Gavin. "I am offered tea so seldom, and you always serve the best."

Cups were served, and the two men settled down into the oversized leather chairs; Monroe sat behind his desk and Gavin by the window. Mackie seemed to be happy standing and exploring the trophies on the shelf.

Sonny and Ruby Mae waltzed into the library, looking ready for the day. Ruby had put on decent clothes, although her skirt seemed short. Sonny appeared happy with her company, but Uma knew he was just showing her off. It was an arrangement that seemed to be mutually agreeable to both of them.

The doorbell rang again, and Uma quietly walked down the hall to the front entrance. She opened the door to find Tom Grasiano with a man she recognized as his father. She could see their pickup truck behind them in the circular drive with a covered trailer in tow.

"Hi, I'm Leo Grasiano," the man introduced himself. "This is my son, Tom."

"Yes, we've met before, Mr. Grasiano," said Uma. "Nice to see you both again. Monroe is expecting you."

She showed both of them into the house and down the hall to the library. Mr. Grasiano followed and looked around with wide eyes. They walked into the library, and introductions were made. Uma did her little coffee and tea ritual. The Grasianos were coffee drinkers, as she had anticipated.

Everyone seemed satisfied at the moment. Sonny stood up, and Uma knew he would be starting his pitch to close the deal.

"Tommy," said Sonny, "let me lay out this opportunity for you. The All-Pro Racing School is a world-class institution for up-and-coming racecar drivers. This scholarship starts with a three-week intensive training program at All-Pro."

Uma didn't need to hear any more of it. She saw the look on that boy's face when he arrived and walked down the hall. She knew that he would sign up for Sonny's program even if he were asked to crawl through broken glass for it. Uma left the room to return to her other activities. She could still hear Gavin talking from down the hall.

She walked to the back of the house, and there it was again—the smell of burnt rubber and freesia flowers. Uma felt the hair tingling on the back of her neck, and there was a chill in the air. She looked around apprehensively.

Bang, bang, bang! A sudden, loud knocking on the front door made Uma jump. She hurried down the hall to the front entrance when the knocking repeated.

Uma pulled open the front door to reveal several men in uniform standing in front of her. She was astonished. Three police cruisers were in the driveway with their blue lights flashing.

"Mrs. Kilgore," a man in a brown suit said, stepping toward her. He held up a badge. "I'm Detective Lowry. We met a few weeks ago."

Uma was surprised and disturbed by the large presence of law enforcement in front of her house.

"Oh! What is going on?" she asked.

"Ma'am, we were told that there is a Thomas Grasiano here," said Lowry.

"Uh, yes. He is here."

234

"Would you ask him to come outside? I need to speak with him immediately."

Uma looked around at the group of armed officers in front of her.

"He's here," Lowry announced, nodding his head.

A wave of tension and anticipation seemed to move over the other officers that accompanied Detective Lowry. Uma certainly did not want any of them coming inside her home.

"Yes, I will ask him to come out," said Uma.

She closed the door and turned toward the library. Very disturbed by the scene in her front yard, she gently walked back to the library where the business meeting was still happening.

"Excuse me," Uma said softly. She could barely get the words out. No one paid any attention to her. "Excuse me!" Uma said loudly. Everyone stopped talking and looked over at her. "There are some police officers outside that asked to speak with Tom Grasiano." This news initiated a flurry of discussion in the room.

"What?" said Sonny.

Uma regretted being the bearer of this news. Gavin walked over to Monroe and whispered something into his ear. Monroe stood up with all eyes on him; he approached Tom and his father.

"I'm sure it's nothing," said Monroe. He gestured for Tom to get up. Tom looked very confused. Tom's father seemed to agree with Monroe and also stood up to leave the room.

"Come on, Tom," his father said.

The two of them walked past Uma and down the hall to the front entrance. The rest of the people and Uma followed after them. Mr. Grasiano opened the door, again revealing the flashing lights and the array of armed law enforcement officers. He stepped outside, and Tom followed him. Everyone else watched from the open door.

"Thomas Grasiano?" asked Lowry of the young man.

"Yes," he answered.

"You are under arrest for Vehicular Homicide for the death of Gillian Anne Mason and for leaving the scene of a fatal accident," said Lowry.

"Wait a minute," said Mr. Grasiano, lunging forward.

In an instant, two uniformed officers put their hands on Mr. Grasiano and held him firmly.

Lowry continued as if he hadn't noticed. "You have the right to remain silent. Anything you say can and will be used against you in a court of law. You have the right to an attorney. If you cannot afford an attorney, one will be provided for you. Do you understand the rights I have just read to you? Say 'yes' if you do."

"Yes," said Tom. He looked at his father with desperation.

Tom then turned to the group of Kilgores huddled in the open doorway. Uma knew that there would be no help coming from inside this mansion. Two other officers escorted the young man away and into one of the police cruisers.

"This is nonsense!" shouted Mr. Grasiano. "Why are you charging Tom with this?" he asked Lowry.

"You drive a white Lexus, don't you, Mr. Grasiano?" asked Lowry.

"Yes."

"With one of these 'K' stickers on the back window?" Lowry pulled a white sticker with checkered flags and a letter K out of his pocket.

"Yes, I suppose so."

"Well, it so happens that we went to your house to ask Tom some questions a couple of weeks back. I noticed your car matched the description given by some eyewitnesses from the Mason investigation. Upon closer examination, there was green paint scuffed on the rear bumper."

"So what does that prove?"

"The observation led to a warrant to take paint samples from your car and that bumper. Analysis of the paint samples showed that your paint was on the Dillanger car, and his paint was on your car. Bingo!"

"So why aren't you arresting me?" asked Mr. Grasiano.

"Because you weren't there. According to your wife, Tom had taken your car to Leeds to see the race on that day.

"Here's my card. Your son will be held at the county jail and then transferred to Auburn, where the case will be prosecuted."

Monroe stepped out of the safety of the doorway and over to Mr. Grasiano after the officers returned to their cars.

"I'm sorry, Leo, but this changes everything," said Monroe.

Uma watched poor Mr. Grasiano just shake his head. "I have to go," he said. He turned and dashed over to his pickup truck.

"Very unfortunate," said Gavin, and he put his hand on Monroe's shoulder. "You certainly dodged that one. I'm so glad this happened before he signed the contract."

"That's for sure," added Sonny, stepping forward to watch the police caravan drive away.

The police cruisers circled around the driveway and headed out the front gate. The pickup truck followed them.

Uma could swear that she saw a figure standing by the gate post under one of the foo lions as the cars were disappearing. It was a man in a white racing suit. She put her hand to her mouth and gasped.

CHAPTER 30

Wood paneling surrounded Chad when he awoke, leaving him confused and disoriented. He sat up and remembered he was staying in the Larsens' guest trailer at the Cottonwood karting park. It was Friday morning at Rodeo-Kart. Today was Practice day. Chad got up, showered, and slipped on his jeans and T-shirt. Hunting around his accommodations, he found a breakfast snack bar in one cupboard in the small kitchen.

He stepped out of the trailer door and looked around while the other park visitors were also waking up. It was still pretty early, but he could see some families stirring around in their motorhomes. The sun was just cresting over the trees in a cloudless sky. The air lay still around him and was already slightly warm for the morning. It would be a hot Texas afternoon for the practice.

Chad started walking, enjoying the morning air while it was still fresh and the grass was laden with dew. The early morning flies were bothering a woman with a cup of coffee outside of her motorhome. She waved hello while she swatted the flies away. Chad happily waved back and kept walking along the pathway by the fence line. The park seemed peaceful, considering all of the activity that would be starting soon. Two birds on the path in front of him were squabbling over some discarded morsel from an early morning breakfast. It was all good.

Bruce Larsen had been very kind to him and seemed to expect nothing in return. Chad enjoyed having dinner with Jessica's family the night before, and he was fascinated with her father's story. It was so different from his own family dynamics. Truthfully, everything felt different now. Chad felt free from worry, and his anxiety was melting away. Despite the uncertainty, some things were becoming clear and vivid. Jessica, karting this weekend, and hope for the future were all on his mind.

He saw a spectrum full of colors all around him. The gray vision was suddenly all gone. Red, green, and yellow racing suits in the distance under the golden and blue Texas morning sky caught his eye. Brilliant colors seemed to be everywhere. The Rodeo-Kart race was going to be exhilarating, and he could already feel the adrenaline rushing through his veins.

Chad wandered past the karting center and came to the arcade. Something familiar. Chad always liked the arcade games that he and his friends frequently played on the weekends after karting events. Maybe a classic game or two would help prepare his mind. Chad checked the door to the arcade and found it open. He went in and looked around. It felt the same as the one back home. Chad put a five-dollar bill in the change machine for a fist full of tokens. He walked over to a video game where he started mindlessly shooting aliens. He played a little pinball and then saw The Claw over on the side.

The claw game had fantastic assorted stuffed animals and toys behind its glass window. This was Chad's specialty. Ha! Now he could win a prize for Jessica and impress her. He spied a two-toned purple and lavender bear that he knew Jessica would like. It might take a few tokens to get the hang of this machine. The shiny stainless steel claw had three fingers, and he maneuvered it cautiously over the bear. Chad hit the button, and the claw dropped perfectly over the prize. Slowly, it lifted… Then the bear managed to slide out of the grip.

"Damn!" he shouted. "You won't escape me. You're mine!" he said to the bear.

He dropped some more tokens into the machine and navigated the grabber over the bear with perfect precision. The claw dropped, then the bear came up and slipped away again the moment it started to move. Getting closer.

Suddenly, Chad was grabbed tightly around the waist.

"Hey, I found you," said Jessica, who had snuck up behind him.

Chad was startled and a little embarrassed to be caught playing games in the arcade. Jessica looked stunning in her pink and white karting suit—the same suit she wore when they first met back in Blue Springs. She gave him a short kiss on the lips.

"What are you trying to do—pay for my college tuition?" she asked.

"What do you mean? I was planning to win this purple bear for you. I am the best at the claw game. I always get my prize."

"You are too funny, and that is so sweet. I love that bear, but I already have one just like it. You know, my dad does own the arcade."

"How am I funny?"

"The claw game—it's rigged. It's just pay-to-play like everything else around here. My dad has this one programmed only to give enough electricity to the claw once in every twenty plays," she explained.

"You mean I would have to grab that bear twenty times before the claw would be able to pick it up and bring it to the prize door?"

"Yup." She smiled.

"Are you telling me that all the arcade claw games are programmed like that?"

"More or less." Jessica started to laugh.

"All these years, I thought I had a unique talent. My friends even called me 'The Claw-meister!' All this time, I thought it was my great hand-eye coordination from karting."

She couldn't contain herself from laughing. "Well, in your defense, it does take some skill to maneuver the claw, but the claw is not much more than a slot machine for kids."

Chad was disturbed by this revelation. Just moments ago, he felt so confident in his skills, and he thought he would prevail as a champion at something. It's just a rigged game. Chad could feel his face turning red with embarrassment. He wondered if everything in his life was like the arcade claw game. Is karting just a rigged game? Is there some ethereal program that says he only wins one race in every twenty races? All that money and time—what does it all matter?

"That just sucks. Damn," he said under his breath to himself.

"Sorry. Did I ruin it for you?"

"More than you know," he said. Chad wasn't interested in playing anything else in the arcade.

"Well, maybe this will cheer you up. I brought you some breakfast. They say it's the most important meal of the day."

Jessica handed him a paper bag that smelled so good. He didn't even have to open it to know that bacon and eggs were inside. Chad reached into the bag to find a delicious breakfast sandwich. He unwrapped it and bit into the egg and smoky bacon, feeling some relief.

"Oh, that is just what I needed. Thank you!" he said with a mouthful. In a moment, Chad had devoured the whole sandwich.

"Wow. Good thing there's another one in there. Come on. Let's get some coffee in the office. Then we have to get you registered for the event."

Chad and Jessica walked through the glass doors of the arcade that connected to the karting center. As they walked past the retail counter, Chad noticed the colorful duct tape in perfect rows on the back wall. Every shade in the color spectrum for any kart was for sale—brilliant!

Jessica led him past the retail store through an open door into a back room. The office was a clutter of supplies, papers, and sticky notes. A woman with curly hair sat in front of a computer, busily tapping away at the keyboard. The printer next to her was churning out pages.

"Good morning, Penny," said Jessica.

"Oh. Hi, sweetie," the woman said, looking up. "It's going to be a busy day!"

"Is Daddy here yet? When does registration start?" Jessica asked. "Penny, this is Chad Gibbons. He's driving the Cottonwood kart this weekend."

Jessica poured two cups of coffee from a large pot on the counter. Chad nodded hello and smiled, hoping his teeth were not full of bacon and eggs.

"Your dad said he was unloading your kart and would be in the pits greeting people. I'll be starting registration in fifteen minutes at 9:30 a.m.," Penny said.

"Thanks," said Jessica. "Here, Chad. Let's go."

She handed Chad his coffee and headed out the office door.

"Nice to meet you, Ms. Penny," Chad said.

The two continued out of the karting center and toward the pit and paddock area. Chad noticed for the first time the sign hanging over the entrance to the pits. He stopped and read.

All persons entering the pit area must purchase a pit pass and sign the insurance waiver. Anyone found without a pit pass will be removed, and the team associated with the offending person will be penalized.

Chad liked the way Mr. Larsen ran his park—clear rules and no riffraff running around the pits.

"Come on," said Jessica.

"Don't I need a pit pass?" asked Chad.

"Yes, of course, but you'll get that when you register."

Jessica led him down the paddock traffic lane to the pit where his cart was now sitting next to hers.

"Here are my wheels," Jessica said, admiring her purple and yellow neon kart.

Chad was surprised. Jessica's kart was identical to his.

"They look exactly the same," he said.

"I know. We have twin karts. Isn't that great! It's like we're a team—the Cottonwood team." She flashed a brilliant smile. "Hey, you have to get ready. Put on your karting suit and meet me at the karting center for registration. We have tech inspection after that."

Chad started to feel a little anxious and wanted to get himself ready. He didn't have time to look at his shifter kart, and he hoped that Jayden knew what he was doing with it. On his way to the trailer to get ready, Chad ran into Bruce Larsen shaking hands and welcoming the karters.

"Good morning, Mr. Larsen," said Chad when he approached.

Jessica's father turned and smiled. "Looking forward to the event?" he asked, joining Chad on his walk toward the trailer.

"Most definitely. I've always wanted to race in Rodeo-Kart. It's a little daunting, though, with the pro drivers also on the track."

"Have some fun with it," said Mr. Larsen. "Today is just a practice day."

"I want to thank you for letting me use your spare kart. It was much easier traveling from Blue Springs without the old kart in the back of the truck."

"Chad, my daughter is a pretty popular kid, but let me tell you this one thing. I built her that extra kart a few years back, and in all this time, she's never let anyone else race it."

Chad didn't know what to say. He just looked at Mr. Larsen.

"She's given you something," he continued, "so handle it with care. And I'm not talking about the kart. Now go and get ready." Mr. Larsen patted Chad on the back.

Chad trotted off, and his pulse started to quicken. He didn't want to disappoint Jessica, and now Mr. Larsen gave him a lot to think about. Chad climbed the stairs into the trailer and changed into his karting suit. He had brought the pit bag ready to go, but he double-checked the contents—gloves, neck brace, balaclava, helmet, and timing watch. Chad opened the door and stood ready to face the track and the competition. His racing suit had the Kilgore team name and green letter "K" logo on it, but he didn't feel like he was racing as a Kilgore karter. He was there for the first time as Chad Gibbons, representing himself today.

Taking deep cleansing breaths, he could hear an engine starting off in the distance. He felt his heart racing as if an engine inside him was starting. He walked down the trailer steps with renewed confidence. It didn't take long to walk back over to the karting center, but Jessica wasn't there.

Chad joined the end of the registration line and looked around at the other karters standing with him. It was an assorted mix of teenagers and adults in their twenties or maybe older. Chad remembered that Tom Grasiano said he would be racing at the event.

He looked around to see if he could spot Tom or anyone else from the Kilgore team, but he didn't know anyone else there. It was easy being anonymous. He didn't have to explain anything to anyone. He could simply concentrate on practicing that day and focus on the task at hand.

"Hey, Gibbons," said a voice from behind him.

Chad turned to see Reggie Johnson, his old rival from his Junior class karting days. The last time he saw Reggie was at the races on the weekend of Gary Lee's accident.

"Hey, Reggie," replied Chad, disinterested in the coming conversation.

"So you're finally racing with the big boys. Are you here with the Kilgore team? Where's your entourage you usually travel with? I never see you without that Gary Lee kid."

Chad realized that Reggie did not know about Gary Lee's crash or Gillian's death. A lump formed in his throat, and he had to pause before speaking.

"Gary Lee's in the hospital. It's just me here today."

Chad was barely able to speak, and he couldn't even mention Gillian. This was the last thing he wanted to be talking about.

"Oh, that's too bad. I hope nothing too serious."

"His car went off the road that weekend we saw you in Leeds."

"Wow! Sorry, man, I hadn't heard. I hope he's recovering."

Chad took a deep breath. "Yeah. He's getting better."

Reggie put his hand on Chad's shoulder. They had now come to the front of the line, and Chad needed to end the conversation.

"Well, see you out there," said Reggie.

Chad turned toward the registration table in front of him, and Penny from the front office looked up.

"Oh. Hi again, Mr. Nice Guy," she said. "What was your last name, again?"

"Chad Gibbons," he replied.

"Okay, here you are," she said, going through a list of names in a notebook. She checked him off. "Looks like your fees are paid already. Do you have your waiver notarized?"

"Sorry, ma'am, I don't have a waiver filled out."

"No matter. You're eighteen, so here is an adult waiver. Fill this out, and I can notarize it for you. I also need to see your driver's license."

Chad took the clipboard and form from Penny and started to read it. The text, *INJURY TO THE PERSON OR PROPERTY RESULTING IN DEATH*, jumped out at him. Chad had never read and signed a liability waiver before. Having just turned eighteen, his father had always handled the legal stuff for him as a minor. Chad signed the form and showed his license to Penny. She stamped and signed the notary and then pulled out a packet with his name on it.

"Here is your pit wristband. Fasten that on your right wrist now so you don't lose it," said Penny, opening the packet for him. "These are your front and back numbers for your kart. You are Number 20. According to the master sheet, you've been assigned Pit 17. That's the Cottonwood pit."

"Yes, I've already seen the kart. It's awesome."

"The schedule is in the registration packet, and this is your tech inspection form. Follow the signs to the inspection area this morning. Make sure you get it signed off before noon. This is your practice group sticker. You're in the Red practice group. See the schedule for your practice time slots, and please remember that you can't go out on the track without your inspection sticker. You're representing Cottonwood today, so keep it civilized out there. Good luck."

"Thank you," said Chad. "Oh, is there a Tom Grasiano on your list?"

"Let me check. Hold on a second, sweetie. Oh, yes. He's signed up, but he hasn't registered yet."

"Okay, thanks again." Chad nodded.

He took his packet and headed toward the open door. A wave of anticipation came over him, and Chad felt a tingling in his spine. He kept thinking anything is possible and maybe this weekend would be life-changing. What if he actually made it to the podium? That would be so incredible. Goosebumps followed him out through the open doors.

CHAPTER 31

The scene outside the karting center was filled with the sights, sounds, and smells that Chad loved. He stood under the Cottonwood Karting sign and paused to take it all in. The kart engines whined while they zipped along the track. He smelled the fair food and motor fumes and saw people in colorful race suits carrying their helmets. Chad was now a registered racer for Rodeo-Kart, a competition that he had only dreamed of entering. Today was the practice day and qualifying. Tomorrow would be the Rodeo-Kart races. The purse was huge by karting standards—$10,000 for first place—but Chad's real hope was to be seen by sponsors and media people so he could break into auto racing. Rodeo-kart was his chance, his big break.

There was a flurry of activity at the main entrance to the park. Chad could see Jessica and her father, Bruce Larsen, surrounded by a small crowd. Jessica waved Chad over as soon as she caught sight of him. Chad approached, and it became apparent that a photo shoot was in progress. A large bounce flash umbrella was set up, and there was a photographer giving directions. Jessica was posing next to her kart and two other men in racing suits.

"I'm having some new pictures taken for advertising," Mr. Larsen explained to Chad when he arrived. "That's Todd Cunningham and Danny Doyle. Do you know them?"

"I know they're professional drivers, but I've never met them."

"Their team owner owed me a favor, so this photo session is payback," he explained. Now, I'll have two professional racing drivers on my new billboard.

"Are they also racing this weekend?"

"Oh, yes. Should be good."

Chad watched Jessica pose. She seemed like a professional model. It was fun to watch until Jessica walked over and pulled him beside her in the photo.

"Just stand up straight and turn your head a little to the right," the photographer said to Chad. "Perfect."

Jessica leaned in close to Chad and kissed him on the cheek as the umbrella flash lit up. A few more flashes and they were finished with the photo shoot.

"Why did you do that?" Chad asked her.

"Don't worry about it. They probably won't use your photo. I just wanted a picture of us for myself. I can send you a copy of the picture if you like."

"Todd, Danny, this is Chad Gibbons, Jessica's guest for the weekend," said Mr. Larsen, making introductions.

"Great to meet you. I'm a huge fan," said Chad, shaking hands with the two racers.

Suddenly, Jayden came running up to Chad.

"Hey, man, they're going to close the morning tech inspections soon. Do you have the form?" he said out of breath.

"Yes," said Chad, picking up his packet.

"Go, get inspected and get some practice laps in," said Jessica.

They both ran back to the Cottonwood pit in the paddock. Chad lagged behind while he was reaching into his information packet to find the inspection form. He dodged running into a kart on its dolly crossing the lane. Jayden handed him a pen, and Chad passed the numbers to Jayden. Jayden put the number stickers on the kart, Chad filled out the form, and they wheeled the kart and dolly down the lane.

It was almost noon when they arrived at the inspection area. The two inspectors appeared irritated at their inconsiderate delay, but Jayden had convinced them to wait.

"We were just about to break for lunch," said the first man, who was dressed in gray overalls.

"I'm sorry. My girlfriend had me taking photos. Thanks for waiting," said Chad.

"Do you have the form?" the man asked.

"Yes, here it is."

Chad thought about what he had just said—*girlfriend*. He had never had a girlfriend like Jessica before. Was this real? He wasn't even paying attention to the inspectors as they weighed the kart. Jayden was answering questions, and he seemed to have it all covered.

"Come on, man," said Jayden. "What's the matter? You seem to be in a daze."

"Sorry."

"We're done. The kart passed without a problem. Time to get out there."

Chad now realized that the inspectors had already left. He slapped himself on his cheeks as if he needed to wake up.

"Okay, I'm good. Let's get going," said Chad. "The schedule says that the Red practice group starts at 1:00 p.m.

Chad and Jayden wheeled the kart on its dolly back to their pit. They set the kart down on the lane in front of the pit area and fueled it up. Jayden handed him a radio headset.

"Here," said Jayden. "We use these for practice. Headsets are not allowed during the competition."

"I know. My dad and I use them, too." Chad put the headset over his ear and positioned the microphone. "Test, test," he said.

"Loud and clear," came the voice back in his ear.

Chad put on his balaclava hood, neck brace, and helmet. Lastly, he pulled his racing gloves on and looked at his watch. The engine started effortlessly. The purple kart began rolling down the lane, and he proved the engine with a couple of taps on the throttle.

Chad started picking up speed on the track entrance ramp and felt the g-force pushing him against the back of the seat. Checking for track traffic over his shoulder, he heard Jayden give him the all-clear to enter. Chad stepped hard on the gas pedal. He shifted gears and was at sixty miles per hour in a few seconds. Reaching Turn 1, he gently tested out the brakes. Although the new kart had its absolute uniqueness, there was something very familiar in the feeling of a 125-cc shifter kart around him.

Slinging around the "S" turns with ease, this borrowed kart felt incredible. It had much more grip than his old kart. He liked the tightness in the steering. It was an exhilarating drive.

"Chad, you're looking good," said Jayden over the radio. "You're making headway on that pack of slower karts ahead of you."

Chad pulled up on the tail of Number 18, with silver and black trim. Moving to the left on the inside of the next turn, he passed that kart with ease.

"Nice!" said Jayden.

The blue and green Number 31 and the red Number 99 were in front of him. Chad held the inside line and passed those karts without a problem. A Junior class kart, Number 63, at the front of the pack was holding everyone up. This time Chad took the long way around him on the outside. This last pass felt like the best practice he had ever had.

Suddenly, another purple and yellow kart zipped by Chad on the inside, with Number 17 on the bumper. Chad recognized the kart immediately and saw a little pink glove waving over the driver's head.

"What—no warning?" asked Chad over the radio.

"Hey, man, I can't help you when it comes to Jessica!" said Jayden. "You won't have any warnings when you're racing tomorrow."

Chad shifted again, coming out of the turn onto the straightaway.

"You've got Number 14 coming up on your right," said Jayden.

"Thank you—finally some help," replied Chad.

He punched the throttle and shifted up as quickly as he could. Reaching over a hundred miles per hour on the straight, Chad thought he could keep ahead, but it was no use. The blue Number 37 kart overtook him and cut into the first turn ahead of him, forcing

Chad to the outside. Chad saw the "Team Cunningham" name across the back of the kart when they came around the turn.

"Oh, man!" said Chad. "That was Todd Cunningham. He's a pro racer."

"Well, learn from the pros because that pass was textbook perfect."

"I'm going to need as much practice as I can get!"

Chad's strength rose inside of him, and he had new determination. He should be passing the pro! He pushed his foot all the way down on the accelerator and then shifted again. In a moment, he was now on the tail of Number 37. Turn 6 was the best place to make his move, and he crossed over to the inside of Cunningham, passing him handily.

"Whoo-hoo!" shouted Jayden. "I didn't know you had it in you, man."

Chad was not finished. He was just getting warmed up. Ahead he was closing on Number 17, the other Cottonwood purple and yellow kart—not intending to pass Jessica but something even better. He maneuvered into position behind Jessica, following her every move, and they began passing other karts together.

"Wow! Now that's what a karting team should look like!" said Jayden.

Jessica waved her pink glove to signal Chad to move ahead of her. He passed her on the inside on the next turn. She fell in line behind him, and he punched the accelerator. Now it was his turn to run in the lead on their exploits. They moved in behind a yellow and white kart, and as soon as they came around the last turn, Chad opened it up on the straightaway. Someone was waving a white flag while his speedometer read eighty-three crossing the lap marker. Together they passed the other kart rounding Turn 1.

"Last practice lap for the Red group," said Jayden over the radio.

Chad knew what the white flag meant. He didn't want it to end. They made their way around the track for the last time, still passing other karts. There was one last green kart, Number 5, in front of Chad that he was determined to overtake before the lap was over.

The three karts came around the final turn, and all engines were at full throttle. Approaching redline, Chad shifted through the gears, trying to squeeze every bit of power out of the 125 cc engine. He pulled to the outside of the Number 5 kart, inching up alongside. Chad looked left and saw that Jessica had also maneuvered to the outside of him. They were three-wide! All three of them crossed the finish line, neck and neck, and the race steward waved the checkered flag. Too bad it was only practice—what a finish that would have been!

"Oh my God!" Jayden shouted in Chad's ear. "I can't believe you guys did that!"

As they reached Turn 1, a yellow flag was waved, and a sign was indicating to exit the track. The karters slowed down and made their way around to the track exit, and one by one pulled into the pit entrance.

Jayden came running over while Chad climbed out of the kart.

"That was a crazy finish," said Jayden. I think you might have won if it was actually a race."

"If it were a real race, I would have won," said Jessica, whipping her hair out after taking off her helmet.

She came over to Chad and pulled him close to her.

"That was quite a finish," he said, with his helmet now off.

"We make a great team," said Jessica, "but don't think I would let you cross the finish line ahead of me!"

She gave him a congratulatory kiss, then turned and ordered her helpers to put her kart on the dolly. They were the same boys Chad had met when he first arrived, but he no longer felt any competition from them. Chad and Jayden lifted his kart up and on the dolly. Chad then turned around and saw that Danny Doyle was the driver of the green Number 5 kart.

"Very nice driving," the pro racer said to Chad. "You've been doing this long?"

"Only twelve years," said Chad.

Doyle laughed in surprise. "Well, it has paid off," he said. "See you out there." Doyle patted him on the shoulder and followed his own kart crew back to the pits.

When Chad returned to their pit, he found it a flurry of activity. Mr. Larsen was there, along with others already busily working on Jessica's kart. He reached out and shook Chad's hand.

"Well, that looked like fun," said Mr. Larsen. "You know we don't normally wave a checkered flag for practice, but our race steward said it was so exciting that he couldn't help himself. So how did you like the Cottonwood kart?"

"It was so awesome," said Chad.

"Feel free to make any adjustments you want with Jayden. He's a wiz with anything mechanical."

"Yes, come over and help me," said Jayden. "We have another practice run at 5 p.m., so I'd like to get some adjustments in."

Chad turned to Jayden and the kart, and they began an afternoon of mechanical work. Chad loved working with his hands and figuring out the machinery. Once he got in the zone, nothing would distract him. He and his dad had spent so many weekends together tearing apart and rebuilding his old karts. Chad wished his father could have been there with him now, but Jayden was fantastic. He would do precisely what Chad was thinking of doing. It was like they could read each other's minds. Together they balanced the car with lead weights, changed out the sprockets, and tuned the carburetor. By the end of the day, Chad was so pleased with their preparations for racing in Rodeo-Kart. But nothing could have prepared him for what would happen that weekend.

254

CHAPTER 32

There was a knocking on the trailer door that woke Chad. He sat up in a sudden panic, worried that he had overslept race day. Looking at the window, he could see by the early light that the sun had not even risen yet. The knocking on the door continued.

"Are you decent?" Jessica called out, opening the trailer door.

"No," said Chad from the bedroom, hoping to get five more minutes of sleep.

He pulled the covers over his head, but Jessica came in anyway. Chad peeked from under the covers and could see her in the kitchen area. She was fully dressed for the day in her pink and white race suit and was setting out a breakfast that she had brought.

"You know what they say about breakfast," she began.

"I know. It's the most important meal."

Jessica walked into the bedroom and sat down on the bed next to Chad.

"Are you really decent under there or not?" she asked.

She smiled and started pulling the blanket down, revealing that Chad was wearing a T-shirt and boxers.

She glided her hands up and across his chest, then leaned in and kissed him. Jessica climbed onto the bed on top of him. Chad was hardly awake, but when he felt the weight of her body on him and her lips on his, his blood started pumping. Chad put his arms around her and slid his hands down to her bottom.

"What do you wear under your race suit?" he asked.

"Well," she whispered into his ear. "It's hot in Texas in August, so not much." Jessica was nibbling on his ear.

Chad started to kiss her passionately. He tried to roll over on top of her, but then Jessica sat up.

"I thought that would wake you up," she said with a smile. We have a drivers' meeting at 7:30, so get dressed, and let's have breakfast."

"Oh, you tease!" He bopped her on the shoulder with his pillow.

Chad sat up also. The two sat there for a moment on the edge of the bed, just looking at each other. Jessica was silhouetted by the morning light through the window behind her. Chad reached over and gently stroked the perfect shape of her face. She smiled, and Chad suddenly felt a surge of emotion come over him. He almost came to tears, but it wasn't sadness. He was thankful to be alive. This was how he wanted to wake up every day. He didn't mind that they had somewhere to go. Jessica was the person he wanted to be with.

"Come on," she said, standing up.

Jessica took his hand in hers and lingered there, her green-hazel eyes looking back at him. Chad stood up also and embraced her, their arms around each other, lips on lips. Time stood still as they held each other and kissed.

"I think we're already late now," Jessica said softly, continuing to kiss his lips.

She finally tore herself away and headed into the kitchen.

"Will you please put some clothes on so we don't completely miss the drivers' meeting?" she said, biting her lip.

"I'm just getting even." Chad laughed, and Jessica danced around the tiny kitchen. He put on his racing suit, and after a quick breakfast, they headed over to the stands for the meeting.

Heads turned when Jessica and Chad walked up the steps. Someone even whistled. Jessica just gave Chad a look that said, "I get this all the time, so get used to it." They joined at least two hundred people in the stands, all looking down at a man standing on the track with a microphone.

"All right, everyone," he said into the mic. "My name is AJ Rodriguez. I am your racing steward for Rodeo-Kart. Please look at your schedules, and we're going to go over the heats."

Papers shuffled, and the drivers pulled out their printed schedules. Chad and Jessica only had one copy, so they shared. Chad could tell that more eyes were on them. *What's the big deal?* he thought. *We're just sharing a schedule.*

AJ went through the classes and heats, explaining and answering questions. The Kid, Cadet, and Junior classes would be up in the morning. The Seniors, including Chad and all the adults, would have their heats starting at noon. The top three from each heat would move on to the finals that afternoon. The award ceremony was at 7:00 p.m., followed by the Rodeo-Kart party with live music.

AJ then introduced a pastor who led the audience in a prayer for the day, asking for safety over all the drivers and everyone involved.

"Thank you, and have a fantastic and safe race day!" AJ shouted to close out the meeting.

Everyone filed out of the stands. The Seniors had plenty of time before their races, and there wasn't much to do in the first three hours. Chad and Jayden had finished all their tuning and tweaking yesterday. Chad was able to make a good lap time during qualifying last night, so he had a decent starting position for his heat. He would be in eighth position, and Jessica would start in sixth.

"You know, I kind of like to watch the little kids race," said Chad to Jessica.

"Really? That's one of my favorite things to do. Let's get some funnel cake and go up into the stands to watch," she said.

The two of them spent the morning pulling apart a funnel cake and watching the younger age groups zip around the track. Jessica couldn't stop laughing at the nicknames Chad gave the different drivers—Peppa Pig, Thomas (his kart sounded like a train), and Ben & Holly.

"Oh, there goes Dora the Explora," he said, pointing.

"Stop it. I can't stop laughing," Jessica complained. "Anyway, I loved Dora."

Finally, the Juniors came out on the track for their racing heats, which was much more serious.

"How did you like racing in the Junior class?" Jessica asked.

"It was my life back then. I had to get through my mom's sickness and death, so I just totally immersed myself in karting. I almost won a championship when I was fifteen."

"Impressive. I know what you mean. I think I did that somewhat myself. My mom had moved back to Paris when I was younger, but it didn't really hit me until I turned thirteen, and then we moved here. My dad had just opened the park, so I became super competitive in Juniors. I wore my racing suit like armor and only let a few people into my world."

Jessica reached for Chad's hand and smiled. Chad then realized what she was saying. He was in her world right now. The moment was interrupted by Jessica's phone chiming. She looked at the screen.

"My dad is looking for me," she said. "I wonder what's up." She texted him back.

A minute later, Mr. Larsen walked up into the stands where they were sitting.

"Jessica!" he said. "You need to get ready for the superkart demonstration. That's in thirty minutes."

"Oh shit!" she shouted. "I forgot all about that."

"Language," Mr. Larsen added.

"Sorry, Daddy. I'll be ready in just a minute. Where is it?" she asked, heading for the stairs.

"It's right in the main walkway. It's been on display all morning. Didn't you see it? The crew will be wheeling it into the pit to fuel up."

Mr. Larsen sat down next to Chad, who was now anticipating another discussion but had no idea what about.

"I'm glad she's only driving the Junior superkart," Mr. Larsen said. "I get concerned about the Senior version."

"What do you mean?" asked Chad.

"Well, how would you feel about driving a 250 cc kart at 140 miles per hour down this straightaway?" he asked, pointing in front of them.

"Wow. I bet that would be quite the thrill. Although I think I would rather have a full-size racecar around me."

"Exactly," Mr. Larsen nodded. "I know the idea is to maximize the adrenaline rush. When you're going that speed at ten inches off the ground, I'm sure the thrill is over the top. But I don't want Jessica driving one."

"I don't think I would like her to drive one either," said Chad, thinking about it.

"Good answer." Mr. Larsen put his hand on Chad's shoulder. "It was Sonny Kilgore's idea to add a superkart series to the Florida Motorsport Resort project. The project looked like a great investment for a motorsports park, so why did they have to add superkarts? Imagine a twelve-year-old driving a hundred miles per hour or a sixteen-year-old driving 140 miles per hour. What do you think those kids are going to do when they get their learner's permits or driver's licenses?"

Chad just shrugged. "I guess they might drive fast?"

"Very smart. That diploma did pay off," said Mr. Larsen. He patted Chad on the shoulder and stood up. "Excuse me, but I have to go and announce the new superkart series."

Chad sat in the stands for a few more minutes thinking about his conversation—it left him confused. He decided he should go and see Jessica off before she headed out onto the track. Chad walked through the park in a dreamlike state, puzzling over what he had learned in recent weeks. It was so different from how he had perceived life and everything for the last eighteen years. He was turned upside down. The sounds of engines and commotion were all just background noise to him. He came to the Cottonwood pit, which was now abandoned, empty of people. The superkart entourage had already moved out to the track entrance, so Chad headed out there.

Chad approached the entrance into the track where the amazing racing machine sat. It was as Chad remembered it, a full red body covered with decorative decals and a spoiler in the back. Jessica was about to put on her helmet when she saw Chad. She stopped and smiled at him, then blew him a kiss. Everyone around the kart turned to look at Chad.

"Hey, there you are," said Jayden to Chad. "Isn't it fantastic? It's like a mini Grand Touring car."

Chad nodded. "I love GTs," he said. Chad could hear Mr. Larsen announcing the superkart over the loudspeakers in the stands. The engine started up, and she took off faster than he expected. Chad felt like he was experiencing a pit stop in an actual race.

"Come on, let's grab some lunch," said Jayden. "My mom is grilling, and we can watch Jessica while we eat."

They walked along the track fence line toward the camping area, which had a nice view of the backside of the track. They could hear the sound of Jessica's kart engine making its way around the course.

"Here she comes," Jayden said. They stopped walking and watched the bright red mini-GT appear around a turn. It zigzagged through the chicanes and then pulled around the last Turn 9.

"Oh, watch this," Jayden said. Jessica opened the engine up on the straightaway, quickly upshifting through the gears. They watched the tiny racecar fly down the track. The crowd erupted in a cheer when it crossed the lap line in front of the stands. The kart disappeared around Turn 1.

"That must have been 110 miles per hour," Jaden said, shaking his head. "Pretty impressive what they can do with a 125 cc engine, huh?"

"I know. I've been on the track behind that kart."

"Really? How was that?"

"Well, it was quite a chase until I spun out."

Jayden resumed walking. "Personally, my favorite part is the way it looks."

The smell of delicious meats and other savory foods cooking was in the air as they walked past the motorhomes. The two hungry boys came upon the Larsens' camp area where Jayden's mom was grilling.

"You boys like some burgers or some sausages?" Aunt Liddy asked.

They each picked up a plate with some chips and sausages. Chad squirted a line of mustard down the middle and took a big bite. That's what he needed!

They walked back over to the fence to watch Jessica fly by a few more times. She pulled off the track, and the demo was over. Chad and Jayden returned to the camp area and sat down with Jayden's parents at the picnic table with their lunch.

"Do you want another?" Liddy asked.

"No thanks, ma'am," said Chad. "I don't like to be too full when I race, but I will have a Coke."

"Chad," said Uncle Chuck, "Jayden tells me you are very talented with a wrench."

"Thanks. I get that from my dad," said Chad. "He owns Rusty's Wrench and Tire back home, and that's where I learned everything about working on cars, trucks, and karts."

"What are your plans after high school? Are you headed to college?" asked Chuck.

"Well, I was going to try auto racing next," said Chad, "but I didn't get the scholarship I wanted. I'm now hoping to get a job in a pit crew. Jessica's father's story was very inspiring. I'd love for something like that."

"We could really use someone like you to help with our oil pumping equipment," said Chuck. "It pays pretty well—better than those volunteer racing gigs. You could start at twenty dollars per hour if you'd be interested."

"Wow. That's very kind of you, Mr. Larsen."

"Call me Chuck. I'm serious about the job, too. I'm not a big fan of kids working in the entertainment industry. Jayden, make sure you get his phone number."

"Sure," said Jayden. "Hey, we have to go, Chad. We need to scope out the competition and get ready for our heat."

"Best of luck out there," said Aunt Liddy. "We'll be cheering for both you and Jessie."

A blast of prerace jitters suddenly hit Chad. He jumped up from the table and thanked Jayden's mom and dad for their hospitality and the job offer. This was it! Would he make a great showing or just fizzle on the track? His racing future depended on this next race.

CHAPTER 33

"Evan, I'm so sorry to put you in this position," said Elle to her business partner, Evan Waitts. They had just finished their Saturday lunch at the Radar Brew and Steak House, which was right around the corner from the DD&W offices in Blue Springs. This restaurant was probably her favorite place in town, at least for lunch. There were so many work-related memories of brainstorming over steak and beer. Takeout included burgers and Radar steak fries at the office when work was piled a mile high. Her all-time favorite was always on the special menu—Alabama pulled pork sandwiches with white barbecue sauce. She was going to miss the exhilaration of their business venture and their many projects. The sense of accomplishment from their success never was tiresome or boring.

"Oh, don't worry about me. I'll be fine," said Evan. "I'm happy for you. I think it's exactly what you need."

Elle had found a good-paying position at a design firm in Auburn, and this was her last business lunch in Blue Springs. She had just handed off her last project to Evan, and he would take it from there.

"I still don't know if I'm doing the right thing," said Elle.

"Stop beating yourself up over this. With Gary Lee coming out of rehab soon, and after all you and Drew have gone through, I think this is precisely what you need. You have to pull your life together— your new life."

"But what will you do? There hasn't been any new work coming in since the accident. Are you going to be okay?"

"You know, I did have high hopes for us and this firm that I had talked you into starting with me. I guess we won't be hanging my portrait up in the Founding Partners wing." Evan snickered while he munched on his steak fries. "You know me. I land on my feet well. Remember how I always managed to get by in college?"

Evan was right. When they were in college together, he skated by using his unique combination of powers: good looks, charm, luck, and intelligence. Elle didn't know how Evan could get such amazing grades without ever seeming to study and frequently staying out late with friends. Elle had to work hard just to get an average grade.

"So how are you getting settled in with your new apartment?" asked Evan. "You'll have to throw a housewarming party."

"It's still a mess, but it's getting better each week. I don't think I'm up to any entertaining, at least not yet."

"I thought so. That's why I brought you this." Evan pulled a wrapped gift box out of a bag that he had concealed by the table.

"Oh!" Elle was surprised. "Evan." She smiled.

"Go ahead and open it. I do enjoy seeing you smile."

Elle unwrapped the gift and opened the box. Nestled in white tissue was a beautiful rainbow-colored glass bowl. "Oh, my goodness! I love it." Elle studied the piece in amazement. "Is this from that little glass-blowing shop up in the mountains?"

"Yes. It's no Chihuly, but I thought it would go nice by your front door. You know, for keys and mail—that sort of stuff."

"Thank you so much. That's just what I will use it for." Elle stood up and hugged Evan.

"Well, I don't want to tie up any more of your weekend. You probably need to head home and get ready to start that new job on Monday."

Evan covered the check for lunch, and they both picked up their things to leave. Elle suddenly felt a bit teary. She looked around, wondering if there was a little steakhouse restaurant like this one that she could find in Auburn. She felt a little anxious about everything: the new apartment, new job, and a new way of doing things when Gary Lee would come home. She found comfort in the rainbow glass gift from Evan, something that would always remind her of their friendship.

They parted their ways outside the restaurant with another quick hug. Elle was feeling more optimistic about her new living arrangement in Auburn and wanted to do some last-minute shopping for the weekend. She also needed some water and snacks for the road trip to Auburn, so she drove down Main Street and pulled into the parking lot at Calhoun's Market.

Elle picked up a shopping cart and walked through the entrance of the grocery store. She loved Calhoun's and was going to miss it. She knew her way around, and within minutes, her shopping cart had all the essentials for the weekend. Elle became preoccupied with thoughts about her new job and life. She would have to find a new favorite grocery store and learn where to find everything around Auburn. Living as a single mom with an injured son would not be easy. She distinctly used the word "injured" and not "handicapped" when talking about Gary Lee.

Elle looked in her basket; it was more than enough for now. The last items she needed were some fresh fruit and orange juice. The market was busy with Saturday afternoon shoppers stocking up on their groceries for the week.

Elle turned to find her way to the orange juice. Suddenly, standing in front of her was Colleen Mason, Gillian's mother. A wave of anxiety passed over Elle. So many times she had thought about talking to Colleen and what she would say. Now here she was, and Elle couldn't think of any words.

"Colleen," Elle said, trying to sound pleasant. "How are you?" Elle studied Colleen's face to try and read the situation. She looked fatigued.

"Elle Dillanger?" the woman who was with Colleen said slowly, staring back at her. Elle presumed she was related by the family resemblance, perhaps her sister.

"I'm sorry I couldn't come to Gillian's funeral. I heard it was lovely," said Elle.

"Lovely?" The sister asked. "We had expected to attend a lovely violin recital this month. We wanted *that* to be lovely.

Instead, all we have to remember is her funeral. It's a good thing you weren't there."

"I'm so sorry—"

"Don't say it," interrupted Colleen. "'I'm sorry for your loss.' I've become tired of hearing that. I'm sorry for *YOUR* loss. Gillian is everyone's loss. This world is a darker place without her."

Elle continued to try and read Colleen's face, which had now become more energized.

"You know," said Colleen, moving closer to Elle. "There are times when I am very angry at your family. I've thought about throwing bricks through your windows, but that's a crime in Alabama."

Colleen had moved a bit too close for Elle's comfort, almost within striking range. Elle started to inch backward slowly while Colleen advanced toward her.

"It was a terrible accident, Colleen," said Elle. "We all are suffering from it."

"Accident? Is that what people are calling it? Was your son driving a hundred miles per hour by accident? Is that how you taught him to live—just do what he wants, when he wants, the privileged life on high cotton? Him and that racing crowd that he runs around with. Everyone living in that circle thinks they're entitled. 'Oh, the Kilgores are here!' They are all going to hell on a scholarship!

"My daughter didn't deserve to be treated without honor and respect! I wish she had never met your son. He sure had me fooled! He seemed like such a nice boy. Who would have thought that he would kill my beautiful Gillian with his recklessness?"

Elle had backed up her shopping cart and was slowly pulling it in reverse. She was trying to think of a way to escape the confrontation. People around the produce section had started to overhear the conversation and were murmuring while they watched. Someone pulled out a cell phone and took a video.

"I think this is a time when we need to come together to heal," Elle said softly, trying to calm the situation.

"Oh, you're one of *them*," said the sister. "We've heard that line. Forgiveness, right? Forgiveness heals the soul." The woman was raising her voice. She looked around and saw that there was now an audience. "What about justice?" she shouted. "Our beautiful Gillian is dead! She was taken away from us by your reckless son!"

The angry red-haired sister took a package of eggs out of the shopping cart and threw them toward Elle's feet. At this point, Elle thought she had better abandon her shopping trip and make a run for the door. She grabbed her purse from her shopping cart and started moving quickly down the aisle.

"God has a plan for hooligans, all right!" the sister shouted after her.

Elle was now hurrying for the first exit. She dashed across the front of the store to find the exit door. She slowed down to an average pace as she left. She didn't want to look like a criminal running. Elle burst out crying after she walked through the automatic doors.

Elle was gasping for air and needed to rest, but she dared not stop. She continued walking quickly through the parking lot. Having forgotten where she had parked, Elle kept clicking the remote on her key fob and looked for the flashing lights. At last, she could see them.

Elle jumped into her car and locked the doors. At least she felt safe for the moment. She leaned her head down over the steering wheel and let loose a fit of loud and uncontrollable crying. Still seized by panic, she looked up to make sure no one had followed her from the store.

Elle took a few more deep breaths and started to calm down. More than ever, she was now certain of her decision to move out of Blue Springs. Her life felt broken, at times ruined, but she believed there would be hope for her and Gary Lee in Auburn. Now she knew that she could not live in Blue Springs under the specter of the Mason family wrath.

She started her car and left the parking lot. Goodbye, Calhoun's Market; goodbye, Main Street. She drove past the office building where Evan must have been toiling away. Goodbye, DD&W. The bitter tears continued to stream down her face. Her future was veiled like a doorway obscured by a heavy screen. She could not see what was on the other side, but she knew that she had to pass through.

CHAPTER 34

The Rodeo-Kart paddock was buzzing with activity when Chad and Jayden walked through to get ready for Chad's first race. Chad was in Heat 4, so he had plenty of time to get prepared. Chad could feel the butterflies inside his stomach again as his adrenalin level rose. He was agitated that he couldn't control his nervous anticipation. He reached into his racing suit pocket to find his amber tiger's eye. It was his good luck stone that his mother had given him years ago. He kept it nestled inside his zipped pocket and found himself fiddling around with it nervously. Chad held the stone in his hand and said a short prayer. This was a big day for him, racing in Rodeo-Kart. The sound of chattering coaches reminded him that it was just like so many other races that Chad and his dad participated in on the East coast.

"Jacob, listen to me. Don't pass too soon. Wait for the moment and get inside," one dad was loudly coaching his son while Chad and Jayden walked by.

The man continued to drone on with orders. It reminded Chad of the endless stream of instructions his father used to give him before a race. Chad would always remember those words even if his dad was miles away. The sounds around him were like the same blah-blah-blah that he heard at his home track in Blue Springs.

"Poor kid," said Jayden as they kept walking. "How'd you like to have that father?"

"That *was* my father," said Chad. "He would say to me, 'Winners drink milk and losers go home' or 'That is what racecar drivers do. They win.' Ugh!"

"Sorry, man."

"Too much micromanagement. It made it difficult for me to make my own racing judgments. I always heard his voice in my head."

"How did you deal with that?" asked Jayden.

"I had to learn to ignore it. I love my dad, but I had to kick him out of my head. I had to hear my own thoughts."

"Hey, we've got some time," said Jayden. "Why don't we go over and watch how others are driving in the first two heats."

Chad agreed. They walked to the side of the paddock facing the track and leaned against the fence. The Senior level karters were already whizzing around the track. The first heat ended with Danny Doyle in his green Number 5 kart crossing the finish line. Two other karts also moved up to the finals. The next heat ended with Todd Cunningham in the top three. Jessica joined them on the fence, watching the karting action.

"You guys are going to have some tough competition if you make it through your heat," said Jayden.

"What do you mean *if?*" said Jessica with a smile.

"I looked at the list for Heat 4," said Jayden. "There's a couple of them you'll need to watch out for. Alicia Reinhold and Reginald Johnson—they're listed online as top karting contenders in the US."

"I know Reggie from karting in Alabama," said Chad. "I didn't know he was that highly renowned."

"Yeah. I looked him up. He placed in the Super Nationals last year in Vegas. I didn't see any pros in your heat, so you guys may do well."

"Yeah! We got this," said Chad, giving Jessica a quick smile and a wink. "Go Team Cottonwood!"

They walked back to the pit where the two twin purple and yellow karts were sitting on the dollies. Jessica's helpers were already filling up the fuel in her kart. Chad and Jayden tanked up the other kart. The crews pushed the karts out to the double column of

270

starting spaces on the track. Strong shoulders hoisted the two twin karts and set them on the ground in their painted spots—Chad in the eighth spot and Jessica right in front of him in the sixth. Twenty karts in all for the heat.

Jayden took a picture of them together in front of the karts. Jessica and Chad completed the usual ritual of suiting up with balaclava, neck brace, helmet, and gloves. Jessica put her helmet against Chad's and said sweetly, "Like we practiced yesterday." Her emerald green eyes were peering out of the helmet.

"Exit speed is everything," said Chad, and he tightened her pink helmet strap.

"Toodle-oo, kangaroo." Jessica laughed. She walked over and climbed into her kart.

Chad took a sip of water to stay hydrated before getting into his kart. He looked back and saw the younger boy, Jacob, get into the Number 31 kart. He remembered the boy's father giving out directions earlier in such a loud voice. They all had overheard the dishing out of directives. Jacob looked so young, his baby face showed signs of acne, and Chad thought he looked no more than thirteen years old. He needed to be at least fifteen to race in this heat, but his father should have kept him in Juniors. Chad hoped that the less experienced driver wouldn't be a problem on the track.

The racers were lined up and anxiously waiting for the green flag, engines revving. The announcer read through the names of the drivers for Heat 4 and reminded them to drive for safety. Chad could feel his heart beating in anticipation.

The green flag waved, and the whole field of karts lunged forward. The roar of the small motors was a pleasant, familiar sound to Chad. He heard some commotion behind him and presumed that someone stalled on the start. He didn't have time to look behind him—just forward, trying to stay close to Jessica in front of him.

The karts accelerated through the gears up to top speeds down the straightaway, everyone trying to maneuver into a better position for Turn 1. Chad could see the banners and the crowded stands out of the corner of his eye as he passed them. His speedometer showed seventy-one as they braked for the turn. Jessica was forced to the outside, and the kart that started seventh pulled ahead of her. This is exactly where Chad wanted to be—back-to-back with Jessica, ready to press through the field of karts.

"Come on, Jess! Line them up and let's push through on the inside," he said out loud as if she could hear him.

She did exactly that. Jessica pulled into the inside of the turn, and Chad followed on her bumper, forcing the other kart to the outside. Together they seemed unstoppable. Over the course of several more laps, they passed all but the Number 11 kart, who was in the lead. This one was not going to be as easy. Another two laps of chasing, and they inched closer to the Number 11 kart in front of Jessica. They were getting a little nearer each time they braked for a turn.

"Do it on Turn 4," Chad yelled. "Do it!"

As if she had heard Chad, Jessica outmaneuvered the lead kart on Turn 4, leaving just enough room for Chad to follow her. Together they had the lead with still eight laps to go! No time to celebrate, though—there was a huge pack of karts trying to chase them down.

Jessica followed a perfect line through the course, and Chad's kart seemed smoother than he had ever raced before. They were able to add some distance from the kart behind them in third place. Chad was thankful for whatever brilliant engineering Mr. Larsen had put into those machines.

Jessica had now reached the last kart in the back of the lap. It was Number 31, Jacob. She had pulled up close behind him and needed to pass, but he was driving so erratically. He didn't follow a clean line, which would be a risk for anyone trying to pass him. Chad now realized that faster karts had also moved up into the passing zone behind him and were looking for an opportunity to take the lead.

"Come on, Jess," said Chad. "If you don't hurry up and pass Jacob, the kart behind me is going to make a move and split us up."

The pack of karts rounded the last Turn 9 into the straightaway, and all the drivers punched it. The karts behind Chad pulled to the outside, and suddenly, they were three-wide on the straightaway.

Chad glanced at his speedometer—only seventy-three miles per hour. They were boxed in. Jessica had no room to pass Jacob, and Chad was also forced to stay behind her by the karts next to him. Unobstructed, the blue kart next to him kept accelerating past them, and another red kart, Number 23, flew by even faster.

Chad noticed the front wheel of the Number 23 kart passing him was wobbling, and suddenly, the whole red kart began to shake. Chad felt frozen in the moment as he watched Number 23 lose control and drive up the side of Jessica's purple kart. It became airborne and sailed over the front of her kart like a skier launching off a ski jump. Chad let off the gas and started pressing the brakes, hoping to give Jessica some room to dodge the flying kart. He veered left, not knowing if another kart was going to careen into him. He only knew that he had to get away from the crash about to erupt. Jessica's kart went into a spin from the side collision. She had no way to avoid the mayhem. The airborne red kart sailed over Jacob's head and came crashing down on the front of his Number 31 kart. *No, no, no,* Chad kept hearing in his head. Jessica was still spinning and headed into the pileup.

Suddenly, a kart rammed into the back of Chad and pushed him into the barrier on the outside of the track. He came to a sudden stop but had lost sight of Jessica's kart. Chad could hear some more karts colliding farther back on the track. After a few seconds, all the engines were silent. There was just smoke and carnage all around. People came onto the track waving red flags.

Chad sat in his kart, straining to see where Jessica had ended up, but he could not see her anywhere. Normally, drivers were not allowed to get out of their karts on the track, but the race was red-flagged, and Chad had to find Jessica. He climbed out of his kart and looked back on the roadway. The karts lay all around the straightaway like fallen soldiers in a Civil War battlefield. Pillars of blue smoke drifted among the wreckage. Half of the karts were involved in the pileup, but he didn't see Jessica's purple and yellow Number 17 anywhere.

One by one, the drivers stood up and climbed out of their karts. Chad took off his helmet and started running.

"Jessica!" he shouted, looking frantically around.

"Chad! Over here," Chad heard a call from the grassy infield.

He ran across the track into the grass, calling out Jessica's name. Jessica's kart must have stopped spinning and rolled into the track infield. He came upon her purple and yellow kart stopped in the open grass. The left body panels on the kart were all crunched up. Jessica had taken off her helmet and was trying to get out when Chad ran up to her.

"Jessica! I couldn't find you—I was freaking out. Are you okay?"

"I think so," she said. "Help me get out of this thing."

Chad grabbed her arm to lift her up.

"Ow, ow! Owie, not that arm," she said.

Chad came around the right side of the kart and lifted her by her right hand. She stood up and stepped out of the kart, poking at her left arm to check it out.

"Oh my God! That was the worst one I've ever been in," she said. "Come on."

Jessica trotted over to the major pileup thirty yards down the track. Chad was stunned for a moment and then followed. They came upon the red kart sitting on top of Jacob's Number 31. Chad could hear screams of pain from the wreckage. Jacob was pinned underneath, and two men were trying to lift it off of him. Jessica ran over and tried to help, seemingly oblivious to her own pain that she complained about seconds ago.

"Chad! We need you. I can't help," she shouted.

Chad ran over and helped lift the crashed Number 23 red kart out of the wreckage. The driver wanted to get out, but the men told him to hold still until they could separate the karts. With the extra hands, they managed to lift the whole kart into the air and carry it over to the side, driver and all. Other people were trying to extract Jacob, whose cries of pain had now faded into sobbing moans.

Chad stared at Jacob's kart. The front had been completely crushed with the boy's legs pinned under the metal tubes. It looked impossible to free him. Every time someone tugged on him to try and extract him, he would scream with pain. Finally, someone arrived with a portable cutting blade and sliced through the tubes of the flattened chassis. By this time, a man and a woman had driven up in a medical vehicle and took out an emergency stretcher for Jacob.

Mr. Larsen arrived. He was walking quickly while talking into a radio. Chad could hear someone squawking from the speaker. Bruce Larsen spoke briefly. The two people from the medical team were now putting Jacob on the stretcher, and then Bruce Larsen turned to Jessica.

"Are you okay?" Mr. Larsen asked her and Chad.

Jessica nodded but started to cry. Mr. Larsen put his arms around her.

"He's such a little boy," she said.

"They are going to airlift him over to the hospital," Mr. Larsen assured her. "It looks like he's the only one who was seriously injured. I'm so glad you're okay," he said, and he gave her another squeeze.

"Ow, ow," said Jessica, freeing up her left arm from his embrace.

"What's this?" he asked.

Jessica cradled her left arm in her right hand.

"I think that red kart drove over my arm," she said.

Mr. Larsen gently touched her left forearm, and Jessica winced. He pulled out his phone and started texting.

"I'm going to have Uncle Chuck take you over to the emergency room for an x-ray," Mr. Larsen explained.

"Daddy," she complained.

"No questions about it," he insisted.

"I'm going with you, too," said Chad.

"No, Chad," said Jessica. "The heat was red-flagged, and you will get third place. You can move on to the final."

"I'm sure my kart is messed up," he said, pointing at it.

They all turned to see Jayden wheeling Chad's purple Number 20 kart around back toward the pit.

"Hey, good news," Jayden shouted across the track, unaware of the conversation. "Your kart is fine."

Jessica turned back to Chad and took his hand. "You came all the way out here for this event, and now you have a chance to make it to the podium!" she implored him.

Chad shook his head. "I came all the way out here to be with you. Rodeo-Kart can wait."

A helicopter appeared in the air above the track infield. Everyone around them was scurrying in the wind from the chopper as it landed. Jacob was loaded on, and the helicopter took off with him and his father.

Chad ignored the activity and looked into Jessica's eyes. She leaned in and kissed him. Chad and Jessica just stood there holding each other tightly while the Medevac flew away. Chad didn't stop or even look up. He just held Jessica in his arms and kissed her again.

CHAPTER 35

The four-door pickup truck bounced along the road while Chuck Larsen drove Jessica and Chad across town to the emergency room at the nearby hospital. Jessica didn't like the idea, but her father insisted that she go for x-rays after the karting smashup. Mr. Larsen had to stay at the track and take care of the situation, and Jessica's forearm appeared to be bruised and swollen. Chad and Jessica sat in the back seat together, quietly holding hands, almost in shock.

"You should be racing right now," said Jessica, breaking the silence.

"No. I figured out my priorities, and I am right where I should be," Chad replied. "Maybe I've learned something from your father." He looked at her with great intent, and she finally gave in with a smile.

Uncle Chuck dropped them off at the emergency room entrance. Chad walked Jessica up to the reception desk while Uncle Chuck parked his truck. The E.R. in Texas looked the same as the one in Alabama, he thought. It was all too familiar: beige walls and vending machines in the back of the waiting room. It even smelled the same. The suppressing antiseptic filled the air. For a moment, he remembered his many trips to the hospital back in Alabama visiting Gary Lee. Chad was so relieved that Jessica walked away from her crash.

A small woman in a long white coat greeted them.

"What is the reason you are here? Do you have a life-threatening condition?" she asked.

"I hurt my left arm," Jessica explained. "My dad said I need to have it x-rayed."

The woman extended to Jessica a clipboard full of papers. It was as if they were already waiting for Jessica to walk in through the front doors. The emergency room was ready for them.

"It won't be long until you can see a doctor," the receptionist said with a smile. "Please fill out these forms and bring them back up to me so I can get your examination process started."

Chad gladly accepted the clipboard for her, and the two young karters, still dressed in their race suits, found their way to vacant seats in the emergency center waiting room.

"I'd be happy to sign for you—with your permission, of course," said Chad, waving the black ballpoint pen as he was pretending to sign the initials "JL" on the clipboard.

Jessica smiled in response, but she didn't look like she wanted to smile; it was strained. Jessica was obviously in pain.

"Give that to me," she said. "I have to fill it out."

Chad handed the clipboard over to Jessica.

"Sorry," he said. "I'm just trying to cheer you up."

"I know. I don't like emergency rooms."

Jessica concentrated on filling out the paperwork and then brought it back to the receptionist. Uncle Chuck came through the entrance and joined Jessica. They walked together back to where Chad was sitting.

"So what happened out there?" Chuck asked. "It looked like a war zone on the track."

"A kart veered into me, drove right up the side of my kart, and flew over the one in front of me," explained Jessica.

"He had some kind of steering or axle failure," added Chad. "His right wheel went crazy just before he lost control."

"I'm just glad you're in one piece here, Jess," said Chuck, and he put his arm around her. "Are you all signed in to get that x-ray now?"

"Yeah, sort of. She said I could be treated, but they need Dad's insurance info."

"I'll send him a text now," said Chuck, and he pulled out his phone.

"What do you think happened to that boy?" Jessica asked Chad. "He was so little. Why was he driving in the Senior class?"

"Jacob? I don't know. His dad probably thought he was too old for Juniors," said Chad.

"I saw him in the wreckage, and his legs were so mangled and bloody." Jessica started to cry.

She leaned on Chad's shoulder, and he put his arm around her. Jacob was in the Number 31 kart, the kid whose father was lecturing him before the race. The droning sound of that voice played over in Chad's head again, "Don't pass too soon, son. Don't pass too soon." But Jacob never had a chance to pass anyone.

Jessica looked at him with teary eyes and said, "Two years ago, a girl was killed at our track, but they didn't pronounce her dead until she was at the hospital. Everyone put flowers and stuffed animals outside of the gates of the park. It was so sad. Her kart flipped over, and she was ejected into traffic. Her helmet flew off, too. Other karts tried to avoid her, but it was gruesome." Jessica started to weep again as she recalled the details. "I don't even remember her last name."

"I am so sorry that this happened to you today, Jess," said Chad. "I'm sure that our boy Jacob will be okay. He had his helmet on, and he was conscious." Chad tried to be positive. "Don't worry. Think good thoughts."

"That's what everyone always says. He was screaming in pain, though." Jessica wiped her eyes with a tissue that her uncle handed to her.

"He's here, you know," said Uncle Chuck.

"What?" asked Jessica.

"The boy you were talking about," said Chuck. "I saw the helicopter that brought him in when I was parking the truck."

The large automatic doors into the medical area opened, and a woman in blue appeared. She called for Jessica Larsen.

"You all can come with me," Jessica said, standing up.

The three of them followed the triage nurse into the heart of the E.R. They walked past exam rooms filled with equipment and an occasional patient. Chad wondered if they might see Jacob while they walked down the hall. The nurse led them into an empty room and asked Jessica to sit on the exam table.

Jessica unzipped her race suit down to the waist, revealing a soft cotton T-shirt that hugged the curves of her torso. She gracefully slid her arms out, folded the top of the suit under her, and sat down. This was a surprisingly sensual display for Chad, but he wished it was under different circumstances. Jessica noticed Chad staring and gave him a squinty look with a sly smile. He was embarrassed by his arousal among the others in the room, but he couldn't take his eyes off her.

The nurse took Jessica's vitals and left the room. A man came in wearing a similar light blue outfit and introduced himself as her doctor. He proceeded to ask Jessica about her accident. He held her left forearm in his hands and gently probed along its length. Jessica winced several times during the process.

"We'll take an x-ray, but I already know what it's going to show," said the doctor. "You have a middle fracture in your ulna, and there doesn't appear to be any dislocation."

Jessica let out a grunt of disgust.

"Cheer up," said the doctor. "This is one of the simplest breaks I've seen in a long time. There's almost no bruising, not too much swelling around the bone. You'll be as good as new in about six weeks."

Jessica was still not happy about it. The doctor left, and the nurse returned to take Jessica down to Radiology.

"You all can return to the waiting room," the nurse said to Chad and Uncle Chuck. "This will take about forty-five minutes."

The two walked back down the hall of the E.R. Chad was still curious if he might find out something about Jacob. They exited out into the waiting room and sat down.

"Well, that's pretty much what I expected to hear," said Chuck. "Have you ever broken any bones, Chad?" he asked.

"Oh, yeah. I've been karting since I was seven, so I've been in the E.R. many, many times. The really bad one was a broken leg, but I've busted fingers and such."

"Hobbling around on crutches?"

"Yep."

"Our family, too," said Chuck. "Being a roughneck in the oil field, you get your share of injuries."

Chad nodded. Broken shoulders, broken legs, and bruised knees were just a part of the racing experience. Chad had seen all kinds of injuries on the karting track in his short life, but today's crash was definitely the worst.

Chad and Chuck sat there with others who were either waiting for loved ones or waiting for the triage nurse to call their names. The afternoon wore on, the waiting room had gained more people, and each one had their own story of pain and suffering.

Chad checked his phone and saw that many messages had been piling up over the weekend. He didn't want to be interrupted and had been ignoring the vibration of reminders. His father had called a few times and finally had sent a message: *911 PLEASE CALL HOME ASAP*. He started to call the number back, and the phone suddenly shut off. The battery was completely dead. Chad tried to turn it back on, but it would just shut off again before he could do anything. He would have to use a car charger and call later. ASAP would have to wait.

Waiting for anything was always annoying for Chad. He decided to go to the vending machine out of anxiousness to look for something to eat and pass the time. He scanned the selection, but his mind was on bigger things. What comes next? His Rodeo-Kart weekend would fade away soon enough. Jessica would go off to college, she would completely recover, and he would go back to doing what? His heart was suddenly racing, and nothing made sense. Leaving tomorrow didn't seem right. Going back to life in Blue Springs without Jessica would be so empty. Did his future plans include her, and how would that work out? So many questions. His heart and mind were racing without a finish line in sight.

Mr. Larsen arrived through the E.R. entrance almost breathless and came over to Chad and Chuck. Uncle Chuck explained what had happened, and Mr. Larsen went over to the registration desk to fill out any remaining paperwork. Jessica finally appeared from behind the big automatic doors. She came strutting out with a bright pink cast on her forearm, holding it up for everyone to see.

"Look what I get to wear for six weeks," she said facetiously.

"There you are," Mr. Larsen said, and he kissed Jessica on the forehead. "That's what I thought you were going to need."

Jessica was grateful to see her dad. He held her face in his hands and then gave her a long and loving hug, making sure not to touch her arm.

"Don't mess up my hair, Dad," she said after the hug lasted for more than twenty seconds.

"Let's go," said Mr. Larsen. "We have the award ceremony in thirty minutes."

Jessica held her father's hand like a small child, and they walked out the double doors to the parking lot. A reporter and TV cameraman were waiting outside the E.R., and when they saw Jessica and Chad in their race suits, they hurried over.

"Mr. Larsen," the woman said into a microphone with the camera pointed at them. "What can you tell us about Jacob Daniels?" She shoved the microphone in front of him.

"All I can say is that he was injured in an unfortunate karting accident during the Rodeo-Kart competition. The doctors told me he was in stable condition."

"Is it true that he lost his leg in the crash at your karting park?" the reporter asked.

"I'm sorry," he said. "That's a private matter for his family. Please excuse us."

Mr. Larsen pushed past the reporter. Jessica had a look of horror on her face.

"Is that true, Daddy," Jessica asked him while they walked to the car.

"I heard that from our emergency team as well, so it probably is true," he replied.

She put her hand over her mouth and gasped. "I tried to help him. I just couldn't lift the kart off of him," she said.

"Jess, you had a broken arm!" Chad came to her defense. "It took four of us to lift that kart off him. You did everything you could and more."

Chad's explanation didn't seem to console her, and she appeared to be in a daze until they reached the car.

"Thanks for all your help, Chuck," Mr. Larsen said to his brother.

"Yes, thank you. I love you, Uncle Chuck," Jessica added, and she gave him a one-armed hug.

"I'll see y'all back at the park," Chuck said and headed for his truck.

Jessica claimed the front seat in her father's car with an attempted smile, and her hazel eyes twinkled a little bit more. She looked tired but still as beautiful as ever. Chad wanted never to forget how Jessica Larsen looked at that moment—like a celebrity on a magazine cover in her half-unzipped race suit. His desire for this girl racer was overwhelming. He hoped that she had that same tingling feeling that seemed to take over his body every time she was close to him.

CHAPTER 36

Chad, Jessica, and her father returned from the hospital to the Cottonwood Karting Park just in time for the Rodeo-Kart awards ceremony at 7 p.m. The parking lot was packed, and the twinkling, colored party lights by the grandstand were just becoming visible. The smell of pulled pork, barbequed ribs, bonfire burgers, and corn on the cob filled the air. Chad was starving, and he was glad that the weekend wasn't over yet.

Jessica had walked out of the emergency room cleared for most activities. She had some bruises on her knees and a fracture on her left forearm. The doctor sent her home with her arm in a short cast, some Tylenol, a sling, and a strict order to rest. The sling came off before she stepped out of her dad's car.

"Jessica," her father said to her, taking the sling out of the car. "You know that your health is important to me." He placed the sling around his daughter's left arm to cradle it. "The sling will support your arm while it heals, and you need to treat your arm gently," he said, and they all started walking into the park.

Jessica looked at her father and rolled her eyes. "It's not like anyone is going to throw me down or slam me into a fence while I'm line dancing."

"I don't think you will be dancing tonight, Jess. You have to take it easy—doctor's orders. Remember?"

"We are not missing the party, Dad. Chad and I are going to the celebration tonight. I am fine."

Mr. Larsen laughed and said, "Well, just keep your sling on your arm and don't take it off. I will be watching you like a hawk. Now I have to get on over to the podium and give out the awards. I want you to take it easy. No fooling around."

They had arrived at the stands. A podium had been set up on the track in front of the grandstand, which was brimming with people. Mr. Larsen headed over to the group gathered at the podium while Chad and Jessica went up the stairs into the stands. She took off the sling and tossed it over the edge. The two made their way up through the rows looking for someplace comfortable to sit. Suddenly, Jayden appeared, standing up and waving at them. He had some seats saved for them, and they crossed over and sat down with him.

"Oh my God, I love it," said Jayden, checking out Jessica's pink cast. "Can I?" he asked, pulling out a pen. Jessica nodded, and Jayden drew a picture of a band-aid across her cast with a big "Ouch" in cartoon letters. She smiled.

"So you broke your arm," said Jayden. "Nothing more?"

"Not for me, but I think that little kid Jacob was really hurt," she said. "A reporter asked if he had lost his leg."

"Oh, that's terrible! Do you think that happened?"

Jessica nodded. "I don't know. I hope not, but Dad seemed to think so." Jessica was squeezing Chad's hand as she spoke. "He shouldn't have been racing in that group. It's so stupid for kids to drive above their level. Their parents think it will make them a better driver, but it just makes them dangerous."

"I'm really thankful you're okay," said Jayden.

Chad looked out over the track and the infield. It had been transformed into a fantastic themed party, a *Night of Stars*. There was a Winners' Circle podium set up facing the stands. Farther back in the infield was a large stage set up for a band with big silver stars shining over the backdrop. It was a great setting for a celebration.

Chad didn't want to miss the announcement of the Rodeo-Kart winners and the presentation of the cash prizes and trophies. The top cash was traditionally given out rolled up in hundred dollar bills in a felt Stetson cowboy hat.

Mr. Larsen was on the podium and introduced the karting organizations and major companies that sponsored the event. He started naming the winners of the younger age groups in runner-up order: third, second, and first.

"So what did we miss," Jessica asked, trying to see who might be on the podium for Seniors. "Did Chad blow his chance to win ten grand?"

"Wow. The finals were crazy," said Jayden. "Good crazy— nothing like what you guys experienced. Cunningham was dominant. He kept running teenagers off the course right and left. AJ should have flagged him, but you know how it is with the pros."

"So who won?" shouted Chad over the applause in the stands.

"Cunningham, another pro racer, Sanchez, and then some karting kid from Houston."

"How did Reggie Johnson do?" asked Chad.

"Well, he would have done better if Cunningham hadn't run him off on Turn 9. By the time he was back up to speed, five more karts had passed him."

"See," Chad said, turning to Jessica. "Don't even worry about me not racing. I would not have done any better than Reggie. The highlight of my karting this weekend was racing with you, the Cottonwood team. The finals wouldn't have meant as much without you." He offered her a gentle fist bump, which she took with a smile.

Mr. Larsen began the introductions of the sponsors for the Senior class prizes. Various people shook hands on the stage with mild applause from the audience. Finally, he announced for third place Sofia Novak from Houston, Texas. Jessica stood up and shouted with her pink cast in the air.

"Yeah, Sofia! Go, girl power!"

Mr. Larsen continued announcing the winners—for second place, Renaldo Sanchez, from Charlotte, North Carolina. Jessica just looked at Chad and smiled uneventfully. Chad felt obliged to clap for second place.

"You know what they call second place, don't you?" she asked a loaded question.

"First loser," Chad and Jessica said in unison. They laughed.

Finally, a giant six-foot check was brought out on the podium. Mr. Larsen announced that the winner of the $10,000 grand prize would be…Todd Cunningham. The stands erupted in applause and cheers. Chad and Jayden clapped for the winner, but Jessica continued just to sit and smile.

"What is with you?" asked Chad. "Isn't he your dad's friend?"

"A pro racer always wins this event. I'm not a big fan of the pro racers edging out the teenage karters who work so hard to race and try to win. Cunningham doesn't need to do that."

"But that's part of the excitement of Rodeo-Kart. You get to race with your racing heroes," argued Chad.

Jessica shook her head. "Maybe it could be great, but they usually are more like big bullies out on the track. Imagine if a pro football player went out to play with the high school kids."

"That would be great. They would love it."

"Not if the pro lineman was flattening the poor high school kids like he had to beat the pants off of them."

Chad made a face. "I see what you mean. Is it really like that?"

Jessica nodded. "Not everyone, but enough to make it suck."

The crowd cheered again when the Stetson felt hats were presented by the local high school Dixie Darlings. The rolls of cash were quickly stashed in the drivers' racing suits.

Once the award ceremony was over, Mr. Larsen announced the *Night of Stars* party, complete with barbeque, music, and dancing in the track infield. Behind him, musicians were arriving on the stage. The karting paraphernalia had been cleared out of the infield, and the dancing area was all decorated with stars and twinkling lights.

"I have got to get out of these clothes," complained Jessica about her race suit. "Why don't you get changed and meet me over by the chuck wagon in half an hour?"

She pointed to an authentic chuck wagon that was serving dinner at the side of the infield. Jessica stood up and made her way out of the stands. Jayden said that he would see them down there and took off, also.

What a wild day, thought Chad, sitting in the stands alone while the people filed out. Ever since his racing scholarship plans had fizzled, he had been mentally in neutral gear, just coasting along and trying to figure out what he should do next. He knew that his dad would like him to work at Rusty's Wrench and Tire with him. Chuck Larsen had made him an offer to work on their oil equipment in San Antonio. Maybe he still had a good connection with the Kilgores and could work on Mackie's pit crew for the rest of the season. Chad could even move to Auburn, get a job, and help Gary Lee get back on his feet. So many options, but how could he know where any of them would lead? Even more important, how could he make this new relationship with Jessica work?

He could hear that the band started playing some Texas swing music, and Chad realized he was burning through his thirty minutes to get changed and meet Jessica. He headed over to his trailer to trade in his race suit for some jeans.

Chad was famished by the time he returned to the track infield. The air was full of the aromas of a wood smoker and barbeque. There was a long line of people at the chuck wagon waiting to pick up some dinner. Near the front of the line, Chad saw a flash of pink—Jessica's cast. She was insanely cute in her cutoff shorts and a dark blue checkered shirt. Predictably, some other boys in the line were busy talking with her. She ran to him and tried to wrap her arms around Chad's neck as soon as he came closer.

"Sorry," she said with a kiss after bonking him on the side of his head with her cast.

Jessica introduced Chad to the other boys in line, who she apparently had just met. They all had signed her cast, too. Chad tried to remind himself there was nothing to worry about or be jealous about.

Chad and Jessica picked up their dinners and walked over to the picnic table area. The Larsen family were all seated there and waved them over. Chad felt relief as he devoured his ribs. The worst of the day was behind him. He and Jessica laughed at each other with barbeque sauce on their faces.

"Wait. Don't wipe that off," said Jessica. "Barbeque Kiss," she announced and gave Chad a very saucy kiss.

"Eww, gross," said Jayden, laughing.

"Quite a day, huh, darlin'?" said Aunt Liddy. Jessica nodded and cleaned her face off. "I'm so glad you're going to college and won't be doing so much of this karting stuff anymore."

Jessica got up and walked over to hug her aunt. "That is so sweet, Aunt Liddy. I'm not sure if I am ready to give it up, but I am glad to be taking a break from it."

Jessica walked back over to Chad, who had cleaned himself up after devouring the ribs. The band was playing some classic country, and the line dancing had started.

"Come on, cowboy," she said to him, holding out her hand. "Let's see you dance!"

They held hands while they made their way over to the dirt dance floor.

The singer announced, "Here's a special request for all our friends visiting from Alabama."

The band started up the classic anthem, singing, "Sweet home, Alabama…."

"Is that for me?" Chad asked Jessica.

She smiled and said, "Who else?"

They joined the lines of people dancing in front of the band—stomping, turning, and clapping. There were all kinds of folks dancing: some older, some teenagers, some little kids, some in race suits, and of course the new Cottonwood duo. The song ended, and Jessica let out a "Whoo-hoo!"

The two stood there clapping for the exceptional dancing music, and the band started to play a slow western ballad. Chad stepped up to Jessica, whose loving hazel eyes looked back at him. He put his arms around her waist, and she put her arms over his shoulder, gently resting her cast on him. They began to sway with the soft lilt of the fiddle and strum of the guitar. The two danced together until the stars came out, moving to the songs of a good ol' Texas band. It was a night that Chad would remember for the rest of his life.

CHAPTER 37

The wood-paneled ceiling above Chad's bed in the trailer now looked familiar when he awoke the next morning. It was Sunday morning, and there was nothing to rush off to. The sun was up, and the light was streaming in through the window, making patterns on the wall. Chad remembered the morning visit from Jessica yesterday and hoped she would show up again this morning. He could tell it wasn't early and wondered what time it was. Chad picked up his phone, which he had fortunately remembered to plug in last night, and saw that it was 8:30. There was a voice mail waiting. He listened.

"Hey, Chad, this is Dad. I wish you would pick up your phone! I have great news for you. There is a racing contract waiting for you here in Blue Springs. Call me when you get this and be sure you're home by Monday morning," the message said.

Chad immediately called his father back, but there was no answer. They were probably out to breakfast or maybe an early church service. No matter—he now knew that he should return home right away, and he would see them that night. Chad was suddenly thrilled with the possibilities. He could be racing real racecars in the next season, and his mind was flooded with thoughts. He would need to start practicing; that would cost money, but he could get a job; living at home would keep his costs down—on and on.

Chad got dressed. His head was spinning, and he couldn't wait to tell Jessica. He rummaged around the kitchen and found all the basics for making coffee. There was a knock on the door, and Jayden came in.

"Hey, Chad. I saw you were up."

"Yeah, I was just going to make some coffee. Do you want some?" offered Chad.

"No, thanks. My mom sent me over to invite you to breakfast. She has the outdoor griddle heating up and will be cooking eggs and other stuff."

"Sure. That sounds better than another snack bar."

"Oh, you found the emergency food stash. So that was some day yesterday, huh?"

"It was incredible—both scary and thrilling. Do you guys do that every year?"

"Rodeo-Kart rotates around to different tracks each year. This was Uncle Bruce's second year hosting it." Jayden paused. "So I need to talk to you about Jessica."

"Sure."

"You know, she doesn't have an older brother, so I kind of do the job of looking out for her. I like you, so don't freak out. I see how she looks at you, and she's kind of vulnerable right now. She had some serious heartbreak from her last boyfriend."

Chad felt a little defensive. "Jayden, I've only known her for like three weeks."

"That's not what she told me. She said she met you back in June when she was out in Alabama. She said that she fell for you in June."

Chad was now really shocked. "Yeah, she was at the karting practice showing off the superkart. I did meet her then, but it was no big deal."

"Well, I think it was a big deal to her. She told me about a sweet guy she had met. She never uses that word, so you must have made an impression on her. So let me ask you this: When you first met Jessica, did she make an impression on you?"

Chad realized that he had to come clean with Jayden. "Yes. Absolutely. I thought she was the most amazing girl I had ever met, and it's only getting more amazing. Honestly."

"Okay, now we're getting somewhere. I want to know what your intentions are."

Chad had expected a talk like this from Mr. Larsen. He stopped and thought for a moment. "I can tell you this: I don't want it to end right now." Chad was trying to be as honest as he could. "Being with Jessica is like nothing I've done before, but I'm just trying to figure out what I'm going to do with my life next."

"Okay."

"You won't believe it, but just this morning, I had a voice mail from my dad telling me that I have a racing contract waiting for me in Blue Springs tomorrow."

"A racing contract? That sounds pretty significant. That is what you've been hoping for, right?"

"Look, I can do a long-distance relationship with Jessica for a while, and then once the racing season starts, I can afford to move to Texas," explained Chad. He was now winging it—trying to figure it all out on the fly, but the idea actually sounded pretty good.

"You're saying 'I' a lot. You need to talk to Jessica about this."

Just then, the trailer door opened and Jessica stomped in. She looked fantastic. Her hair was pulled back, and she had on a peach summer dress, but there was no smile on her face.

"You guys are late! You're holding up breakfast," she said sternly.

"Sorry, Jess. We were just about to head over," said Jayden. "Chad was telling me here about the racing contract that he's been offered back in Blue Springs."

"Oh, congratulations!" she said in a strange way.

Jessica walked up to Chad. He was expecting a kiss or something, but she thumped him on the chest with her hands and her cast, startling him.

"That's exactly what you've been hoping for, right?" she said.

Chad looked into her eyes and saw resentment. He tried to hold her, but she pulled back and walked over to the kitchen area. She slammed the coffee can on the counter.

"I hope you get into every race you dream of and get to the podium every time," she said.

"Jessica," Chad pleaded, "what's gotten into you?"

"Oh, she's annoyed that you're leaving," explained Jayden.

"Shut up, Jayden!" said Jessica, slamming a coffee cup on the counter. "He doesn't need a relationship translator to figure that out."

"Jess, you were mad even before you found out he was going to be racing," said Jayden.

Chad was bewildered. Jessica paced back to him. "So you're headed back home to Alabama to your dad and your family and your best friend," she said, taunting him. "Hmmm?" she questioned, still fiery-eyed.

Chad looked over at Jayden behind her, and he was nodding.

"Jessica, stop. I love you," Chad confessed. He grabbed onto her so she couldn't pull away. "I don't want to leave you."

Jessica struggled for a moment and then gave up. With her face buried into his shoulder, she let out a groan. Jayden was nodding again in the background. Chad surprised himself. He had been hesitant to reveal his true feelings.

"I don't want to be that girl," said Jessica, "who just amused some boy who floated into her life, melted her heart, and then left, never to be seen again." She sobbed with her face again in his shoulder.

He held her tightly. "I could never do that." Chad himself was overwhelmed with emotion, and his eyes filled with tears.

Jessica lifted up her head and looked at him. He could not hide his feelings, and the anger was gone from her eyes.

"I love you, too," was all she could say, and she kissed him passionately.

"I'm going to wait outside," said Jayden, and he slipped out the trailer door.

Chad ran his fingers through Jessica's hair, and she touched his face with her hands. Jessica paused and took a deep breath.

"So here's the deal," she started. "If we are going to try and make this work, I need to see you every now and then." She smiled at how silly that sounded. "I mean, I'm going to be living in College Station, Texas, going to school. It would make me so happy if you were there, but I can be flexible," Jessica said while she played with Chad's shirt collar.

"Hey, I get it," Chad interrupted her. "That's what I want too, but we may need to work something out until the spring. I have a lot of options, but this racing thing could be my big break. I won't know until tomorrow morning."

"I don't want to ruin anything for you," she said. "I love you too much to do that. I'm not a selfish person." She started to weep again.

Chad held her close. "You have the biggest heart I know. That's something I love about you. Listen, a racecar driver can live almost anywhere and just travel during the racing season. If this works out and I start making some real money, I can move to College Station."

Jessica's face lit up. "Really?"

"Really," he assured her, nodding.

Jessica took a deep breath and put on a serious face. "If this doesn't work out," she said with a long pause, "I won't hold it against you." She put her finger on his lips. "Because I know the racing business is grueling, and if you can't get away and visit me and be in my life, I will understand. I will. I promise."

She steadfastly looked into Chad's eyes; her expression was still serious, and a tear rolled down her cheek. "I hope that you will visit me every week," she said and held on to him tightly.

Chad held her in his arms but was terrified by what she said. Long-distance relationships often didn't work out. He wanted to be hopeful, but he dreaded the thought of losing her.

"I believe," said Chad, "that when two people love each other, they will find a way to make it work. It's all good."

Chad worried that he sounded like a greeting card message, but he needed to keep himself positive. Jessica nodded with a slight sniffle. She took a tissue from the box by the couch and gently wiped her eyes.

"So that's the plan," she said, taking another deep breath and then smiling at him. "Come on. Let's go get some breakfast."

Chad felt a sudden sense of accomplishment and relief. For the first time in many weeks, he had something to look forward to beyond this weekend. He actually knew what he was going to do.

Chad and Jessica walked out the door of the trailer into a beautiful Texas Sunday morning. Jayden was patiently waiting, tossing pebbles at some squirrels. He looked at Chad, and Chad gave him a thumbs-up sign. Jayden smiled.

CHAPTER 38

Everyone was already sitting down for breakfast at the Larsens' camp area when Chad, Jessica, and Jayden arrived. It smelled delicious once more—that hickory smokehouse aroma. Aunt Liddy asked them how they liked their eggs cooked, and she cracked some onto the griddle.

"We've got bacon, sausage, potatoes, and there's some toast over on the table," Liddy said.

Chad brought his plate of eggs with everything over to the table and sat down across from Mr. Larsen, Jessica's father. Jessica and Jayden also joined them.

"I really want to thank you, Chad," said Mr. Larsen, "for going with Jessica to the hospital yesterday."

"I couldn't imagine not going with her," said Chad.

"Well, Jayden informed me that you would have moved up to the finals if you stayed and raced. That says a lot."

"I still feel terrible about that," said Jessica, with a piece of bacon in her hand.

"Chad," continued Mr. Larsen. "You know we have rental karts here at the park, and they really could use some attention. I know you have a lot of things up in the air right now, but I would like to extend you an offer to work here at Cottonwood for the rest of the summer. You can stay in the Palace while you're here."

"Oh, Daddy, that is so sweet of you," said Jessica, "but I think Chad may have some new plans coming together."

"Yes, thank you so much, Mr. Larsen," said Chad. "That is a very generous offer, but I did find out from my dad this morning that I've been offered a racing contract, and I have to get home right away." Chad received congratulations from everyone around the table.

"Very nice. Is that offer from the Kilgore team?" Mr. Larsen asked.

"I don't know yet. I'll find out when I get home tonight."

"Well, if you don't need to start right away, or if the deal doesn't work out, the offer still stands," said Mr. Larsen. "Just a word of caution. Not all racing deals are great for the driver, and some contracts are not worth the paper they are printed on."

"Daddy!" grumbled Jessica.

"Now, just hear me out," he continued. "This is for Chad's benefit. I know that you probably have never seen an actual racing contract, and there are warning signs to look for.

"For example, if your income is based on the number of people you recruit into the company and not the sales of products to real customers. If you are required to buy lots of inventory or other things that you don't want or need to stay in good standing with the company. Also, watch for possible indebtedness or if they offer to pay you in Monopoly money."

"Monopoly money? Do you mean like the Kilgores' kartcoin?" questioned Chad.

"Yes. Smart kid. Just like in the board game, that's fake money—all those kartcoins that Kilgore offers to the karters who bring in new customers. You can't buy groceries with kartcoin or pay rent with it, so don't expect to be able to live on a contract like that."

Chad nodded. "Thanks for the advice," he said.

"If you have doubts about a contract, have a lawyer take a look at it," Uncle Chuck added. "Didn't your friend Ricky get stuck in a bad contract?" he asked his brother.

Mr. Larsen nodded. "Oh yeah, that was a lesson learned! My friend Ricky continued on in racing after me and signed into this awful contract. They had promised him the world, but his main job

298

was cold calling businesses to see if they would sponsor him. He didn't reach the minimum sponsorship obligation and wound up owing the team owner tens of thousands of dollars. After two years, Ricky's dad, who fortunately was well off, had to bail him out."

Chad was horrified.

"Any racing organization worth working for will have their own marketing people and not rely on the drivers to do all the sales work," said Uncle Chuck.

Chad had finished his breakfast and washed it down with a glass of orange juice. He wasn't going to let himself worry too much about his contract until he found out more about it.

"You look awfully pretty this morning, darlin'," said Aunt Liddy to Jessica.

"Thank you," she answered. "I got dressed up for the service at the karting park. The chaplain is going to hold a prayer time for Jacob. I wanted to make a donation to the fund they are collecting for him."

Chad was surprised, but no one else seemed to be.

"The park is closed for karting on Sunday morning," Jessica started to explain. "Since all the people are still here from Saturday night, Daddy has some church folks come over, and the chaplain holds an informal Sunday service in the stands."

"So you want us to go there? When is it?" asked Chad.

"Yeah. I hope you don't mind. I thought it might be a nice thing to do since it's your last day here," she said. "It starts at 10:00 a.m., so we should walk over there in a few minutes."

"I'm afraid it will be just you two unless Jayden wants to join you," said Mr. Larsen.

"Sorry, guys, but I'm on vacation," said Jayden.

Jessica stood up and waited for Chad. "You look so nice, but I just have this T-shirt and shorts," said Chad.

"Don't worry about it. You're fine," said Mr. Larsen. "You guys go. It is a come-as-you-are kind of activity."

Chad stood up and thanked Aunt Liddy for breakfast. Liddy nodded thoughtfully and took Chad's hand. "I tell people in your shoes to follow your heart," she said. "Figure out what the one thing is in the world that you love the most and go for it. Everything else will fall into place. It was so nice to have you here this weekend." She gave him a quick kiss on the cheek.

Chad took Jessica's hand, and they started walking together out of the camping area. They walked through the gate out onto the track and headed toward the stands. Jessica had a pleasantness in her stride, a warmth of confidence and beauty.

"The real reason I wanted to go to the service is to pray for Jacob," said Jessica. "I didn't want to say that in front of everyone at breakfast."

"Don't you think God can hear you pray anywhere?" asked Chad.

"Well, yes, but somehow it feels like a prayer sent up in a setting with faith would have more weight. Maybe that's just my perspective. After all, I'm no saint."

Maybe she was not a saint, but she seemed pretty angelic to Chad.

"I have trouble with prayer," Chad confessed.

"How so?"

"My mom used to take us to church. When she became sick, I would sit in the church pew and pray so hard for God to heal her."

"I see. So you feel like God didn't hear you."

"Think about the pastor who prayed for safety yesterday morning at the drivers' meeting. That didn't stop Jacob from being in a terrible crash."

"Well, how do you know that prayer didn't save his life?" asked Jessica. "Or mine? A few inches over and that kart could have easily crashed on his head instead of on his leg."

"I don't know why bad things happen." Chad shrugged. "When my mom was getting sicker, I started to get angry. She would tell me, 'Now don't be mad at God. It's not his fault, no matter what they say.'"

"Wow, she sounds like quite a mom," said Jessica.

Chad nodded, getting a little choked up. "She would say, 'In all the stories you learned about Jesus, when did he ever make anyone sick?'"

300

"She's got a point there." Jessica paused. "You're very lucky. I wish I could have had a mom like that."

"Really? From what I've been hearing, your mom sounds fantastic. Did I miss something?"

"You didn't, but I did. Mothering is what I missed out on. Sure, my mom is an amazing woman, tenacious in business, a real Parisian role model. You could say she leads by example, but she doesn't do mothering." Jessica sighed. "She doesn't believe in God, either."

"Wow. I see what you mean. That's like the total opposite of my mom. At least you still have her."

"She's no more with me than your mom is with you," said Jessica, pointing to his heart.

Chad smiled. She was right. So many of the things he cherished in life were connected to his mother, who now lived on in his heart. At that moment, Jessica with her huge heart reminded him a little of his mom.

They had reached the stands by now and could see that a small crowd had gathered for the Sunday service. A man and a woman were on the podium; he was strumming out some music on a guitar. Jessica and Chad came to the stairs, and a young man handed them a piece of paper. It had the words to the songs on it. They climbed up the stairs and found a nice spot in the center, a few rows up.

Chad sat listening to the music for a moment, savoring the peaceful sound. He turned to look at Jessica. She was sitting with her eyes closed. Chad watched her for a minute or two, studying the lines on her face and wondering what she might be saying in her prayer. Jessica opened her eyes and looked at him. Chad reached over and took her hand.

"Today, my prayer is one of thankfulness," he said. A wide smile appeared on Jessica's face, and she squeezed his hand.

The man playing the guitar stepped to the microphone on the podium. He thanked everyone for coming out, and they started to sing the first song of praise. All of the songs were simple. A mixture of hymns, praise songs, and traditional ones he remembered from when he was younger. All these things brought Chad back to a time when he was happy as a young boy. It gave him hope that he could be happy again and that his adult life didn't have to be a tragic story.

Chad looked around at the people in the stands. They ranged from little children to great-grandparents, all singing together in their own simple way. Yesterday they were all competing on the track, and this morning they were all holding hands.

They closed out with a prayer and an offering for Jacob Daniels, who was recovering in the local hospital. The service ended on a happy note with cheerful songs, and the guitar player had a chance to show off his flat-picking.

Afterward, everyone stood up in the stands to leave except Jessica. "I don't want it to end because I know what comes next," she said. "You're leaving now, aren't you?"

Chad nodded. "You're not going to get mad at me again, are you?" He sat down next to Jessica.

She shook her head. "I was mad because I thought our time together was ending. I started to think you didn't care about me."

"Jess, that is the furthest thing from the truth. We are going to make this work. You will see."

"I'm in," she said, turning toward him. She took Chad's face in her hands and leaned her forehead into his. "I'm into you with my whole heart."

"I'm in, too."

"Come on. Let's go." Jessica stood up and took a deep breath. "I don't want you getting into Blue Springs too late tonight."

The stands had all cleared out, and they walked alone across to the set of steps going down. Jessica stopped and turned back to Chad.

"Remember what I said in the trailer," she said, leaning into him, her face an inch away from his. "If this does not work out, I know it will not be because you didn't try. Do not hold yourself down because of me. I want you to take your opportunities and soar like an eagle."

"Don't let me or anything get in the way of your dreams, either," Chad replied.

They looked at each other for a moment, and then he sealed their pact with a kiss—a promise of unselfish love for each other. Jessica turned and continued down the stairs. Chad followed.

"You don't think I would actually quit school because of you?" she teased him.

He just smiled back.

"Hey, you should hurry up and take that job here at Cottonwood," she added. "My dad needs someone to pick up all these papers and clean up this place." She looked back at him, checking for a reaction.

Chad just still smiled. She had a mean tease, though.

"Can you clean toilettes?" she asked.

"Shut up!" Chad finally broke down and responded with a little bit of irritation.

Jessica laughed and took his hand.

"Keep on the sunny side, always on the sunny side…" she started singing.

Her cheerfulness was infectious, and Chad started to sing along with her. They walked together that way, swinging their hands to the melody of the last song until they came up to the Larsens' camping area. Chad said his goodbyes and his many thank-yous for everything—the generosity, the meals, the job offers. Chad wondered what he had done to merit such kindness. He picked up his duffle bag from the Palace, and Jessica walked him out of the park. They stopped under the Cottonwood sign to take a few pictures with her phone and his, then continued on over to his truck.

"Remember, I love you," she said softly to him.

Tears were welling up in her eyes, and she kissed him. Chad felt the gentle touch of her tongue on his, another invitation of intimacy he could look forward to someday soon.

"You will inhabit my mind every waking minute," Chad answered and kissed her again, returning the sensual kiss.

He climbed into the truck and rolled down the window. Jessica stood there smiling with her piercing, green eyes—a mental picture for Chad to cherish.

"Toodle-oo, kangaroo," she said, and he drove off toward the highway.

CHAPTER 39

Chad drove back from Longview, Texas, to Blue Springs, Alabama, in record time. He took only a couple of pit stops for food and bathroom breaks, and it gave him plenty of thinking time. His appetite was satisfied with a drive-through double bacon cheeseburger. He liked the drive. The taste of Jessica's kiss still lingered, his phone was plugged into the radio playing his favorite country playlist, and he sang along without a worry in the world.

Chad had grown up more this past weekend than he had in the entire previous year. It seemed that he had looked up at the stars coming out in the evening sky in Texas, and his adulthood emerged. He used to think of people in two basic categories: racers and fans— the people who raced and the people who watched. That was his childhood view of the world. Now Chad had begun to see that life as an adult was much more complex. The racing hero that he and Gary Lee fantasized about as kids didn't really exist. Instead of feeling shattered, Chad was flowing with excitement.

What had he learned this weekend? Jessica was a great kart racer, but she wasn't pursuing a racing career. Her father, Bruce Larsen, was in the karting business, but he wasn't indoctrinating kids into his karting club. Mr. Larsen was cool with the kids in his club and not always demanding performance. The Larsens were surprisingly not obsessed with auto racing; instead, they were a tight-knit family always interested and investing in new business ideas. Jessica's uncle and cousin had found success in the oil business and even offered Chad an opportunity to start working with them. Chad didn't finish Rodeo-Kart, but he didn't care. Life wasn't just about karting and racing, although he still loved it.

The opportunities seemed as infinite as the stars in the universe. High school was now behind him, and he had his whole life ahead of him. He had a racing contract waiting for him at home. The girl who meant the world to him loved him back. His best friend was no longer in trouble and going to be okay. His dreams seemed to be falling into place.

It was around 9 p.m. when Chad pulled into Blue Springs. He slowed down and turned off the radio when he got to his driveway. Chad pulled up to the lit garage, and his dad came into his view, wiping his hands with a rag. Chad assumed his dad had been waiting for him to come home and anticipated a lecture since he had not called his father back as asked. He slowly climbed out, pulling his duffle bag from the passenger seat, and closed the door.

"Why didn't you call me back right away?" his dad said. "Don't you know what ASAP means? As Soon as Possible—it means right away! Immediately."

"My phone went dead," Chad replied and turned to go into the house.

"Come on. I called you yesterday. Did you get my message about the racing contract?"

"Yes. I did try to call this morning, but there was no answer. Then I was driving, and I needed time to think. Anyhow, I'm home now, right?"

"So… How was Rodeo-Kart? You had always wanted to go to that."

"It was incredible. I have so much to tell you and Carole," Chad said, turning back toward his dad. "Do you remember that girl Jessica Larsen who drove the superkart in June?"

"Yeah. She certainly had you distracted."

"Well, she's my new girlfriend now. And her father, Bruce Larsen, let me drive his kart in Rodeo-Kart. And then Jessica was in a crash, and I went with her to the emergency room."

"Well, that's quite a story," his dad said. "I had a call from Sonny Kilgore on Saturday. Apparently, you were listed on the

Rodeo-Kart website as a 'Cottonwood' racer, and he was furious that you went and drove for Bruce Larsen instead of Kilgore Karting."

Chad was surprised that his story reached Blue Springs before he even made it home.

"What is wrong with you, boy?" His father shook his head. "You know that loyalty is important in this business."

Chad dropped his duffle bag and said, "I'm not a boy. I'm not Kilgore's wheelboy. I'm not anyone's boy. I'm eighteen, I finished high school, and FYI, I have to sign my own papers now. So stop calling me boy."

Chad's mood had turned sour. He picked up his duffle bag and stormed through the kitchen door on the side of the house. He no longer felt like this was where he belonged. He wished he could just get back in his truck and drive back to Texas without any arguments about karting.

"Hey, Shug," his stepmom said when he came into the kitchen. "So glad you are finally home. We missed you." Carole hugged Chad enthusiastically. "You hungry? You want some dinner?"

"Sure," replied Chad.

Carole's warmth made him feel more at home again. Carole sat him down at the kitchen table and put some chicken-fried chicken and green beans on a plate in front of him. Chad's father came in from the garage.

"Did you hear that Tom Grasiano was arrested?" asked Carole. "They are charging him for hit-and-run in Gary Lee's crash. It all happened just after you left."

"That's what I've been trying to tell Boy Wonder here all weekend, but he doesn't answer his phone," said Chad's dad.

"That is crazy!" said Chad. "So Tom is the one who was racing Gary Lee and drove him off the road? He left Gary Lee on the side of the road when Gillian was killed? Wow! Tom Grasiano really is an ass!"

"This is why I have been calling you all weekend," said his father. "Tom Grasiano lost his chance for the All-Pro Racing School scholarship, and now they are going to give it to you!"

Chad looked at his dad in shock. "I can't believe it! But your message said I had a racing contract."

"Chad Gibbons, All-Pro Racer," said his dad.

He dropped a large envelope on the table in front of Chad.

"What's this?" Chad asked.

"This is the contract from Kilgore Racing that goes with the scholarship. You're not just going to learn to race autos; you're going to start your racing career."

Chad fell silent. This was the opportunity he had been waiting for all of his life—maybe. Chad pulled the papers out of the envelope and started to flip through them.

"I at least need to be able to read something like this for myself. I want to read this first," said Chad.

"Fine, fine. Look through that, and we'll go over to the Kilgores' in the morning."

"Shug, your father read it over. He thinks it's good. I think it sounds exciting," added Carole.

Chad smiled at his stepmom. She always tried to make everything better.

"Carole, at this point, I don't even know what I am signing up for, and nobody seems to care what I want. I have to think for myself."

"Well, I can tell you what it says if you could be quiet and listen for a moment," said his dad. "It's a five-year contract, and all you have to come up with is $25,000 in cash or sponsorships each year. Kilgore Racing covers the balance of the racing costs. I will go over there with you, and we can seal the deal."

Chad was beyond disappointed. He had expected to be paid as a racer. Instead, he would have to be paying to race for five years?

"So Kilgore Racing doesn't pay a salary? This sounds just like karting, only more expensive. I can't live on nothing but Sonny Kilgore's big promises," Chad said. "Can I just take the All-Pro scholarship without the contract?"

"Son, it is a package deal. There are many ways to earn money as a racecar driver, and there are ways to cover the $25,000 obligation. The contract for the All-Pro Racing School and Kilgore Racing is for you to sign, and there is only one spot left right now."

"If I sign this, I'm on the hook for twenty-five grand—every year! Why don't *you* sign up, since you want a racing career so bad?"

Chad's father walked back a few steps and said, "What is wrong with you, Chad? Do you think I have been paying all of this money for karting for nothing? I was doing it to get you to the next level, and this is the next level! You have a great offer from a professional racing team right in front of you, and now you're turning into a crybaby? This is your career!"

Chad laughed out loud and shook his head. "How is this a career? If I take this scholarship, I will owe Sonny Kilgore big time. I don't like the idea of being another act in his dog and pony show for the next five years."

"Two months ago, you were sweating over your chances for that scholarship. I thought you would be ecstatic to have this opportunity. You've been dreaming about this since before you started karting in Juniors."

"Sure, I have dreams. I wanted to be a racecar driver. But this— this is just more of the same crap I've been putting up with for the last five years. Hustling for Sonny Kilgore. Working his booths, his parties, his events—never seeing a dime. Just a carrot on a stick. This racing deal might be your dream, Dad, but I've aged out of it."

"That's the racing business, Chad. Grow up and get with the program!"

"I'm trying to tell you, Dad, I am growing up. The Kilgores only want me to make them money. They demand loyalty and offer little in return. Sonny Kilgore only cares about his pathetic racing racket. There are other important things in life.

"I'm glad that Gary Lee isn't going to pay for a crime he didn't commit. He loved Gillian. Someone I really cared about died, and my best friend was left on the side of the road to die. Why should I grovel to race for people who don't have a clue?"

"Shug, your father is only looking out for your future," said Carole.

"Really?" said Chad. "All you want is to live out your racing dreams in this script you have written for me. What if it were me on the side of the road? Would that make a difference?"

"Shug, you shouldn't say that," said Carole.

Chad sat down in frustration.

"Well, sorry you feel so put out," said his father. He took a deep breath. "Listen. Sonny Kilgore is at Big Mo's mansion tomorrow until noon, and he wants to talk to you. Why don't you get a good night's sleep and go over there in the morning? I think you're going to like what he has to say—I'll go with you."

His father walked out of the kitchen, and Carole followed him.

Chad could hear him say to her, "I just don't understand. We have been planning this racing career for years now."

Chad didn't know how to explain his new perspective to his father. He saw everything so differently now. Chad cleared his plates to the sink and took his duffel bag upstairs. He pulled his phone out and looked at his messages: Dad, Gary Lee, Annie, Jessica—it was a long list of unread stuff.

He sent a message to Gary Lee, *r u still up? I just heard the news about Tom.* No response.

Chad sat in his room and started to read through the contract again. Sponsorships, obligations, termination, etc. It seemed to be more about him selling and bringing in revenue than it was about racing. There was a whole section on "Kilgore-Kash" and different ways to earn the "kash" credits toward his obligations. It all made Chad very upset and exhausted. He didn't want to think about it anymore.

He texted Jessica, *I have a racing contract in my hand. Something to talk about. I'll call in the AM,* and he got ready for bed.

He checked his phone before turning out the lights and saw, *Love you.* He could at least close his eyes in peace.

*****

Chad woke up in the morning to the smell of bacon and coffee. He looked at the clock; it was 8:00 a.m. He looked at his phone; no new messages. He texted Jessica again, *I think your dad was right—it's just Monopoly money.* No response, so he got dressed and went downstairs.

"Good morning, Shug," said Carole while she was busy around the kitchen. "Your father has already left for work, but he wants you to meet him at the shop on the way over to the Kilgores' place."

"Okay," said Chad, and he poured himself some coffee.

His little brother, Grant, was sitting at the kitchen table with a bowl of cereal. Chad sat down at the table across from Grant and put his phone face up by his coffee cup, anticipating a call or text.

"Carole, Chad has his phone out," said Grant.

"Swanee, don't tattle. Shug, you know the rule. No phones at the table."

Chad put his phone in his shirt pocket, annoyed. He collected his coffee cup and spoon and left it all in a spilled mess by the kitchen sink.

"What's the matter, Shug?" said Carole.

"I'm waiting to hear from Jessica."

"Oh, is that your new girlfriend? Your father told me you had met someone new."

"Yes, Jessica Larsen, she is amazing," said Chad. His bad mood melted away when he started to talk about her. "She's smart and talented. She's going to Texas A&M. You will really like her."

"Chad's in love," said Grant, making kissing sounds.

Chad ignored Grant.

"Oh, bless your heart. She sounds so nice. Are we going to have her over?" asked Carole.

"Soon. She lives in Texas, but I'm sure she'll be coming to Alabama again."

"Oh, that's pretty far away. Are you going to be okay with that?"

"I wouldn't mind if she lived on the moon, as long as she calls me back soon."

Chad took the large envelope with the contract and headed out the door. He drove over to his father's shop and parked. There were stacks of tires in front of the building. He got out of his truck and went inside. His father was standing under a car on the lift talking to one of his employees.

"Dad," Chad called out.

His father stopped and came over to him.

"Dad, I want to go over to the Kilgores' and talk to Sonny myself."

"I think I should be there with you, Son. You've never signed a contract before, and you need to be careful about what you say to the Kilgores. Loyalty is important, and you need to patch things up with Sonny."

"I'm going over myself. I have to learn how to take care of these things as an adult."

Chad got in his truck and started driving down the street toward the Kilgore mansion. He could see his father's red Mustang following him. His father's determination was something that he could not prevent or control. He resolved to accept his father's interference in his meeting with Sonny Kilgore. He drove down the straightaway a little faster and collected his thoughts. He thought about Jessica Larsen and remembered their parting kiss.

CHAPTER 40

Chad's drive to the Kilgore mansion took him past the Babylon Karting Park and the large, painted number "87" that served as a reminder of his childhood dreams. It made his heart ache to know that Dillanger-Gibbons Racing would never be a reality. His childhood dream had taken a turn, but at least he still had his best friend.

Chad felt a knot in his stomach driving up the long driveway of the Kilgore estate. He was murmuring to himself, trying to rehearse what he would say to Sonny Kilgore when he asked about his weekend at Rodeo-Kart. He just wanted to tell the whole world that he was in love with Jessica Larsen, but he recognized that probably nobody else cared.

Judging by the expensive cars parked on the side of the circular part of the driveway, there must be a full house of Kilgores. Chad remembered his days back when he and Gary Lee used to play the *Name That Car* game, trying to identify luxury cars by sight. A black Porsche Cayenne, a candy apple red Lamborghini Gallardo, and a pearl white Audi R8—he picked them off as he rounded the driveway. Gary Lee would have been proud.

Chad wished that he and his friend could have been entering this next phase of life together, but life had taken a turn. Chad knew that Gary Lee was lucky to be alive, and he was glad to have his friendship still. This All-Pro racing scholarship had once been Gary Lee's dream, too.

Chad waited for his dad to pull up and park the Mustang next to his truck. They walked together toward the front steps without saying a word. Big Mo Kilgore answered the door.

"It's about time, Checkers!" he bellowed. "Come on in. We are all waiting for you."

"Good morning, Mr. Kilgore," said Chad, a bit surprised being called Checkers.

Rusty Gibbons greeted Big Mo also, and they all walked back through the main hallway to the library. They entered the room filled with helmets and trophies on the shelves. It smelled different this day, a faint odor of old burned rubber and cigar smoke.

Chad was surprised to see four people already in the room. Big Mo introduced Chad to everyone as "Checkers Gibbons," which made everything start to seem surreal. Sonny Kilgore was there, Mr. Butkis, a gentleman named Gavin, and a butterfaced woman with a low-cut blouse. Her name was Ruby Mae. They all seemed very friendly like they had known Chad for years. There was iced tea served on a tray, and Chad's parched throat welcomed the tall glass of southern hospitality.

"Checkers!" said Mr. Butkis, putting his arm around Chad and squeezing him. "I love that name."

"Let me lay out for you this opportunity," started Sonny. "First of all, every great racecar driver needs a nickname, which is why we want you to race as Checkers Gibbons. You know, like Dixie Michaels, T-bone Tarzana, or Cracker Jack Adams."

"Okay then, Checkers," his dad said, patting Chad on the shoulder.

"Next," continued Sonny, "you'll be in a three-week intensive training program at the All-Pro Racing School in Leeds starting in September, at no cost to you."

"That's the scholarship," added Mr. Butkis.

"Now comes the exciting part," said Sonny. "You're going to be racing in the K-2000 series races starting next April! That is kind of like an American Formula 3 series—a great place to start."

"You know, I started in Formula 3," added Big Mo.

"You'll be driving for Kilgore Racing, and you'll have five years of guaranteed opportunity to move up into different series," said Sonny.

"As long as you maintain the minimum requirements," added the man named Gavin.

"Minimum requirements?" asked Chad.

"Yes, like not being arrested for hit-and-run!" said Big Mo.

"Ah, you're referring to Tom Grasiano," said Chad's dad.

"Yes," answered Sonny. "We would have signed up Tom as our racer, but unfortunately, he has forfeited his contract. We have to be mindful of the Kilgore reputation."

"You can find the various provisions for forfeiture in the contract," said Gavin.

Chad wondered what Tom's nickname would have been. Tom "The-Ass" Grasiano? Chad almost laughed out loud.

"It sounds really great, and you know that this is what I've been working toward in all my years of karting. I need to know if I can earn a living with this contract," said Chad.

"Earn a living?" said Big Mo, almost laughing.

"Yes, you know, buy groceries, pay rent," explained Chad. "I don't want to live at home forever."

"Look, Checkers," said Sonny. "This program is not just your first job after high school. If that's what you want, then you should try flipping burgers or delivering pizza. This is a career launch opportunity, and it's going to take some effort on your part to make it pay off."

"If you play this right," said Big Mo, "there's no limit to how much money you can make in racing."

"It costs over $100,000 to run a car in the entry-level series," said Sonny. "This is a great offer and just the start. You get your foot in the door. Most of our drivers are earning six figures through sponsorships and endorsements. As a Kilgore driver, we'll represent you in endorsement deals."

"Plus, you get to keep forty percent of all your winnings," added Gavin.

Chad took another sip of iced tea and sat back and contemplated. It sounded almost too good to be true, but he still wondered how he was going to afford to move to Texas and live on his own. What was the downside of this deal that no one was telling him?

Mrs. Kilgore came in and asked if anyone needed refills or some more biscuits.

"Thank you, Uma, but we're all good," said Big Mo.

Uma distracted everyone for a moment when she extended a warm welcome to the young woman in the library.

"So glad to see you, Ruby Mae. You truly are a beautiful jewel that Sonny brought into our home."

Big Mo laughed and said, "Now Uma, don't go stealing this precious gem; we need more jewels like her around!"

Ruby Mae smiled at Uma and said, "Thank you, Ms. Kilgore. Your iced tea is so uplifting and refreshing." She turned to Chad and gave him a wink, which seemed awkward at the moment.

Chad nervously continued to look around the room and said, "I'm still confused as to how I'm going to make ends meet when I'm first starting out before all this money starts rolling in."

"That's a good question, young man," said Gavin. "We give you a $50,000 line of credit and a debit card to draw against it. That way, you can have money to spend."

Gavin opened a briefcase, pulled out a stack of papers, and handed them to Chad.

"Here," said Gavin. "This is the same as the copy we gave your father. You can keep that one, and this is the one you'll need to sign."

Chad looked through the document that was handed to him. It looked the same as the one he had read last night. There were red stickers on the back pages, indicating "sign here."

"Chad," his father said, "I'm ready to write the Kilgores a check for $25,000 today to get you started. I've arranged for financing through our tire shop."

"Dad," said Chad, "that's a lot of money!"

"It won't be without benefit," said Sonny. "Rusty's Wrench and Tires will be the first sponsor on your car."

"But I have to come up with that every year," said Chad.

"We can provide you with a list of businesses to reach out to," said Sonny.

"Do you mean for cold calling?" asked Chad.

Sonny laughed. "No, I wouldn't call it cold calling. We purchase a special list of businesses known to donate to charity or sponsor sports or entertainment events. Trust me; once you make a name for yourself, it won't be hard to sell. You'll be swimming in sponsors by your second season."

"Not just sponsors," added Butkis, "but all the perks of being a celebrity! You'll have gorgeous girls throwing themselves at you."

"Oh, that's really the fun part," interjected the woman named Ruby Mae. "I've had so much fun with the racers and the Luxurious Lifestyle people. They have parties all night long sometimes. I had no idea how much fun it would be when I started. You just need to draw the blessings of the Universe to yourself."

Sonny turned to Ruby Mae. "When were you involved with the Luxurious Lifestyle people?" asked Sonny, changing the subject.

"Oh, I thought you knew," she said. "I was a masseuse for the LL for a long time before I became a sports massage therapist. That's how I know Mr. Butkis."

Sonny turned to Big Mo. He seemed very disturbed and distracted.

"Let's not get off the subject, Sonny," said Big Mo. "We can talk about that later."

Ruby Mae smiled happily, but her large breasts had become the center of attention. The men in the room ogled the poor woman. Chad thought it was strange that she was there while they were discussing the contract. The others were comfortable enough, but it made him feel embarrassed.

"Checkers," said Big Mo, "what do you think of all this?"

"There's a lot of details in this contract," said Chad. "Maybe I should have a lawyer look it over before I sign it."

"Well, I have good news for you," said Sonny. "Gavin here is the team lawyer. He represents all of our drivers. He can answer any questions you have about the contract. He can also help you set up side deals for endorsements."

Chad wanted some more time to think, and he wished he had someone like Bruce Larsen to talk to. He had been bombarded by everyone in the room with good reasons to sign the contract; even his own father was pushing him. Was anyone really on his side, watching out for him? Chad took another sip of iced tea and asked to be excused to use the bathroom.

Chad walked down the hall through the mansion on the creaky wooden floors. The smell of cigar smoke had made him a little queasy, but when he walked toward the back patio, a new odor enveloped him—the strong smell of fresh flowers and burnt rubber. Before he turned into the pool bathroom, he saw a peculiar man through the French double doors. The strange man in a white racing suit standing out by the pool was smoking a cigarette. The gray smoke enveloped the man's image. Chad finished in the bathroom and exited out to the pool area.

The intriguing man in white was still there, lurking in the shady corner of the patio by a large potted plant. He looked over at Chad and then blew a perfect ring of smoke into the air. It suddenly felt chilly for a summer morning.

"Do you know anything about racing contracts?" Chad asked the man.

The man nodded, and Chad approached him.

"I have to make a decision about signing my first contract. Should I be paying money in order to race?" Chad asked.

"Winning is everything," is all the strange, dark-haired man said. The phantom visitor shrugged and tossed his cigarette butt. "Winning is everything," he repeated.

Chad stood there for a moment, gazing around the pool patio. He turned and looked again, but the stranger was out of sight. Chad went back into the house through the patio doors. He passed by the kitchen and saw Uma Kilgore.

"Who was that man in the white racing suit with the strange accent?" Chad asked her.

Mrs. Kilgore stopped and gasped, "Pederson? Did you talk to him?"

"Yeah, but just for a minute."

"You must bc going through something very stressful if you talked to Pederson."

"Yes, I am. I have some big decisions to make," said Chad.

Uma nodded thoughtfully. "Oh, don't tell anyone you saw Pederson. They will think that you are crazy."

Chad nodded and continued back toward the library. This racing deal definitely did not feel like it was his honest destiny. Chad entered the library again, where everyone was laughing over stories, but they all quieted down upon Chad's return.

"So, Checkers Gibbons, are you ready to sign up and start your racing career?" asked Sonny.

Chad paused, standing in the dark wooden room surrounded by racing regalia. "I can't sign it. At least not yet. I need to think about it," he said.

The room burst into argument and outrage. Sonny started to shout at him, and his father berated him.

"You ungrateful little boy!" hollered Big Mo.

"You know, I've put up with an awful lot of your nonsense," said Sonny. "What was that stunt you just pulled with going to Rodeo-Kart? You should know that you owe us a couple of hundred dollars for your Kilgore event fee."

Chad watched and listened without saying a word. These people were not his friends. It was just all about their business. He started to wonder what the business was really about. Maybe he was just a commodity being sold like the hoochie mama, Ruby Mae.

Chuck Larsen called it an "entertainment" business. Maybe it was just advertising space on a car that goes around the track, and Chad would have to sell that—a lot of it. The whole thing was still just a pay-to-play scheme, only it was way more expensive than karting. Chad would still need to get a job just to have spending money.

Chad reached over to the desk and picked up the contract. He headed for the door, and everyone stopped talking.

"I said I'll think about it," Chad said, and he left the room with the unsigned racing contract in his hand.

Everyone returned to arguing without him even present. Chad could hear his father promising, "He'll sign. Don't worry."

Big Mo Kilgore was getting so loud, and he could hear the anger in his tone of voice all the way down the hall.

"I expect loyalty," Big Mo shouted. "There are more kids on the team with real talent! Real talent and skills—not this crap!"

Chad walked to the front door and out to the large front porch. The warm summer morning air greeted him. He thought about his childhood dreams of racing. Was this the deal he had been waiting for? Paying the Kilgores to let him race? After meeting the Larsen's, Chad didn't even like the Kilgores anymore.

A foul odor of old burned rubber drifted in the cool breeze from the other side of the house. The smell matched the unsettled feeling that Chad was left with from this contract fiasco. He turned and saw Pederson in his white racing suit again, leaning against the stonework. Chad walked up to him.

"Here," said Chad, and he handed the contract to the stranger. "I won't be needing this millstone around my neck."

Pederson took the contract from Chad, smiled faintly, nodded, and whispered, "Winning is everything."

A chill ran up Chad's arm and across his neck.

He walked back over to his truck and climbed in. He was so glad that he had his own truck, and he didn't have to listen to his dad lecturing and complaining. Time to get out of Blue Springs. His essential things were still packed in the camo duffle bag from the Rodeo-Kart weekend.

He started the truck, put it in reverse, and backed up slowly. He could still see Pederson standing there when he looked over his shoulder. He took off and looked again behind him through his rearview mirror. All he saw was a whirlwind of papers blowing around in the front yard of the mansion.

Chad's father came out the front door and started running around, trying to pick up the pages of the racing contract. Poor Rusty's dreams were all swirling around in the air and slipping through his fingers. His father looked so small to Chad at that moment. His dad turned and waved his arms frantically for Chad to stop. The papers continued to blow around in the wind, all strewn out across the front lawn of the mansion.

Chad needed a new start, and he was anxious to get on the road again. His life in Blue Springs would become a collection of memories that Chad would pack away along with his dreams of professional racing. He would always revisit his memories of karting, high school, and friends. Maybe there would be a spot in his future with professional racing, but it would have to be with people who had some integrity.

Chad stopped at the end of the driveway. He took out his phone and texted Jessica, *The deal wasn't right for me.* Then he added, *See you soon. xo Chad.*

He put the phone away and pulled out to the long private road. In his rearview mirror, all he could see were the two white concrete Imperial foo lions that adorned the front gate of the Kilgore mansion. He watched as they grew smaller and smaller in the distance, and then they were gone.